The Return From Troy

The Return From Troy

LINDSAY CLARKE

CollinsPublishers

HarperCollins*Publishers*
77–85 Fulham Palace Road,
Hammersmith, London W6 8JB

www.harpercollins.co.uk

Published by HarperCollins*Publishers* 2005
1 3 5 7 9 8 6 4 2

Map by Andrew Ashton © HarperCollins 2005

A catalogue record for this book
is available from the British Library

ISBN 0 00 715027 X

Typeset in Bembo by
Palimpsest Book Production Limited,
Polmont, Stirlingshire

Printed and bound in Great Britain by
Clays Limited, St Ives plc

7151

For Phoebe Clare

Contents

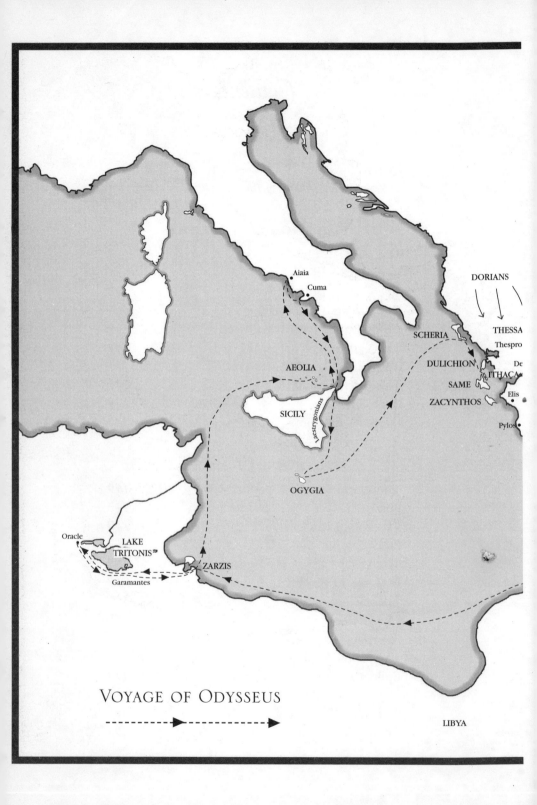

Aiaia
Cuma

DORIANS

SCHERIA
THESSA
Thespro

AEOLIA
DULICHION
De
ITHACA

SICILY
SAME
ZACYNTHOS
Elis

Lestrygonians
Pylos

OGYGIA

Oracle
LAKE
TRITONIS
ZARZIS
Garamantes

VOYAGE OF ODYSSEUS

LIBYA

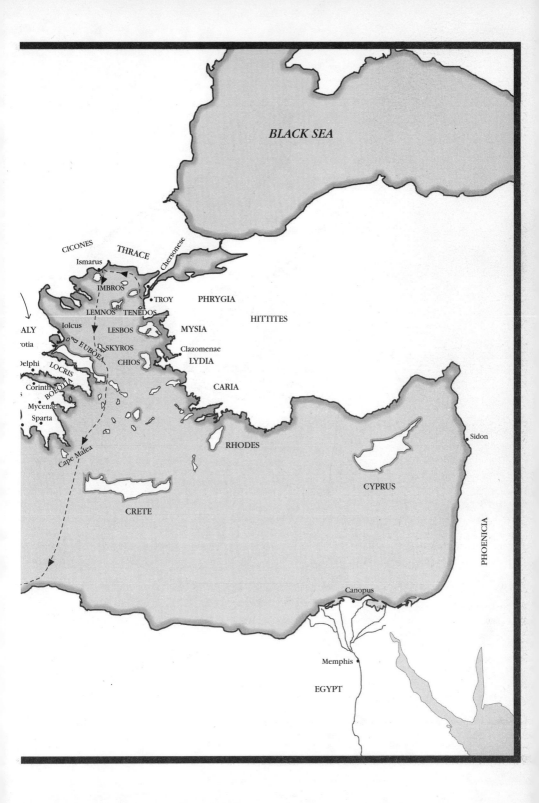

ΕΥΧΗΝ ΟΔΥΣΣΕΙ

'A Prayer to Odysseus'

*(Inscription found on a terracotta fragment
in 'the Cave of the Nymphs' on Ithaca)*

The Justice of the Gods

Nearly fifty years have passed since the fall of Troy. The world has turned harder since iron took the place of bronze. The age of heroes is over, the gods hold themselves apart, and my lord Odysseus has long since gone into the Land of Shades. It cannot now be long before I pass that way myself; but if honour is to survive among mortal men, then pledges must be kept, especially those between the living and the dead.

Whoever finds these papyrus scrolls will see from the inscription on their urn that they are offered in prayer to Odysseus. They contain a reliable account of the ordeals and initiations he underwent on his return from Troy, along with the story of the fate of the House of Atreus and the other Argive heroes. By the end of the day I shall have concealed these scrolls in the Cave of the Nymphs, hoping that they will be found in better times when men may be ready to listen to tales other than those sung in praise of the glories of war. Meanwhile, they must stand in fulfilment of a pledge that I Phemius, bard of Ithaca, made one winter night when Odysseus was seeking to make peace with his own turbulent past.

Earlier that evening a few of us had sat by the fire in the great hall discussing whether or not justice was to be found among the gods. I insisted that few traces of divine order were discernible in a world where a city as great as Troy could be reduced to ruin and yet so many of its conquerors were also doomed to terrible ends. What point was there in looking to the gods for justice when the deities could prove as fickle in their loyalties as the most treacherous of mortal men?

'That Blue-haired Poseidon should have wreaked his vengeance on the Argive host is unsurprising,' I declared. 'He had favoured the Trojans throughout the war. But Divine Athena had always been on our side, even in the darkest times. So how could she have forgotten her old enmity with Poseidon for long enough to help him destroy the Argive fleet? Such perfidy would be appalling in a mortal ally. How then can it be excused in an immortal goddess?'

Odysseus studied me in silence for a time. The expression on his face reminded me plainly enough that I might know all the stories by heart but I had never been at Troy myself and was speaking of matters that lay far outside my experience.

'Even a god's heart can be shaken by the sacking of a city,' he said. 'Even enemies can conspire when they find a common cause. As for myself, I believe that the gods see more deeply into time than we do, and what appears to us as mere caprice may eventually prove to be a critical moment in the dispensation of their justice.'

I saw him exchange a smile with his wife Penelope, who turned to me. 'Consider,' she said, 'what Grey-eyed Athena must have thought as she saw Locrian Aias trying to ravish Cassandra even in the sanctuary of her own shrine. Consider how the goddess must have felt when Agamemnon ordered her sacred effigy to be taken from Troy and carried off to Mycenae.'

'And those were not the only crimes and desecrations committed that night,' Odysseus added. 'If Divine Athena turned her face against us, it was with good cause. I can well imagine that she looked down through the smoke on the destruction of Troy and felt that she had seen enough of the ways of men to know that there could never be peace till they came to understand that the desolation they left behind them must always lie in wait for them elsewhere.'

A reflective silence fell across the hall for a time, in which the fire shifted and sent a constellation of sparks rising on the chimney draught. Then Penelope lightened the moment by saying that fortunately peace and justice were both to be found on Ithaca. 'And they will always be so,' she concluded, 'so long as our young men show proper reverence for the gods.'

Later that evening Lord Odysseus summoned me to his side. 'You are an honest man, Phemius, if not always as wise as you believe yourself to be. But you are my bard,' he said, 'and the time has come for me to share with you things that I have told to no one else except my wife. I do so trusting that one day you will make a fine song of my story — a song by which the world will come to know what kind of man Odysseus truly was. And it will be a song unlike all the other songs because it will show that the ordeals he endured at Troy and on his return to Ithaca were more marvellous, because more human, than all the extravagant inventions of the poets.'

When he asked me if I would do him this service, I vowed that I would.

'And who knows but that if you find wisdom enough to equal your skill,' he said, 'it may even prove to be a song that vindicates the justice of the gods?'

Remembering those words, and hoping that my own will be remembered in a future time, it is my earnest prayer to the shade of my lord Odysseus that the pledge I gave him has now been faithfully redeemed.

PART ONE

THE BOOK OF
Poseidon

The Fall

Odysseus stood in the painted chamber high inside the citadel of Troy, listening to the sound of Menelaus sobbing. Spattered in blood, the King of Sparta was sitting on a bed of blood with his head supported in his blood-stained hands. Helen cowered at his back, white-faced. The mutilated body of Deiphobus lay sprawled beside him. Though the streets outside rang loud with shouts and screaming, here beneath the rich tapestry of Ares and Aphrodite it felt as though time itself might have halted to hear Menelaus weep.

Even Helen, whose delinquent passion had precipitated all these years of suffering, had ceased to whimper. Having been so appalled by the sight of warm blood leaking across the bed that she might have screamed and been unable then to cease from screaming, she was now staring at her husband with a kind of wonder. For the first time in many weeks she was thinking about someone other than herself, and feelings that she had long thought petrified began to stir with an almost illicit tenderness. Was it possible then that, for all the offence she had given him, and all the anguish she had caused, this gentle-hearted man still loved her?

Afraid that she might break the spell that had so far spared her life, she raised a bare arm and stretched out her hand to comfort his quaking shoulder.

Instantly, as though that touch had seared like flame, Menelaus pulled away. He leapt to his feet and turned, lips quivering, to stare down at the woman lying beneath him. Unable to endure the naked vulnerability of her breasts, his gaze shifted away to where Deiphobus lay with his eyes open and blood still draining from the ragged stump of the wrist. Menelaus bared his teeth and uttered a low growl. Dismayed that he had been so visibly overcome by weakness, resolved to countermand all signs of it,' he picked up his sword from where it had fallen to the floor and began to hack once more at the lifeless flesh.

Watching Helen cower across the bed, Odysseus knew he had seen enough. If, in his madness, Menelaus desired to murder the woman who had betrayed him, that was his business. Odysseus would not stay to witness it. Silently he turned away and passed through the door, leaving his friend to do as he wished with the dead body of his enemy and the terrified, living body of his wife.

As he stepped out into the night air, he caught a smell of burning drifting upwards from the lower city. From somewhere in the distance, beyond the walls, he made out the din of swords beating against shields: a host of Argive warriors were still climbing the ramp and roaring as they poured through the open gate. Hundreds – perhaps thousands – more were already inside the walls, taking command of the streets and extinguishing whatever resistance the bewildered citizens were managing to muster. The nearer sounds of screaming and shouting were hideous on his ears. Yet it would all be over soon, Odysseus thought as he crossed the courtyard of Helen's mansion; the Trojans would come to their senses and lay down their arms in surrender of their captured city. Even to the bravest and most fanatical among them, any other course of action must soon come to seem futile and insane. But he was worried by that smell of burning.

When he came out into the street he found the cobbles underfoot slippery with blood and he was forced to pick his way among the corpses. Here they were mostly top-knotted Thracian tribesmen who lay thrown over one another in lax postures, with slack jaws, like too many drunkards in the gutters. There was no sign of movement anywhere among them. From the top of the rise, beyond their silence, came the shouts of Argive soldiers and a terrible screaming.

Afterwards Odysseus would wonder how he could not have been prepared for what awaited him there. After all, he had sacked towns before. He had killed men and taken women into slavery. In the heat of battle he was as ruthless as the next man and had never lost much sleep over what he had done. It was the way of things. It had always been so and nothing would change it. Yet when he turned the corner and saw three Spartans laughing as they tugged at the legs of a white bearded-old man who was trying to climb over a wall, then thrust their spears through his nightshirt into his scrawny belly, he was not prepared. He was not prepared for the way, all along the street, doors had been broken down and the terrified, unarmed figures of men and boys were being driven from their homes at spear-point and cut down by the warriors waiting for them.

When Odysseus saw their sergeant swing his sword at the neck of a sobbing youth with such force that it almost severed the head, he grabbed the man by the shoulder, shouting, 'In the name of all the gods, what are you doing? These people aren't putting up any resistance.' But the sergeant merely shrugged and said, 'So what? They're Trojans, aren't they?' and turned away to pull the next cowering figure towards the sweep of his sword. Odysseus saw the naked man's throat splash open as he crumpled and fell. He looked up through a slaughter-house stench of blood and saw such deft butchery repeated again and again along the length of the street while women with their hands in their hair stood screaming as they watched. One of them threw herself over the body of her husband only to be dragged away while a burly axe-man finished him off.

Odysseus shouted out a demand to know who was in command here, but his voice was lost in the shrieking of the women and he received no answer. He pushed his way along the street, making for the square outside the temple of Athena, and saw Acamas, son of Theseus, who had ridden inside the wooden horse with him, holding a man by the hair as he twisted his sword in his guts. Hearing Odysseus shout out his name, Acamas looked up, smiled in recognition, let the man drop, and stepped back, wiping the sweat from his brow.

'It's going well,' he said as Odysseus came up to him.

'But none of these people are armed,' Odysseus shouted above the din. 'There was an agreement.' He took in the warrior's puzzled frown. 'We gave Antenor our word!' he shouted. 'We said we'd spare the lives of all those who surrendered.'

Acamas glanced away at where his men were working their way like dogged harvesters through a huddled crowd of Trojan men and boys trapped in a narrow corner of the street. 'That's not what I was told,' he said. 'We're under orders to kill the lot and that's what we're doing. It's the same all over the city.'

'That can't be right,' Odysseus protested. 'Where's Agamemnon?'

'Probably strutting through King Priam's palace by now. I haven't seen him.' Acamas wiped a bloody hand across his mouth. 'Come on,' he said, 'there's still a lot of work to do.' Then he turned away, lifting his sword.

In what should have been the most glorious hour of his life, Odysseus was seized by a numbing sense of dread. To fight in open combat across the windy plain of Troy had been one thing: this slaughter of defenceless men, stinking of piss and panic as they stumbled from their sleep into narrow alleys from which there could be no escape, was quite another. Yet the havoc in these streets had already run so far beyond control it was clear that any male Trojan, man or boy, would be lucky to survive the night.

In a fury of disgust, Odysseus turned to push his way through the throng, looking for Agamemnon. The smell of burning was stronger now and through a thickening gush of smoke a lurid flame-light glared out of the darkness of the lower city. If fire had broken out among the weaving halls with their bales of cloth, reels of yarn, and timber looms, then more people might be burnt to death or trampled in the scramble for safety than would fall to the sword. The dogs of the city barked and whined. Coarse laughter surrounded a frantic screaming where a man was being tormented somewhere. Women cried out as they were pulled from the sanctuary of holy altars and driven like geese along the streets. Children sobbed above the bodies of their fathers. And when Odysseus strode into the square before the temple of Athena he saw the immense moonlit form of the wooden horse, like a monstrous figment from a dream, looming in silence over the spectacle of a city in its death throes.

Sick with shame, he remembered how he had harangued the troops on the day when it looked as though they might refuse to follow Agamemnon when he called for a renewed assault on the city. That had been months ago but he remembered how he'd incited them with the thought of the women waiting to be raped inside these walls. How easily the words had sprung to his lips. How little thought he'd given to the price they would exact in human suffering. But now Odysseus stood in the shadow of the horse that had sprung from his imagination, watching men kill and die in helpless multitudes. In conceiving his clever stratagem to breach the unbreachable walls of Troy, he had released ten murderous years of rage and frustration into the streets of the city. Never had he seen so many people cut down like cattle in a hecatomb. Never before had he felt so entirely culpable. When he looked about him, there seemed no limits to the horror he had wrought.

Still shaking from having seen her husband's head lopped off by that monstrous boy Neoptolemus, Queen Hecuba was among the first of the women to be dragged beneath the open portico in the square. Her younger daughters, Laodice and Polyxena, were supporting her feeble frame while the women of the palace followed behind, wailing and tearing at their hair. Neither Cassandra nor Hector's widow, Andromache, were anywhere to be seen.

Not long ago, for a few brief hours, the Trojan Queen had lain beside her husband in a dream of unexpected peace. Now the world had turned into a phantasmagoria around her aged head and so intense was the feeling of nightmare, so violent the alteration in her circumstances, that she could no longer trust the evidence of her senses. It was impossible that Priam lay dead with his regal head severed from his body. It was impossible that these streets and squares, which only a few hours earlier had been filled with thankful prayers and jubilant with revelry, should now echo to the brutal shouts of foreign voices and the anguish of her frightened people. It was impossible that the bronze helmets and armour of the soldiers dragging her away were anything other than the figments of a dream. Yet she knew from their gaping eyes and mouths that her womenfolk were screaming round her and, after a time, Queen Hecuba came to understand that she too was keening out loud with all the strength of her lungs.

Lifted by the breeze from the burning buildings in the city below, smoke gusted across the square so that the staring head and arched neck of the wooden horse seemed to rise out of fog. The women were left coughing as they moaned. Spectral in the gloom, their faces blemished by the streaks of paint running from their eyes, they looked more like creatures thrown up from the underworld than the graceful ladies of royal Troy they had been only an hour earlier. Then they were screaming again as the armoured figure of the herald Talthybius strode out of the torch-lit smoke. He was clutching the slender, half-naked figure of Cassandra by the arm.

The girl's eyeballs had turned upwards and she was singing to herself, not for comfort but in a crazy kind of triumph. Hecuba recognized the words from the Hymn to Athena. As though unconscious of the terror around her, Cassandra was singing of how, when the armed goddess sprang with gleaming eyes from the head of Zeus, all the gods had been awe-struck and the earth itself had cried out and the seas had stood still.

Pushed out of the swirl of smoke into the throng of women, Cassandra too might have sprung in that eerie moment from some unnatural source. But the suave pragmatist Talthybius had his attention elsewhere. Seeing Hecuba shivering in the night air, he berated their guards for putting the health of these valuable captives at risk. He ordered one of them to raid the nearest house for throws and blankets before the women caught their death of cold. Then he turned to confront the Trojan Queen where she stood with the cloth of her gown hanging open to reveal her depleted breasts.

'Forgive me for not observing your plight earlier, madam. The guards should have shown greater courtesy. But I beg you to calm these women.' Talthybius raised both his staff and his voice to silence the captives. 'The High King himself has commanded that you be brought here to safety and kept under guard. No harm will come to any of you. You have my word on that.'

'No harm!' Hecuba's thin grey hair had come unbound. It was blowing about her face like rain in wind. 'You think it no harm to see our men struck down? You think it no harm to watch our city burn?'

'Such are the fortunes of war.' The herald glanced away from the accusation of her eyes. 'Your husband would have done well to think of this when he threw our terms for peace back in our teeth all those years ago.'

'Do not dare to speak of my husband, Argive. The gods will surely avenge what has been done to him.'

'Isn't it already clear that the gods have set their faces against Troy?' Talthybius sighed. 'Be wise and endure your fate with all the fortitude you can.'

Reaching out to take Cassandra into the fold of her arm, Hecuba said, 'The Queen of Troy has no need of Agamemnon's lackey to teach her how to grieve.'

'The Troy you ruled has gone for ever, madam,' the herald answered. 'You are Queen no longer. When this night's work is done, you and your kinswomen will be divided by lot among the

Argive captains. I pity your condition but things will go easier with you if you school yourself in humility.'

'Do as you like with me,' Hecuba defied him. 'My life ended when I saw Hector fall. It was only a ghost of me that watched my husband die. What remains here is less than that. Your captains will find no joy in it.'

Talthybius shrugged. 'It may be so. But I give Cassandra into your care. Be aware that my lord Agamemnon has already chosen her for his own.'

'To be at the beck and call of his Spartan queen?'

'To be the companion of his bed, madam.'

Hecuba looked up at him with flashing eyes. 'I would strangle her with my own hands first.'

But at that moment Cassandra reached her fingers up to her mother's face and held it close to her own. She was smiling the demented smile that Hecuba had long since learned to dread. 'You have not yet understood,' she whispered. 'This is what the goddess wants of me. I have seen her. I saw her in the moments when they sought to ravish me beneath her idol. Divine Athena came there to comfort me. She told me I would be married to this Argive king. She told me that we must light the torches and bring on the marriage dance, and go joyfully to the feast. So that is what we will do. And you too must dance, mother. You must dance with me. Come, weave your steps with mine. Let us rejoice together and cry out *evan! evoe!* And dance to Hymen and Lord Hymenaeus at the wedding feast,' – her voice dipped to a whisper that the herald could not hear – 'for Athena has promised me that this marriage will destroy the House of Atreus.'

And then, as Hecuba looked on in dismay, Cassandra broke free of her grasp and began to stamp her foot and clap her hands above her bare shoulder, crying out to the bewildered Trojan women to join her in the dance and honour the husband who would shortly share her marriage bed.

'Look to your daughter, madam,' Talthybius warned. 'I fear she is not in her right mind.' Then, commanding the guards to keep a watchful eye on both women, the herald left the square to go in search of his master.

Slowly the hours of that terrible night dragged past. The women trembled and wept together. As if drugged on her own ecstasy, Cassandra slept. Exhausted and distraught, her throat hoarse from wailing, her breasts bruised where she had pummelled them in her grief, Hecuba entered a trance of desolation in which it seemed that no more dreadful thing could happen than she had endured already. And then Hector's widow, Andromache, was brought through the gloom.

Hecuba did not see her at first because her eyes were fixed on the twelve year old warrior Neoptolemus, who strode ahead of Andromache wearing the golden armour that had once belonged to his father Achilles. The last time she had seen this ferocious youth he had been standing over Priam's body looking down in fascination as blood spurted from the severed arteries of the neck. Still accompanied by his band of Myrmidons, Neoptolemus was carrying his drawn sword but he had taken off his helmet so that for the first time Hecuba could see how immature his features were. Only a faint bloom of blond hair softened his cheeks, and the eyes that surveyed the captive women were curiously innocent of evil. They were like the eyes of a child excited by the games.

Unable to endure the sight of him, Hecuba glanced away and saw Andromache held in the grip of two Myrmidon warriors. It was obvious from her distracted eyes and the uncharacteristic droop of her statuesque body that they were there to support rather than restrain her. The women of Hector's house followed behind, weeping and moaning. Evidently hysterical with terror, the body-servant Clymene seemed scarcely able to catch her breath as she gripped and tore the tangles of her hair.

Neoptolemus gestured with his sword for the women in his train to be brought forward and herded with the others. But when

Hecuba held out trembling hands to receive Andromache into her arms she was appalled to see her daughter-in-law stare back at her without recognition through the eyes of a woman whose memory was gone.

Though Andromache said nothing Hecuba could hear her breath drawn in little panting gasps as though she was sipping at the air. Her cheeks and throat were lined with scratches where she had dragged her fingernails across the surface of the flesh. A bruise discoloured the skin around the orbit of her right eye, and there was such utter vacancy in the eyes themselves that Hecuba knew at once that this woman had already been made to endure the unendurable.

'Where is your son?' she forced herself to ask. 'Where is Astyanax?'

Andromache's eyeballs swivelled in panic as though at sudden loss. Then memory seared through her. Again, as though the scene were being played out before her for the first time, she saw Neoptolemus dragging Astyanax by the lobe of his ear across the upper room of her house. Again she saw the deft sweep with which the young warrior lifted her child above the parapet of the balcony. Again she released a protracted scream of refusal and denial, and again it was in vain. Neoptolemus opened his hands and Astyanax vanished, leaving only a brief, truncated cry on the night air.

Unable to stop herself, Andromache had run to the balcony and gazed down where the small body of her son lay twisted on the stones twenty feet below. A pool of blood oozed from his head like oil. In that moment she would have thrown herself from the parapet after him if Neoptolemus had not grabbed her by the arm and pulled her away. So she had stood with that gilded youth bending an arm at her back, screaming and screaming at the night.

But even the mind has its mercies and, for a time, Andromache had slipped beyond the reach of consciousness. When she was pulled back to her senses, she woke into an alien land of torchlight, noise and violent shadows. If she had been asked her own name she could not have recalled it. Still in that primitive state of near oblivion, she had been conducted through the streets of Troy until she was brought to the moment when Hecuba asked after Astyanax. At the sound of the name a whole universe of pain flashed into being again.

Wiping the back of his hand across his nose, Neoptolemus stepped forward to look more closely at the terrified group of women huddled beneath the portico. Wrapped in blankets now, their heads held low in the gloom, they were hard to distinguish from each other. He used the blade of his sword to edge one woman aside so that he could see the girl cowering behind her. 'The boy had no father,' he was muttering, 'and now the mother has no son. But I have a remedy for that.'

Hecuba reeled where she stood. She felt as though she was striding against a dark tide and making no progress. She had seen her firstborn son Hector slain before the walls of Troy. She had seen her second-born, Paris, lying on his deathbed pierced and half-blinded by the arrows that Philoctetes had loosed at him. Others of her sons had failed to return from the battlefield. She had seen one of the youngest, Capys, die that night, cut down trying to defend his father. Then Priam himself had been murdered under her bewildered gaze. Now her six year old grandson Astyanax, Hector's boy, who had been the only solace that remained to her in a world made unremittingly cruel by war, was also dead. Somewhere she could hear Neoptolemus saying, 'One of you must be Polyxena, daughter of King Priam. Come forth. The son of Achilles wishes to speak with you.' Had she not already been exhausted by atrocity, every atom of her being would have shouted out then in mutiny against the gods. As it was, this latest devastation had left the Trojan Queen reduced to the condition of a dumb animal helplessly awaiting the utter extinction of its kind.

And no one among the women moved.

'Come, Polyxena, what are you afraid of?' Neoptolemus cajoled. 'I understand that my father was fond of you. It's time that we met.'

Still there was no movement among the huddle of blankets.

From somewhere Hecuba found the strength to say, 'Haven't you brought evil enough on Priam's house?'

The boy merely smiled at her. 'We Argives didn't seek this war. Troy is burning in the fire that Paris lit. We're looking only for justice here. As for me, remember that this war took my father from me. He might still have been living at peace on Skyros with my mother if your son hadn't taken it into his head to meddle with another man's wife. Now tell me, where is your daughter, old woman?'

But at that moment the sound of Agamemnon's voice boomed from across the square, shouting out his name and demanding to know where his generals were. As Neoptolemus turned to answer, Odysseus stepped out of the shadow of a nearby building, holding his boar-tusk helmet in the crook of his arm. Immediately Agamemnon demanded to know where he had last seen Menelaus.

'I left him with Helen,' Odysseus answered. 'Deiphobus and his household are dead. The Spartan Guard have control of his mansion.'

'Has he killed the bitch?'

'I don't know. Not when I left.'

Detecting an unusual shakiness in the Ithacan's voice, Agamemnon looked at him more closely. 'What's the matter with you? Have you taken a wound?'

'Have you seen what's happening down there? Have you seen the blood in the streets? I gave them my word – I gave *our* word to Antenor and Aeneas that we would spare all the lives we could. But this . . .'

Brusquely Agamemnon interrupted him, 'Aeneas and his Dardanians have already gone free. Antenor is safe enough if he stays indoors. And I've got my mind on other things right now. Memnon's Ethiopians have broken out of their barracks. Diomedes and his men are having a hard time containing them.'

He would have turned away but Odysseus seized him by the shoulder and stopped him. 'Antenor only agreed to help us because I gave him the most solemn assurances. I gave them on your behalf with your authority. Now you have to get control of this or they're going to kill everybody. You have to do it now.' But then he caught the shiftiness in the High King's eyes. His heart jolted. 'Are you behind this bloodbath?' he demanded. 'Is this what you want?

Agamemnon shrugged the hand from his shoulder and walked away to where Neoptolemus had abandoned his search for Polyxena and was now assembling his war-band for action.

'Move your Myrmidons down into the lower city,' Agamemnon ordered. 'If you look lively we should be able to trap Memnon's men between your force and Diomedes. I want it done quickly.'

The young warrior raised his sword in salute and, to a rattle of bronze armour, the Myrmidons jogged out of the square down a narrow street that would bring them out in the rear of the Ethiopians.

Agamemnon looked back with displeasure over the city he had conquered. 'We need to start fighting this fire before half the treasure of Troy is lost to it.'

He was speaking to himself but Odysseus had come up behind him, determined to get the truth from him. 'You intended this all along,' he said. And when no answer came, 'You never meant to hold on to Troy as we planned, did you? You were just making use of me to deceive Antenor and Aeneas.'

'I've no time for this,' Agamemnon scowled. He was about to walk away when he was snagged by a need to justify himself further. He looked back at Odysseus again. 'Your stratagem of the horse worked well, old friend. Troy is finished. Poets will still be singing of this victory a thousand years from now. And you'll be back home on Ithaca soon enough, a rich man, tumbling your wife on that great bed of yours.' He grinned through the smoke at the grim face that frowned back at him, white as wax, in the moonlight. 'Think of it, Odysseus. Just think of it. We are immortal, you and I. Whatever happens, our names are deathless now.'

And with that, Agamemnon, King of Men, summoned his bodyguard around him once more and advanced towards King Priam's palace.

All night long, not speaking, refusing to be touched, Menelaus prowled the bloody chamber where the bed had begun to stink like a butcher's stall. Helen crouched in a corner, stifling her whimpers. Sometimes, as the night wind gusted, smoke blew into the room, charring the air. After a time the oil-lamp that had been left burning on a tripod guttered out. Now the darkness was almost complete.

Menelaus went to the balcony once to look for the source of the fire and saw that the mansion was in no immediate danger. Beneath him, a tumult of screaming people ran along the street, looking back over their shoulders to where a company of spearmen advanced towards them rattling their shields. But he took almost as little interest in what he saw as did the many corpses already cluttering the gutters. He was remembering those moments in the bull-court at Knossos when he had first heard the news of Helen's defection – how the roaring of the crowd had dimmed in his ears so that it sounded like the distant throbbing of the sea; how time had wavered strangely, and he had been possessed by the feeling that nothing around him was quite real.

Now it was much the same, for he was as little moved by the sacking of this city as he had been by the antics of the dancers in the hot arena or by the sleek rage of the bull. All this din and terror amounted to nothing more than an incidental accompaniment to the unappeasable clamour of his grief.

Menelaus could no longer see what was to be done. He had come to Troy with a single clear purpose in mind. But Paris had escaped him, fleeing from their duel in the rain like the craven coward he was. And though he had fallen later to the arrows of Philoctetes, it was an end in which Menelaus could take no pleasure because it deprived him of the personal satisfaction he had sought. And then, when the sickening news came that

Deiphobus had taken Helen to his bed, Menelaus had found a new and still more violent focus for his hatred. Because of this further insult to his heart, he had driven on the Argive generals to fight when it looked, for a time, as if the two exhausted armies might settle for a negotiated peace. He had reminded them of the oath they had sworn to him in Sparta. He had made it clear that he would be satisfied by nothing less than the death of Deiphobus. So the war had gone on and now the war was won. Troy had been taken, as Helen had been taken, by stealth and treachery. Deiphobus was dead, and Menelaus had made sure that he had known in the moment of his death exactly who it was that killed him. But his body lay on the bed like the joints of horse-meat on which the princes of Argos had sworn to defend Menelaus's right to Helen, and his troubles were now over. Yet even as Menelaus had hacked at his body, severing the head and limbs and genitals with his sword, he had found no satisfaction in the act. His arms were sticky with the man's blood. His face was splashed with it. And almost as strong as the grief in the King of Sparta's heart was the wave of disgust that left him retching in the night.

And still Helen lived.

Already Menelaus knew that if he was going to kill her he should have done it when he first found her in bed beside Deiphobus. But he told himself that he had wanted her to see her lover die. He wanted her to know how terrible his vengeful fury was. He wanted her to see what she had done to him, to learn how she had turned his gentle heart into a murderous thing. So the moment in which he might have acted had passed. And still, as she crouched in the corner like a frightened animal, he could not bring himself to finish her.

Nor could he command anyone else to do the deed.

Menelaus walked back from the balcony into the room and stood leaning against the door. He was still holding his sword. With the back of his free hand he tried to wipe the flecks of vomit from his mouth only to realize that the hand itself was wet with blood.

What was to be done? What was to be done? All across the city his comrades exulted in their triumph. Agamemnon must already be sitting on Priam's throne. Young Neoptolemus would be taking bloody vengeance for his father's death. The others would be revelling in the slaughter, toasting each other in captured wine as the women fell into their hands, or stripping the sacked palaces and temples of their treasure. Only he on whose behalf this long war had been fought stood in the darkness, empty and wretched, rejoicing at nothing.

Though the pain of the memory was almost more than he could bear, he was remembering the days long ago, in another time, in another world, when he and his wife had played together with their little daughter Hermione in the sunlit garden of the citadel at Sparta. How could Helen have dreamed of turning her back on such happiness? What must he himself have lacked in manhood that she should have spurned the unquestioning, utterly trusting fidelity of his heart, for a mad act of passion that could only ever have ended in disaster such as this?

Never, in all the long years since Helen had left him, had Menelaus felt so utterly alone.

Odysseus stood alone in the lurid night, beating his brains with the knowledge that this catastrophe was of his making and that he had intended none of it. His plan had been clear enough. He had discussed it carefully with Agamemnon and secured his agreement. Odysseus had always maintained that the long-term gain must be greater if the victorious Argives exploited the trading strength of Troy's position rather than merely despoiling the city of its wealth. With this larger aim in mind he had pursued his secret negotiations with Antenor and Aeneas, and he had done so in good faith, certain that King Priam and Deiphobus would be more easily deceived by the stratagem of the wooden horse if the distrusted minister and the vacillating Dardanian prince were seen to suspect it. So the city would fall by stealth and need hardly be damaged in the taking. Crowned as a client king once Priam was dead, Antenor would owe his throne and his loyalty to Agamemnon. The presence of a strong garrison in the city would underwrite the alliance. And then, with Troy secured as an Argive fiefdom commanding trade with the Black Sea, the entire eastern seaboard must sooner or later fall under Agamemnon's control. Meanwhile, Odysseus would go home to Ithaca a wealthy man, having crowned the Lion of Mycenae as undisputed ruler of an Aegean empire.

It was more than a plan: it was a vision – a vision that would change the map of the known world for ever. Even as he had climbed the ladder into the wooden horse, Odysseus had been sure that Agamemnon understood the dream and shared it. But he had come out of Helen's mansion and stepped into a massacre.

The fire, he was prepared to concede, might have started by accident. But if, with the low cunning and purblind greed of a common soldier, the King of Men had already decided to opt for quick profit rather than the long-term benefits of a less certain vision then the logic became inexorable. To prevent Troy rising again and descending on Argos with the force of the avenging Furies, the destruction must be complete. The city must be burned, its walls torn down, its men exterminated, its women carried away. So even as he licensed Odysseus to give the assurances demanded by Antenor and Aeneas in return for their defection, Agamemnon must have known this was what he would do. He must have been hugging himself with glee when the Trojan defectors accepted those assurances. And why should they not have done when Odysseus had also been deceived?

All his care and craft and guile counted for nothing now. His brain was in flames with the knowledge. If Agamemnon had been standing beside him in that moment Odysseus might have struck him down. But it was another figure that came hurrying towards him out of the night, a huge Ethiopian, one of Memnon's men, half-naked, his black skin glistening with sweat, his eyes wide and very white. Reflexively Odysseus drew his sword and stuck him through the belly.

The shock of the man's weight jarred at his arm, driving the sword deeper. The Ethiopian hung there for a moment impaled, grunting with dismay. Odysseus pulled out the blade and stood back, watching him sag to his knees and fall, shuddering, to the ground. He could hear the black man muttering something in his own tongue — a curse, a gasp of execration, a prayer to whatever gods he served, who knew what those mumblings meant?

Odysseus stared down at the dying man, resentful that he had been drawn into the killing. Then his mind swirled in a blur of rage. If Agamemnon wanted blood, then blood he should have. He advanced across the square towards the sounds of slaughter and once he had begun to kill it seemed there was no stopping. He saw frightened faces gasp and cry as they fell beneath his sword. He saw the wounds splash open. He was killing people swiftly, without compunction, as though doing them a service. At one point he slipped on the entrails of a fat man he had butchered and found himself lying beside him, face to face, with the sightless, outraged eyes staring back into his own. Then he pushed himself to his feet again, driven on by an impulse of disgust, filled with fury and self-loathing.

Almost as deep in delirium as Ajax in his madness had once slaughtered the cattle in their pens, imagining them to be his enemies, Odysseus killed and killed again, working his way through the throng as though convinced that each body that fell before him might prove to be the last, so that he could be liberated, once and for all, from this dreadful duty. His mind was numb. His arm ached from the effort. His throat was parched. It all seemed to be happening in silence.

A Visitor To Ithaca

So loud was the anguish at the fall of Troy you might have thought the noise must carry across the whole astounded world; yet it would be weeks before the news of Agamemnon's victory reached as far as Ithaca. Of all the kingdoms that sent ships to the war, our western islands were furthest from the conflict. We were always last to receive word of how our forces were faring and by the time reports arrived they were far out of date, never at first hand and, more often than not, coloured by rumour and speculation. To make matters worse, Troy was taken late in the year when all the seas were running high and the straits impassable, so the fighting was over long before we got to know of it.

The view must always have been clearer from the high crag at Mycenae but even the intelligence that reached Queen Clytaemnestra was not always reliable, and she was too busy managing Agamemnon's kingdom in his absence to keep my Lady Penelope apprised of events on the eastern seaboard of the Aegean. Meanwhile the infrequent letters Penelope received from her father, Lord Icarius of Sparta, were always terse in their account of a son-in-law of whom he had never approved. So throughout the war we Ithacans were fed on scraps of information that had been picked up in larger ports by traders who came to the island, or that reached us from the occasional deserter who made it back to mainland Argos. Such men had only a fragmentary picture of events, and who could say whether their accounts were trust-worthy? All we knew for certain was that Lord Odysseus had still been alive the last time anyone had news of him.

As Prince Telemachus emerged from infancy into the proud knowledge that the father of whom he lacked all memory was one of the great Argive generals, this proved to be an increasingly frustrating state of affairs. So as his friend, I Phemius – still only a boy myself – did what I could to supply his need with flights of my own fanciful imagination. Each day he and I, along with a ragged troupe of fatherless urchins, fought our own version of the Trojan War around the pastures and coves of Ithaca. From hill to hill we launched raids on each other's flocks, singing songs and taking blows. Meanwhile, far away in windy Phrygia, Odysseus used all his guile to steer his comrades towards victory over a foe that had proved tougher and more resilient than anyone but he had anticipated.

Then, in the ninth year of the war we learned that an incon-clusive campaign in Mysia had ended with the Argive fleet being blown back to Aulis by a great storm. For a time we lived in the excited hope that Odysseus might seize the chance to visit the wife and child he had left so many years before, but all that came was a long letter which was delivered under seal directly into the hands of Penelope.

The next day she summoned my mother and some of the other women into her presence and with the gentle grace that always distinguished her care for our people, she told them that *The Raven,* the ship in which my father Terpis had sailed from Mysia, had failed to appear at Aulis. There remained a small chance that the crew might have made landfall on one or other of the islands scattered across the Aegean but the women should prepare them-selves for the possibility that their husbands were drowned at sea and would not return.

The island rang loud with wailing that day. For me, for a time, it was as though a black gash had been torn in the fabric of things. But remembering how my father, the bard of Ithaca, had sung at the naming day of Prince Telemachus, I converted my fear and grief into a solemn vow that, if he did not return, I would honour his memory by becoming the island's bard myself.

Meanwhile Penelope gave her son as sanguine an account of the letter as she could. How else was she to speak to a ten year old who knew nothing of his father except her love for him and the fact that almost all those he had left behind on the island spoke of him with affection and respect?

Only many years later, long after the war was won and Odysseus still had not returned to Ithaca, was Telemachus allowed to read the letter for himself. He told me that it contained warm expressions both of undying love and of agonized regret that a hard fate had kept him so long from his wife and son. But it was also filled with bitter criticism of the way the war was being fought. In particular, Odysseus was at pains to distance himself from the decision that had just been taken to sacrifice Agamemnon's daughter Iphigenaia on the altar of Artemis in order to secure a fair wind back to Troy.

He attributed the blame for that atrocity to Palamedes, the Prince of Euboea, a man for whom he cherished an abiding hatred. It was Palamedes who had demanded that Odysseus take the terrible oath that had been sworn at Sparta to protect the winner of Helen's hand from the jealousy of his rivals – an oath which Odysseus (who was not a contender for Helen's hand) had himself devised. It had been Palamedes who accompanied Menelaus to Ithaca and compromised Odysseus into joining the war against his will. Now it was Palamedes who had thought up the scheme to lure Iphigenaia to her death in Aulis with the pretence that she was to be married to Achilles, and Odysseus could no longer contain his contempt and loathing for the man's devious mind.

Small wonder then that Penelope had been deeply troubled by the letter, for the roguishly good-humoured, ever-optimistic man she had married was entirely absent from its words. In his place brooded an angry stranger about to return to a war which he had never sought. And he did so with his mind darkened by the conviction that the evil shadow of that war was corrupting all on whom it fell.

So the fleet had put to sea again in the tenth year of the war, and we in Ithaca heard nothing further about the fate of those aboard until the spring afternoon several months later when a black-sailed pentekonter with a serpent figurehead put in at the harbour. It bore the arms of Nauplius, King of Euboea.

Nauplius was not the only visitor to Ithaca at that time. Earlier that week Prince Amphinomus had sailed over from the neighbouring island of Dulichion to pay tribute on behalf of his father, King Nisus, who owed allegiance to Laertes, King of Ithaca. This agreeable young man had proved such an entertaining companion that Penelope persuaded him to remain a while after his business with her father-in-law was done. She claimed that he lifted her spirits in what was, for her, a lonely and anxious time. I also grew fond of Amphinomus. He was possessed of a charming, easy-going manner, was eloquent without showiness, and did not condescend when I revealed in answer to his friendly question that it was my intention to become a bard like my father before me. But Telemachus took against him from the first and to such a degree that his mother felt obliged to admonish the boy for his rudeness.

'Don't be too hard on him,' Amphinomus mildly chided her. 'After all, he has lacked the guidance of his father's hand.'

'Sons have lost their fathers in this war and fathers their sons,' Penelope sighed. 'Sometimes I can see no end to the woes it brings.'

'My own father feels the same way.' Amphinomus gave her a wry smile. 'He often thanks the gods that I was too young to go to Troy with Odysseus – though there have been times when I bitterly reproached them for the same reason.'

'Well, I pray that the war will be over long before you are called upon to serve,' Penelope replied, 'and not least so that my husband will come back soon to take this skittish colt of mine in hand.'

At which remark Telemachus scowled, whistled his father's dog Argus to his heel, and left the chamber.

'Go with him, Phemius.' Penelope favoured me with the smile that always made my heart swim. 'See if you can't improve his ill humour before we dine.'

But when I did as I was bidden, Telemachus merely glowered at me. 'You should have stayed and kept an eye on him,' he said. 'I don't trust that man. He's too eager to be liked.'

'I like him well enough anyway,' I said. 'He's asked me to sing for him tonight.'

But Telemachus was already staring out to sea where the distant sail of an approaching ship bulged like a black patch stitched into the glittering blue-green. 'Who's this putting in now?' he murmured, throwing a stone into the swell. 'No doubt some other itchy hound come sniffing at my mother's skirts.'

Until that moment such a thought had never crossed my mind. Penelope was the faithful wife of the Lord Odysseus and everyone knew that theirs was a love-match. While most of the other princes of Argos had lusted after Helen, Odysseus remained constant in his devotion to her Spartan cousin, the daughter of Icarius. Their marriage had been a cause for great joy on Ithaca and though its early years had been shadowed by a grievous number of miscarriages, no one doubted that the shared grief had deepened their love, or that it was only with the most anguished reluctance that Odysseus finally left his wife and newborn son to fight in the war at Troy. Then, as the war dragged on and King Laertes and his queen Anticleia grew older, Penelope had become the graceful Lady of the island. She was always a reliable source of comfort and wisdom to those in need, revered throughout all Argos for her constancy, and utterly beyond reproach. So I don't know whether I was more shocked by the vehemence of what Telemachus had said or troubled by my sense of its astuteness.

I was fifteen years old at that time. Telemachus was four years younger, yet he had seen what my own innocently cherished infatuation had failed to see – that the fate of Odysseus was at best uncertain and if he failed to return to Ithaca then Penelope would become the most desirable of prizes. I also realized in that moment that if Telemachus had seen it, then others must have seen it too. And with that thought it occurred to me that he must have overheard someone else uttering some such remark as the one he had just made. In any case, my angry friend stood scowling out to sea, too young to defend his mother's honour but not too young to worry over it.

However the black ship bearing down on our island that day did not carry some hopeful suitor making a speculative bid for Penelope but someone more devious – a bitter old man motivated neither by love nor by lust but by an inveterate hatred, which he did not at first reveal.

I clearly remember King Nauplius coming ashore on the island that day – a scraggy, bald-headed figure in his sixties with a hawkish nose and an elaborately barbered beard. There was a gaunt and flinty cast to his features, and the shadows webbed around his eyes darkened the critical regard with which he studied both our undefended harbour and the homely palace on the cliff. But what most impressed my young imagination were the conspicuous mourning robes he wore. I remember thinking that whatever news this king was bringing, it could not be good.

King Laertes, the father of Odysseus, was not present in the palace to receive this unexpected visitor. In those days the old king had taken to spending more and more time tending the crops and animals on his farm, or simply sitting in the shade, fanning himself with his hat and wishing that his son would return from the foreign war to assume the burden of kingship over the western islands. Laertes had been famous among the heroes of Argos in his day. As a young man, he had sailed to far Colchis with Jason on the raid that brought back the Golden Fleece. He was also among those who hunted the great boar that Divine

Artemis had loosed to ravage the lands around Calydon, but he was growing old and weary now. Earlier that week he had received the year's tribute from Dulichion, Same and Zacynthus, and then done what he could to give fair judgement over the various disputes that had arisen between them while their leaders were away. Now, once more, he had retreated with his wife Anticleia to the peace of his farm.

Having apologized to the unexpected royal visitor for the king's absence, Penelope was ordering a runner to call Laertes back to court when Nauplius raised a restraining hand and gravely shook his head. 'There is no need to trouble him,' he said. 'Let old Laertes enjoy such peace as this world allows. In any case, it is you I have come to see.'

The words fell on the air as stark and grim as the robes he wore. Sensing that grief had turned to a mortal sickness inside the man, Penelope said, 'I see you have suffered some great loss, my lord.' But she was remembering how she herself had suffered at the last visit from the royal house of Euboea. Already she was fearful that the ill news that Nauplius brought with him must press closely on her own life too.

'A loss from which I do not expect to recover,' Nauplius answered. 'This war has cost me my son.'

'Palamedes is dead?'

The grey eyes studied her as if in reproach. 'You have had no word from Troy?'

'We have heard nothing since the fleet sailed from Aulis.' Opening helpless hands, Penelope shook her head. 'I grieve to hear of your loss. Tell me, how did this thing happen?'

Nauplius made as if to answer, then seemed to change his mind, shaking his head at the immense burden of what he had to utter. 'I have sailed far today,' he sighed, 'and my heart is heavy with evil tidings. Let me first rest a while and regain my strength. Then we shall speak of the grief that this war has brought to us.' Nodding with the absolute authority of a sovereign who had decided that everything that needed to be said for the time being had now been said, he turned away, raising a ringed hand to his body-servant for support.

'Of course,' Penelope answered uneasily. 'My steward will escort you to your chamber. But first . . . Forgive me, but I must ask you, Lord Nauplius . . .'

Frowning, the old king tilted his head to look back at her. Penelope forced herself to speak. 'Do you have word of my husband?' She saw how one flinty eye was narrower than the other and its lid quivered like a moth beneath its brow. Into a silence that had gone on too long she said, 'Does Odysseus live?'

Nauplius drew in his breath and stood with his mottled head nodding still.

'Oh yes,' the voice was barely more than a hoarse wheeze, 'Odysseus lives still. Odysseus lives.' And again, with a sigh that seemed to rebuke the relief that broke visibly across her face, he turned away.

When Nauplius and his attendants had left the hall, Amphinomus approached Penelope, smiling. 'Good news at last, my lady.'

'Yes.' Penelope stood with the fingertips of her right hand at her cheek. 'But I fear that Nauplius has more to say.'

Amphinomus shrugged. 'It may only be that his grief has darkened his view of things. You mustn't let his shadow dim your own fair light.'

Penelope shook her head. 'The truth is that I didn't greatly care for Palamedes. He was a clever man, in some ways as clever as Odysseus, but he lacked warmth. And I have often wished that he had never set foot on this island. If he hadn't come here with Menelaus all those years ago, Telemachus would have a father to watch over him and I a husband in my bed. Yet one must pity any man who has lost his son.'

'One must indeed,' Amphinomus pursed his lips, 'even though he brings a deathly chill into the hall with him!'

Penelope reproved the arch smile in the young man's handsome face. 'It wouldn't surprise me to learn that the King of

Euboea sickens from more than grief. Also he is as much a guest of the house as you are, sir. We will be civil with him.' But she was glad of her friend's company in what threatened to be a difficult and demanding time.

Her apprehensions were confirmed at dinner that evening when Nauplius merely frowned in response to Penelope's warmly expressed hope that he was well rested, and then went on to express his surprise that a young woman of the royal house of Sparta had not long since grown discontented with the dull round of life in rustic Ithaca.

'I regret that our plain ways are not to your taste,' Penelope answered. 'I myself have always found the simple life here wonderfully refreshing after the rivalries and gossip of the court in Sparta. With each day that passes I learn to love this island and its people more.' Nor did she entirely conceal the reproach in her voice as she added, 'Indeed I sometimes think that were all the world to emulate such dullness, it might be a happier and more peaceful place.'

'Your husband has been gone for nearly ten years, madam,' Nauplius replied. 'Have those years not taught you that happiness and peace are not to be found anywhere for long?'

Penelope shrugged her delicate shoulders. 'I respect the wisdom of your years, my lord, but it may be that Ithaca has something to teach you still.'

'However,' Amphinomus put in, 'we are all eager for news of the war, and not much reaches us here. Will you share with us what you know of its progress?'

'Troy still stands,' Nauplius glowered. 'Men fight beneath its walls and die, and it would seem that Agamemnon and Achilles are fiercer in their quarrels with each other than they are with the Trojans. Meanwhile prudent counsel is ignored and honest men are traduced by liars. In short, the Argive army is led by knaves and fools. What more is there to say?' Undismayed by the flush he had brought to Penelope's face, he looked away.

Amphinomus said quietly, 'I think you forget that Lord Odysseus is among those who command the host.'

'No, sir, I do not forget,' Nauplius answered shortly.

From further down the table Lord Mentor, whom Odysseus had entrusted with the management of his affairs on Ithaca uttered a low growl. 'Then you will except him from your remarks, I trust?'

But either Nauplius did not hear him or affected not to have done so. He took a trial sip from his wine-cup, wrinkled his nostrils in a barely concealed grimace of disappointment, and smiled at Penelope. 'Our Euboean vintage is mellower, my dear. I must make a point of sending you some.'

Her voice uncharacteristically tense, Penelope said, 'My husband is no man's fool, sir. Do you suggest he is a knave?'

Nauplius opened his hands in a mild gesture of protest. 'You were daughter to my old friend Icarius long before you became wife to Odysseus. Believe me, I have no desire to say anything that would cause you pain or displeasure.'

Aware that the answer was neither a withdrawal nor an apology, Penelope made an effort to still her breathing. If she had suspected earlier that this dour old man had come with mischief at work in his embittered mind, she was convinced of it now. Looking for space to gather her thoughts, she turned to Amphinomus. 'Did you not ask Phemius to sing for you tonight? Perhaps his voice will please our royal guest?'

And so I was required to stand before this uneasy table and raise my voice in the silence. I had been looking forward to this moment all day but any bard will tell you that few can sing at their best before those whose minds are elsewhere. My ambition had been to sing from *The Lay of Lord Odysseus* on which I had been working, and in the circumstances it would have been the courageous thing to do. But I was reluctant to expose a still raw and tender talent before a judge as stern as King Nauplius, so I chose instead to sing some of the traditional goat-songs sung by shepherds on the island. Amphinomus and Lady Penelope received them warmly enough, but those bucolic airs appealed no more to the visiting king's ears than our island's wine had done to his palate.

'My son told me that you liked to keep a simple life here on Ithaca,' he said dryly, 'but I'm surprised to find that the court of Laertes lacks a bard even!'

'The boy's father is our bard,' Penelope answered quietly. 'There is some fear that his life was lost at sea after the Mysian campaign.'

'A campaign against which my own son strongly advised,' Nauplius said with narrowed eyes, 'but other counsel was preferred, and with what disastrous results we may all now plainly see.' Then he cast a searching look my way. 'The boy sings sweetly enough,' he conceded. 'I hear the grief in his voice. It is hard for a son to lose a father, but it is in the natural course of things.' Nauplius shook his gaunt head. 'For a father to lose a son however . . .'

Amphinomus said, 'Surely a father can take comfort from the knowledge that his son died honourably in battle?'

But Nauplius turned a cold stare on him. 'My son was denied such honour. And denied it by those whom he had loyally sought to serve.'

The silence was broken by Lord Mentor. 'As the king has observed,' he said, 'we are simple souls on Ithaca. Perhaps he will make his meaning plainer.'

Nauplius met the controlled anger with a bleak smile. 'In good time,' he said, 'in good time. My business here is with the Lady Penelope. If she will grant me private audience when this meal is done, we will talk more of these things.'

'You are the guest of our house,' Penelope answered. 'It shall be as you wish.'

And so, with the only subjects about which people wished to speak thus firmly confined to silence, this awkward meal progressed. Amphinomus did what he could to ease the atmosphere by extolling the contribution that Euboea had made to the art of navigation. In particular he praised that island's introduction of cliff-top beacons beside dangerous shoals, an invention which had caught on across Argive waters and proved a boon to mariners everywhere.

Nauplius nodded in acknowledgement. He and Amphinomus chatted together for a while. 'It pleases me,' he said, 'to learn that the Lady Penelope has found a diverting companion in her husband's absence.' And at the fireside pillar where we sat with the dog Argus stretched between us, kicking his hind-legs in a dream of chase, I saw Telemachus scowl.

Eventually, having eaten well for all his disdain for rustic fare, Nauplius declared himself replete, washed his hands in the bronze bowl and indicated his desire to speak alone with the lady of the house. We watched them leave the hall together, he gaunt and frail, she taller by almost a head, yet they felt worryingly like an executioner and his victim.

'Come, Phemius,' Amphinomus called across the hall, 'sing for us again.'

Not for many years, not indeed till after her husband's return, did Penelope utter a word about what was said between her and King Nauplius that night. The following morning, shortly after dawn, that disagreeable visitor put out to sea without offering thanks or saying farewell to anyone. No one on the island regretted his departure though we were all troubled by the shadow that he had evidently cast across Penelope's mind and face, and not even Amphinomus could persuade her to share the burden of her cares.

Not many weeks would pass, of course, before we learned that this was only one of many visits that Nauplius was to make to the chief kingdoms of Argos, and everywhere he went, including, most dramatically, Mycenae itself, he left the contamination of his vengeful grief. And from reports of what happened elsewhere it was not difficult to guess what must have passed between Nauplius and Penelope that night.

Nauplius would have begun by singing the praises of his dead son Palamedes. Was his not the swiftest and most orderly mind in the Argive leadership? Had he not come to the aid of the duller-witted Agamemnon by recommending an order of battle which would take full advantage of the diverse forces assembled under his command rather than allowing their rivalries and customs to weaken their strength and cause disarray? Had he not devised a common signalling system that could be understood and exploited equally well by tribesmen from Arcadia, Crete, Boeotia and Magnesia? Had he not unified the systems of measurement used throughout the host so that there could be no confusion over distances and arguments over the distribution of rations and booty might be kept to a minimum? Wasn't it Palamedes who had kept the troops in good heart by teaching them his game of dice and stones? Hadn't he always done what he could to make sure that the voice of the common soldiery was heard among the council of the kings? In short, Nauplius insisted that if it had not been for the presiding intelligence of Palamedes, anticipating difficulties and finding means to overcome them, Agamemnon's vast army would quickly have degenerated into a quarrelsome rabble with each tribal contingent looking only to its own interests even though the entire campaign might founder on such narrow pride.

Penelope would have listened patiently to all of this. After all, the man was her house-guest and it was understandable that a father's grief should exaggerate his dead son's contribution to the arduous effort of a war in which he'd lost his life. She had no doubt, of course, that the intelligence and experience of Odysseus must have played at least an equal part in that effort, and probably a greater one, but she had already sensed that to speak up for her husband at this juncture could only arouse a hostile response from this lugubrious old man. So she preferred to hold her peace and wait to see what menace still lay concealed behind his show of grief.

It was not long in coming. Frowning into space as he spoke, Nauplius told how, late in the previous year, when their supplies began to dwindle and raids along the Phrygian and Thracian coasts produced little by way of grain and stores, the Argive host had been faced with a choice between starving outside the walls of Troy or turning tail with little to show for all those long years of war. Odysseus had been in command of one of the raiding parties that returned with its holds empty. When he was met by the rage of Agamemnon, he publicly defied any man to do better. The harvests had failed everywhere that year, he claimed. The granaries were bare.

'Palamedes took up the challenge,' Nauplius said, 'and when he returned to the camp only a few days later, his ships rode low in the water, heavy with grain. You would have thought he deserved the heartfelt thanks of the entire host, would you not? And the common soldiers were warm enough in their praise. My son had always championed their cause. Now he had saved them from hunger. But with the generals it was a different story.' Fiercely the old man drew in his breath. 'Whenever there had been conflict among them as to the most effective course of action, Palamedes was invariably proved right. The high command sometimes paid a high price in blood for ignoring his advice and now, once again, my son had succeeded where others had failed. Their envy turned first to spite and then to malice. At least one of them was determined to blacken his name.'

By now Penelope must already have guessed the direction of Nauplius's story. She knew very well that Odysseus cared for Palamedes no more than she did herself. But nothing could have prepared her for the charge that Nauplius was about to bring against her husband.

'My son used to send me frequent reports of the progress of the war,' he said. 'After all, I had been one of Agamemnon's principal backers from the first. To fight this war he needed the wealth of Euboea as well as our ships. Without the huge loans I made him, he could never have mustered half the force he did. And both my son and I were well aware that those loans would not be repaid unless Troy fell. So Palamedes went to the war as the guardian of my investment. I relied on him to make sure that the campaign was effectively pursued. I relied on him for news. When he fell silent I began to suspect that something untoward had happened.' After a grim silence Nauplius said, 'I sent urgent messages to the Atreides brothers. When no word came back I decided to sail for Phrygia myself.'

After a deliberate silence Penelope asked, 'And what did you learn there?'

'I learned that my son had been dead for some time. But he had been denied an honourable death in battle. Palamedes had been traduced by men he took to be his friends. Envious men. Men who worked in darkness to do him harm. A conspiracy of lies had been mounted against him. He was accused of treason. Evidence was fabricated. It purported to show that he had taken Trojan bribes. He was tried and found guilty by the very men who had perpetrated this foul calumny. Palamedes, always the most prudent and honourable of men, met a traitor's end. He was stoned to death by the host he had sought to serve to the very best of his ability.' Nauplius was shaking as he spoke. His lips quivered but his eyes were dry as in a hoarse whisper he said, 'My son's last words were, "Truth, I mourn for you, who have predeceased me."'

The words lay heavily on the silence for a time. They could hear the sound of men carousing in the hall below. Eventually Penelope raised her eyes. 'You are impugning the honour of Agamemnon and Menelaus?' she demanded.

'I am,' Nauplius answered, 'and I am impugning Diomedes of Tiryns and Idomeneus of Crete who conspired with them against my son.' He paused to fix her with his flinty stare. 'And I am impugning your husband Odysseus who was the father of these lies.'

'Then I will hear no more of this,' Penelope said steadily, 'for it seems to me that anyone can vilify another man's name when he is not present to defend himself, but there can be no honour in such slander.'

'Which is precisely what your husband did to my son,' Nauplius retorted, 'and his shade still cries out for justice. Do not turn away from me, Penelope. I have never felt anything other than affection in my heart for you. Yet I confess I have long shared your father's doubts about the man you chose for your husband. Odysseus was always a plausible rogue, yes, but a rogue nevertheless. And now I know him to be more and worse than a rogue – he is a villain, one who will stoop to any deceit to secure his own ends. Do not turn away, my dear, for as you will soon learn to your bitter cost, you are as much the victim of his duplicity as I have been.'

But Penelope was already on her feet and crossing the room to leave it. She stopped at the door to confront the old man with the cold rebuke of her eyes. 'You have already said too much.'

'The truth is often painful, I know,' he began to answer, 'but it must be heard if justice is to be done.'

'You are the guest of my husband's house,' Penelope interrupted him, 'and you are also old, sir. So I will not ask you to leave this place at once. But I advise you to take to your ship at dawn. Otherwise I will not answer for your safety.'

'Hear me,' Nauplius beseeched as she turned to open the door. 'I speak only out of care for you. This war has corrupted all who lead it. Why do you imagine that not one of them has come home in all these years? It is not because they are constantly in the field, I assure you. Far from it! Those errant gentlemen have long been living a life of licence and debauchery out there in Phrygia. From all the many women they have taken to their tents, each has now selected his favourite concubine. And there is more. They mean to make queens of their oriental paramours when they return to Argos. Pledges have been given before the gods. Believe me, my dear, Odysseus is as faithless as the rest.' He took in the hostile glitter of Penelope's eyes and refused to be abashed by it. 'You do well to look for comfort elsewhere. Amphinomus is a handsome fellow.'

Penelope drew in her breath. 'Now I am sure that you lie,' she said. 'May the gods forgive you for it, for I cannot. Let me never see your face on Ithaca again.'

She left the chamber, banging the door behind her. Yet for all her defiance I doubt that she slept that night. Nor can she have known much rest in the days and nights that followed, for secrets and lies are defilers of the heart and once the trust of the heart is breached it knows no peace. So Penelope was often to be heard sighing as she worked her loom by day, or again when she made her offerings to Athena and prayed that the goddess might teach her patience of soul. And often she would walk alone along the cliff, gazing out to sea as she wondered what had happened to her husband beneath the distant walls of Troy.

The Division of the Spoils

Dawn, when it finally came, was little more than a ruddy gleam blackened by smoke and made redder by the flames still rising from the burning buildings. Again and again throughout the night the nerves of the Trojan women had been shaken by the noise of roof-beams collapsing and the harsh clatter of falling tiles. Here and there the hoarse gust of a blaze still sent its vivid exhaust of sparks upwards through the smoke, but most of the fires were now under control, all resistance had ended, and only occasional screams rose from men under torment to reveal where their riches were concealed.

The streets stank vilely of blood and excrement. With the trap-door still hanging open at its belly, the wooden horse looked down on a dense litter of corpses. Already kites and vultures circled. Somewhere, indifferent to everything but the glory of his own existence, a cockerel crowed his clarion to the day.

A few of the women had briefly taken refuge in oblivion, but only Cassandra had truly slept that night, and it would have been wrong to deduce from the subdued sound of their sobbing that the captives were calmer now. Rather, with the coming of the light, they felt more than ever to be the victims of a fate so violent and capricious that it numbed their frightened minds. Yesterday Troy had been intact behind its walls, having withstood all the strength the Argive host could bring against it. Today the city was a ruin and its royal women were waiting like stockyard cattle to be apportioned among foreigners they detested and feared.

Yet the sun seemed content to preside over such outrageous fortune and the sky might have been void of gods for all the notice it took of their imprecations. So these women were far from calm. They huddled together, exiled from the past, afraid of the future, seeking from each other the solace that none had to give, and deprived even of the means to kill themselves.

Polyxena crouched among them, knowing that sooner or later Neoptolemus must come in search of her again. She had been present by the altar of Zeus when that terrifying youth had struck off her father's head, and she had guessed already that he would seek her out. The sixteen year old girl had huddled behind her sister Laodice in the portico earlier that night, listening to his voice cajoling her to reveal herself. She had cast about for a form of words that might convince him that she had been only the unwitting bait in the trap that had been set for Achilles. But she had seen the torchlight glancing off his sword and knew that words would make no difference. The boy was fanatical in his desire to avenge his father. Her only chance of survival was to conceal herself among the other women in the hope that he might be struck down by the hand of a merciful god before he could identify her. Then, when Agamemnon had called Neoptolemus away, she had begun to wonder whether the fates might prove kindly after all. But as the night wore on there was no evidence of kindness in this stricken city and when daylight broke, her terror returned with greater force.

Polyxena could not prevent her teeth from chattering as she crouched beside her mother who sat nursing Andromache's head in her lap. Beside them Cassandra whispered prophecies that the Trojans would prove more fortunate than their enemies. They had at least died in defence of their sacred homeland, while thousands of the barbarian invaders had perished far from their homes, and

those who made it back to Argos would find a cruel fate waiting
for them.

'Agamemnon will see that he has taken death into his bed,'
Cassandra chanted. 'Already the lioness couples with the goat. A
blade glints in the bath-house. A torrent of blood flows there. I
too shall be swept away on that red tide. But the son of
Agamemnon shall bring a bloody end to Neoptolemus. He will
leave his impious body dead beneath Apollo's stone. As for that
ingenious fiend Odysseus, Blue-haired Poseidon will keep him
far from the home while others junket and riot in his hall. The
Goddess will seize his heart. Hades will open his dark door to
him. Death will crowd his house.' But none of the women believed
the mad girl any more than they could silence her. So they sat
together under the portico, watching the sun come up and
dreading what the day must bring.

Exhausted from the efforts of the night, most of the Argive leaders
were relaxing in the palace across the square. The first elation of
victory had passed and the rush of wine to their heads brought,
at that early hour, only a queasy sense of what they had achieved.
Odysseus had wandered off alone somewhere. Apart from
Menelaus, who still brooded in the mansion that Paris had built
for Helen, the others were carousing together, but there were
grumbles of dissent from Acamas and his brother Demophon
when Neoptolemus claimed the right to take Polyxena for his
own before the lots had been apportioned.

Annoyed that even in this hour of triumph, discord should have
broken out so quickly among his followers, Agamemnon stood
uncertainly. He knew there was some justice in the complaint but
he was reluctant to offend Neoptolemus who had shown a ferocity
in the fight against the Ethiopians that had astounded older, battle-
hardened men. Also he knew what fate lay in store for Polyxena
if he acceded to this demand, and his thoughts had involuntarily
darkened at the memory of what he had done to his own daughter
Iphigenaia.

Seeing his hesitation, Neoptolemus declared that the shade of his father had demanded in a dream that the girl who had betrayed him should be sacrificed on his tomb. 'Does the High King not believe that the man who did so much to win this war should be accorded such justice? Would you deny my father's shade?'

Immediately Agamemnon made the sign to ward off the evil eye. A quarrel with Achilles had almost lost him this war once. He would not risk another with his angry ghost. 'Take her,' he said. 'It is only just.'

So Neoptolemus came to claim Polyxena in the early morning light. Again he summoned her out of the huddle of women. Again Hecuba rose to protect her youngest daughter. But the weary young warrior was in no mood to listen to her pleas and insults. 'If you don't want to feel the flat of my sword on your old bones,' he snarled, 'tell your daughter to show herself.'

Polyxena rose from the place where she had been crouching. 'I am here,' she declared in a voice that shook as she spoke. 'Achilles asked for me more gently. If you hope to emulate your father, you must learn to speak with something other than your sword.'

'Come into the light,' Neoptolemus answered. 'Let me take a look at you.'

Loosing the hand of Laodice, Polyxena stepped between the women huddled round her and stared without flinching at the youth. Being his senior by three years or more, she might, in other circumstances, have taunted him for parading in the suit of armour that had been made to fit his father's broader shoulders. But she knew that her life stood in graver danger now than when she had met with Achilles in Apollo's temple at Thymbra. Her face was flushed with fear. Her breath was drawn too quickly. When Neoptolemus smiled at the swift rise and fall of her recently budded breasts she glanced away.

'I understand that my father sought to befriend you,' he said. 'Is that not so?'

'Achilles asked to speak with me, yes.'

'But it was you who made the first approach.'

Nervously she whispered, 'My father asked it of me.' Polyxena's gaze had been fixed on the ground beneath her. Now she looked up hopelessly into those cold eyes. 'We thought it the only hope of having Hector's body returned to us.'

'And because my father had a noble heart he acceded to that hope, did he not?'

Polyxena nodded and averted her eyes.

'Yet that was not the last time you saw him?'

Her arms were crossed at her breast. Now she was trembling so much that she could barely speak. 'But it was Achilles who sought me out.'

'Perhaps you had given him cause to do so?'

'I swear not,' she gasped. 'The priest told me he had come looking for me many times. The thought of it frightened me. I didn't understand what he wanted.'

'But still you came.'

'Yes.'

'And you didn't come alone. You told your treacherous brother Paris that Achilles was to be found unguarded at the temple of Apollo. You told him exactly when he would be there. You told him to bring his bow and kill my father in vengeance for the death of your brother Hector.'

'That is not how it was!' Polyxena cried.

But Neoptolemus was not listening. He was remembering that Odysseus had told him how, in a quiet hour together, Achilles had confessed his tender feelings for Polyxena. Looking at the girl now – the tousled ringlets blowing about her face, the delicate hands at her shoulders, the shape of her slim thighs disclosed by the pull of the breeze at her shift – he thought he understood how this alluring combination of poise and vulnerability might have tugged at his father's heart.

It did so now, seditiously, at his own.

Yet this girl had betrayed his father, whose shade cried out for vengeance.

'And is not Thymbra under the protection of the god?' he

demanded. 'Isn't it a sacred place of truce where men from both sides – Argive and Trojan alike – were free to make their offerings without fear?'

Seeing that her truth and his must forever lie far from each other's reach, Polyxena lowered her head again and consigned herself to silence.

Accusation gathered force in his voice. 'But you and your brothers lacked all reverence for the god. Together you violated the sanctuary of Apollo's temple. Your brothers were afraid to face my father in open combat like true men, so they set a trap for him. And you, daughter of Priam, were the willing bait in that trap.'

In a low whisper Polyxena said, 'I knew nothing of what they planned.'

Neoptolemus snorted. 'I think you're lying to me – as you lied to my father before me. I think, daughter of Priam, that it's time you were purified of lies.'

He turned away from her and gestured to the two Myrmidons who stood at his back. The women who had listened with pent breath to their tense exchanges began to moan and whimper as the Myrmidons stepped forward to seize Polyxena by her thin arms.

Swaying where she stood, Hecuba screeched, 'Where are you taking her?'

'To my father's tomb,' Neoptolemus answered coldly. 'There is a last service she can perform for him there.' Then all the women were wailing again as they watched Polyxena dragged off through the gritty wind blowing across the square, past the impassive effigy of the horse, towards the Scaean Gate.

Walking at dawn through ransacked streets where only the dead were gathered, Odysseus disturbed vultures and pie-dogs already tugging at the silent piles of human flesh. They cowered at his approach or flapped away on verminous wings, peevishly watching as he stared at the horror of what had been done.

During the course of the night a living city had been transformed into a vast necropolis. Its very air was charred and excremental. As though some swift, inexorable pestilence had struck out of the night sky, all its men folk had lain down in droves, their necks gaudy with wounds, their entrails flowering in garlands from their bellies, their eyes gaping at the day. Here lay a man who might once have been a jolly butcher, now with his ribs split open like a side of beef. There, in a slovenly mess, crouched two twin boys – they could only recently have learned to speak – with their infant brains dashed out against a wall. And over there a youth sat propped against an almond tree, evidently puzzled by the broken blade of a sword that had been left protruding like a handle from his skull. And still, in the boughs of that tree, a linnet sang.

When he came out into a small square strewn with bodies, Odysseus saw three men who had followed him to Troy from Dulichion. They were quenching their thirst at a fountain while another milked a nanny-goat into an upturned helmet clutched between his knees. Across the square a half-naked woman with blood splashed at her thighs sat weeping in the doorway of a house.

The soldiers leapt to their feet at his approach, pressing knuckles to their brows as though expecting a reprimand. When Odysseus merely asked if he might share their water, he was offered goat's milk but said that water was all he wanted. Before he could reach the fountain however, the weary men relaxed and began to congratulate him on the success of his ruse. Only a man out of the Ionian isles, they declared, could have been canny enough to dream up a scheme as clever as that of the wooden horse.

'We shall have tales to tell when we get home, sir,' lisped the oldest of them, a grey-headed man who had taken a scar across his mouth and lost half his teeth in the rout at the palisade much earlier that year.

'Do you think there was ever a night of slaughter such as this?' asked another.

Odysseus shook his head, unspeaking.

The man who had been milking the goat said, 'There's been times I've wondered whether I'd ever get to see my wife again, but thanks to you, sir, I expect to come home a rich man now.'

The first man nodded, grinning. 'It seems the gods were with us after all.'

Around them, the bodies of the dead paid scant attention to these ordinary men, their murderers. And when Odysseus opened his mouth he found he could not speak. His hands were trembling again. When he lifted them to where water splashed in the basin of the fountain he realized that his arms were still stained with blood up to his elbows.

Hurriedly he washed them clean, then cupped his hands at the spout and lifted them to his lips. Water splashed across his tongue like light. He stood swaying a moment, possessed by brief startling intimations of another life in which, with a frenzy entirely alien to his nature, he too had joined the massacre. He saw the Ethiopian mumbling in his blood; he saw the fat man's eyes staring back at him.

Then he returned to time. He heard the water splashing in the bowl and the woman sobbing still.

Nodding at the soldiers with a weary, distracted smile, Odysseus walked out of the square towards the gate, making for the sea.

At a wind-blown dune not far from the burial mound of Achilles he came to a halt and stood alone beside the sea, watching a flight of pelicans flag their way across the bay. Then his gaze shifted westwards with such concentration that his keen eyesight might have travelled out across the turbulent Aegean and over the mountains of Thessaly to focus on his small homestead island of Ithaca. He was thinking about his wife Penelope and his little son Telemachus, who must now be almost as old as Neoptolemus. With a fervour that amazed him, Odysseus heard himself praying that, unlike the son of Achilles, his own boy would never rejoice in a night of slaughter such as the one he had just endured.

Hunched against the wind, he remembered the dream that had

come to him on Ithaca — the furrows of his fields sown with salt, his infant son thrown down before the ploughshare. Ten years, the sibyl at the Earth-mother's shrine had said, ten wasted years must pass before Troy fell. And now Troy had fallen, destroyed by his own ingenuity, and those long years of war seemed waste indeed, for he had lost more in a single night than all the gold of Troy could redeem. He had done such things as would chill his wife's blood should she ever come to hear of them.

The white caps of the breakers rolling in off the Hellespont clashed against the shore. The wind banged about his ears. Odysseus swayed where he stood. His breathing was irregular, his tongue dry as a stone in his mouth. Shivering, he lifted a hand to his brow and found that his temples were rimed with sweat. His fingers trembled. He sensed that his nerves had begun at last to mutiny.

He had been standing alone by the clamour of the sea for perhaps an hour when he saw the small party making its way towards the burial mound of Achilles. Two lightly armoured Myrmidons were pushing along the slight figure of a girl whose hair was winnowed by the breeze. Clutching a blanket about her shoulders, she trod the shingle gingerly in bare feet. Behind them walked a smallish warrior in a golden breastplate: Neoptolemus.

Instantly Odysseus knew what the youth intended to do. In the same moment Neoptolemus recognized him and called out that Agamemnon had been asking for him. 'The division of the spoils will take place soon,' he said. 'Let me do what I have to do, then we can walk back together.'

Shielding his eyes against the glare from the sun, Odysseus said, 'Is that Polyxena you have there?'

'The whore that betrayed my father, yes. I mean to sacrifice her on his tomb. Come and stand witness.'

'Have you questioned her?' Odysseus demanded. 'Have you heard her side of the story?'

Neoptolemus frowned at his comrade across the space between

them. 'She claims she had no idea what Paris and Deiphobus were up to. But then she would say that, wouldn't she?'

'It may be the truth,' Odysseus urged. 'Think about it. You don't want innocent blood on your hands. Your father was fond of her. He gave me reason to think that Polyxena was fond of him too.'

'Such are the wiles of women. She's tried the same game with me. The bitch is all temptation.' Neoptolemus spat onto the sand. 'Are you coming or not?'

Odysseus looked across to where the girl stood desolate in the morning light, He found himself remembering Iphigenaia on the altar at Aulis – how she had been brought to her death on the pretence that she was to be married to Achilles. Then he was thinking of Deidameia, the mother of the baby who was to become Neoptolemus, and how bitterly she had grieved when Achilles left Skyros. And then about Briseis, over whom Achilles had quarrelled with Agamemnon in a dispute that almost wrecked the Argive cause. Whenever Achilles let his fierce radiance fall on a woman it seemed that disaster must ensue, as though he had inherited his mother's glamour like a curse. Yet above all Odysseus was thinking about his own wife and what judgement she would pass on a man who stood by and watched a helpless girl dragged to her death by a half-demented boy.

He looked up and saw Polyxena staring at him. Where he might have expected to find a desperate appeal in her eyes, he saw only the glazed terror of a trapped hare. The world was an immense snare, and she was caught in it, and struggle was of no avail.

'Let her go, Neoptolemus,' he shouted.

When only a dubious silence came in reply, he added, 'I'll buy her from you if you like, out of my own share in the spoils.'

'Fancy her yourself, do you?'

Odysseus shook his head in pained incredulity. 'I can't believe that your father would want this.'

'Oh but you're wrong.' Neoptolemus smiled. 'He came to me in a dream. He told me that his shade would know no rest until the whore who betrayed him lay dead on his tomb.'

Odysseus stared across at that fanatical young face, already aware that nothing he could say or do would ever penetrate such certainty. 'But you never knew your father,' he protested. 'You were too young. How can you be sure it was him in your dream and not just some shadow of your own rage?'

Neoptolemus merely jeered again. 'And I thought you were the one who put his trust in dreams.' With a flash of sunlight off his breastplate, he turned away, ordering his men to push the girl on towards the top of the great mound where his father's ashes lay buried in a golden urn, mingled with those of Achilles' beloved friend Patroclus.

Odysseus stood trembling as he watched them go. Having always prided himself on his ingenuity, his resourcefulness, his intelligence, he saw in those moments that he possessed no more than a callow understanding of the aptitude for evil lurking in human nature, doggedly awaiting its chance to thrive. And the failure was a failure of self-understanding also, for as the past night had just shown he was in no way exempt from this terrible propensity. Yet after ten years of war, he remained, it seemed, the merest novice in those ordeals of anguish through which deep wisdom might be learned; and if he had been so easily made Agamemnon's dupe, it was only because for far too long he had duped himself, proclaiming things in which he had no belief, acting as he had no wish to act, capering before the world as a clever, but morally derelict, cipher of a man.

Overwhelmed by a stultifying sense of his own futility, Odysseus knew that what he was about to see must be seared for ever on his mind, but he lacked the will even to avert his eyes. When the figures reached the summit of the mound, he saw the girl pushed roughly to the ground. He could hear nothing, for if words were spoken, the wind snatched them away. He saw Neoptolemus draw his sword, but before he could raise it to strike, Polyxena got to her feet. She stood with the wind wrapping her thin dress taut about her limbs, lifted her chin, and tore open the cloth at her chest so that her small breasts and neck were bared. Momentarily

Neoptolemus seemed disconcerted by the act. Her pride, her refusal to be cowed, must have struck him as impertinence. To his strict mind there was something shameless in the way she flaunted before his sword. It was as if she was choosing death as her lover in preference to him. Then with a curt tilt of her head Polyxena swept her hair back and lengthened her neck before the blade. Her eyes remained open. Odysseus felt sure that she was looking precisely in his direction as the sword sliced through the air.

Meanwhile an urgent, increasingly ill-tempered restlessness had possessed the victorious host. Most of them wanted to get away as quickly as possible from a place where evidence of their crimes lay rife around them. Already the air was tainted with the stink of decaying flesh. Soon it must prove insufferable. Yet after those years of struggle, each man was determined to grab as much as he could before leaving and there was a prodigious bounty of loot in the captured city.

In the early hours of the sack, a gang of Lapiths caught pillaging a small temple on their own account had been summarily executed, but once the generals were called into council and became locked in their own disputes, all attempts to organize an orderly and equitable way of dividing the spoils broke down and each contingent of troops sent out its scavengers in packs. Requisitioning carts and pack-animals wherever they could find them, they loaded them with golden effigies, silver cauldrons, copper ingots, tripods, ewers, dishes, rhytons, chalices, torques, pectorals, jewelled diadems, rich tapestries and drapes, anything of value that could be moved. Arguments broke out over the choicer items of spoil. Old rivalries turned vicious with greed. Blood was shed. Meanwhile the gale that had got up across the Phrygian plain began to blow harder and men were injured in the drive to load herds of stolen cattle and horses onto ships that dipped and lurched in the choppy waters of the bay.

By late morning of the first day after the fall of the city,

Agamemnon was in a filthy temper. He hadn't slept for two nights. He was exhausted from the effort of trying to control his rampaging troops. Wine had left him with a thunderous headache, and now he seemed doomed to listen to interminable wrangling in the council about how a fair division of the spoils could be achieved. Not for the first time he found himself missing the cool, discriminating mind of Palamedes. The young Euboean had applied himself to this very problem after the fall of Smyrna and had come up with a solution; but his system had been so complicated that no one could remember quite how it worked, and now he was dead. Nor, with the possible exception of the still-absent Odysseus, was there anyone else who commanded sufficient respect to act as arbiter. So the arguing went on.

Meanwhile Agamemnon had things on his mind which he had not yet shared with his squabbling council. Prominent among them were thoughts of Cassandra as he had seen her, several hours earlier, in the temple of Athena. She stood, grasping the Palladium in her slender arms for protection while Locrian Aias lifted her shift from behind to reveal her naked flesh. Agamemnon had entered the temple in time to prevent the rape but the image was seared on his mind. And he had spoken to Cassandra. He had seen her breasts through the torn shift and looked into her face and found himself beguiled by the wild, penetrating gaze with which her eyes defied him. It was like being looked at by a wounded lynx.

Driven by an impulse of desire, Agamemnon had turned to his herald Talthybius, ordering that Cassandra be kept aside as part of his own portion in the spoils. As swiftly, as unconsciously, as that, the thing had been done.

And he wanted her now. He wanted her very badly, but he must sit here in this half-wrecked throne-room, listening to Acamas complain that there could be no justice if those who had fought throughout all ten years of the war were to see no more profit from their pains than those, such as the stripling Neoptolemus, who had only recently arrived.

Then Demophon, who had slipped earlier in a pool of blood and cracked his forehead, was declaring that as this relative newcomer had already seized Polyxena for his own purposes, should the others not be offered adequate compensation from his share for her removal from the lottery?

Neoptolemus, of course, would hear not a word of this. Why should a man be penalised for piously avenging his father's murder? No personal gain had accrued to him from Polyxena's death. Lesser men should be grateful that their own names would live for ever in the reflected glory of Achilles' fame rather than seeking to defraud the hero's son of a portion of his just reward.

Agamemnon groaned as the argument went on. Rueing the day that Odysseus had persuaded him to have Palamedes stoned, he was wondering where the Ithacan had got to now that his advice was needed. 'Let us at least agree to the division of the women!' he shouted. 'I have taken Cassandra for myself. Does anyone question that?'

Far from questioning it, most of the council were as relieved by their leader's eccentric choice as they were astonished by it. Who else would want a mad girl prowling round his house? So Agamemnon reclined back on Priam's throne, drumming his fingers with satisfaction. 'Let lots be drawn for Andromache then.'

Again Neoptolemus stepped forward. 'I have a prior claim to Hector's wife. Why should I trust her to chance?'

'How so?' Old Nestor wearily demanded. Still grieving for the death of his son Antilochus in a brutal skirmish only days before the war ended, the King of Pylos had taken little pleasure in the victory. This undignified squabbling appalled him.

'Andromache is mine on two counts,' the young warrior declared. 'Firstly, because she fell to me at the sacking of the city. She is the captive of my spear. But she is also mine by right of inheritance from my father who slew her husband in fair fight. Had Achilles lived he would certainly have claimed her for his own. I claim the wife of Hector in his name.'

'But your father's dead,' Acamas protested, 'and you've already claimed Polyxena in his name.'

His brother Demophon turned his bandaged head to the rest of the council. 'Does this boy mean to have all the women for himself?'

Neoptolemus bristled. 'Polyxena was offered in sacrifice to my father's shade.'

'You had your choice,' Demophon came back. 'The sword wasn't the only weapon you might have stuck her with. Or were you afraid the other wasn't yet keen enough.'

'Silence!' Agamemnon roared as he saw Neoptolemus' hand move towards his sword. 'Haven't we spilled enough Trojan blood that we must fight each other now?' When the murmurings in the hall had died down round him, he said, 'There are women enough to go round. And the treasure we have taken will make all of you rich for life. So be patient and let's try to sort this thing in an orderly manner.'

'But if we are to argue the claims of the dead as well as those of the living,' Acamas protested, 'the women will all be as old as Hecuba before we're done.'

'In any case,' Diomedes put in, 'this division cannot fairly take place until Menelaus and Odysseus are here to guard their interests.'

'Then let them be found at once,' Agamemnon growled. 'We cannot haggle like this for ever.'

He gestured to Talthybius who was about to leave the throne-room when Menelaus strode through the space where the two great gold-plated doors had already been removed from their hinges. Unlike any of the other men assembled there he had found time to bathe and change out of his battle-gear and looked so spruce in the looted vermilion robe he wore that his appearance stunned his grimy comrades to silence.

'So you've decided to show your face at last,' Agamemnon said. 'It looks as though you've been relaxing at the barbers while some of us were fighting a war.'

'The war is over, brother,' Menelaus answered. 'We have prevailed. I see no reason why one should not behave like a civilized man again.' But there was less confidence in his voice than in the defiant gaze he cast over the other lords.

Agamemnon studied him in disbelief. 'Can we presume,' he returned, 'that your business is concluded and your faithless wife is dead?'

'She is under close confinement. Deiphobus, however, is despatched.'

Narrowing his gaze, Agamemnon was about to say more but then decided it would be wiser to pursue this matter in private. His intentions were forestalled, however, by Demophon who asked eagerly, 'Does this mean that Helen will be included in the lottery along with the other captive women?'

The question was addressed not to Menelaus but to Agamemnon, who scowled at his brother, saying, 'I'm not sure what it means.'

Seeing his difficulty, Nestor intervened. 'You are speaking of the former Queen of Sparta,' he said sharply to Demophon. 'Her fate is surely for her husband, the King, to decide?'

Once more everyone looked to Menelaus, who had blanched at the exchanges.

The hall fell silent round him. The noise of men loading wagons ready for delivery to the ships could be heard from the court-yard. Somewhere an ass brayed under a beating from a stick.

'Well?' said Agamemnon.

'Helen's fate is not yet decided.' When the silence in the room sharpened to a new pitch of dissatisfaction, Menelaus saw that more was required. 'I am considering taking her back to Sparta and handing her over to those who have lost their loved ones in this war. I doubt she will last long in their hands.' Sensing that most of the men assembled in the hall would prefer either to witness Helen's death immediately or enjoy the pleasures of her body at leisure, he looked up with a pugnacious jut to his chin. 'But this much I promise you: my wife will never stand like a harlot in the public street for men to haggle over.'

'So if she lives you keep her?' Diomedes said.

'I know you've lusted over her for years,' Menelaus snapped back at him. 'But believe me, Diomedes, she'll never be yours. Nor shall any other man here lay hands on her.'

A general muttering broke out among the members of the council, above which rose the angry voice of Demophon. 'So, Agamemnon has already taken Cassandra for himself. Neoptolemus has killed Polyxena and lays claim to Andromache. Now Menelaus tells us that Helen will be withheld from the lottery. That leaves precious few of the royal women left for the rest of us, except that raddled hag Hecuba, of course, and who in his right mind would choose to be saddled with her?'

'I will take Hecuba.'

The voice had come from the back of the throne room near where the gold-plated double doors once stood. Everyone turned to see who had spoken.

It was Odysseus, who had just come from two painful encounters, both of which had further shaken his already troubled mind.

The most recent was with Antenor who had accosted him outside the palace and told him how he had been thrown down the palace steps by guards who were under orders not to admit him into Agamemnon's presence.

'Have you neither shame nor honour, Odysseus of Ithaca?' he shouted, white-faced and trembling. 'You swore to me that all Trojan citizens who laid down their arms would be spared, yet there is scarcely a man left alive in this whole city. You swore it to me and are now forsworn before the gods themselves. They know you for a fouler villain in this evil than even that foul brute in there.'

Odysseus held out a hand to steady the desperate old man, but Antenor spurned him as if contaminated by the touch.

Knowing that his words could make no difference, Odysseus said, 'Believe me, this was never my intention.'

'You gave me Agamemnon's word. You swore you spoke with his full authority.'

'I believed that I did. I truly believed it. But it seems I was deceived.'

'You're asking me to believe that he lied to you as you have lied to me? Why should I believe a word that any of you say? And what difference can it make? The dead are still dead whether you desired it or not. There is no mending that. And I curse you, Odysseus of Ithaca, for the fool's part you made me play in it.'

'We are both Agamemnon's fools,' Odysseus said, 'and both his victims too, though the gods know my suffering is as nothing compared with yours. Come inside with me, Antenor. Let us face him together.'

'He won't see me.' Antenor shook his white head. 'I've been demanding to speak with him since I came out of my house and saw . . . this.' He gestured hopelessly towards a pile of corpses. 'But he won't answer to me. His guards have kept me from the palace. Look.' He raised his robe to show where his pathetically thin shins were barked and bloody.

'We shall go in together, friend,' Odysseus urged him. 'They won't refuse you entry if you are at my side.'

But he was wrong. An armed troop of Agamemnon's Mycenaean Guard stood at the entrance to the palace and though they acknowledged Odysseus with a respectful salute, their commander was resolute that Antenor should not pass. 'The High King has more urgent matters on his mind,' he said. 'He will deal with this fellow in good time.'

'Without this fellow's help,' Odysseus protested, 'we could never have entered Troy. He is king here now and deserves your respect. Now let us through.'

'There is only one king here that I know of,' the commander answered, 'and he gives me my orders. I know he's been expecting you for some time, sir. But if this Trojan values his life he would do well to keep out of the High King's sight.'

Angry and humiliated, Odysseus was left with no choice but

to enter the palace alone. Having forced his way through the crowded vestibule, he stood in disbelief for some time, fingering his beard as he listened to the ill-tempered wrangling in the throne-room. A single glance at the flushed face and bleary eyes told him that Agamemnon was drunk, but he was amazed at the contrast between the dapper figure now cut by Menelaus and the dishevelled wreck of a man he had seen in Helen's bedroom. Everyone else in the hall had been so intent on the discussion of Helen's fate that his own arrival passed unnoticed. But now he had spoken and Agamemnon turned a scowl his way, demanding to know where he had been hiding himself.

Odysseus moved forward to stand before the King. 'I've been taking the measure of our achievement here,' he answered steadily.

Agamemnon chose to ignore the note of sarcasm in the Ithacan's voice. 'Well, there's one thing on which we're all agreed: that thanks to your guile we've just won what is probably the greatest victory of all time.'

'It will certainly rank among the greatest crimes.'

As others gasped around him, Odysseus held Agamemnon in his cold gaze. 'Last night you had the chance to become a truly great king. You already rule all Argos and might have ruled half of Asia out of Troy. Instead you seem content to be thought a brigand and a liar. You have betrayed your own honour and defiled mine. I find it small wonder that you can't look Antenor in the face.'

Momentarily shaken by the accusations, Agamemnon glanced away. Then he glowered back at his accuser. 'Let Antenor go home and count himself lucky he had the sense to betray his king rather than die with him.' Before Odysseus could utter a retort, he raised a menacing hand and struck back at the insult he had been offered. 'Nor should you trouble me with your cheap talk of honour. I heard none of that when you urged the death of Palamedes on me.'

'Palamedes was a traitor.'

'So you say. So you say.' Agamemnon narrowed his eyes in a

dangerous squint. 'In any case, what is your Trojan friend Antenor if not a traitor? Beware, Odysseus, lest you become one too.'

Around them, the silence of the hall intensified. The two men glared at one another. Odysseus was about to speak again when Menelaus stepped forward to forestall him, declaring out loud to the whole company that no one doubted the honour of Odysseus or his loyalty to the cause. He turned to smile uneasily at the glowering Ithacan. 'This is our hour of triumph, Odysseus. Rejoice in it.'

'No sane man rejoices over a massacre,' Odysseus replied. 'My heart quails at what we've done in this place.' He glowered back at Agamemnon. 'You wanted to know what I've been doing? I've just come from Queen Hecuba who threw herself at my knees and told me something I didn't know till now: that it was she who interceded with King Priam to spare my life. Yes and your life too, Menelaus, when we came as ambassadors into Troy. If it had not been for her and Hector, speaking up in our defence, Deiphobus would have murdered us in our beds that night. And now Hecuba was beseeching me to save the life of her daughter Polyxena. But I had to tell her that her plea came too late. I had to tell her that Polyxena was already dead. She died because Neoptolemus wanted her dead and because King Agamemnon assented to her death. And she died bravely with her breast bared under the sword because she *wanted* to die rather than endure any more of the suffering we have inflicted on her people. So I had no comfort for that wretched queen, and she had only curses for me and for the entire Argive host.' By now Odysseus was shaking as he spoke. 'It was from those curses that I learned how Locrian Aias tried to rape Cassandra in the temple of Athena. Of *Athena*, I say – the very goddess who came to me in a dream and gave us victory. Yet we have defiled her holy place with our lust and taken her sacred image as spoil. And this on top of the slaughter of countless men who lay down their arms because they saw no hope except in our mercy. *And all of this in breach of our given word.*'

Out of the silence someone jeered, 'You did your share of the killing, Odysseus. I saw you going at it like a man possessed.'

Odysseus turned and held the man's stare. 'To my shame I acknowledge it. But I for one take no pride in such a victory. I accept my share in guilt. And I will be amazed if the gods fail to punish us for the crimes we have committed here.'

'Enough,' Agamemnon bellowed. 'Would you call down the wrath of the gods on all our heads?'

When Odysseus answered grimly that he feared that was done long before he spoke, Agamemnon leapt to his feet. 'I've heard enough of this. Keep your shame to yourself, Odysseus of Ithaca. War is war and men fight and win it as best they can. We have done nothing that Priam and his Trojans would not have done to us had the gods given them the chance. Nothing, do you hear me? Now this council is over. I'll summon it again when you're all back in your right minds.'

Throwing his cloak over his shoulder, the King of Men commanded Menelaus to follow him and strode from the throne-room with an angry din of dissension breaking at his back.

The Strength of Poseidon

Menelaus, meanwhile, was also in trouble with his conscience. Always aware that his brother's ambitions had extended as far as Troy even before Paris came to Sparta, he still cherished the belief that the war was fought principally on his own behalf. Hadn't all Argos rallied to help him regain his lost honour? Yet here, at the end, when the city had finally fallen to the cunning of Odysseus and the onslaught of the Argive host, he had played almost no part in the triumph.

True, he had been among the band who risked those dangerous hours riding inside the wooden horse. True, he had personally killed Deiphobus who was the leader of the Trojan forces in all but name. But since that convulsion of fury in the bedroom of Helen's mansion, he had done nothing. Least of all had he been able to bring himself to kill his faithless wife, for where Helen was concerned, his spirit had succumbed to a stultifying lethargy so debilitating that he believed some god must be present between them in that chamber, forbidding her to flee and him to act. But how to convince anyone else of this, particularly his own brother, who sat scowling across from him now in the state-room where Priam had kept his father's charred throne as a reminder of the disaster that had once befallen Troy?

'You see what has begun to happen?' Agamemnon said, throwing his weight down on that throne. 'No sooner have they triumphed over the common enemy than they begin to fight amongst themselves. And Odysseus openly insults me. I tell you it's going to be harder asserting my authority now than it was before the walls were breached.' Then he raised his voice in a menacing growl. 'And what kind of example does my own brother set? Where were you during all those hours when I could have used you at my side? And why in the name of all the gods does that faithless Spartan bitch still live?'

'Need I remind you,' Menelaus said quietly, 'that my wife is your wife's sister?'

'You still think of her as your wife, do you, after she's dragged the good name of the House of Atreus through all the dirt from Epirus to Egypt? Have you forgotten how she cuckolded you with that Trojan peacock Paris? Or how she had no more shame than to let Deiphobus paddle his fingers in her pool as soon as Paris was dead?' Agamemnon brought his fist down on the table. 'The whore is not fit to be spoken of in the same breath as her sister. But, believe me. if Clytaemnestra had done to me what Helen has done to you, she wouldn't have lived a minute to tattle of it in the women's quarters. Have you no pride, man? Don't you care that you've become a laughing-stock out there, or that they're already laying bets on which of them will be the next to take his pleasure in Helen's bed if you're fool enough to let her live?'

During the years of the war Menelaus had lost much of the flowing head of red hair that had been his most striking feature. Flushed now under this withering assault from his brother's tongue, he passed a hand over his bald crown and down through the curls that remained above the nape of his neck. His eyes shifted around the painted chamber which still smelled of the pungent incense that King Priam had recently burned. He saw the Hours and Graces dancing there among the asphodels and the world seemed to sway around him like a sickly dream. He was biting his bottom lip hard enough to make it bleed.

And things were never meant to be like this. He had always imagined that once he was inside Troy he would swoop to his vengeance like an angry god. Yet he had brought the largest army that men had ever seen half-way across the world to seize his faithless wife, and thousands of men had died in the struggle, and still he dithered.

He was filled, in those moments, with a violent hatred for his brother. Yet he knew that Agamemnon spoke the truth. After Helen had so egregiously betrayed him, he could not take her back into his bed without making himself ridiculous before the hard-bitten men who had risked everything to help him to his vengeance. The humiliation he was suffering now would be multiplied a thousandfold when others, unconstrained by brotherly pride, began to smirk and jest behind their hands.

'The only question,' he conceded gruffly, 'is whether she dies here in Troy or at home in Sparta where her shame will be greater.'

Agamemnon shook his head. 'The only question is why she isn't dead already. Can't you see it? The longer she lives the more dissension her beauty will cause. We already know it has the power to make men mad.'

And here again, Menelaus saw it at once, his brother was in the right of it.

The power of that beauty had arrested his own sword-hand in the very moment when he had the chance to extinguish it for ever. Only here, away from her, beyond the reach of her allure, could he see how the glamorous enchantment worked and why he had been unmanned by it. Just to look at her again had been like sipping on a drug that paralysed his will.

But now his head was clear. Everything was clear to him again. Helen must die. She must die in a public place before the entire Argive host. Like a man waking from a bewildering dream he wondered how he could not have seen it sooner. Helen must die. And she must die by his own hand. His manhood depended on her death. The honour of the House of Atreus depended on it.

Helen's beauty had already dragged the world into a war longer and more terrible than any that mortal men had endured before: it must not be allowed to do so again.

'Yes,' he said as if speaking to himself, 'she has to die.'

Agamemnon's thoughts were already drifting elsewhere. He was thinking about Cassandra and the peculiar allure she exercised on his own senses. Too much of the day had already been wasted wrangling with words.

Impatiently he looked back at his brother. 'You will attend to it then?'

Menelaus swallowed, and nodded his head.

'Today?'

'Not today.' Menelaus withstood his brother's irascible glare. 'I want them all to witness it . . . the whole host. But they're looting the city still. I think she should be executed in a public ceremony . . . just before we take to the ships.'

Agamemnon considered the proposal for a moment. Such a last vivid memory of Troy would send the host of Argos back home with the knowledge that the honour of his house had not gone unredeemed. It would leave no one in doubt that the sons of Atreus accomplished what they set out to do. 'Very well!' he nodded. 'But you must let the captains know what you intend. Tell them at once and put an end to their fantasies. And make sure that Helen is kept under close guard. I don't want her wheedling her way round any of them. Now leave me. I have other things on my mind.'

But the Lion of Mycenae was not yet to be allowed the freedom of his desires, for Talthybius was waiting in the doorway as Menelaus went out, and there was a troubled frown on the herald's face.

'What is it now?' Agamemnon growled.

'Not good news,' Talthybius said. 'A ship has just put in from Iolcus. It was sent urgently by Peleus nearly a week ago. There's been an invasion into Magnesia from the north. A siege was closing round Iolcus when the ship put out. Its captain fears that the city may already have fallen.'

'Am I to be allowed no peace?' Agamemnon roared. 'Let Peleus look to his own troubles. I have problems enough here.' He got up and crossed to a window where he looked down on a gang of men who were struggling to lift the golden statue of Phrygian Aphrodite they had dropped while loading it into the back of an ox-cart. One arm had snapped off in the fall. The lovely thing was ruined and would have to be melted down.

Talthybius coughed discreetly. 'Need I remind my lord that Peleus sent almost his entire force of Myrmidons to our aid.'

Agamemnon turned to frown at him. 'What's been happening back there?'

'The situation isn't entirely clear but there are rumours that the sons of Acastus have joined forces with the Dorians and are out to wrench back Magnesia from Peleus's control.'

'Acastus? Who's he? I don't remember him.'

'Old Nestor is the only one left who knew him. He was king in Iolcus once but he's been dead for many years. He and Peleus were friends when they were young, but then his crazy wife falsely accused Peleus of trying to rape her when he spurned her advances. Acastus tried to have Peleus put to death but failed. Then he was killed himself when Peleus advanced an army out of Thessaly to settle his score. Peleus seized the whole kingdom of Magnesia at that time.'

'This is all ancient history,' Agamemnon snapped impatiently. 'What has any of it to do with me?'

'Perhaps a great deal,' Talthybius answered. 'With the Myrmidons fighting over here for us, Magnesia was left wide open to attack from a well-organized force. No such force was threatening Iolcus when we left, of course, but it seems that while we've been busy here in Troy, the Dorians have gathered their strength west of the Axius River and now they've moved south. They're ferocious fighters . . . and there's something else.' Talthybius hesitated, worried by what he had to tell. 'There's talk that some of them carry weapons made of a magical new metal. One that is much harder than bronze.'

The herald saw the creases deepen on the High King's brow. Agamemnon said, 'What else do we know about them?'

'Not much, except that they're barbarians. Until now they've stayed far enough to the north not to bother us. But it seems the world's been changing in the last ten years. We'd scarcely heard of the Dorians before we left for Troy and now look where they are. I can't imagine they care much about the sons of Acastus but they'll be happy enough to use them as figureheads. And once they've secured a foothold in Iolcus, they'll be poised to advance further south.'

'Unless they're stopped,' Agamemnon sighed, beating his fist against the arm of the throne as though hammering a nail into the blackened wood.

'Yes,' Talthybius nodded, 'unless they're stopped.'

'And Peleus can't hold them?'

'Not without the Myrmidons.'

'And he's an old man, long past his best.' Agamemnon narrowed his eyes. 'Do Neoptolemus and Phoenix know about this yet?'

'They're in council with Philoctetes right now. His citadel at Meliboea is also under threat. I doubt they'll be with us much longer.'

Agamemnon nodded, thinking quickly. It seemed that enemies were like the fabled dragon's teeth: you dealt with one only to see others spring up in your face. He said, 'It could have happened at a worse time, I suppose. Troy is ours now and I've no further need of the Myrmidons here. In fact, they'll be more use to me holding off these Dorians than arguing over plunder with the rest of the host. And I shan't be sorry to see the back of Neoptolemus. He's almost as dangerous as his father and less predictable. The sooner we're rid of him the better.' He looked up at his herald, frowning. 'A magical new metal, you say?'

'Their smiths smelt it from some ore they dig out of the earth. The rumour is that bronze swords break against it.'

Agamemnon shrugged uneasily. 'Well, a man's strength and courage count for more than the weapons he wields. And warriors don't come any tougher than the Myrmidons.' He gave a little, scoffing laugh. 'Let them and the Dorians slug it out across Thessaly together while we look to our own interests in the south.'

'There is still a difficulty,' Talthybius said, and glanced away when Agamemnon glowered at him. 'The question of Andromache remains unsettled. Neoptolemus still lays claim to her.'

Agamemnon scowled. Was there no end to the demands on him? His first impatient thought was that he had no personal interest in the woman's fate. Then a further thought occurred to him. 'I don't want that argument opened up again,' he decided. 'If we put Andromache to the lots then sooner or later someone will question my right to take Cassandra without doing the same. Let the boy take her – and much pleasure may she give him!'

Talthybius pursed his lips. 'It will cause trouble. Acamas and Demophon already feel they are being treated unjustly. They are not alone in this.'

'Then if they want Hector's wife so badly let them chase Neoptolemus across the Aegean for her. Tell him to stow her below decks and put to sea at once.'

'But . . .'

'I shall deny I knew anything about it when he's gone, of course.' Agamemnon smirked at his herald. 'In any case, they'll forget about women once they start counting out gold. Now have Cassandra brought to me, and get me some wine.'

Alone among the Trojan women Cassandra was not devastated by grief. On the contrary, a hectic elation had possessed her spirit almost from the moment when she heard the invading army enter Troy. Such further evidence of madness appalled her mother, for Hecuba had no understanding of how the catastrophic events of the night had brought, for this, the strangest, least congenial of her daughters, a final vindication of her long derided powers of prophetic insight.

Even while she had stood clutching the ancient woodwork of the Palladium, with the breath of Aias hot on her neck and his hands tearing at her shift and his gang of spearmen coarsely egging him on, Cassandra knew herself as safe in the possession of the goddess as if she had been surrounded by a ring of astral fire. So it had been no surprise to her when Agamemnon strode into that violated sanctuary, saw the unholy thing that was happening there and immediately put a stop to it. What astonished her, however, was the silent exchange of sensual energy that took place between herself and the Lion of Mycenae as they stared into each other's eyes.

She had expected to be filled with hatred for the man. She had willed all the venom she could muster into her voice when she hissed out her brief answers to his questions. And this show of implacable hostility was the only thing evident to those around them. But for the two of them the deep truth of the encounter was quite different. They were like souls disturbingly familiar to each other from another time, another country – another life even – come together once more in a mutual shock of recognition. Yet where Agamemnon sensed only the tense, erotic charge in that meeting, Cassandra's deeper gaze flashed on a darker assignation lying in wait for them. She saw it so clearly that it frightened her. But then the goddess had spoken through the silence and the bewildered young woman understood that she alone was now invested with the power to wreak destruction on the House of Atreus. It was only a question of time.

None of the other captive women believed Cassandra when she tried to share her secret, just as no one had believed her when she warned of the doom that Paris must bring on Troy. But she was no longer demoralised by their disbelief. Already parts of the city were in flames. Soon, just as she had long prophesied, the whole of Troy would be reduced to a rubble of stones and smoking ash. And just as certainly Agamemnon would take her into his bed, utterly ignorant that in doing so he was embracing his own death. So Cassandra came to the king that afternoon with the serene docility of an animal consenting to the sacrifice.

For his own part, Agamemnon expected to see her cowering

before him, but the moment she entered the royal chamber, he knew himself in the presence of a powerfully composed young woman. Her eyes countered his appraising gaze as though it was he, not she, who had been summoned to this encounter. Smiling, she put her palms together, raised them to the delicate cleft of her chin and said, almost as if it was some conspiratorial joke between them, 'To think it has taken ten long years of war to bring us together!'

He uttered a gruff little snort of surprise. 'You think that's what it was all about? I understood it had something to do with my brother Menelaus and his wife's lust for your treacherous brother Paris.'

She smiled again. 'And with your desire for the wealth of Troy, of course.' She shrugged her narrow shoulders. 'But that is mere mortal fiddle. The gods have always had deeper intentions.'

Dryly he said, 'And they keep you informed of them?'

'They do.'

Agamemnon took a swig at his wine. 'Then you'd better come and sit down and tell me what they have in mind for us.'

'Union,' she said without moving. 'They mean to consecrate me as your bride.'

He stared at her in shock for a moment, and then, not knowing what else to do, he laughed.

'They mean for us to live together and die together,' she declared.

Uneasily he said, 'I already have a wife.'

Cassandra crossed the floor to stand before him. 'You have a queen,' she contradicted him, 'and your children have a mother. But I am the destined consort of your soul. It was for me you came to Troy.'

She reached out a finger to trace the contours of his face – the broad, bull-like brow, the scar at his temple, the craggy orbit of his eyes and cheekbone. He gasped a little as it came to a halt at his bearded chin. 'Can you deny,' she said, 'that you recognized it when we met in Athena's temple?'

Agamemnon could deny nothing. So closely was his heart knocking against his tonsils that he was, in fact, having some difficulty speaking at all. There remained a wary recess of his mind which suspected that he might be falling under some form of bewitchment, but the rest was vertiginously attracted to that condition.

In so far as wounds and an excess of wine permitted it, Agamemnon had taken brief pleasure throughout the years of the war with a constantly changing harem of concubines and slave-girls. Most of them he could not remember, and in none had he met much more than an anxiety to please him that was bred only of fear and dread. But there remained, it seemed, an unanswered loneliness at the centre of his soul, and this woman had both divined and answered it. Here at last might be someone who recognized the man he truly was.

That had never been the case with Clytaemnestra. He had long since come to depend on his wife's shrewd intelligence and the skilful, pragmatic command she exercised over tedious details of finance and the subtler twists of court intrigue. But that was the only good in their marriage now. He had long since accepted that she would never for a moment worship him as he, when he was a shy youth exiled in Sparta, had once worshipped her. He had even learned to fear her severe, autocratic spirit, for though he had sired three children on her, he had never found any warmth in their marriage bed. There had always been too much which Clytaemnestra could never forget. And ever since the day he had put their daughter to death on the altar at Aulis, he had known that, whatever triumphal show the people of Mycenae might mount for him, his true eventual reception in that city would be far colder still.

Yet was it possible that for all the arid years he'd endured, and for all the bitterness still to come, there might just, in his hour of triumph, be a measure of consolation here?

A wary part of his mind could not quite bring itself to credit it.

Smiling, Cassandra whispered, 'I know what you're thinking. And I will answer your thought. Long ago I warned my father of what must happen if he took Paris back into his house, but he would not hear me. I warned him again when Helen came to Troy, and still he would not listen. So he brought destruction on himself, and though I spoke for the god, I could not prevent it. As for you, in destroying his house you are as much an instrument of the gods as I am.' Smiling, she added, 'We are not to blame, Agamemnon, if our true power goes unrecognized.'

Standing gravely before him, Cassandra removed two ivory combs and shook loose the piled tresses of her hair. Then she crossed her hands at her shoulders and pulled down her gown along slender arms.

Breathless, lips slightly agape, Agamemnon stared in wonder at her small bared breasts. He saw the nipples appear, dark almost as figs against unblemished flesh. 'Come,' she said and reached out an inviting hand. Then the King of Men was suckling gratefully at her bosom like a hungry child.

Helen, meanwhile, remained a prisoner in the city where she had always been a prisoner. Even in the days when Paris was alive and the two of them were still lost in their dream of love, she had never felt free to roam the streets of Troy or venture alone into the wooded hills beyond the plain of the Scamander as she had done in Sparta when she was a girl. Too many Trojans envied and resented her, so Paris was reluctant to let her stray far from his sight. And then the Argive host had come, and her enemies inside the city found larger cause to hate her. Helen had felt herself besieged inside a city under siege, and now that city had fallen and she was merely one among a throng of captive women, but kept apart from the others for fear they might vent their despair on the beauty that had brought them so much grief. And she lacked a single friend to comfort her, for even her old bondswoman Aethra, the mother of Theseus, had been joyfully released by her grandsons Acamas and Demophon, and would soon be on her way home to pass her dying years at home in Troizen or Athens.

Because the mutilated body of Deiphobus still lay in the chamber she had shared with him, Helen sat alone in the smaller room where Aethra had slept.

She had found in the bondswoman's care the nearest thing she had known to a mother's love since she had been a very small child, and she imagined that some vestige of that security might still be found among the things that belonged to her. But without Aethra's presence the things were only things, and for many hours Helen had been terrified by the knowledge that, for her, there was no security anywhere in this devastated city.

She had tried to prepare herself for death but she had no talent for philosophy and there was no comfort to be found in prayer. It seemed that her father Zeus had turned his face from her, and to which of the goddesses could she pray with any hope of being heard? Aphrodite, on whose altar she had thrown away her life, had failed her already. Hera would not countenance the violation of the marriage bond, and Divine Athena, whose votive horse looked down across the city, had brought destruction on Troy and all who dwelt there. There remained Artemis, the goddess Helen had revered as a girl, but Artemis had not saved her all those years ago when Theseus abducted her from the woodland shrine. Nor had that goddess spurned the offering when the innocent Iphigenaia was put to her father's knife on the altar in Aulis. There was, it seemed, no pity there.

There was no pity anywhere.

Outside she could hear men shouting as they plundered the house that had once belonged to Hector and Andromache. Somewhere a hungry baby cried. Black smoke gusted on the wind that rattled the shutters and agitated the trees. The whole world was in turmoil and she sat at the centre of it, isolated and afraid.

Soon it would be dark and with the darkness Menelaus would return and both her greatest fears and her only hope were fixed on that moment. If she could prevail on him to spare her again, then she might survive the fall of Troy. But if, as she suspected, Agamemnon were to bully his brother with primitive talk of honour and revenge, then she would never leave this room alive.

And there was no saying which way things would go, for when the world was turned upside down, all things were prey to the random chance of war.

How to better her own chances then?

Should she remain like this, unkempt and bedraggled by weeping, and thus make a last appeal to whatever reserves of pity might be left to Menelaus? Or should she brush out her hair, put on a gown that enhanced the light in her eyes, coax the colour back into her cheeks, and present herself to his senses as the woman he had always adored?

Either choice might work. Either could prove disastrous. She was incapable of decision. Then she remembered that what had stayed his sword in the moment when he might have killed her was the sight of the breasts she had instinctively bared. The beauty which had always been her curse had become her salvation. Perhaps it might save her again.

She had been sitting at her dressing table for only a few moments and was tying back her hair before applying the paint to her face when the door of the room banged open and Menelaus was standing there. She could detect no hint of mercy in his baleful stare.

He took in the signs of weeping round her blotchy eyes. He saw how pale and distraught her face. He saw that the hands she lowered from the nape of her neck were trembling. Menelaus felt an answering faintness at the back of his knees when she sighed like a woman renouncing all hope and said, 'You have come to tell me I must die.'

'Yes.'

'Is it to be now?'

'No, not yet. But tomorrow. You should prepare yourself.'

Her throat was dry, her smile wan as she said, 'And how am I to do that?'

He glanced away from the beseeching reach of her gaze. 'As best you can,' he said tersely, and left the room before she could unman him once more.

With the naked bulk of Agamemnon's body sleeping beside her, Cassandra lay awake far into the night, elated by the knowledge that at last she was coming into the fullness of her powers. This grim man, the Lion of Mycenae, High King of all the Argives, enemy and destroyer of Troy, was as pliable in her hands as clay.

Before he slumped into sleep, she had lain placidly on her parents' great bed while he nuzzled at her breasts and kissed the soles of her feet, abasing himself before her body. Earlier, she had watched him mount to the climax of his passion like a man battering at the gate of a city that he believed he would never take; and when – already chafed by the force of his thrusts – she saw how his frustration must soon turn to rage, she whispered a spell in his ear that might have come to her from a god. His eyes had widened. The grim set of his mouth eased into a gasp, and he was crying out in gratitude as he released all the tension of his body into her unresisting warmth.

As for herself, the only pleasure Cassandra took from the act resided in the knowledge that strength was being purchased by her pain. And the shedding of her virgin blood had been a kind of investiture. Already she had known that sexual congress was charged with magical power, but now she had felt that power rising within her at every thrust, and in the moment when Agamemnon shuddered his seed into her loins, a net had been thrown over him that was as fine and inescapable as the net in which Hephaestus once trapped Aphrodite and her lover Ares. Utterly unaware of what was happening, the King of Men lay gasping in its trammels like a landed fish.

Again Cassandra smiled to think how the spell which he had taken for the key to his release had been, in truth, a binding spell. Agamemnon was hers now. He was hers as she would never be his.

Smoke and moonlight drifted through the window casement. The still night breathed about her head. Troy, the capital city of death, was filled with sleepers and the dead. For much of that night only Cassandra lay fully awake, gazing down the galleries of time to where her final consummation waited: Agamemnon dead; the House of Atreus deeper mired in its heritage of blood; the city of Mycenae reduced in turn to ruin. Far-sighted Apollo might have rejected her all those years ago so that no one would believe her when she spoke. But soon, quite soon, every one of her prophesies would be fulfilled.

Cassandra was smiling as she entered sleep.

Towards dawn, she jumped awake, her head dizzy with a pain that felt both sickly and thunderous. Agamemnon still snored, untroubled, at her side. The drapes at the casement were blowing in the wind and a jagged light, the colour of sulphur, stained the darkness of the sky outside. Whether it came from the moon or a pallid sun she could not say, for it had a drastic, raw sheen she associated with neither. Her nose distinguished the mingled smells of burning and decay. Every cell of her body started to quiver with alarm.

Then the sound rose round her, a sound such as she had never heard before. She imagined the muffled groans of an imprisoned titan locked inside the earth; but then it broke louder on her ears, a harsh grinding as of monstrous millstones disrupted in their toil. Dust fell in a fine powdery shower on her face. The bed was shaking. The walls seemed to stagger before her gaze. Cassandra leapt from the bed and found the floor moving beneath her feet.

Agamemnon sat up clutching at the blankets as the bed-frame juddered round him. He was shouting like a drunken man woken from a dream. 'What is it? What is it?' But his voice was buried under the groan of the quaking earth.

The noise increased in volume, shuddering through her flesh, blurring her vision, hurting her ears. She winced at the panicked rattling of shutters, the creak and jarring of the beams. As though it was about to faint, the palace swayed.

Then it stood still again. The dawn air held its breath.

After several seconds she heard voices shouting in the street outside. A cloud of dust gusted across the room. Agamemnon jumped naked from the bed. 'We should get out of here. The shock may come again.'

Cassandra turned to him and smiled. 'That was Poseidon warning of his strength,' she said quietly. 'But calm yourself. It's not yet our time to die.'

An Audience with the Queen

Unaware of the stratagem of the wooden horse and, therefore, that Troy was about to fall, Clytaemnestra stood on her balcony in the palace at Mycenae, gazing out across the olive groves and farms of the fertile valley at the foot of the crag. She was holding a wax tablet onto which her most trusted secretary had deciphered a message sent by one of her agents – a minister in the Hittite court whom she had suborned many years earlier when he first came to Mycenae as an imperial legate. The message informed her that Hattusilis, Emperor of the Hittites, had finally dealt with the unrest on his eastern border, and because he was unwilling to countenance a permanent Mycenaean presence in Troy, he was now considering committing the entire western division of the Hittite army to King Priam's aid.

And if that were to happen, Clytaemnestra thought as she gazed into the hazy light that hung like a veil across the bay of Argos, Agamemnon's expeditionary force was doomed.

Not quite a year had passed since she had taken her daughter Iphigenaia to Aulis, but her face had aged by much more than the months that had elapsed since then. These days Clytaemnestra slept so little and ate so little that her severe features were honed as spare as a windblown shell, and the vivid glitter of paint she applied around her eyes only accented the pallor of her skin. She might have been thought a decade older than her thirty-seven years.

The Queen of Mycenae had never been a woman to laugh easily or take pleasure in the trivialities of life, but not even her remaining children had seen her smile since she had returned from Aulis. More than ever, they were afraid of her.

Throughout the long night before Iphigenaia was put to death and during the day of the sacrificial ceremony itself, Clytaemnestra had been kept under guard in the fortress at Aulis. Had she possessed the strength, she would have struck her husband dead where he stood sooner than let him lay violent hands on her child. But this formidable queen, who had grown used to commanding the court of Mycenae in Agamemnon's absence and wielding all the instruments of civil power in his name, was now surrounded by forces with which she could not contend. Those forces were masculine and brutal and would baulk at nothing – not even the murder of a child – to impose their will on the world. And so, for all the power that had accrued to her, the Queen of Mycenae knew herself reduced to what she had always truly been – a woman in a world ruled by men. She was as helpless before their strength as a nymph ravished by a god.

Once the first frenzy passed and she realized that no one would answer her shouting and screaming and beating on the door, she had slumped into a trance of self-harm, tearing at her hair and dragging her nails along the flesh of her arms. Then she had resorted to prayer, but to which of the gods could a woman confidently pray when Artemis herself, the virgin goddess of unmarried girls and protector of the young, had demanded the life of her daughter as the blood-price of her husband's stupidity?

Both her daughter and her sister Helen had lavished their devotions on Artemis before all other gods, and what good had she brought to either of them? Helen had been abducted by Theseus even as she danced at the shrine of Artemis; and now, in only a few hours, Iphigenaia would lie dead across her altar.

And what of herself? Clytaemnestra had always given her first allegiance to Sky-Father Zeus, but she had fared no better. A long time ago Agamemnon had come to her in Elis and killed the husband she loved and commanded that her baby's brains be bashed out against a wall. Her prayers and imprecations had been of no more avail then than they were now at the imminent loss of this second child to the cruelty of men and gods. Her heart boiled with the pain of it.

She had finally fallen asleep out of sheer exhaustion, and in the small hours of the night a vision came to her.

In the vision she had strayed outside the city into the foothills of the mountains. She could hear birdsong and the clatter of wild water among stones. Her nostrils took in the smell of a damp green world. Unlike Helen, Clytaemnestra had never been at ease out in the wilds and she was trembling as she walked. Thorns scratched the skin of her calves. Gorse tore at the short tunic she wore. Flies droned about her ears. The sun lay heavy on her head. The whirr of crickets ratcheted to an unnerving pitch of intensity. When she looked up, black birds were wheeling above her in the glare. She sensed animals around her, inquisitive and hostile, aware of her as prey.

All her life Clytaemnestra had been a creature of the city. She was at home inside the busy world of court intrigue. Politics, diplomacy, commerce, trade relations, the intellectual traffic of art and cultural refinement, all such civil discourse was the very stuff of life to her. And because her chosen world began and ended inside city walls, she had taken little interest in the natural terrain beyond except in so far as it furnished the material necessities of life. Yet here she was, exiled from all things congenial and familiar, in a wilderness where the single law was that one devoured only to be, in turn, devoured.

Clytaemnestra began to run and the faster she ran the more afraid she became. Somewhere at her back a horn sounded. Her heart thudded against her ribs as the world swept past her in a dazed green swirl. She was sobbing as she ran and when she looked down she saw that her arms were covered with black bristles. There were bristles at her face and she was squinting out over a lengthening snout through which, like complicated music, passed a whole medley of scents. Then she was down on all fours, travelling quickly now, thrusting her dense bulk forward into the cover of the brakes.

For a moment she stood panting there, torn ears pricked, eyes peering at the light, hearing sour juices swill in the low-slung, churning cauldron of her belly. Then she caught the sharp, hot stink of hunting dogs. A pack of them howled and bayed behind her now. Clytaemnestra knew that she had been transformed into a boar, a wild sow, bristly, tusked and muscular, and she was now the single quarry of this forest-chase.

So she turned and ran again, scrambling among stones as she splashed her shoulders along a muddy water-course to scramble up a steep bank of scree. With the pack yelping and the hunter hallooing close behind her, and her breath no more than a hoarse, wheezing squeal, she burst through the thickets into the dim declivity of a cave she knew. Here she could turn and make her stand. Here she might hold the frantic pack at bay. But where she had expected to find a footing of solid rock, the soft earth sagged beneath her. Then she was falling, and turning as she fell, deeper and deeper into a vertiginous black pit where her bones must shatter when the falling stopped.

Clytaemnestra came to her senses in a place so dark and raw and ancient that it chilled her blood. She was alone except for a stone figure, only remotely human, that loomed above her. The charred bones of votive offerings lay scattered at its feet. There was, she knew at once, no exit from this place.

In a dim light emitted from the rock itself, Clytaemnestra looked up into the face of the Goddess. She found nothing radiant there, no virgin sheen, no curving silver bow. This was no maiden daughter of Zeus. She was far older than the Olympians, born of another primeval generation, an aboriginal survivor of the gods before the gods. A lion and a stag dangled helplessly in her grip.

Through hollows in her breasts protruded the sharp, rapacious curve of vultures' beaks.

Quailing, Clytaemnestra delivered herself over to an archaic power that was both the creator and the immolator of everything that dared to live. Her own face became a face of stone. Her tongue shrivelled to a stone. Her heart was stone and her ribs had turned to a cage of stone about it. She was the Queen of Stone in a place of stone. She could hear the hiss of snakes writhing about her feet. Her breasts had grown sharp as vulture's beaks.

By the time Clytaemnestra was released from confinement in Aulis, the contrary wind had turned, and the King of Men was sailing back to Troy with the blood of his daughter on his hands. His wife had not seen him since. Nor had she received any letters except those bringing instructions for the administration of the state he had left in her charge. She was secretly informed by her spy Talthybius that his master was drinking heavily and had a costive stomach; he was also short-tempered and slept badly. Otherwise the Lion of Mycenae was getting on with his war.

But as far as Agamemnon's dealings with his wife were concerned, the death of Iphigenaia was buried in a silence so deep the child might never have existed.

In the months since that vision had come to Clytaemnestra not a day passed without her renewing the cold strength that she derived from it. She drew on that strength as she placed the tablet on her desk and turned to confront the visitor who entered her chamber with a respectful bow of his gaunt head. King Nauplius of Euboea was more welcome in Mycenae than he could have guessed.

'It was good of your majesty to grant me a private audience so quickly,' he said. 'I know that the demands of state press heavily in the absence of your lord.'

'They do indeed,' she answered dryly, sitting at a large desk on which many papyrus scrolls and inscribed tablets were piled, 'so I beg you not to waste words preparing the ground, as I am quite sure you did with Penelope in Ithaca, and at the court of Diomedes in Tiryns, and in the House of the Axe on Crete.'

For some time before his arrival in Mycenae, Nauplius had been worrying about what course this encounter might take. Though his confrontation with Penelope had turned out badly, he had found Agialeia, the credulous young wife of Diomedes, entirely pliant to his will, and Queen Meda of Crete was already so voracious in her appetites that she had needed no encouragement to cuckold her absent husband Idomeneus. But Clytaemnestra was a more dangerous quarry. All Argos knew how much of Agamemnon's authority she had arrogated to herself. It would take a rash man to risk causing her offence and Nauplius had never been rash. But he was old and furious with grief and weary of life, and his single interest was in avenging the death of his son, for which satisfaction he was prepared to take whatever risks might be required.

Even so, as his litter was carried past the kingdom's great ancestral tombs, beneath the huge stone-built bastions, and on through the Lion Gate into the citadel, the shadows of Mycenae had closed down round him. Not having visited the city for many years, Nauplius had been impressed by its mighty show of power and wealth. The ramparts were formidable, of course, but the porphyry friezes and richly painted porticoes bespoke a vision of which that dull boor Agamemnon was surely incapable, and which must therefore be attributed to the ambition, taste and intelligence of his queen.

To come into her presence he had passed through a busy antechamber filled with ministers, legates and suppliants, all of whom were impatient to secure her attention once this audience was over, and then on through a warren of sentried passages. And those documents on her desk were not for show. Nauplius knew that her correspondence reached from Posidonia in the far west to the eastern kingdom of Mesopotamia, by way of the mighty

Hittite Empire and Pharaonic Egypt. And it was this woman whom he sought to make the instrument of his will.

Finding himself already outflanked in the first exchange, he masked his surprise with a wry smile. 'I see your majesty is well-informed. Does the mistress of the Lion House keep spies in place across all Argos?'

Clytaemnestra motioned for the old man to sit. 'Why should I need spies?' she shrugged. 'Your mission has been aimed at the wives of my husband's captains, and wives have a way of sharing secrets, especially where their husbands' misdemeanours are concerned.'

'Misdemeanours?' Still smiling, though with diminished confidence, Nauplius fingered the curls of his beard. 'You think of them so lightly.'

But Clytaemnestra merely appraised her visitor with faintly disdainful hauteur. 'I did not require my husband to swear a vow of celibacy when he took ship for war. He has his appetites. I expected him to sate them.' Having noted the unhealthy shadows round his eyes, she had already decided that there was not much time left in which to make use of this dying man.

Nauplius watched her reach for a wax tablet and glance at it as though already bored by this conversation. Having studied her negligent air for a moment, he said quietly, 'And did you also expect him to bring home an oriental concubine and make her his queen in Mycenae?'

Clytaemnestra lifted her gaze. 'I presume you can put a name to this rival for my throne?'

'Chryseis,' Nauplius answered at once.

'Chryseis?'

'A Trojan captive taken in the raid on Thebe, She is daughter to a priest of Apollo. Very beautiful, I understand. And also young.'

Clytaemnestra shook her head. 'But your news is old, Nauplius. Haven't you heard that Chryseis was returned to her father many weeks ago?' She uttered a further dismissive sigh and glanced back at the tablet, reading as she spoke. 'Not for the first time my husband offended a god. He was forced to surrender her in recompense. But I assure you he planned nothing more for the girl than a place among the many harlots who warm his bed.' Her painted eyes shifted back to the discountenanced King of Euboea. 'In some matters my husband is a fool, I acknowledge it freely; but women are of small importance to him. No, Nauplius. Your unsavoury gossip may have troubled the wives of Diomedes and Idomeneus, but I'm as little impressed by your lies as was my cousin Penelope.'

The corners of the old man's mouth drooped in an offended moue. Putting his weight on his staff, he made a show of getting to his feet. 'I came here in good faith. But if the Queen does not care to hear what I have to say . . .'

'Sit down,' Clytaemnestra interrupted him. 'You are not yet dismissed our presence.' She put the tablet down. 'You came here to make mischief. We both understand that. Let us not pretend otherwise.'

Nauplius narrowed his eyes. He might have overestimated this woman's readiness to hear him but he did not underestimate her power. His position was now fraught with danger. The palace was difficult to enter: it might prove far more difficult to leave, for this was Mycenae, a city as dark as it was golden, and there were guards at every door. Yet he thought he had detected something almost reassuringly conspiratorial in her last remark.

Thinking quickly, he said, 'I have a just grievance against your husband.'

'I have many,' she answered, 'though I find it wisest to keep them to myself.'

'I am speaking of the death of my son.'

'Palamedes was a traitor.'

'No more than I am myself,' Nauplius protested.

Clytaemnestra uttered a humourless, scoffing laugh. 'And this is loyalty?'

Nauplius clenched his fist at his knee. 'Agamemnon forfeited my allegiance when he commanded the wrongful death of my son.'

'If it was indeed wrongful.'

'My son was the innocent victim of slander and envy.'

'No one is innocent, Nauplius. In any case, it makes no difference.'

For a moment he thought everything lost. He too was about to be charged with treason. He too must brace himself to meet a traitor's death. But her eyes softened a little. A frown passed across her face like the outward sign of pain. 'Though there is no more grievous hurt,' she conceded, 'than the loss of a child.'

And quite suddenly he saw what this devious woman was about.

'Iphigenaia!' he whispered.

'Yes,' she hissed, 'Iphigenaia.'

'Then your majesty will understand the fury of my grief.'

'Oh I do, Nauplius. I understand it very well.'

'And wasn't there another child killed before her?' he risked. 'Long ago when you were queen in Elis.'

The green and gold paint around Clytaemnestra's eyes glittered in the light. When she looked up at him the hollows at her cheekbones seemed more deeply drawn. 'He was not yet six weeks old.' Her voice was almost without expression as she added, 'He too is among the many ghosts that haunt this place.'

By now Nauplius was contemplating possibilities that had been far from his mind when he set out for Mycenae. How absurd that he should have been worried about stirring up this woman's feelings against her husband when for so many years she had been cultivating her own patient hatred of the man.

As though complete understanding had now been established between them, he nodded in a show of sympathy. 'We have a common interest, it seems.'

But his presumption had been too eager. Her grief felt contaminated by proximity to his.

For what felt like a very long time Clytaemnestra studied the old king with distaste. In other circumstances, she might have been pleased to put a speedy end to his deceitful and vindictive life. But she had need of him now.

Mistaking the gist of her appraisal, a dreadful thought struck root in his mind. Surely she did not intend to appoint him as the immediate instrument of her vengeance? He was an old man, and sick. He was not the stuff of which assassins were made.

She let him sweat a moment longer before saying, 'You came here today with the intention of persuading me to betray my husband with some other man. Is that not so?' And when he glanced uncertainly away, 'That was your strategy with Penelope. You offered the same temptation to Queen Meda and Agialeia. Am I to under-stand you had a less attractive proposition to put to me?'

Uncertain of his ground once more, Nauplius replied evasively. 'Would you not agree that such humiliation is no less than a disloyal husband deserves?'

'And you would have been content with that? It would have satisfied you merely to see me cuckold the man you hold respon-sible for the death of your son? You disappoint me, Nauplius. I credited you with larger ambition.'

He was aware of her eyes taunting him to think the thoughts that she had put into his mind. But his breath was fetched short with anxiety and his face was grey. How to be sure she wasn't inciting him to condemn himself out of his own mouth? If she were to arraign him as a traitor, she would certainly be believed, as he would not should he seek to accuse her of complicity.

Again, without humour, she smiled. 'Are you afraid of me, Nauplius?'

'A man would be a fool,' he said, 'not to hold you in great respect.'

'Good,' she answered. 'Then we understand one another.' With a brisk, light touch, her fingers tapped the edge of the desk. Then she surprised him again with a change of direction. 'You know the whereabouts of Aegisthus, do you not?'

Nauplius looked up at her in amazement. Aegisthus had been on the run ever since his father, the usurper Thyestes, was toppled from the throne of Mycenae by Agamemnon's army many years ago. It was Aegisthus who, while still a small boy, had murdered

Atreus, the rightful king. Since Agamemnon had regained the Lion Throne, every attempt to find and kill his father's murderer, and thus put an end to a gruesome cycle of vengeance, had failed. How could Clytaemnestra know that Nauplius had made contact with him? What were her intentions now?

Irritated by the mute gape of the old man's mouth, Clytaemnestra tapped the desk with greater impatience.

Hoarsely, thinking quickly, Nauplius said, 'And if I did?'

'Then you might speak to him on my behalf.'

'And what would your majesty have me say?'

'Perhaps that the Queen of Mycenae does not look upon him with the same inveterate hatred as its king.'

Nauplius swallowed. 'I feel sure the heart of Aegisthus would be gladdened to hear this news.' His eyes shifted with his thoughts. 'But he has good cause to be wary,' he risked. 'How can he be sure of its truth?'

'Do you take me for a liar, Nauplius?'

'By no means. Yet Aegisthus will surely remember how his father Thyestes was once invited to return to Mycenae in what seemed a gesture of reconciliation . . . with what truly terrible consequences your majesty will certainly recall.'

Clytaemnestra's lips narrowed. The old man had dared to refer to an event that had been so horrifying in its impact on the imagination that no one in Mycenae had spoken of it for years. Yet even that silence seemed to taint the city's air.

Sharply Clytaemnestra said, 'That was in another time.'

Nauplius shrugged. 'But the shadows remain.'

'And will, as long as the House of Atreus rules in Mycenae.'

The implications of her statement astounded him. He knew he must be very careful now. In a voice as low as hers, for who could tell if these walls were recording every word, King Nauplius hissed, 'Does the Queen foresee a time when it may not?'

'Nothing lasts for ever.'

'Least of all a man's life.'

'Exactly so.'

'And for that reason Aegisthus will not put his own at risk unless he is given very strong assurances.'

Aware how momentous the step she was about to take, Clytaemnestra drew in her breath. 'Then let us be plain with one another. You may tell Aegisthus that if he has the stomach for it, I, and only I, can help him to regain what was once his father's throne here in Mycenae.'

Nauplius could feel his heart knocking at his ribs, but he merely nodded as though she had made no more than a further gambit in haggling over the price of some desirable commodity.

For the moment she offered nothing further, so his throat was dry as he said. 'If I were Aegisthus, might I not be wise to ask how I could be certain this was not some ruse devised by the High King's wife to lure her husband's most inveterate enemy out of hiding?'

Clytaemnestra nodded. 'Would an assurance sealed in blood satisfy him?'

'I would think,' Nauplius answered with a bleak smile, 'that would entirely depend on whose blood was shed.'

Having already anticipated every development of this wary conversation, Clytaemnestra nodded calmly. 'Even before my husband sailed to Troy, many of those in positions of power and influence in this court owed their good fortune entirely to my favour. There were others, of course, retainers of the House of Atreus from before my time, men to whom the High King feels a certain loyalty. Men he would not replace even though I urged him to do so. But ten years are a long time.' She lifted her eyes. 'There have been deaths, you understand.'

'As is only natural.'

'Yes. As is only natural. So there has been a need for new appointments.'

Nauplius recalled the intense young ministers and secretaries he had seen conferring in quick, low voices in the ante-room outside, every one of them no doubt loyal only to the formidable woman to whom they owed their preferment.

'However,' Clytaemnestra continued, 'a few remain who are not entirely under my control. There is one in particular. I am thinking of the court bard, Pelagon.'

'I know his reputation of old,' Nauplius said. 'I hear he is the greatest of singers.'

'So they say. The question is, for whom does he sing and on what theme?'

'You have found reason not to trust the bard?'

'He is Agamemnon's spy, left here in the court to keep me under surveillance. There are limits, you see, to the trust the High King places in his queen. It will not be long, therefore, before Agamemnon is informed of your visit to Mycenae. For that reason I shall, of course, inform him of it myself. Today, as soon as you are gone. I will write to him explaining why it was only because of your status as a royal guest of the house that I let you depart with your life.'

Nauplius held her dry stare for a time, thinking quickly ahead. 'But were your husband to learn that you were in communication with Aegisthus . . . ?'

'Precisely. Which is why he must never learn of it.'

'Then Pelagon must sing no more.'

'Neither must Agamemnon suspect his sudden silence.'

Nauplius considered this for a time. 'Does the bard ever leave Mycenae?'

'Pelagon is an old man with little interest in travel. But he is also vain and has a secret weakness for beautiful young men.'

'Then he might he be lured from the city by reports of such a person willing to grant him favours?'

'I think it more than possible.'

'Then I will speak with Aegisthus. Perhaps such a person could be found.'

Clytaemnestra narrowed her eyes. 'No shadow of suspicion can attend this matter. Whatever becomes of Pelagon, it must appear no more than an unhappy accident – though it would be well, I think, if it were to happen soon.'

'Aegisthus is a man of considerable resource.'

'I expected no less.'

'Indeed, I believe your majesty will find him an excellent match for her own wisdom and discretion.'

Disdaining his flattery, Clytaemnestra said, 'I wish to hear nothing more of this until I receive the distressing news of my bard's departure from this life. After that it will be time for you and I to speak together again. By then I will have decided whether the time is ripe for Aegisthus to return to Mycenae. Is that understood?'

'Perfectly.' Nauplius hesitated. 'But I was thinking . . .'

'There is some difficulty?'

'Aegisthus will be risking a great deal in this matter.'

'Nothing great is achieved without risk.'

'Quite so! But as things stand he will have only my word for this.'

'He knows you for his friend, does he not?'

'Yet he may ask for more. Is there not perhaps some token you might send to him as an earnest of your interest in his future welfare?'

She saw at once what the man was after. Should things go amiss, any identifiable token given as a pledge would render her complicit in the death of Pelagon, and it had always been her policy to keep such things deniable. Yet in an intrigue as perilous as this the demand was not unreasonable.

Clytaemnestra slipped from her finger a ring on which two jewelled serpents were entwined. 'This once belonged to a Lydian queen. My husband sent it to me some time ago with a letter informing me of his great victory at Clazomenae. Give it to Aegisthus. Tell him that it belonged to one of his forebears, as once did Mycenae itself. It is all the earnest he needs.' Dropping the ring into Nauplius' outstretched palm, she said, 'Conceal it about your person and leave this city at once. And do so in a way that makes it plain to all that you have incurred my displeasure.'

Smiling, Nauplius bowed his head.

'Play your part well,' she said, 'and I shall play mine. In good time both of us will have our satisfaction.'

But when he looked up again, Clytaemnestra had already turned her attention back to the wax tablet. It might suit her purposes for her husband to die in Phrygia but there was no relying on it, and it was no part of her plans that he should be defeated at Troy and return empty handed. She was thinking, therefore, that if his army was not to be trapped between Priam's host and the Hittite Empire, Agamemnon must be swiftly informed of the changing situation. So even before Nauplius had bowed out from her chamber, she was ringing the small silver bell that would summon her scribe.

The Last of Troy

Menelaus was woken from a fitful sleep by the trembling of the earth beneath his bed. For a few seconds, expecting the painted walls to collapse around him, he lay listening to the deep grinding roar, feeling it shake his lips and skin. Then there was only dust falling through the silence.

After a time he heard shouting outside and the noise of his own Spartan soldiery as they scrambled to get out of the building. He knew that the tremor might have been no more than a shrugging of the ground before the earth opened up beneath him. He knew that he too should make haste to get out into the clear. But he could not bring himself to move. Listening to the noise of the quake had been like listening to the stupefying pain of the world, and it was too much for him. He lay motionless on the bed feeling as if the moral lethargy that had seized his heart since entering this city had now infected every limb.

Yet the question that had kept him awake for most of the night remained unanswered: having already failed to kill his wife in the heat of passion when he discovered her in bed with Deiphobus at her side, how could he bring himself to kill her in cold blood?

Yet it would have to be done. Once he stood before the host with all that mighty pressure of expectation fixed on him, he would have no choice but to bring the sword down – just as

Agamemnon had been left with no choice when he stood before the host at Aulis. Thousands of men had already died in this war. They had died for the sake of his honour, and if the sack of Troy was the chief reward for those who had come through, the recapture of Helen was certainly another. And because no single one of them could be allowed to take her for himself, all must have the satisfaction of watching her die. Menelaus had assented to that judgement and it must be carried out. It must be done that day.

As he lay striving with these thoughts, he became aware of a sound somewhere outside the room in which he had slept alone. Someone was pummelling on a door with both fists and the knocking was going unanswered. Menelaus got up from the bed, pulled his cloak about his shoulders and went out into the hall. Everyone had rushed from the building for fear it might collapse – everyone but himself and Helen who was hammering at the locked door along the corridor. Her voice was muffled by its thickness but he could hear her crying to be let out.

Menelaus crossed to the door, unlocked and opened it. Helen saw his broad figure blocking the doorway, his face expressionless, his features darkened in the gloom by the greying, gingery beard which covered the familiar scar across his cheek. He was almost a stranger to her now.

When he said nothing she gasped, 'We have to get out of here. You must let me out. Please . . . I'm very afraid.'

'Does it matter so much,' he said dully, 'whether you die now or later?'

Her lips were quivering. She lifted a hand to her mouth. He heard the whimper of her breath behind it. 'Help me, Menelaus,' she whispered. 'You know me. You've always known the depths of my fear.'

'You were not afraid to betray me.' His voice was measured and cold. 'You were not afraid to flee from Sparta and bring shame on my house.'

'But that's not true,' she came back quickly. 'I was terrified. Every step of the way I was in mortal dread.'

'Yet you didn't let fear stop you.'

'I lacked the power. I was in the hands of a god.'

'You are in the hands of a god now. If Poseidon wants us he will certainly take us.' Scornfully he shook his head. 'In any case, any lying whore might claim as much.'

'I have wronged you,' she gasped, 'I freely acknowledge it. But not once, never once in my whole life, have I ever lied to you.'

He saw the truth of it in her eyes. Helen was shivering in her night-shift but her chin was held high. The silence of the plundered mansion waited round them. Sensing his uncertainty, she said, 'Did you think I was lying when I implored you not to leave me alone with him, when I begged you to let me accompany you to Crete that day?'

His hands had clenched into fists. He made to turn away from her, to shut the door on her again, but words crowded at his lips demanding to be spoken. 'In the name of all the gods, Helen, we were happy together in Sparta,' he heard himself saying. 'Our life was good. We ruled together over a contented kingdom. We had our child, the child we loved – the child that you abandoned.'

He might have struck her with the words.

Helen stared up at him, trembling. 'And can't you see that the guilt of it has tormented me all my days?' she cried. 'Do you think I will ever forgive myself?'

Confronting the full scale of her pain for the first time, he felt his own heart shaking. His eyes were casting about the darkness of the room, looking for his rage. He found only confusion.

'Yet you threw it all away,' he gasped. 'And for what? For what?'

At a loss to offer any explanation of a choice she had long since come to regret, Helen shook her head. 'It was madness,' she whispered. 'When Paris came to Sparta he was already possessed by the madness of Aphrodite. Her madness was too strong for me.'

'And Deiphobus?' he demanded. 'Do you blame the goddess for that too?'

'I blame her for nothing. We are what we are and must answer for ourselves.' Hope was absent from her voice, yet when her eyes looked up at him again they were filled with entreaty. 'But there are powers stronger than reason, Menelaus. Are you sure that such a power doesn't have you in its grip right now?'

His hands opened, and closed again, grasping at the air.

'Enough,' he said. 'What kind of fool do you take me for?'

'I have never thought you a fool,' she said. 'I have never believed you to be anything other than the truest and kindest of men. All the folly in this was mine.'

He stood uncertainly, confronted by both her pathos and her honesty. She had not yet asked for his forgiveness but if, as he suspected was about to happen, Helen fell to her knees and did so, he could no longer be sure that his heart would not vacillate. Quickly he sought to harden it.

'I've heard enough of this. Come noon today you'll have the justice of the gods. And so will I. So will I.'

He was about to close the door on her then, locking her in with her guilt and fear, with all her tragic beauty; but through a sudden catch in her breathing emerged a single, urgently uttered word: 'Wait.'

Menelaus stopped, knowing that he should not stop. Unable to prevent himself from hoping that a thing might still be said that would bring their whole wretched story to a better end, he turned to look back at the wife he had loved as he had never loved anyone else before or since.

Helen stood before him with her hands clasped together at her mouth and her shoulders hunched as though hugging herself against the cold.

'No one can escape the justice of the gods,' she whispered. 'What I hope to find is their mercy.'

In the dream Odysseus had come home to Ithaca and Penelope was running towards him down the cliff-path to the bay where his ship was moored. He had jumped over the side into the waves and was walking ashore through the surf to greet his wife with open arms, but as she approached more closely her face fell. She halted in her tracks. He saw her eyes gaping with horror. Puzzled, he looked down, following the direction of her gaze, and saw that the hands and arms he held out to hold her were still drenched with blood. He watched it dripping from his fingers. He saw it staining the water round his thighs. Looking back at his wife, opening his mouth to explain, he saw at once that words could make no difference — such an embrace of blood could never be acceptable. Penelope stood transfixed, shaking her head, holding up her white palms in a gesture of self-protection. Then the sea was rising and his balance was gone. With shocking force, salt-water slapped and splashed around him. Odysseus jumped awake aboard his lurching ship.

Unable to bear the smell of death in the city, he had decided to sleep on his ship where it lay moored on a strand of the bay. But a freak wave thrown up by the tide must have lifted the vessel where it stood on its keel and tipped him from his pallet to the scuppers amidst a boil of surf. Still emerging from the vague region between dream and waking, Odysseus heard how the dark sea sizzled and hissed across the turbulent bay. Then he took in the grinding of the earth beneath the rattle of shingle and knew that Poseidon had stirred.

When the strand was still again, he stumbled to his feet, looking towards the city. In the sulphurous light of the dawn sky it was impossible to tell from that distance how much more damage Troy had suffered. And then, so vivid had been the impact of his dream, he glanced down at his arms, expecting to find them still running with blood. He stood for a time, shaking his head, puzzling over the strange elision between the dream and the world. Had he been dreaming of water before the wave broke over him? Had his dream in fact invoked the wave, or had the sea pre-empted his dreaming mind?

Because there was no answer to such questions they left him uneasy, and he felt queasier still at the thought that the dream was Poseidon's work.

Once, long ago in Sparta, he had called down the curse of Earth-shaker Poseidon on all who failed to defend Menelaus's right to take Helen as his bride. But the oath had been sworn on the joints of a horse that had come reluctantly to the sacrifice, and from the moment in which he was required to swear it himself, Odysseus had suspected that the oath must come home to haunt him.

And so it had proved. Once again, as had been the case countless times since leaving Ithaca, Odysseus was tormented by the memory of the conversation in which his wife Penelope had perceived with devastating clarity the bind in which he found himself.

'So I am to understand,' she had said, 'that you devised this oath as a means to help my uncle Tyndareus solve the problem of choosing a husband for Helen without antagonizing all the other contenders for her hand?'

'That was my intention, yes.'

'And you did so on the understanding that Tyndareus would then persuade my father to countenance accepting you as my husband?'

'I did it for you.' he urged. 'You know how bitterly your father was opposed to me. I thought his brother's counsel might change his mind. And the plan worked.'

'Except that you too swore the oath,' Penelope reminded him.

'Palamedes insisted on it before all the others. I could hardly refuse. And there seemed to be no risk. No one was about to provoke the anger of the god by breaking the oath. As far as I could see, there was no reason why Menelaus and Helen should not be left to live happily in peace.'

'But you don't always see as far as you think you can see. And now the oath you devised to bring us together is tearing us apart.'

It was true, and the truth was underwritten by the logic of the gods who have an insatiable taste for irony. So for ten years Odysseus had devoted all his resources to winning this war, yet his heart had never truly been in it. Not when his twelve ships set sail from Ithaca, leaving Penelope alone on the cliff with the infant Telemachus in her arms. Not when he was luring the young Achilles to abandon his wife and child on Skyros in order to win undying glory in the war. Not when he finally contrived the death of Palamedes, whom he had always hated in his secret heart far more than he hated any of the Trojans. Nor even when he conceived the stratagem of the Wooden Horse as a means for the host to find its way inside walls so strongly built that they might stand for ever. And least of all now when he saw how all his efforts to negotiate a sane surrender of the city had been betrayed.

Odysseus had come to the war with only one intention – to return home as quickly and as profitably as possible to his wife and son. But as he stood in the thin light beside his toppled ship, with the waters of the bay shaking around him, he was possessed by a sickening conviction that returning home might prove as arduous as winning the war had been. And the man who returned to Ithaca would not be the man who had left; and who could blame his wife if she could not find it in her heart to welcome the grim stranger he had now become?

Agamemnon came down from what had once been King Priam's bedchamber to find his men jumpy and anxious to be gone. Having been woken from a drunken sleep by the shaking of the earth, they were afraid that the ground might move beneath them again with greater force. A bitter wind was blowing across the city. Through the livid dawn light, clouds heavy with rain hurtled low above Mount Ida. Some of the Argive ships which had been loosely beached on the night of the invasion bobbed and yawed in the turbid waters of the bay. Others had been knocked from their stays by the wave that came with the quake. Mariners were already down there, assessing the damage to masts and spars, or putting out in fishing smacks to retrieve the vessels that had broken loose. Everywhere he looked Agamemnon sensed the growing agitation to be gone from Troy.

He felt it himself. This city belonged to the dead now not to him. Impervious to everything, having endured the last indignity of a callous death, they had scarcely stirred in their piles while the ground trembled under them. And there were too many to move. Even if anyone had the stomach for the task, it would take days to clear the streets and burn all these corpses and there was still looting to be done.

Meanwhile the shrieks and moans of the women captives had begun to play on Agamemnon's nerves. He was standing at the wall of the citadel looking down across the lower city when Calchas came striding towards him, staff in hand, with Antenor at his side, grim-faced and recalcitrant. They were the last people he wanted to deal with now, but they had taken advantage of the confusion caused by the earth-tremor to force an encounter and there was no escaping them.

'Is this how the High King of Argos keeps his word?' Antenor demanded. 'Are we to believe that boys and pitiful old men went down fighting rather than plead for their lives? There are ten thousand ghosts in Troy. I pray that every one of them will come out nightly from the Land of Shades to haunt your dreams.'

'If your friends are dead,' Agamemnon growled, 'it's because you gave them into my hands.'

'On the strength of your word that their lives would be spared.'

'War is war, Antenor. You are king in Troy now. Learn what it means to be a king. If you would rule men, make them fear you first.'

'There's no one left for me to rule,' Antenor almost shouted the words back at him. 'Troy is dead. It's become a city of the dead. I have no desire to be a king of corpses.'

'Then go your ways, man, and count yourself lucky that you have your life still.'

Confronted by such indifference, Antenor's will collapsed in that moment. Helplessly he opened his hands and all the agony of Troy was resumed in his voice as he gasped, 'I can't find my wife. I've looked for her everywhere.'

Again Agamemnon snorted. 'I've had trouble enough these past ten years pursuing my brother's wife. I have no time to look for yours.'

Calchas said, 'Theano is priestess to Athena. Her person is sacred to the goddess.'

'Then let the Goddess protect her. She's no business of mine.' Agamemnon turned to stride away but he had taken only a few paces when he was halted by the cold authority in the priest's voice.

'The High King would do well to take care how he speaks of the gods. Already they begin to turn away from him.'

A tangle of broken veins flushed at Agamemnon's cheeks. He turned to glower at Calchas with narrowed eyes. 'Are you threatening me with curses, priest?'

'Earth-shaker Poseidon has already made his displeasure plain,' Calchas answered. 'The omens now say that he has made his peace with Athena.'

'Divine Athena has always taken my side.'

'There has been sacrilege in her temple,' Calchas answered. 'Her image has been plundered. Her priestess is missing. And the gods pursue their own ends,' he added quietly, 'not ours.'

Agamemnon's rage combusted then. 'The gods have given this great city into my hand. What clearer message do you need of their favour?'

'What the gods give,' Calchas answered, 'they can also take away.'

'The same holds true of kings,' Agamemnon snarled. 'If you value my favour, Calchas, you'd better look for more propitious omens. And you, Antenor – be certain of this – Troy, as you truly say, is dead. Before we Argives leave this land we shall do what Heracles and Telamon failed to do. We shall tear down these walls, stone by stone, so that they can never rise to trouble us again. Priam is no more. His seed is extinguished from the earth. We have seen the last of Troy. Now there is only one King of Men.' Agamemnon stood panting in his rage. 'Be thankful for his mercy.'

Then he turned away again, shouting for Talthybius. 'Call my captains together,' he demanded of the herald. 'I want them all in council. The last of the looting must be done by noon and the ships loaded. Then the host will gather at the Scaean Gate to witness Helen's execution. As soon as she's dead and the offerings are made, every ship's company will start work demolishing these walls; and once they're razed to the ground, the city will be put to the torch. I want to see nothing here but smoking ash and rubble. Then, and only then, shall we make sail for Argos.'

An hour later all the captains except Odysseus and Menelaus were gathered in the ransacked throne room of Priam's palace where they were waiting for Agamemnon to appear. Though the earth had not shifted again, Acamas and Demophon hovered uneasily within reach of the doorway. Even garrulous old Nestor was unusually silent except when he muttered impatiently about this waste of time. He demanded an explanation of the delay from Talthybius, but the herald merely glanced away, answering that the High King was in conference and would join them shortly.

'In conference with who?' Acamas asked dryly.

But before Talthybius could speak, Demophon said, 'Or is he still making his offerings on Cassandra's altar?'

Diomedes was sitting at the edge of the huge round hearth, nursing a thick head from the previous night. Impatient of the younger men's laughter, he demanded to know where Menelaus and Odysseus had got to, and whether there was to be a council that morning or not?

'Word has gone out among the Ithacans to bring Odysseus here,' the herald answered. 'He should join us quite soon. As for the King of Sparta . . .'

'The King of Sparta is here.'

All the men in the room turned to look at Menelaus who stood between the twin pillars of the doorway, wrapped in a vermilion cloak, his face anxious and drawn. 'Where is my brother?'

'The High King has not yet deigned to join us,' Diomedes scowled.

Menelaus nodded, sensing the impatience in the room. 'It's just as well. I need to speak with him before this council meets.'

'I wouldn't interrupt him just yet if I were you,' Demophon smirked.

But Menelaus was already making his way through the hall and up the stairs to the upper floor. He came out onto the wide landing just as Agamemnon emerged from the apartment where he had been alone with Cassandra since returning from his encounter with Antenor and Calchas.

'All right, I'm coming,' the King muttered gracelessly, brushing back his hair with big hands. 'Is everybody here?'

'I need to talk to you —' Menelaus said, '— privately, before you go down.'

Agamemnon appraised his brother with narrowed eyes, sensing his urgency. 'Is something wrong?' Without answering, Menelaus followed him into the apartment where he saw the slight, dark figure of Cassandra pulling on a dressing-gown as she walked past the open inner doorway of the bedchamber. He looked at his brother, who nodded and crossed the room to shut the inner door.

'Well, what is it?' Agamemnon frowned.

Swallowing, Menelaus said. 'I have changed my mind.'

'What do you mean — you've changed your mind?'

'About Helen.'

Agamemnon's face darkened. 'It's too late to hand her over to the Spartans, if that's what you're thinking. The word has already gone out that Helen will be executed here at Troy. It's what you led me to understand would happen and the entire host is now expecting it. I'm not about to disappoint them.'

Menelaus said, 'You don't yet understand me. There will be no execution. Not here and not in Sparta. Helen will not die. Not by my hand or by anybody else's. We are reconciled, she and I.'

Agamemnon stared at his brother in disbelief. Visibly his breathing quickened. He looked around the room as if to make sure that he was quite awake and all of this was actually happening.

His nostrils flared, but still, as he walked towards a table where his unbuckled sword-belt lay, he said nothing. He stood for a time, patting the table with the flat of his hand. Then he looked back at his brother with a thin, derisive smile at his lips.

'You are reconciled?'

'Yes.'

'I see,' Agamemnon nodded. 'So you asked your brother to raise all the armed might of Argos and bring it across the sea in a thousand ships so that we could spend ten miserable years fighting for your honour over a faithless wife who has humiliated and disgraced you, only to tell me that you've changed your mind?'

'This war was never about Helen,' Menelaus said quietly. 'No one knows that better than you. You wanted Troy's wealth and Helen gave you all the excuse you needed to seize it.'

Agamemnon glared across at his younger brother with violence in his eyes.

'Do you think I care nothing for the honour of the House of Atreus?' His voice was shaking as he spoke. 'Do you think I care nothing for you? Do you think I didn't wake in my sweat night after night thinking of how that cockscomb Paris was making a mockery of your name in every squalid tavern from Epirus to Ethiopia? Believe me, if Troy had been of no more account than a brigand's filthy rat-hole, I'd have crushed it just to show the world that no one lays a finger on anything that belongs to me or mine and gets away with it.' Agamemnon was panting now. 'And what return do I get for my loyalty? Apparently untroubled by the fact that your wife opened her legs for Paris, and then again for his brother Deiphobus and, for all I know, might have played the two-backed beast with old King Priam himself – untroubled by any of this, you stand before me like a sickly boy and tell me that you mean to take her back!' A vein throbbed at his temple as he shouted 'Have you gone quite mad? Have you lost all sense of honour?'

Menelaus stood with closed eyes under the withering assault.

His hands were clenched, his knuckles white as he said, 'There are things that count for more than honour in this world.'

Agamemnon brought his fist down on the table-top and shouted, 'Without honour a man is nothing. Nothing! He is less even than a worm. Men piss on those who do not prize their honour. In the name of all the gods, Menelaus, don't you remember what our father did to our mother when she betrayed him? Didn't you stand beside me watching her drown? Everyone there could see that Atreus loved the woman and that she had broken his heart, but he knew what his duty was to the honour of our house. He knew she had to die and that the world must watch her die.'

There were nights when still, as a grown man, Menelaus woke sweating with the anguish of that memory. He could clearly see the way his mother's hair had splayed beneath the surface, and how her breath bubbled from her open mouth, and the outline of her body wobbled in the green depths as though merging into water as the act of drowning protracted itself. His eyes were closed now, gripped in darkness, rejecting the memory as he had sought to do many times before.

Through clenched teeth he said, 'I am not our father.'

'Indeed you are not,' Agamemnon shook his head in disgust. 'Atreus would be ashamed to acknowledge you as his son.'

'If I am indeed his son,' Menelaus retorted. 'If either of us is, for that matter. Who knows who our father was? Certainly Atreus didn't, which is why he turned against us. Have you forgotten that? Or have you never dared to look it in the face?'

In fact, only silence filled the room, though it felt in that moment as though the whole space had burst into flame. Neither brother had ever admitted such a thought to the other since that night, nearly thirty years earlier, when the question of their paternity had first been raised. They were still small boys then, watching the quarrel between their father Atreus and his brother Thyestes, who had been vying for the throne of Mycenae after old king Sthenelus had died. When Atreus won the contest, Thyestes had vented his fury by poisoning all their minds.

'The throne might be yours now, brother,' Thyestes had shouted, 'but are you so sure about your sons? It may interest you to know that your Cretan whore of a wife has warmed my bed more times than I can remember while your back was turned.'

The boys had seen those drunken words cause the immediate banishment of Thyestes, the death by drowning of their mother Aerope, and the start of a gruesome cycle of vengeance that would contaminate their imaginations for the rest of their lives. Yet neither of them had spoken of them until now.

Trembling at what had happened, Menelaus snorted and glanced away. 'In any case,' he gasped, 'I would die sooner than become the monstrous sort of man that Atreus became.'

In a blaze of rage, Agamemnon seized the scabbard of his sword-belt in his left hand and drew the sword with his right. The blade hissed against the leather. His voice was shaking as he said, 'Humiliate yourself before me if you must, but I'll cut the breath out of your throat sooner than let you shame the House of Atreus before the host.'

Then the door to the bedchamber opened and Cassandra was standing in her robe, studying them, dark-eyed.

Without turning to look at her, Agamemnon crossed the room, holding the blade out before him till its point was pressing at his brother's throat.

'Tell me that you've heard me,' he said with a trembling fervour. 'Tell me that we'll shortly go down together and you will inform my captains that Helen's execution will take place before the Scaean Gate at noon.'

With the bronze point pressing so closely that it puckered the skin of his neck, Menelaus shook his head.

'Do this thing for me, brother,' Agamemnon gasped, his hand quivering a little, 'because I swear I will kill you if you do not.'

Menelaus said quietly, 'As our father was killed by the will of *his* brother?' He endured the menace in Agamemnon's gaze. 'Is that what you want – for the curse on our house to carry on looking for death after death down all the generations? Then kill me if you must. I can't prevent you and I have honour enough not to beg for my life.' He stood, panting with defiance. 'But this much I tell you: for all her frailties, I have always loved my wife. Even when I stood above her with a sword in my hand, I knew that I loved her and the knowledge was strong enough to stay my hand. Helen is as life itself to me. I've been a dead man all these long years since she left me. And I would rather die now than live without her for another day.'

Agamemnon stared along the blade of the sword in disbelief. A single panting sigh disturbed the spittle at his lips. Unable to countenance the unflinching gaze confronting him, he turned his head and looked, as if for guidance, to Cassandra, who observed the scene with an aloof, sibylline smile.

'What shall I do?' Agamemnon gasped.

Cassandra shrugged. 'Of all the Argives who came to Troy, this was the only man we had wronged. But you are the King. You must give him the justice you think fit.'

Absolving herself of the matter, she turned away into the inner chamber. The sons of Atreus were left alone together with the ghosts of their tormented ancestry beating about their heads. Downstairs the captains waited. The bitter wind blew across Troy, gusting in the alleys, disturbing the hair of the dead. And all that Agamemnon need do to make this wasteland complete was push the point of his sword into his brother's throat. The honour of the house would be served and men would fear his power all the more for having seen him take his brother's life. Meanwhile – he saw it almost as clearly as if the thought had summoned it – in some dark corner of the Land of Shades, the vindictive ghost of Thyestes would be smiling at this further harvest of the curse that had haunted their house since it had been founded, more than half a century ago, by the ruthless treachery of King Pelops.

The rage racing through Agamemnon's veins had become indistinguishable from pain. He was remembering how, as boys, he and Menelaus had sworn never to violate each other's trust. It was on the night when they had hidden in the darkness of the water stair at Mycenae before being smuggled out of the postern gate to seek refuge with Tyndareus in Sparta. Earlier that night their father Atreus had been murdered, Thyestes had seized his throne, and the two frightened boys could only vow always to be true to each other as they fled. But now, all these grim years later, after all they had endured, they had arrived at this bleak moment where Agamemnon stared at his brother in silence, trying to love him as a brother should love his brother and found that he could not.

But neither could he bring himself to murder him.

Agamemnon lowered the blade and threw it clattering across the room. 'Get from my sight,' he snarled. 'Take ship with your Spartan harlot if you must. But let neither of you ever set foot in Argos while I live.'

Having walked hurriedly in silence through the gathering of fractious and puzzled captains in the throne room, Menelaus came out of the palace just as Odysseus began to climb the steps towards him. Both men were dazed and distracted, staring at each other, almost as though struggling for recognition, like friends unexpectedly re-met after a separation of many years.

With the sudden, liberating realization that he was throwing off a shadow that had oppressed his life for far too long, Menelaus spoke first. 'This is well met,' he said. 'I couldn't have left Troy without speaking to you.'

Odysseus listened in bewilderment as Menelaus tried to explain himself, but so strong was the memory of this same man looming over Helen with a bloody sword in his hand that he found it difficult to take in what was happening.

'So Helen still lives?' he said.

'We are leaving together on the tide.'

'And Agamemnon knows this?'

Menelaus nodded, almost impatiently. 'Odysseus, I don't know if we'll ever meet again,' he pressed. 'Helen and I can never return to Argos after this.'

Again it took a little time for the truth of things to penetrate.

Odysseus felt a drizzle of rain blow at his face as he said, 'Where will you go?'

'I'm not sure. Eastwards I suppose. Perhaps to Egypt.'

Reflecting wryly on the ironies that seemed to rule all things now, Odysseus said, 'Then may the gods go with you.'

He would have walked on by, but Menelaus lifted a hand to prevent him. 'I have done you a great wrong,' he said. 'I should never have brought you out of Ithaca to this war. It was envy, more than need, that made me do so. Envy of the love that I saw between you and your wife.' Biting his lip, he looked up into his friend's troubled frown. 'When you get back home to her, tell Penelope that I beg her forgiveness.' Swallowing, he offered his hand.

Odysseus studied it with neither reproach nor sympathy in his eyes. Around them, on the steps of the palace and out across the square lay the lax bodies of the dead. From beyond the temple of Athena the head of the wooden horse looked down on them with a few tattered garlands still blowing from its mane. Menelaus saw the raindrops shining among the hairs of his friend's beard. Then he was amazed to hear Odysseus uttering a bitter chuckle as he walked away.

Aeacus had done his job well sixty years earlier when he built the walls at Troy, for as well as withstanding the shock of more than one earthquake they had resisted the longest siege in the history of warfare; and though the Trojans had themselves weakened one section when they broke open the masonry of the Scaean Gate in their eagerness to admit the wooden horse, everywhere else those gleaming limestone ramparts still stood strong. So it took longer than Agamemnon had hoped to tear them down.

As he laboured among his men, Odysseus was thinking that if the High King had given the matter any thought, he would have let the men of Troy live long enough to do this demolition job. As it was, the weary Argive army, anxious only to get away with its loot as quickly as possible, must now set to with rams and crowbars, battering and prising at the stones. Odysseus knew it was more than mere chance that his Ithacans had been assigned the formidable task of pulling down the eastern bastion with its deep well from which the citadel had drawn its water supply. The high brick superstructure had been toppled easily enough but as they chipped and heaved at the dressed stonework amidst a cloud of dust, Sinon could be heard muttering that this was what came of questioning the morality of that vindictive brute Agamemnon. Once a man's blood was shed, you couldn't squeeze it back in, he said, and the same held true for a whole host of corpses. Odysseus would have done better to keep his mouth shut rather than trying to salve his conscience by publicly arraigning the High King's ruthlessness.

Meanwhile, on the far corner of the bastion, Odysseus and Eurylochus were supervising an attempt to bring the masonry down by undermining it; but the foundations had been laid so deep, and the blocks were so large and closely fitted, that after an hour of digging they had made no larger profit from their work than to turn up the cracked skull, mottled bones and rotten leather corselet of some unlucky foot-soldier who had died in that place in an earlier war.

At the sight of that vacant skull, Odysseus was overwhelmed again by a black sense of the futility of human endeavour. Who could now tell how much wit and love and courage might have flourished inside that cup of bone before its owner came to fight and die beneath the walls of Troy? And the Troy at which he had fought was older than Priam's Troy, probably older than Laomedon's too. So how many wars must have been fought hereabouts, over how many centuries? And must another Troy rise one day above the rubble of these walls only to be destroyed in turn as some new army raised its might against the city? Did nothing change? And would his own skull be dug up like this one day, unrecognized?

The Lion of Mycenae was already congratulating himself that

his name must live for ever, and already the bards were at work, turning history into myth, slaughter into song; but as he stared back at the cracked eye-sockets of the skull, Odysseus looked forward only to the redeeming obscurity of a time in which there would be no living memory of the terrible thing that had been done at Troy.

So when Eurylochus broke the haft of his spade against another course of limestone footings and threw the useless tool away, grimacing up at Odysseus, he saw to his astonishment that his leader was standing above him, stripped to his breech-clout in the heat, with tears brimming at his eyes, as though the skull he held in the palm of his hand had once belonged to a well-loved friend.

Not till the late afternoon of the following day were they ready to set fire to the ruins of the city. All the women who were to be taken into captivity had been led away, wailing, to the ships. Everything of value that the ravaged capital had to offer was stowed in the holds beneath the oar-benches, and what the ships could not carry lay abandoned like so much rubbish on the strand or was dumped overboard in the choppy waters of the bay. Dry timber, bales of wool and straw and other combustible materials were arranged along the wider streets to encourage the spreading of the blaze, while men with scarves at their faces stacked the sullen multitudes of the dead in piles and dowsed them in oil. A wind rising to gale-force from the east promised to make the flames thrive even though the dense, swiftly moving storm-clouds threatened further rain.

Teams of men with torches started fires in every quarter and by dusk the whole noble city of Troy was one vast funeral pyre. The night sky flushed to an incandescent orange-red. The bruised clouds charred to ruddy-black above it. Smoke extinguished half the known stars, while new constellations of sparks gusted on the wind. Meanwhile, even where they stood at a far distance from the blaze to gaze with awe at what they had accomplished, the heat and stink of burning came at men's faces like a pestilence.

Odysseus was standing on Thorn Hill with his dark-skinned herald Eurybates, looking towards the inferno with shielded eyes when he saw Agamemnon's chariot hurrying across the plain towards him. As the driver reined in the sleek team of blacks that had once belonged to Paris, Agamemnon shouted up to Odysseus that he wanted to have words. Uncertain whether the tone of his voice was anxious or elated, Odysseus made his way down to where Agamemnon's horses sweated and fretted, rolling their eyes towards the roar of the inferno.

'I've been looking for you everywhere!' Agamemnon shouted. 'There's something I need to tell you. Something you need to know.' Odysseus was able to make out the gleam of triumph in his eyes. 'We've done the right thing. In destroying Troy, I mean. I'm sure of it now.'

'I thought you always were,'

'Well, yes, I was, of course.' Agamemnon frowned at his obdurate comrade. The buckles on his harness seemed to blaze in the reflection of heat from the burning city. 'But I've just had a despatch out of Mycenae and it confirms I was right. The Hittites are on the march. They're coming westwards, heading for Troy. They'll be here in a matter of days.'

'The Hittites? I thought they were still at war in the east.'

'I'm told that Hattusilis has settled things on his eastern front and now he's decided to send the whole western half of his army to the aid of Troy. He doesn't yet know that Priam's finished.'

Odysseus stood in silence for a time, taking in this unexpected development, thinking quickly. 'When was the despatch sent?' he asked.

'I'm not sure. Why?'

'Because Hattusilis may not have known that Troy had fallen when the pigeon was released, but if his spies are any good he'll know by now. Presumably he's not about to risk losing control of the Hellespont to Mycenaean power.'

'Exactly.' Agamemnon fixed Odysseus with his smirk. 'And if

we'd stuck with your plan we'd have a big new war on our hands any time now. A war I'm not at all sure we could win. Do you understand?'

'Yes,' Odysseus answered dryly, 'I understand.' He looked back at where one of the oil magazines under the citadel had just combusted with a whooshing roar of yellow flame. 'And the fact that you didn't know this when you decided to kill everyone in Troy is a matter of no moral consequence whatsoever, I suppose?'

Agamemnon flushed with exasperation. He had won a great victory, perhaps the greatest victory in the history of warfare, yet his own brother had frustrated him, his captains were increasingly truculent around him, and this man, his most trusted counsellor and one of his oldest comrades, evidently held him in contempt. Where was the justice in all this? Why would no one honestly acknowledge him for what he had proved himself to be, the King of Men?

'The fact is, I was right, wasn't I?' he demanded. 'We were stretched to the limit coping with Priam's western alliance. There was no way we could take on the whole Hittite Empire. So we've done well out of this. We're going back with all the treasure of Troy stowed in our holds. There's no danger of reprisal from this pile of ash and rubble, and Hattusilis will be content to keep his Asian empire intact. He won't risk crossing the Aegean to avenge Priam any more than we're about to outstare him here. By the time his army reaches Troy our ships will be well gone. The Hittites are welcome to what's left after this fire has burned out!'

Odysseus stood in silence, letting the bluster blow past him. When it was done, he turned away and called up to his herald. 'Do you hear this, Eurybates? It seems that the High King has come to crow over me.' Then he glowered back at Agamemnon. 'Is that it?'

'No, that's not it,' Agamemnon scowled. 'I came here as an act of friendship. I came to tell you this because I thought it might ease that delicate conscience of yours. Think about it, man. Can

you believe that Antenor and the Dardanians would have stayed
loyal to your treaty once the Hittites turned up with a force large
enough to drive us into the sea?' Before Odysseus could answer,
he pointed upwards over the Ithacan's shoulder. 'Look! Do you
see what that is?'

Odysseus turned his head and saw where a bonfire had burst
into a bright conflagration against the blackness of the night sky
on the summit of Mount Ida.

'It's the first of the chain of signal fires.' Agamemnon's eyes
were themselves smouldering with pride. 'In a minute or two the
detachment on Lemnos will see it and light their fire, and from
there the signal will leap to the rock of Zeus on Mount Athos,
and then it'll be passed on from beacon to beacon till all Argos
knows that Troy has fallen.' Agamemnon looked back with a smile
of satisfaction. 'The gods know that we've done what we came
here to do.' But when he failed to find any sign of assent in the
anguished intelligence of the face across from him, he shook his
head impatiently. 'You're a dreamer, Odysseus! You're a dreamer
and I'm glad of it. I doubt there's another man on earth who
could have thought up the stratagem of the wooden horse. So
everything we've loaded in our ships we owe to you and your
imagination. I don't deny it for a moment, and I thank you for
it. I thank you from the bottom of my heart. But admit it, man
– if we'd tried to handle things the way you wanted, we would
have ended up with nothing. We'd have been lucky to save our
skins from the Hittite host. So remind yourself of what's stowed
in your ships and be grateful for your good fortune. Then go
back home to Penelope in the knowledge of a job well done.
That's what I came to say. If you've any sense, you'll sleep well
tonight because of it.'

Without waiting for a response, Agamemnon signalled to his
driver to turn the chariot away. Odysseus watched it speed across
the plain, a fleeting dark shadow against the fierce, incendiary
glare in which, hour by hour, the city of Troy was vanishing from
the face of the earth. Meanwhile, high at his back, the beacon on

Mount Ida proclaimed to the world in tongues of flame that the King of Men was victorious and nothing would ever be the same again.

The Ghosts of Mycenae

The drowned body of the bard Pelagon was found washed up on the shore of an uninhabited island in the bay of Argos. The last time he'd been seen alive he was in the company of a young Corinthian poet of conspicuous beauty who had come as a pilgrim to the court at Mycenae declaring himself to be a passionate admirer of Pelagon's art. At the young man's suggestion the two bards had taken a small boat out onto the gulf for a pleasure cruise. But some misadventure must have happened, a freak gust of wind driving them onto a shoal perhaps, for the wreckage of their craft was discovered later that day with no one aboard.

Because the Corinthian's body was never recovered, a degree of mystery and scandal surrounded the affair. But Queen Clytaemnestra ordered a time of mourning in Mycenae, not least because the chief bard's regrettable death left unfinished the great Lay of Agamemnon on which he had been working for many years. The High King's eventual return from Troy would be, she insisted, the poorer for the lack of it.

Not long afterwards a traveller turned up in Mycenae, bearing rich gifts and asking for an audience with the Queen. Aegisthus had been only a boy of twelve when he fled the city more than twenty years earlier, so no one recognized this suave, intense stranger as the son of Thyestes, who had ruled Mycenae for a number of years until Agamemnon and Menelaus, the vengeful sons of Atreus, had returned with the Spartan army at their backs to reclaim their father's throne. So if there was some surprise that the stranger was speedily granted the private audience he sought, there was no immediate understanding, even among the better-informed citizens, that the blood-drenched course of Mycenaean history was about to undergo a further violent change.

'That you were powerful I already knew,' said Aegisthus, settling himself on the proffered couch, 'and King Nauplius warned me at some length that you are also formidably intelligent. But he neglected to inform me that you have the further advantage of being a very beautiful woman.'

Knowing that she was some years older than the refined man across from her, and that he must already have enjoyed much success with younger women on whose faces the cares of state were not indelibly inscribed, Clytaemnestra raised a languorous hand to brush the remark aside. 'There is no appetite for flattery here,' she said. Yet it was evident in her smile that she was not displeased.

Exiled from power by his father's defeat and death, Aegisthus had clearly learned that the attractive exercise of charm might supply many deficiencies of a fugitive's life. His vivid blue eyes were still smiling as he said, 'Nor was there any thought of flattery here. On the contrary, I understand very well that my only hope of leaving Mycenae alive resides in your respect for my honesty as one who has also suffered at your husband's hands.'

'So you believe you have my measure already? And what if you are wrong?'

'Then at least I will have died proudly trying to recover what is mine.'

'Rather than running from bolt-hole to bolt-hole ahead of Agamemnon's men?' Clytaemnestra gave a little, humourless laugh. 'My husband left me with very clear instructions. *Aegisthus is as dangerous as his father was,* he warned me. *Hunt him down while I'm gone and, once you have him in your power, show him no mercy.'* And then, almost as though this were a matter on which she should take his advice, she asked, 'Was he right, I wonder? Is that what I should have done?'

Opening his hands, Aegisthus said, 'Doubtless that would have been the proper course, if you were no more than an obedient wife. But I imagine you have always prided yourself on being rather more than that.'

'Yet you should understand,' Clytaemnestra arranged the many folds of her viridian gown, 'that once my agents traced you to the court of that sickly weasel on Euboea, you would not have lasted long if I didn't have a use for you.'

Unfazed, Aegisthus studied her with admiring eyes. 'I always considered Agamemnon a fool. Now I know he was never more so than when he failed to secure your loyalty.'

There was no arrogance, merely a casual acceptance of simple fact, in the Queen's nod of assent. 'Yet there was a time when he could count on my absolute support,' she said, 'in matters of state at least.'

'But Aulis changed all that?'

Clytaemnestra sighed. 'It began long before then, but yes, at Aulis everything changed.'

'Not only the wind,' he dared.

'No, not only the wind.'

'And you are no longer obedient?'

'Oh yes,' she said, 'but not to Agamemnon.'

'Then to whom?'

'Not to any man, I assure you.'

'A god then?' He paused for a moment over the severity of her frown. 'Or a goddess perhaps?'

Though she said nothing, he caught a glint of acknowledgement in her eyes.

'I confess that my own devotions are to Divine Artemis,' he volunteered. 'I intend to make offerings to her while I am here, in the hope that she will look with more favour on Mycenae.'

For a moment Clytaemnestra had felt transparent under the glitter of those eyes, as if he had looked into the cold cave of her heart and seen the altar at which she worshipped there. Only then did she understand just how dangerous this man might be. Beneath his charm lurked a soul that had been forged in a dark smithy. It further occurred to her that the two of them together resembled the twisted serpents on the ring she had given him for a pledge, the ring which Aegisthus was fingering conspicuously now as he smiled across at her. It was time she took control of this conversation.

'You must not imagine,' she said coolly, 'that I am unaware of your following here in Mycenae. I know that not everyone in this city rejoiced when my husband overthrew your father. There are those here who still think of you as their rightful prince.' She paused before adding, almost as an afterthought, 'Their names are known to me.'

Because some instinct of his survivor's soul had already detected a kindred air of corruption in this woman, Aegisthus smiled. It was to that corruption he spoke when he answered with a lightness that surprised her, 'But not to your husband?'

'Not yet. Their lives are in my hands, not his. As is, of course, your own.'

The smile dissolved at his lips. He waited for a moment, gazing at her with an intensity that she would have found impertinent in any other man. 'Then I think,' he declared quietly, 'that it has found its destined home.'

Both voice and eyes were so patently sincere that she was astonished by the utterance. Either this man was a consummate actor or, and with every moment this began to feel more likely, he had been brought here not merely at her behest but by his own unshakable sense of destiny. Not a word she had spoken had surprised him. Still less had it made him afraid. By some divinatory power born of a lifetime spent on the perilous edge of things he seemed to know her soul almost as intimately as she did herself.

Already they were deeply complicit, twinned serpents capable of renewing each other's life, or of ending it with a toxic kiss.

Her own instinct had been true then. Here was exactly the accomplice she needed for the most dangerous enterprise of her career. And if, for a moment, she had almost been in awe of this man, Clytaemnestra now felt an equivalent power rising inside her like a snake.

From a silver mixing bowl chased with a design of nymphs and satyrs, she poured wine into two goblets and crossed the room to sit closer to Aegisthus. 'Now you will tell me about yourself,' she smiled. 'I want to hear your whole story. In particular I wish to know what feelings passed through you as a child on the night when you murdered King Atreus.'

'But I cannot tell my story,' he returned her smile, 'without also telling my father's; and that cannot be done without raising all the ghosts of Mycenae.'

'Then raise them,' she said. 'Let me hear what they have to say.'

So nightmarish was the story Aegisthus had to tell that, when she thought about it afterwards, Clytaemnestra was uncertain whether his cool, ironical voice made it harder or easier to accept its appalling truth; for in the dangerous smile on his handsome face could be seen the latest flowering of a curse that had haunted his family since his grandfather's time. So much power had accrued to old King Pelops that most of the mainland of Argos was eventually named for him, but that power was won by treacherous means, and the curses he invoked were passed on, like evil seed, from one generation to the next. So Aegisthus told how even before the death of Pelops, his estranged sons, Atreus and Thyestes, who had fled the shadow of their imperious father to seek fortunes of their own, were set against one another by that legacy of curses. Their quarrels came to a head when Atreus was made king of Mycenae. Furious at being cheated of his own claim to the Lion Throne, Thyestes exposed his brother's wife Aerope as his whore, thus calling the paternity of Agamemnon and Menelaus into question; and though Atreus eventually recalled his brother from the banishment to which he consigned him, it was only with the intention of perpetrating the most horrific act of vengeance that his mind could conceive.

Thyestes, of course, was unaware of this. Delighted by his brother's change of heart, he returned to his wife and children in Mycenae. That night he was treated as the guest of honour in the banqueting hall of the Lion House and made a good meal of the delicious stew that was served up for him. Assuring him that he had not yet tasted the daintiest portions, Atreus pressed him to eat more. Another salver was placed before him and, when the lid was lifted, Thyestes found himself staring in bewilderment at a neatly arranged pile of little hands and feet. They lay in the blood that had leaked from them, small bones and severed gristle protruding from raw, vividly red flesh. Then his eyes were caught by the splashes of silver paint on the tiny fingernails that his four-year-old daughter had held up for his admiration on his arrival home in Mycenae only a few hours earlier.

'Can you imagine how Atreus smiled as the colour drained from Thyestes' face?' Aegisthus said. 'Think how cold his voice must have been when he said, "Console yourself with this thought, dear brother – the confidence that my sons are indeed my own has been stolen from me; but from this hour forth, you will never be in any doubt that you and your children will always be one flesh." But by then, I suppose, Thyestes must already have been out of his mind with the shock of what had been done to him. And what loathing for his own body must such knowledge have stirred? Yet he was condemned to live with it as he fled from Mycenae. Nor did Atreus himself emerge from that hideous banquet with his mind unscathed. Increasingly he grew obsessed by guilt at the thing he had done. His dreams became so troubled that he scarcely dared sleep at night. Then his anxieties increased when a long drought parched the countryside for miles around the city. Weeks passed without rain; the crops withered in the fields. When the harvest failed and famine threatened everyone's survival, Atreus succumbed to the general belief that his dreadful crime was the cause of the disaster. Under pressure from the city's priesthood, he was driven to consult the oracle at Delphi for guidance on how best to cleanse himself of the pollution of that crime. He was told it could be done only by recalling Thyestes to Mycenae.'

At that point Aegisthus left a silence in which he composed himself to speak of the circumstances surrounding his own birth, for in all his years of exile he had never previously confided in anyone. He might have found it impossible now had he not been urged on by this queen's insatiability for truth.

Sensing his uncertainty, Clytaemnestra said, 'My own life is well acquainted with horror. We are kindred in that, you and I. The truth can only bring us closer.'

Aegisthus smiled in assent and went on to tell how Thyestes had sought refuge at the court of King Thesprotus in Sicyon. On a visit to that city many years earlier he had fathered a daughter who had since grown up to become priestess to Divine Athena. Though he had not seen her since she was a babe in arms, it was to Pelopia that Thyestes now turned for consolation. Afraid that she must instinctively recoil from him as he recoiled from himself, he was overwhelmed with gratitude at the unexpected warmth with which Pelopia received him.

'She was a consecrated priestess as well as his daughter,' Aegisthus said. 'Perhaps she came to believe that she could heal her father's troubled soul? Whatever the case, Thyestes began to nurse an unholy passion for this beautiful young woman who had brought hope to his blighted life. That passion became an obsession, and when Pelopia realized that her sympathy had been mistaken for some stronger emotion, she sought, as best she could, to withdraw.'

Sensing the agitation that must lie in the fissures beneath his dry, ironical regard, Clytaemnestra listened in fascination as Aegisthus went on to tell how Thyestes, denied his daughter's company, had taken to stalking her. On a night when she was due to make her offerings to Athena, he concealed himself in the shadows of a grove from where he could spy on the sacrificial rites. He watched in a state of intense excitement as she drew the knife across the throat of a black ewe. When the offering was made, Pelopia clapped her hands and led the temple maidens in the dance to the goddess. Thyestes saw her lose her footing as she slipped in a pool of blood that had drained from the severed arteries of the ewe. When she rose to her feet her tunic was splashed with stains. Covertly he followed her to watch her wash away the bloodstains in the temple fish-pond; and there, crazed by the sight of her nakedness, Thyestes masked his face with his cloak, pressed his sword at her throat to silence her, and took her by force.

He must have woken from that demented trance of passion to see his daughter sobbing on the ground beneath him. Dropping his sword, Thyestes backed away. Unable to speak, scarcely able to breathe, he turned and ran. With his mind descending into ever deeper turmoil, he kept on running until he was gone from Sicyon, and when he came to the sea he took ship for distant Lydia.

'Some days after Pelopia had been found in a dumb state of shock,' Aegisthus said, 'Atreus arrived in Sicyon looking for Thyestes. No longer virgin by then, and therefore no longer priestess to Athena, Pelopia had been taken into the king's care. When Atreus saw her sitting sadly in the court, he too seems to have fallen under the spell of her strangely familiar presence. Assuming that the girl was the king's daughter, he asked Thesprotus if he might take her for his new wife.

'For some time Thesprotus had been worrying over how to keep at bay the imperial might of his powerful neighbour in Mycenae, so he immediately saw the value of such an alliance. But he also knew that Atreus would recoil from the proposal if he learned the truth of what had happened to his ward. So Thesprotus cannily decided to say nothing of Pelopia's tragic fate. Atreus returned to Mycenae with his bride and nine months later Pelopia gave birth to a son.'

Aegisthus paused again, reaching for his wine. When he resumed, his voice was held under still colder control. 'Having already turned his back on Agamemnon and Menelaus,' he said, 'Atreus was delighted by the birth of a new heir. But shortly after recovering from her confinement, Pelopia took the baby from its crib and carried it into the hills around Mycenae where she left it to die. Imagine the consternation here in the Lion House! Atreus told himself that his young wife must have been over-whelmed by the madness that can sometimes possess a new mother. But as he sent out people to search for the child, he was fearful that the gods were still conspiring against him. To his enormous relief, the infant was found unharmed in the care of a goatherd who had given it to one of his nanny-goats for suckling.'

Clytaemnestra said, 'So that is how you came by your name!'

Aegisthus smiled. 'Atreus named me for the strength of the goat that had shown me more tender mercy than my mother did. And so, entirely unaware that my conception, birth and survival were all the work of a malignant fate invoked by a chain of curses binding one generation to the next, I grew up in the citadel at Mycenae as the half-brother and unloved companion of Agamemnon and Menelaus, who had withdrawn into a conspiracy of mutual support after the execution of their mother. As you can imagine, they did not greatly care for me!'

Looking at the man he had become, Clytaemnestra could see that even as a child Aegisthus must have been troublingly beauti-ful. His corn-coloured hair, intense, periwinkle eyes, and lean body, delicately boned but with the promise of an athlete's swift strength, would have contrasted with the brawnier, more rumpled features of his two stepbrothers. Accordingly they would have taken pleasure in informing him that he had the vacant eyes, rancid stink and doubtless the randy morals of the she-goat who had suckled him. Yet, however painful the insults he took, Aegisthus said, he remained confident that he was the favoured heir of Atreus. Sooner or later a day must come when he would be given the power to make his tormentors eat every word with which they had wounded him. In the meantime he was content to scheme alone, looking for ploys to darken their father's mind against them without ever appearing openly to do so.

Thyestes, meanwhile, had grown restless with his state of exile in Lydia. He was driven by the single obsessive thought that all the evil fortune in his life had been engendered by his brother Atreus. So Atreus must die. And when he was dead, Thyestes would seize the throne of Mycenae. And then there would be sanity and justice in the world again.

Seven years after he had fled from Sicyon to Lydia, Thyestes learned from traders putting in at Smyrna that discontent was rife in Mycenae. Long years of drought had taken a dreadful toll on the surrounding countryside. As crops failed and livestock perished, people murmured that no land had ever suffered such prolonged misfortune unless its king had offended the gods, and there could be no more monstrous crime than the one that Atreus had perpetrated on his brother. The pollution of that crime must be cleansed; but the oracle at Delphi had long ago proclaimed that the drought would not lift until Thyestes returned. So how much longer must the people wait for the god's demand to be answered?

Confident that the wind was now blowing in his favour, Thyestes took ship back across the Aegean. His intention was to put in at Euboea where King Nauplius, who had no love for Atreus, would give him shelter. From there he would proceed to Delphi and seek guidance on how best to avenge himself on his brother.

'At Delphi,' Aegisthus said, 'he received what was, perhaps, the strangest oracle ever pronounced by the god. *How else should a man take vengeance on his brother*, he was told, *except by raping his own daughter?*'

'But in his madness he had already done that,' Clytaemnestra said.

Aegisthus smiled. 'Which was exactly the confusing thought that came to my father when he heard the judgement of the god. Surely such madness could not be required of him again? So he came out of the temple into the glare of the day bewildered and dismayed, scarcely aware of his surroundings. And by a gesture of chance such as happens only through the will of the gods, he did so at just the moment when Agamemnon and Menelaus arrived in the forecourt of the temple. Atreus had sent them there to make placatory offerings on behalf of his stricken city. It was Menelaus who recognized Thyestes first. He pointed him out to Agamemnon who immediately commanded their guard to seize him. Thyestes was brought in fetters to Mycenae; but the gods were far from done with him.'

Aegisthus took a drink from the goblet which Clytaemnestra had replenished for him. 'As it happened,' he continued, Atreus was away from Mycenae at that time, putting down a band of brigands who were causing trouble on the Corinth road; so his sons threw Thyestes into the dungeon to await his return. I remember Agamemnon taunting me about their achievement, bragging that Atreus would now recognize who his true heirs were. They would soon be back in his favour, not some upstart goat-boy who belonged among the stinking shepherds who had found him . . . things of that sort. The oracle had been fulfilled. Thyestes had been brought back to Mycenae. The god had been obeyed. Soon the drought must be lifted. Surely Agamemnon must receive his father's thanks and praise! Imagine his disappointment, therefore, when Atreus merely nodded as though having difficulty digesting the fact that his brother was back in the city and that something must now be done about him. Though I was only seven years old, I saw at once that he could not bring himself to look in the face of the man he had so savagely wronged. Certainly, he could not bring himself to order his brother's death, even though he had no wish to see him live as a continual threat to his own security. And then I think that some god must have whispered in my ear that Atreus was in need of my help. In any case, I spoke up in the silence of the hall. "The oracle decreed that Thyestes must be brought back to Mycenae," I said. "It did not insist that he must be allowed to live. If my father wishes it, I will gladly put an end to his wretched life." I remember that

Atreus looked at me as though seeing me for the first time – a seven-year old boy confidently volunteering to commit murder as if it was the most natural thing on earth. But that was exactly how it felt to me.'

Conscious of the quickening of her heart, Clytaemnestra stared at her guest in fascination. Looking into those intense blue eyes, she had no difficulty imagining the peculiar innocence of the child who had uttered those terrifying words even though not a shred of that innocence was evident in the smile across from her.

'Of course, Agamemnon began to scoff immediately,' Aegisthus continued, 'but Atreus raised an imperious finger to silence him and asked if I would truly do this thing for him. "If the father I love desires it of me," I answered at once. And he said, "I do. I do desire it." And so the thing was decided. Agamemnon sought to protest, of course, claiming that such an important task would be safer in his own hands than those of a mere child. But he could only blush when Atreus demanded to know why he had not done the job already. Was it perhaps because Agamemnon believed that Thyestes was indeed his father?'

Aegisthus smiled at the irony of the gods. 'I think it must have been the first time that the question of Agamemnon's paternity had been so openly raised between them,' he added, 'for he blanched at the imputation and strode from the king's chamber in a blustering sulk of rage. I cannot now say which gave me the greater pleasure, to receive this earnest of the degree to which I was loved and trusted by Atreus, or to see my tormentor Agamemnon so roundly humiliated by the man he had sought to please. Either way, when Atreus offered me the loan of his own sword to do the deed, I proudly declared that my mother Pelopia had already given me a short sword as a portion of my birthright heritage from Sicyon. I was used to its weight, it could be concealed more easily in the folds of my cloak, and I would prefer to use it as the instrument of Thyestes' death. What I did not say was that the sword had exercised a powerful fascination over my mind ever since the solemn occasion when my mother first presented it to me. The bronze blade was finely chased with a hunting scene: a wild boar, a pack of hounds and men with spears; and the pommel was delicately fashioned in the form of the head of Artemis. I had never displayed the weapon in public where my half-brothers might learn to covet what was my most prized possession, and my heart was excited now by the thought of putting it to use in what must be the most noble of all causes, the defence of my father's life and honour.'

Aegisthus fell silent for a time. Aware that he was now approaching the climax of his story, Clytaemnestra poured more wine into his goblet. She watched him stare into its depths before drinking. She saw the shadows of memory move across his dark, angular features. She waited patiently for him to speak.

Without telling his mother what he was doing, the boy Aegisthus had taken his sword from its place of concealment and made his way down the stairway to the vaulted store-room beneath the citadel which served as a prison in those days. Having seen no one but his gaoler for days, Thyestes looked up at the unexpected sight of a small boy approaching him through the gloom with an oil-lamp in his left hand and his right hand tucked inside the folds of his cloak.

'We had never seen each other before,' Aegisthus said, 'and when he saw from my clothing that I was well-born he demanded to know whether another of his brother's brats had come to crow over him. I held the lamp so that I could study his face and was struck by his resemblance to Atreus. This man was younger, and there was a hungrier look about his cheeks and eye-sockets, but he was unmistakably the brother of the man who had sent me to murder him. He sat crouched against a wall that had been carved out of the solid rock, with his hands firmly tethered at the wrists and one leg shackled by a bronze chain fixed to a cleat in the wall. The store-room stank of his piss and shit. "You are my father's enemy," I said, "and I have come to put an end to your life." Of course Thyestes snorted at that, and shook his head as if to convince himself that he wasn't merely dreaming. But then I put the lamp down where it would shed most light and advanced towards him, taking my sword from the folds of my cloak. He said, "Is my brother so great a coward that he sends a child to do his dirty work these days?" Then he pulled himself up to his feet, saying, "Come on then, little boy, you'll be doing me a kindness." He held his bound wrists up above his head, exposing his stomach to my blade, but then, as I drew back the sword ready to plunge it deep into his flesh, he moved with surprising nimbleness, pushed his free leg between my own, and tripped me to the floor. The sword slipped from my grip and the next thing I knew this big, half-naked man was leaning over me with the hilt of the sword gripped in his bound hands staring down at me. "Shall I kill you then, spawn of Atreus," he said, "as Atreus killed my children and served their poor flesh up for me to eat?" I was staring up at him, wide-eyed, with the sword blade trembling above my throat. Then I heard him gasp as though he had been pushed from behind by a god. "Where did you get this?" he demanded. I lay beneath his weight, unable to grasp what was happening. He was staring not at me but at the head of Artemis on the pommel of my sword. "Where did you get this sword?" he shouted. "Tell me or I'll cut the tongue out of your head."

'Thinking he was accusing me of theft, I gasped out that the sword had been given to me by my mother. Immediately Thyestes demanded to know who my mother was. "Pelopia," I stammered, "daughter of King Thesprotus of Sicyon."

'He lowered over me more closely then, shaking his head as he scrutinised my face. "How old are you?" he demanded, and when I told him I was seven, I could see his mind working quickly behind his eyes. "And your mother is Pelopia?" He pressed the point of the sword to the skin of my neck. "You swear you are telling me the truth?" Terrified of this strange, violent man, I swore on my life that I spoke the truth and was amazed when he lifted his weight off me and stood trembling in the gloom. I would have scrambled away then but he held me down with his foot, demanding to know whether Pelopia knew that he was here in

Mycenae under confinement. I said that I didn't know for sure, but I didn't think so because she rarely left the women's quarters and Agamemnon had kept his prisoner secret as a surprise for Atreus when he returned. Then, "Listen to me, boy," Thyestes panted. "If you wish to live you must swear on the head of Divine Artemis here to do exactly as I say. Believe me, more than both of our lives may depend on it." Then he pushed the pommel of the sword into my hand and made me swear a terrible oath that I would obey him. As I stammered out the oath, I could hear the rasp of his breath. I could feel his skin trembling next to mine. "I know your mother," he said. "She is very dear to me. Bring her here to me now. Tell her that the father she once loved begs to have words with her."

'I lay in a state of confusion, wanting only to be out of that evil place, unable to understand what he could mean. But, "You have sworn," he growled. "You will bring a terrible fate down on your head if you fail to keep that oath. Now go. Go quickly. Bring Pelopia to me." He lifted his foot off my chest. I got up, unable to take my eyes off him. Then I turned and ran for the stairs.'

'And your mother,' Clytaemnestra said, 'tell me, how did she respond to this?'

Aegisthus faltered for a moment. 'My mother was a strange, fey creature, who rarely left her apartment unless it was to feed the birds or stare out across the hills as though in expectation of someone or something. And she was prey to fits of black depression, when she would speak to no one but me, even though I could understand almost nothing of what she said.' For the first time he looked up at the woman across from him with a pained frown. 'I loved her very much and was greedy for more of her love than she was able to give me; but I was also alarmed by her strange, distracted ways. And that night she was as confused as I was by what I had to tell her. For a time she would say nothing in answer to the questions I gabbled out. But when I told her of the dreadful oath I had been made to swear on the head of Artemis, she gathered her mantle about her shoulders and accompanied me, shivering all the way, down the dark stair to the dungeon.

'I watched as she peered through the lamp-lit gloom at the shackled man who stared back at her. Thyestes had used the edge of my sword to sever the tethers at his wrists and he was holding the sword still, so I was afraid for both of us. But though nothing was said for what felt like a very long time, it was immediately clear to me that they recognized each other. Eventually Thyestes croaked out my mother's name, almost as though he were asking her a question. I couldn't see my mother's face because it was buried at his shoulder but I caught the glisten of tears at his eyes. "Pelopia," he asked hoarsely, "this sword that you gave to your son, how did you come by it?"

'He was holding up the sword in the lamp-light so that she could see the pommel and the chased engraving on the blade. She turned her face away and then looked down at her feet as she said, "It was dropped by the stranger who raped me on the night when I last made the offering to Artemis at Sicyon." She reached out and took the sword from her father's hand. "The sword was his," she said, gazing down at the blade with revulsion in her eyes. "I gave it to my son in the hope that one day he might avenge my honour."'

Aegisthus drew in his breath. 'I knew nothing of any of this,' he said. 'I can only assume that my mother must have been waiting until I was nearer manhood before telling me her story. But the gods were impatient for the truth to be known. I was still trying to cope with the shock when I heard Thyestes say, "Pelopia, the sword is mine."'

Clytaemnestra saw Aegisthus wince at the memory. There came a long silence, which again, out of a tact that was now touched with a surprising measure of compassion for the tormented man across from her, she chose not to break.

'From that moment things are not so clear to me,' Aegisthus said eventually. 'I felt bewildered by the tension between them in that awful place. I was trembling and I could feel the hairs bristling at my neck as though I was in the presence of a god. Then even before I could understand what was happening, my mother had turned the sword on herself and with a single thrust pushed the blade deep into her stomach. I can see her body swaying as she stares up into Thyestes' face. He is looking back at her, reaching out his hands when she begins to fall. Then they are both slumped on the stone flags of the floor and I can see blood shining like oil in the lamp-light as it seeps into the cracks between the stones. I wanted to be gone from there to a place where I could tell myself that none of this had happened, that it was a nightmare come to trouble my sleep, but my limbs wouldn't move. I was fixed there like a statue of myself, unable to think, unable to feel, scarcely able to breathe. And then, somehow, Thyestes was staring into my face. I could see the hairs in his nostrils. I could smell his breath and see his teeth as he spoke. He had my thin arms gripped so tightly in his hands that I knew they must leave bruises there. I could see my mother's blood spattered on his clothes and chest. My teeth were chattering. I think my whole body must have been shaking. I could hear what he was saying and it made no sense to me. He was telling me that he and I were father and son and that my mother was also my sister. He insisted that he, not Atreus, was my true father, and we were both, therefore, monsters. A monstrous father embracing his monstrous son. My mother lay between us with my sword protruding from her stomach. I watched as he gripped it by the hilt and pulled out the blade with a soft puckering of sound in the silence of that place. A fresh spurt of blood burst out across the floor. I was staring at it when Thyestes grabbed me by the chin and fixed me with his gaze. He demanded to know what name they had given me, and when I gasped it out between my chattering teeth he said, "Well, Aegisthus, you are faced with the first and most important decision of your accursed young life. You must take back your sword and do one of two things with it. Either you can do what you came here to do and plunge it into my flesh, and this time I will not try to prevent you because you will be bringing an end to all my evil days. Or you can use it to kill the man who sent you here to murder me." He was staring so intently into my eyes that I could not look away from him and he must have divined the confusion of my thoughts because he said, "Be assured that Atreus is not your father." Then he gravely offered me the sword.'

Aegisthus stared into space remembering how cold he had felt in that moment. Cold and immensely powerful – a child given absolute power in a world in which the adults knew only how to hate each other. For a few seconds he had felt utterly free to choose. And then, only a moment later, he had known himself under a compulsion that left him with no choice at all. He saw Pelopia lying dead in her blood on the stone floor and Thyestes standing over her, and he knew that the three of them were caught in the trap of their terrible consanguinity. In a place prior to reason, older even than thought, he knew that the three of them were all one flesh; that they were an unholy family living and dying inside a trap that had been set for them by a malevolent fate.

'And there was no escape,' he said. 'I would do what my true father told me to do. I would return to Atreus with the bloody sword, claiming that I had done his will and murdered his brother Thyestes. And then, when his back was turned, perhaps in the very moment when he was making a thankful offering to the gods he worshipped, I would take that sword and drive it with all my strength up through his back and into his lungs and heart. And in so doing I would have fulfilled the Delphic oracle and avenged my father on his enemy.'

'And in that moment,' Clytaemnestra whispered urgently, 'tell me, what did you feel?'

Aegisthus looked up, aware suddenly of the almost sensual appetite with which she waited for his answer. 'Now I shall disappoint you,' he said, 'for the truth is that I felt very little. I think that by then I was beyond all feeling as I was beyond all thought.

Without understanding what was happening to me, I had become an instrument of fate as devoid of moral consciousness as was my sword itself. Perhaps I had given my whole being over to my sword, the sword that Thyestes had purchased with the intention of killing his brother all those years before. The sword he had held at his daughter's throat when he ravished her. The sword with which the mother of his child had killed herself that night. And the sword which I now thrust into the back of the man whom I once believed to be my father and who I now knew to be a greater monster than my true father had ever been. And I did it with no sense of triumph. Nor even with much in the way of fear; merely with the dull certainty that my misbegotten life had fulfilled the purpose for which it was created and it would not greatly matter if I died for it.'

'But you did not die,' Clytaemnestra smiled.

'No, I did not die. There were men in Mycenae who were still loyal to Thyestes, and others who blamed the crime of Atreus for all the evil fortune that had fallen on the city. When my father was released from his shackles and the news spread that Atreus was dead, these people quickly rallied to his cause. By daybreak Thyestes was King in Mycenae and I was honoured as his heir. Agamemnon and Menelaus went into hiding and were eventually smuggled out of the city by their friends. Had he been wiser, Thyestes would have hunted them down before they left, but I think he was troubled by the thought that they too might be his sons by Aerope, and he was reluctant to risk bringing the guilt of their deaths on his head. It was a mistake, of course, as he learned to his cost years later when they came to Mycenae with the Spartan army of King Tyndareus at their backs and took the city by treachery. It was my turn then to flee for my life.'

'But again,' Clytaemnestra said, 'you did not die.'

'No, it seems that the gods still had a use for me.'

But Clytaemnestra did not answer his smile. She said, 'Can you still believe in the gods after all you have suffered in this life?'

'It seems to me that there are two possibilities,' Aegisthus answered coolly. 'Either there are divine powers who see more deeply into things than we do and who shape our destinies in larger ways than we can conceive in order to work their justice in the world; or there is no meaning and no justice in our lives and we are merely the absurd creatures of our own appetites and ignorance. If I am honest with you, I have to say that I have no idea which of these versions of the world is truly the case. But in either dispensation I am content to follow my own will rather than bow to the will of any other man. And because it seems to me that if the gods do exist, it would be a foolish man who failed to honour them, I make my offerings to Artemis, as the divine incarnation of that savage power which I see at work in the world around me whichever way I turn my eyes.'

To his satisfaction Aegisthus saw the woman across from him nodding as he spoke. 'However,' he added smiling, 'I recognize that in so doing I may be worshipping nothing more than a ruthless drive for life inside myself. Is not that, after all, why you invited me here?'

'It is,' Clytaemnestra assented, content in the knowledge that she had found the perfect instrument of her own cold-minded passions.

Getting up from her couch, she crossed the marble floor to stand before him and took between her own hands the hand on which he wore the serpent ring that she had sent to him. 'Now come,' she whispered, lifting that hand and pressing it to her breast, 'let you and I cleave together as these serpents do. And I shall help you to have your justice as you shall help me to have mine.'

And in the cold stones that lay behind the painted plaster of the chamber she had made beautiful, all the ghosts of Mycenae were stirring as she spoke.

The Bitch's Tomb

Even as the Argive ships pushed out into the bay of Troy it became clear that Poseidon would grant them no easy passage home. The weather had darkened since the night of the earth-tremor. Blackish-grey clouds, bullied across the sky by a hard wind out of the east, had broken into rain, and many of the vessels were so laden with spoil that they began to ship water even before they broached the mouth of the Hellespont. Once out on the open sea, the wind gathered force and as ships tipped and yawed among the waves, men regretted that they had not followed the examples of Menelaus and Nestor and left Troy two days earlier. Soon they began to fear both for their treasure and their lives.

Odysseus had thought twice before putting out to sea that day; but he could smell lasting trouble on the wind and wanted to be away from Troy, so he decided to risk the crossing back to Argos rather than be kept landlocked on that desolate shore. Yet unlike Diomedes and Idomeneus, who chose to risk the direct crossing by way of Lemnos, Odysseus remained with Agamemnon's fleet as it hugged the coast between Imbros and the long peninsula of Thrace. The voyage home would certainly take longer by that route, but he hoped that a few additional days at sea might allow time for his troubled mind to settle once more. He was as haunted now by the dream that had come to him on the night of the tremor as he was by his memories of the slaughter in Troy. Once or twice he had found himself washing obsessively as though a tide of blood kept rising through his skin. At other times he trembled uncontrollably. More deeply than ever he yearned for Penelope's embrace, but he was convinced that she must recoil from the hot broil of anger, guilt and self-disgust still swirling inside him. So he shied from the thought of presenting himself before his wife, and kept to himself as much as possible, hoping that time might quieten the turmoil in his mind.

While his crew strained at the oar-benches under shortened sail, their captain stood at the stern, staring back at where thick smoke still rose from the ruins of the city. The conflagration had been so vast, and its heat so tremendous, that it had taken on the force and scale of a natural disaster; but there was nothing natural about that murky haze. A world was burning there and men had set fire to it. The smoke billowing upwards from the ruins across a livid sky seemed to reflect the darkness still burning in his mind. It sickened him to look at it.

But when he turned away he saw Queen Hecuba standing at the rigging with her silver-grey hair blowing about her face. She said, 'Do you think the gods will look with favour on your work, Odysseus of Ithaca?'

To the best of his knowledge this was the first coherent sentence the old woman had spoken since the murder of her daughter Polyxena. Nor had she eaten since the fall of the city and her once majestic features were scrawny and hollow now. She looked less like a queen than a mad woman such as could be seen hanging about temple courtyards, chanting prophecies and beseeching alms. Yet there was an unforgiving sanity in the accusation of her eyes.

'I do not presume to speak for the gods,' Odysseus answered.

'Then speak for yourself,' she demanded. 'Are you proud of what you've done?'

'I take pride in the courage of my friends,' he prevaricated.

'And if you were to come home,' she said, 'and find that your son had been murdered and your wife carried off into slavery – would you still take pride in what men such as these can do?'

Odysseus made the sign to ward off evil and turned his face away from her.

'Be careful of what you say, old woman, or I'll have you kept below decks where no one can hear you.'

Hecuba brushed the hair from her gaunt cheeks. 'You find the truth of things too painful? Then perhaps one day we will understand one another, you and I.'

She gazed back at the burning city again and winced as a twisting pillar of lurid smoke gushed skywards from the citadel of Ilium. For a moment the despair in her face was so intense that he thought she might pull herself up by the rigging and throw herself over the side. But Hecuba remained where she was, rising and falling with each lurch of the ship, watching Troy vanish in charred ruins and a smear of smoke. She began to sing then, a low, heart-stirring lament for the city and its exterminated world. Her knuckles whitened at the yards. The grief in her song lifted on the stiff breeze, carrying across the oar-benches for all to hear, and when the women cowering beneath the afterdeck saw that Odysseus could not bring himself to silence her, they too joined in the refrain.

So the ship passed on past Cape Sigeum out of the bay of Troy. The scarlet prow of *The Fair Return* dipped and climbed among the white-caps but with no hint of triumph in her progress or any sign of the joy that might have come from the thought of returning home. Even the coarsest man aboard seemed burdened by a doleful sense of the transience of things.

They had not been long at sea when the wind turned and it became ever harder to make way through the swell. Hours passed in a back-breaking, slow tussle against wind and waves. Odysseus knew that they would have to put in at some haven before nightfall but this coastline remained hostile terrain. Throughout the ten years of the war only Achilles had seen much success fighting along the Thracian shore, and plenty of men in the Argive ships nursed bad memories of hard-fought encounters in these parts. Queen Hecuba was herself the daughter of a Thracian king, and though many of her father's warriors had died fighting for Troy, many more of the most ferocious tribesmen in the known world remained to guard their homeland against Argive marauders. Yet the seas were too high to risk the rigours of this coastline by darkness when the ships would be little more to each other than an unstable constellation of oil-lamps flickering in the blackness of the Aegean night.

Then, in the late afternoon, the small pinnace that Agamemnon used for delivering messages throughout the fleet pulled up alongside *The Fair Return*. The herald Talthybius stood clutching the rigging with one hand while holding the other cupped at his mouth against the wind. 'The fleet can put in safely here on the Thracian Chersonese,' he shouted. 'King Polymnestor has declared an end to hostilities rather than risk what he thinks might be a full-scale invasion.'

'You're sure about this?' Odysseus shouted back.

'Absolutely. He's given the High King proof of his shift in loyalties. Signal your ships to follow you into shore. There's to be a feast tonight.'

The pinnace put its head about to approach the Locrian ships that were battling the swell further out towards Imbros. The helmsman pushed over the steering oar of *The Fair Return* to make for the shore and, having seen to the trimming of the sail, Odysseus went down to lend a hand at the oars. As he was settling himself at the bench he heard an anxious muttering and suppressed moans from the Trojan women under the afterdeck. He could make out nothing distinctly except two names – Polymnestor and Polydorus. Clearly the women had heard what Talthybius had said and the news was causing consternation among them. But then Odysseus was heaving on the oar and could hear nothing more above the creak of the rowlocks and the slap of the waves against the side of the ship.

★   ★   ★

By the time *The Fair Return* made landfall on the Thracian Chersonese, Agamemnon's Mycenaeans were already pitching their tents outside the fortified stronghold which was the hilltop citadel of King Polymnestor. The camp was only lightly guarded and the troops seemed relaxed enough, so Odysseus made his way to Agamemnon's tent to discover how this unexpectedly friendly welcome had come about.

'Panic,' Agamemnon answered, smiling, when he looked up from where his scribe was penning a brief despatch that would be carried by pigeon back to Clytaemnestra in Mycenae. 'The destruction of Troy has shaken everyone's nerves in these parts and our progress has been watched all along the coast. Polymnestor must have thought we were planning to launch an attack against him because he hadn't expected the fleet to come this way. And it turns out that he had a particular reason to fear my wrath.'

Irritated by the complacent smirk on Agamemnon's face, Odysseus wilfully declined to ask what that reason might be. He was remembering how this man had swollen like a bullfrog to receive the triumphant acclaim of the host outside Troy. He was remembering how the King of Men had dragged his own reluctant figure up before the Scaean Gate to share in that acclaim. He had no interest in yielding him further satisfactions.

Aware of the rebuff but refusing to be discomposed by it, Agamemnon pressed the lion stamp of his signet-ring into the seal of the missive and dismissed the scribe. 'Have you heard of Priam's youngest son Polydorus?' he asked.

Odysseus nodded. 'He was only a boy, wasn't he? Didn't he come out onto the field against his father's wishes and fall to the spear of Achilles?'

'That's what I thought too,' Agamemnon smiled. 'But it seems the Polydorus that Achilles killed was only one of Priam's bastards. He'd been given the name as cover for the real Polydorus who was Hecuba's youngest son and of the true blood. Priam sent the boy away from Troy early in the war so that his line didn't die out completely if the city fell. He's been living here in the court of Polymnestor and his Queen Iliona, who's one of Priam's daughters and sister to Polydorus.'

'So Polymnestor thought you'd come here to smoke him out?'

'Exactly; and when he saw the size of the fleet bearing down on his headland he decided the game wasn't worth the candle. So he did the job for me himself.'

'He intends to hand the boy over to you?'

'He's already done so. When he saw my ship approaching he pushed his body out to sea with a message attached to it explaining the situation.'

'So he's already dead.'

'Very dead.'

'And now we're all good friends?'

Agamemnon frowned at the sarcasm. 'Personally, I wouldn't trust this Thracian kingling as far as I could throw him. But he knows that the balance of power has shifted across the Aegean once and for all and he's looking for allies not for enemies. In the meantime we have a place to beach the ships till the wind changes. I don't expect any trouble from him.'

'How old was the boy?' Odysseus was thinking – as Hecuba had challenged him to do – about his own son, Telemachus.

'Twelve? Thirteen? All I know for sure is that there's no way he's going to grow up and come looking to avenge his father now. So that really is the last of Troy.'

'And what about Queen Iliona?'

'What about her?'

Odysseus sighed at the obtuseness. 'Are we to assume she was content to see her little brother murdered by her husband?'

'Who knows?' Agamemnon shrugged, increasingly annoyed by the Ithacan's refusal to share his pleasure. 'Perhaps she's just thanking her gods that she's better off than her wretched mother.'

'And Cassandra?' Odysseus pressed. 'Wasn't she the boy's sister too? What are her feelings about this?'

Agamemnon lost patience then. 'In the name of the gods, why do you always have to look on the black side of things? Can't you see we've struck lucky again? And the beauty of it is I had no more idea of Polydorus' existence than you did. So cheer up, you miserable Ithacan. We're going to dine at Polymnestor's expense tonight. I want you to come and get very drunk with the rest of us.'

But Odysseus was in no mood for drunken revelry. He was thinking that in some declivity of her pain, Queen Hecuba must have been sustained by the secret knowledge that, for all the grievous losses she had endured, one of her sons still survived, hidden away on this northern peninsula where the Argives would never find him. Now that son had been betrayed. Sooner or later she must learn that Polydorus was among the dead, murdered by his sworn protector, her own royal son-in-law, a Thracian kinsman. Odysseus could not conceive how even a mind and heart as strong as Hecuba's could withstand this final blow.

By the time he joined the feast that the Thracians had arranged for Agamemnon and his captains, the evening had already deteriorated into a rowdy binge over which Polymnestor presided with a canny, bibulous vigilance. A small, tubby man with a ginger moustache forking to either side of his narrow lips, he took pleasure in feeding titbits from the table to a gaudy parrot that was tethered by a golden chain to a perch at his side. The hall was clammy with heat from the huge fire blazing at the central hearth, and many slaves – whose pallid, greyish skins suggested they had been captured in some barbarian territory far to the north – were kept busy, serving the tables from the sides of beef and hog-meat turning on the spits, and pouring wine from amphorae to the mixing-bowls and thence to the goblets of the guests. Eager to be generous with his hospitality, the Thracian king seemed disappointed that Agamemnon remained more attentive to Cassandra, who sat beside him next to her sister Queen Iliona, than to the broad-hipped, half-naked dancing girls whose chains of silver baubles jangled as they rolled their bellies to the plangent sound of pipes and drums.

Having decided he would not remain long in that drunken company, Odysseus was already thinking of leaving when Polymnestor sought him out, demanding that he take more wine and asking to hear more of the strategy of the wooden horse by which all of King Priam's might had finally been destroyed. Repelled by his unctuous manner, Odysseus kept his answers terse, insisting that without the courage of his companions inside the horse his own ingenuity would have counted for nothing. But Polymnestor seemed determined to make a friend of him and would not be deterred.

The din of the revelry buzzed in Odysseus' ears. The smell of too many people crowded in a hot space assailed his nose. His eyes shifted between the rotten teeth in Polymnestor's mouth and the golden torque around his throat. Amid the heave of human carnality around him, his mind flashed back on images of the silent bodies of the Trojan dead. He heard himself saying, 'But weren't you and Priam kinsmen and friends?'

Evidently untroubled by the question, Polymnestor twisted his lips in a weary moue. He opened his hands as though to let something drop. 'The world changes, my friend,' he smiled. 'A man who fails to change with it is nothing.'

'And in such a world,' Odysseus asked, 'how shall a man know who to trust?'

A little ruffled by such seriousness on what was intended to be a light-hearted occasion, Polymnestor stroked his moustache with a heavily ringed finger. 'Ah, we are men of the world, you and I,' he said. 'We know that loyalty can be bought and sold. One need only keep an eye on the going price.'

Odysseus felt the sweat breaking at his brow. The hand holding his drinking-cup was trembling. With a stammered excuse that he was feeling ill, he turned away, leaving his host gaping after him as he pushed through the rowdy throng of men and women dancing round him, and out into the chilly air of the Thracian night.

The cloud-cover had broken, and a gibbous moon hung its

radiance across the turbulent sea. In the silence of the night Odysseus became conscious of a sound filling the channels of his ears of which he had not been conscious before, like a muffled alarm still ringing in an empty city. He had been standing alone for some time, trying to shake his head clear, half-afraid that he was losing his grip on his mind, when he heard a woman's voice behind him.

'Lord Odysseus?'

Turning, he saw Cassandra standing there. She was wearing a cloak draped over her head and shoulders against the night wind. A thin hand held the folds of cloth together at her throat.

She said, 'The entertainment is not to your taste?'

'Neither the entertainment nor the company.'

She stepped a little closer towards him. 'Then will you be patient with me for a moment? There is something I need to ask of you.'

Thinking that this strange young woman had never previously shown the least sign of humility in his presence, he said. 'There's nothing I could grant that you could not extract more easily from your new lord and master.'

'You are wrong,' she answered. 'This thing is in your power.'

Uneasily Odysseus said, 'What is it?'

'I have been talking with my sister Iliona. She has not seen our mother for many years and longs to do so. I have told her that Hecuba is held by you. I have also told her that, alone among the Argive generals, you have shown compassion for the sufferings of the captive women. It is Iliona's wish that you allow our mother to come to the palace so that we can grieve together for the death of Polydorus. I told her that I did not think that Odysseus would refuse this wish.'

Staring through the darkness at the pale, always enigmatic face of the woman across from him, he said, 'Hecuba doesn't yet know that her son is dead.'

'Then be merciful and let her daughters be the ones to tell her.'

'Am I to understand that Queen Iliona had no part in her brother's death?'

'You may understand,' Cassandra replied with alarming honesty, 'that she has as little love in her heart for Polymnestor as do I for Agamemnon.'

'And does Agamemnon know this?'

'The High King knows what he wishes to know.'

'Which may be less than is good for him?'

Cassandra merely shrugged beneath the linen cloak.

After a moment Odysseus said, 'Do you give me your word that the three of you will not conspire together against Agamemnon?'

'It was not Agamemnon who murdered Polydorus.'

'That doesn't answer my question.'

'If I were to give you my word, would you believe it?'

It was already evident to Odysseus that Cassandra had more in mind than a wake for a dead brother. From the unflinching way she held his gaze, he also saw that she was aware of his suspicions. Yet whenever this young woman spoke there was always a palpable air of truth about her as though her powers of prophecy had cursed her with a tongue that could not lie.

'Yes,' he heard himself answering, 'I believe that I would.'

'Then you have it,' she said.

As a matter of simple prudence, Odysseus informed Agamemnon the next day that he had given permission for Hecuba to leave his camp and visit her daughter Queen Iliona in the palace of King Polymnestor. Agamemnon confirmed that Cassandra had already spoken to him of this meeting and that he would do nothing to prevent it. Polymnestor had already suggested that they go hunting in the hills that day, and though he took little pleasure in the Thracian king's company, the expedition would make it possible for the meeting to take place without occasioning a bitter confrontation between Hecuba and her treacherous son-in-law. And so, later that day, accompanied by her serving-women, Hecuba made her way up the steep rise into the citadel.

But when Polymnestor returned from the hunt late that afternoon he found Hecuba waiting for him in his palace. Recovering quickly from his surprise, he stood before her, open-armed, his face a mask of grief and sympathy for all the misfortunes that had befallen her. Profuse with apologies that he had not sought her out sooner, he declared that he had only just learned from Agamemnon that she was held in the Argive camp by Odysseus. That strange fellow had said nothing of it at the previous night's feast or he would certainly have come at once to offer her his comfort and condolences. 'How to account for such calamities,' he lamented, 'except to say that we are all helpless before the will of the gods? Sometimes I wonder whether they deal with us so capriciously merely to make us revere them out of a simple fear of the unknown.'

Without allowing her eyes to settle on him, Hecuba nodded. 'There can be no comfort for my grief – though it has been some solace to know that Polydorus is in your safe keeping still.'

Polymnestor could only mirror her nodding for a moment, wondering what he would say if this half-crazed queen asked to see her son. Before he could think of a way to pre-empt the request, she was saying, 'I would dearly love to look on his face again but Iliona tells me that you wisely concealed him far upcountry when you saw the Argive fleet approach. The beast of Mycenae would not have let him live an hour longer if he had laid his foul hands on him.' Then she leaned her hawkish features forward, gripping his wrist. 'But as long as Polydorus lives,' she hissed, 'all is not over for us.'

'No,' he murmured uncertainly, 'while there is life there is always hope.'

'And you have the gold safe that we sent to you from Troy?'

'Yes, it's all quite safe in my treasury. The Argives know nothing of it.'

Again Hecuba nodded. 'I see that we chose well, Priam and I, when we sent our son to you as our forlorn hope. Few men could dissemble so. If we are patient, dear friend, our hour must surely come.'

Conscious of the pain in his wrist where her fingers gripped him like talons, Polymnestor dared not pull away. He looked down into her face and caught what he thought to be the glint of madness in her eyes. Was this indomitable old woman really still hoping that her last surviving son could mount a campaign against the might of Mycenae with the gold that Priam had shipped from Troy into his vaults? Yet after all she had endured it seemed only charitable to humour her in this last pathetic illusion.

'And when that hour comes,' he said, 'I shall be ready.'

Hecuba released his hand and glanced up at him so fiercely that he thought for a moment that she had seen through his deceit. But then it was as if the strength went out of her. She caught her breath as though to stifle the tears that might otherwise overwhelm her and said, 'Apart from my servants who are as helpless as myself, I am a woman alone in the world. Whether I wish to or not, I must now look for help. I have only you to turn to, Polymnestor.'

What was she going to ask of him? He stood uneasily, wondering now whether it might not be wiser to disentangle himself from this old woman and her desperate dreams. Let her face the stark truth of her circumstances as he had been forced to do once Troy had fallen and the Argive fleet sailed into his waters.

'There is more,' she said.

Despite his consternation, the man was astute enough to pick up the fervour of a silent message in her eyes. If he was prepared to hear, this woman might still have something to say that might prove to his advantage.

'More?'

Her gaze flitted around the chamber, making sure that she could not be overheard. Then it settled on his face again. 'More gold lies buried beneath the ruins of Troy. Buried where all the Argive army could not find it.'

After a moment Polymnestor said, 'King Priam was ever gifted with great foresight. But can this gold still be recovered?'

'I cannot do it. Not while I am held captive by Odysseus. And there is no one left alive in Troy that I can trust.'

Polymnestor allowed a further deferential silence to pass before saying, 'You know that I have always stood at your service.'

'I know it, and may the gods reward you as you deserve. But where there is gold there is also temptation. If I were to tell you how it might be found, do you swear that you would use it only to further my son's righteous cause?'

'As your son lives,' said Polymnestor, 'I so swear it.'

He saw a fierce little smile of gratitude cross Hecuba's face, a smile that might have shrivelled the heart of a more scrupulous man. She said, 'I knew that I could rely on you to respond as I thought.' Then she looked away and began to finger the long strands of her silver-grey hair and chew at her lower lip so that he began to wonder if her wits had gone astray at this most critical of moments.

'This treasure must be buried in a truly secret place,' he said.

'It is. And all who placed it there are dead.'

'Then how shall it be recovered?'

The lines of Hecuba's gaunt features wrinkled in a cunning smile. 'There is a map, a clay tablet inscribed by Priam's own hand. It shows precisely where the treasure lies – on the site where the Temple of Athena once stood. Even among the ruins, it can easily be found with the guidance of this map.'

Polymnestor lowered his own voice to a whisper as he said, 'Then it should be kept securely. Do you have it with you?'

Frowning, she shook her head. 'Had Odysseus seen me leaving the camp with it, he would certainly have taken it from me. And the man is ingenious enough to work out its significance. No, I dared not risk it.'

Suppressing his excitement, Polymnestor said, 'But surely it should be put beyond his reach as soon as possible? Let me send for it.'

'I will deliver it only into your hands,' Hecuba said. 'I trust no one else.'

'I understand.' He fingered his moustache. 'Then I must find some pretext to come to your tent.'

'But if Odysseus sees you there he is sure to suspect something.'

'Then I must come unannounced,' he frowned, 'and under cover of darkness.'

Hecuba clutched at his wrist again. 'The women's pavilion stands apart from those of the men. It is easily found. If you come there by dark no one will see you carry the map away. Dare you do this thing for me?'

'It shall be done tonight.'

'And you must come alone,' Hecuba urged.

Immediately she sensed him stiffen. He was about to demur but she closed her other hand over the one that gripped his wrist. 'We cannot allow anyone else to guess at this secret.' Her voice was urgent, her harrowed eyes were all appeal. 'Where the prize is so great, only kinsmen are to be trusted . . . and I confess to you, even that comes hard.'

'Have I not kept faith with you all these years?' he reassured her. 'Once this gold is secured we shall have the means to see that Troy rises again.'

'With my son on the throne,' she pressed. 'Polydorus is the rightful heir to Troy. Remember you are sworn to his service.'

'Rest assured, madam, this gold will be as safe with me as your son has been.'

'Then I see you swear truly,' Hecuba said and released his hand.

The first that Odysseus knew of the consequences of this encounter was a terrible screaming in the night. Reaching for his sword, he rushed from his tent. The moon was still big and radiant in the night. By the milky light it cast across his camp, he saw a small hunched figure shrinking away from him with grey hair blowing about her face. A sound issued from her lips but whether the gasps were of anguish or of crazy laughter he would have been hard-pressed to say. The canopy of the women's pavilion flapped in the night breeze at her back. It was from there that the sound of screaming came.

'Hecuba,' Odysseus demanded as other men appeared around him, 'what is it? Has someone assaulted you?'

But the old woman did not answer him. She merely stood there in the gloom, looking down in fascination at whatever it was she clutched in her hands. Sinon came up beside Odysseus holding a torch he had lit from the camp-fire. In the same moment another figure staggered into the moonlight out of the women's tent. He was holding a hand across his face, screaming for help and crying out that the bitch had blinded him. When the man lowered the hand to help feel his way, Odysseus saw that his face was streaming with blood. Yet he recognized the forked moustache and portly figure of Polymnestor.

The Thracian king stumbled over a guy-rope and fell to the ground where he lay in torment, shrieking curses at the night. Quickly Odysseus crossed to help him and winced at the hideous sight that confronted him when Polymnestor looked up in the glare from Sinon's torch. Above the clotted strands of facial hair, the eye-sockets were two craters rimmed with bloody flesh and fringed with broken veins. He could hear Hecuba howling in the night behind him – quick, raucous yelps of triumph or of horror – who knew which? – bayed hoarsely upwards at the moon. He knew then what it was that she held in her hands.

More men were gathering round him. Then he heard the voice of Agamemnon demanding to know what all this commotion was. Out of the corner of his eye Odysseus saw Hecuba's serving-women cowering together in the shadows of the tent and guessed that their combined strength must have pinned the Thracian King to the ground while, for the want of any more lethal weapon, their grief-crazed mistress had used her bare hands to gouge out his eyes.

Leaving Polymnestor whimpering under the ministrations of a physician, Odysseus pulled away, feeling his gorge rise. But Agamemnon called him back, demanding to know how this thing had been allowed to happen.

'It happened because we started a war, 'Odysseus answered bitterly. 'I doubt now that there can ever be an end to it.'

'The war is over and won,' Agamemnon snapped back. 'Pull yourself together, and get that woman silenced and bound before she does more harm.'

But as the two men turned to look at her, Hecuba disappeared in the gloom between the tents, making for the ships. Calling Sinon to join him, Odysseus ran after her scurrying figure. He had not gone more than a few yards when he slipped on something in the rough grass under his feet. Looking down, he saw the sole of his foot smeared with the jelly of one of Polymnestor's eyes.

Odysseus was retching as Sinon caught up with him. By the time the two men arrived at the ships, Hecuba had already clambered aboard the nearest vessel, which happened to be *The Fair Return*. She stood with her hand at the rigging, staring up at the moon, singing the lament for Troy that had come to her as they sailed away from the burning city. Against the plunge of the breakers and the hoarse rattle of the shingle racing back into the sea, her voice was little more than a torn and ragged muttering to the night.

'The woman's out of her mind,' Sinon whispered.

'And has been, I think, for longer than we know.'

'What are we going to do?'

'I don't know.'

Sinon said, 'The gods have done their worst with her.'

Odysseus looked at him with narrowed eyes. 'You blame the gods for this?'

Sinon shrugged. 'We are always in their hands.'

Before Odysseus could answer, a change came over Hecuba's voice. At first he thought that the Queen was in tears, overwhelmed by the pressure of her grief, but then he recognized the guttural, panting breaths cracking from her throat as a resumption of the barely human noise she had been making earlier.

'Listen to her,' Sinon whispered in horrified awe.

'Hecuba!' Odysseus called out to whatever might remain of a human soul inside her anguished frame. But for all the notice she took, he might as well have been shouting at a disobedient dog. Hecuba had withdrawn to a region so remote from human reach that she had no use left for language. Only the moon, radiant and cold, commanded her attention. Clutching the rigging in blood-stained hands, she pulled herself up from the deck onto the side of the ship and began to climb towards the masthead. Again Odysseus called out her name. Again, if she heard him at all, she ignored him. Cursing that in his desire to make a quick getaway he had ordered that the mast be left unstepped, he watched her clamber upwards with an agility that belied the frailty of her years.

'The crazy bitch is trying to reach the moon,' Sinon said.

And spoke Odysseus's own thought.

Moments later she was at the masthead, her silver hair blowing like a banner in the breeze, one hand outstretched as though, were she to lean just a few inches further into space, she might have that bright shell in her grasp for ever. Stars glittered among the clouds and went dark again. The surf plunged and boomed against the strand. Queen Hecuba, wife of Priam, First Lady of royal Troy, and among the most tragic women ever to dignify the earth, was still barking like a tethered dog when her fingers lost her grip on the mast and she plummeted – a ragged spectre in the moonlight – to the ship's deck thirty feet below.

Odysseus commanded that Hecuba's remains be buried beneath a funerary mound on a headland of the peninsula that forms the northern shore of the Hellespont across the water from Troy. Ever afterwards the place was known by the name that Sinon gave it – Cynossema, the Bitch's Tomb.

Some days later, the fleet was beating along the Thracian shore past the tribal lands of the Cicones when Sinon's ship, *The Jolly Dolphin,* struck a rock on a shoal concealed beneath the swell and sprang a larboard strake.

Heavily burdened with loot, the vessel was already riding low among the waves. Now she was shipping so much water that she must surely sink unless they could raise the damaged timber above the water-line. Cursing his ill-luck, Sinon watched from the helm as his crew frantically bailed with skins, jars and helmets – whatever they could find. Most of those men were as little able to swim as he was himself and he had quickly signalled for aid, but the sluggish progress of his over-laden ship had left him some distance behind the main body of the fleet. He could see no choice now but to start dumping his precious cargo into the sea.

The Fair Return had immediately put about in speedy answer to the signal. She hove alongside the *Dolphin* just in time for Odysseus to see a golden effigy of Aphrodite topple over the side and plunge beneath the waves head-first in a dispiriting inversion of the manner of her ocean birth. A few minutes later it became clear that the damaged vessel had been saved but only by dint of shedding the vast bulk of her cargo. It was equally clear that she had no hope of coping with heavy seas without first putting in for repairs. But the swell was too high to risk making a run for the distant island of Samothrace, and when Odysseus looked towards the nearer mainland shore, he could make out the Ciconian city of Ismarus perched on its mountain. The Cicones had always been staunch allies of Troy. Were he to leave Sinon's ship unsupported on that hostile coast, his cousin and crew would soon be cut down.

Odysseus cursed beneath his breath. Almost from the first moment he had climbed out of the belly of the horse, everything seemed to have gone wrong for him. He wanted nothing more now than to reach Ithaca as soon as possible, yet with every day that passed, his homeland seemed to recede into a hazy region of serenity and peace from which he might be forever excluded. The ravages of the war had left him in command of only twelve ships – a mere fifth of the sixty he had led out of the Ionian Islands ten years before. Many of his friends were dead. The ghost of Hecuba seemed to haunt his ship. And now it seemed he was opposed by the unpredictable power of Poseidon himself.

Signalling to his other ships to follow, Odysseus ordered his helmsman Baius to put the prow about, and made for the Thracian shore with *The Jolly Dolphin* limping behind. Meanwhile, several miles away by now and unconcerned over the mishap, the rest of the Argive fleet vanished into the afternoon mist.

They made landfall in a sheltered cove along the coast from Ismarus. Odysseus felt confident that the Ithacan force was strong enough to deter anything other than a large and well-organized attack, but they would be holed up there for at least another day before the damage was repaired, so he sent out scouts to assess the strength of any likely opposition. Meanwhile, bored and rest-less, the other crews grumbled resentfully when Sinon declared that it was only just that they should give up a portion of their booty to compensate his crew for their loss.

Their fellow Ithacans grudgingly assented on condition that everyone else agreed to do the same, but the men of Dulichion and Zacynthos grew vociferous in their resistance to the idea. Sinon's hoard had not been lost as a result of their faulty seaman-ship, so why should they be made to pay for it? Old rivalries and grudges quickly flared. As insults flew, Odysseus was beginning to worry that things must come to blows when one of the scouts returned, sent back with the report that they had found Ismarus surprisingly ill-defended.

'There's our answer then,' said Meges, leader of the Dulichians. 'Let Sinon's men lead us in a surprise attack and he can load his ship with Thracian gold.'

'It's not worth the risk,' Odysseus demurred. 'There's enough in our holds to make us all rich for life. We should make for home with what we have.'

The more sober of his followers agreed but Sinon was not among them. 'I need to salvage something from this bloody war,' he insisted, 'or ten years of misery will have gone for nothing.'

'They will have gone for less,' Odysseus said, 'if you end up skewered on a Ciconian spear.'

'I'll take my chances,' his cousin countered. 'Who will back me?'

Among the survivors of the war were a hard-bitten bunch of men who had grown so inured to the exertions of fighting that they were left fractious and ill-at-ease by the onset of peace. Enough of them raised their hands to leave the rest feeling paltry.

'We were all pirates before we were warriors,' Meges grinned, 'and I've heard that Ismarian wine is among the best there is. I look forward to trying it.'

When his Dulichian followers nodded along with him, it was clear that Sinon had his raiding-party.

They fell on Ismarus after dark while most of the unsuspecting citizens were dining. Odysseus had insisted that there should be no indiscriminate slaughter and this time there was no one to countermand him. But those among the Cicones who had time to reach for their weapons mounted a stiff resistance and many of them had to be killed before the others surrendered. Shocked and despondent, the disarmed men looked on as their palace and temples were stripped of their treasures. A band of Dulichians discovered a vast wine-cellar beneath the citadel and many amphorae of the best local vintage were loaded on to the requisitioned ox-wagons with all the gold, silver, copper and bronze that could be quickly gathered. Only a few hours after the raid had begun, and having taken no losses, the elated looters were back in the cove getting very drunk.

That might have been the end of it had not two of the outraged citizens of Ismarus ridden throughout the night stirring up support from the neighbouring cities, towns and villages. Early the next day, when the drunken raiders were barely coming to their senses again, they found themselves confronted by a superior force of Ciconian warriors gathered on the cliff-top above them.

Odysseus and his followers would almost certainly have been wiped out if the narrowness of the cliff-paths had not prevented their enemies from bringing their full force against them in a single attack. Even so, the top-knotted Ciconians fell on them in numbers. Their shouts and ululations panicked the long-horned oxen that had dragged the loaded wagons to the cove, and the Ithacans were caught up in a desperate skirmish across the strand as they tried to cover the retreat to the ships.

With his unseaworthy vessel still propped on the beach, Sinon died in that fight as did most of his crew. Meges was among those trampled beneath the hooves of the terrified long-horns. The black skin of Odysseus' herald Eurybates was torn into a vivid gash where a slingshot grazed his brow. Other men were brought down by archers as they scrambled aboard their ships. Odysseus himself was lucky to escape with his life when a brawny axe-wielding barbarian bore down on him in the fray. A youngster called Elpenor who had slept aboard *The Fair Return* that night saw the ruffian coming and let fly an arrow that pierced his lung before the axe could fall.

Somehow the Argives managed to run their ships out into the sea but it soon became clear that every crew was depleted by losses. As his own vessel rose on the heavy swell, Odysseus looked back from where he strained at his oar and saw the Cicones finishing off the wounded. Further along the beach others were reclaiming the pile of spoil that lay shining in a patch of sunlight near to where the fractured belly of *The Jolly Dolphin* lay careened on the strand. Then the scarlet prow of *The Fair Return* plunged into a trough and when it rose again the sunlight had faded from the beach.

Out across the sea, dense thunderheads rose black against the sky. Odysseus sensed their menace in the change of the light and the smell of the wind. The ship rolled among green breakers. Seabirds canted along the channels of the air. Around him, dismayed by the abrupt alteration in their fortunes, men gasped and groaned. Odysseus tried to fix his mind on the image of his wife Penelope waiting for him at home on Ithaca; but with each pull on the oar he felt himself drawn deeper into Poseidon's grip, and deeper still into despair.

Cassandra

A knocking at the door of her bed-chamber woke Clytaemnestra from her sleep. Cautioning Aegisthus to lie still and be silent, she left the bed, crossed to the door, opened it, and listened as, in a voice trembling with excitement and apprehension, Marpessa, the trusted old beldame who aided the furtive comings and goings of Aegisthus, broke the news.

Aware of the sudden agitation of her heart, Clytaemnestra said, 'There can be no mistake?'

'I had it directly from the watchman,' Marpessa answered. 'The beacon fire was lit on Mount Arachne less than an hour ago. I came to wake you straight away.'

Clytaemnestra stood quite still in the night. After all the uncertain days of waiting and scheming, time was accelerating round her. Impossible at this hour, at this news, to sustain the studied calm that was her customary cold manner. Once again her heart became a cockpit of emotions. She gripped Marpessa in a fierce embrace, unable to repress the surge of elation that came with the news that the Argive host had triumphed in the greatest war the world had ever seen. How many hours had she and Agamemnon spent planning for this victory – prising the warlords of Argos out of their comfortable lives, requisitioning the ships, haggling over the price of supplies, making sure that the troops were well-armed, dealing with the countless logistical problems thrown up by the unprecedented task of moving a hundred thousand men from one side of the Aegean to the other? And there were so many setbacks, defeats and disappointments across the years that there had been times when the whole enterprise felt futile and absurd, a hubristic fantasy of two ambitious minds. Then a catastrophic storm had blown the fleet back to Aulis, and with that had come the atrocity of her daughter's death. Later Achilles had been slain, and Ajax too had died among countless lesser losses. Yet despite everything, Agamemnon had won through. The unbreachable walls of Troy were breached. Priam must be dead already, and the richest city in Asia looted and in flames. It was impossible, utterly impossible, for her heart not to sway with exhilaration at the titanic scale of what had been achieved!

Yet since the day that Aegisthus had come at her bidding to Mycenae, the prospect of Agamemnon returning to her bed in triumph had become more loathsome to her mind and senses than it had ever been. Whatever else he might be, he remained the slayer of her children still. There were crimes on his head that could never be forgiven. So along with the excitement came an almost breathless trepidation at the thought of what she planned to do.

Through an invisible effort of the will, Clytaemnestra stilled the dark elation in her heart. 'Very well, Marpessa,' she said quietly as though the woman had just informed her of some minor success in the domestic arrangements of the palace. 'This news is good. But return to your bed now. There will be time enough to celebrate tomorrow.'

Wondering once more at the strange implacability of the mistress she served, Marpessa nodded and turned away. Clytaemnestra lifted the oil-lamp from the sconce by the door and crossed back through into her bed-chamber where Aegisthus was sitting up against the pillows with a wry smile on his face.

'You heard?' she said.

'The Lion of Mycenae is Lord of Asia at last.'

'For the moment – unless he lingers too long and the Hittite legions push him back into the sea.'

'He must have received your warning by now.'

'No acknowledgement has come. We cannot yet be sure.'

Aegisthus smiled, pulling back the covers for her. 'Not that it makes a great deal of difference. Either way, he's a dead man.'

'It makes a great deal of difference. I want him to bring home the treasure of Troy before he crosses to the Land of Shades.' Clytaemnestra put down the lamp but she did not yet return to the bed. 'How long do you think it will take him to get back to Mycenae?'

'That rather depends on how much time they spend arguing over the spoils. And then there's the weather, of course. The seas are running high on this side of the Aegean and the wind is out of the east, so conditions are not likely to be any better over there and may be worse. I would guess we have at least a week to wait. Probably rather longer.' Aegisthus lay down in the bed again with his hands crossed beneath his head. 'I'm afraid it's going to be a nerve-racking time.'

Gathering a shawl about her shoulders. Clytaemnestra sat down beside him, her eyes narrowing in thought. 'We should send the children away tomorrow,' she decided. 'Helen's girl must go back to Sparta to await the return of Menelaus. I shall put Orestes and Electra in the charge of old Podargus at Midea until things have settled down here in Mycenae.'

'The boy will be difficult,' Aegisthus said. 'He's sure to want to witness his father's triumph.'

'Orestes will do as I tell him.'

'Which is more than I can say. He grows more insubordinate every day.'

Though she felt the heat rising to her throat, Clytaemnestra kept her voice calm. 'He's a tethered bull-calf,' she said. 'He's young, and frustrated that he's missing the war. Be patient with him. Orestes has no great love for his father. He'll come round well enough in time.'

Glancing away, Aegisthus said, 'I wish I could share your confidence.'

'Trust me,' she answered. 'I know my son.'

'Even though you see so little of him?'

When Clytaemnestra stirred impatiently, Aegisthus added, 'You should listen to me. Orestes is a little too full of himself. Just because his voice has broken he thinks he's already a man. And he's rather too close to the sons of people we have no reason to trust. I'm thinking in particular of young Pylades.'

'Pylades will shortly be recalled to Phocis by his father. I have already seen to that. And Orestes will be kept well apart from him in Midea.' She looked down at the angular cheekbones and deep-set, kinetic eyes of the man lying next to her. 'You should be easier with my son,' she said. 'Make allowances for him. Show a little more patience and be his friend.'

Drawing a deep breath, Aegisthus nodded his assent, though privately he considered that, for all the stern control she exhibited, Clytaemnestra's feelings were still too raw and protective where her children were concerned. Nor were they always realistic. There were things he might tell her if he chose, but they would only arouse an anger he had already learned to fear and further increase the invidiousness of his position; so he was reluctant to press the issue of Orestes any further at this time. In any case, there were influential figures at large inside Mycenae who presented a more immediate threat to the success of their plans than did Agamemnon's moody son. With Orestes gone from the city it would be easier to concentrate his mind on dealing with them.

'We should decide,' he said, 'when to make our move against Idas and that tiresome old fool Doricleus.'

Clytaemnestra rested the long fingers of one hand on her lover's shoulder. 'Calm yourself. Everything is in place. We've discussed this already. If we act too soon we'll alert Agamemnon's supporters in Tiryns and elsewhere.'

'And if we leave it too late one or other of them is sure to inform him that all is not as he thinks in Mycenae.'

'The timing will be exact.' There was a hint of impatience in Clytaemnestra's voice. 'Idas and Doricleus are watched. There's no reason why they should suspect that anything is wrong; and I'm quite sure that Agamemnon will give plenty of notice of his arrival so that I can arrange the kind of triumph he expects.' Lightening her tone a little, she added, 'We can leave him to determine the pace of events without knowing what he's doing.'

But she sensed that this unexpected ratcheting of the tension between them had left the man lying next to her more anxious than herself. Clytaemnestra moved further down into the bed to caress his hairless chest. 'Agamemnon is no more than a stone in my shoe,' she smiled. 'And Mycenae is ours already. Come, be easy on yourself. Take me in your arms. Make love to me.'

Far across the Aegean, Agamemnon watched *The Fair Return* go about and sail to the aid of Sinon's stricken vessel, but he had no intention of slowing his own progress along the Thracian shore. There were many reasons why he wanted to get back to Mycenae quickly now and that grisly business on the Chersonese had delayed him long enough. With the seas already running high and dirtier weather threatening from the east, he was anxious to make landfall as far west as he could before darkness fell. At the very least, he might put in on Thasos. With luck he might even find shelter for the night in the lee of Mount Athos.

When he turned to gaze ahead he saw Cassandra standing at the prow of the ship where the wind blew through her hair and spindrift softly broke against her face. Since her mother's death she had withdrawn into long elusive silences that would have troubled him more if the strength of their improbable alliance had much depended on the power of words. As it was, Agamemnon made allowances for her grief and told himself that she would soon grow warm at his side again when she heard him lauded by the adoration of the crowds.

He recalled the image of Cassandra weeping with her sister Iliona beside their mother's funeral mound as the final offerings were made. A cold wind had sliced out of the north, tugging at their robes and blowing smoke into their eyes. At the foot of the cliff, wave after wave smashed against the rock-face, each shaking the air with the force of its impact and falling back with a thunderous detonation. Seabirds clamoured overhead. With the wind thudding and sucking about her ears, Iliona shivered at her sister's side, venting her grief but, as yet, a mere novice – as Cassandra was not – in the mysteries of pain.

To avoid further trouble, Agamemnon had insisted that the serving-women who had helped Hecuba with the blinding of Polymnestor should be put to the sword. So with the possible exception of that increasingly strange fellow Odysseus, it had seemed to him that of all the people assembled on the bare headland, the two sisters were alone in mourning the queen's bleak death.

Again, standing at the stern of his flagship, Agamemnon stamped his feet against the cold. Remembering how discomfited he'd been by the sullen stare of Polymnestor's sons, he was wondering whether he should have finished them off lest one day they come to Mycenae with vengeance on their minds. But it was their crazy grandmother who had blinded their father, not he, and he wanted as little as possible to do with the whole unchancy affair. The sooner this accursed Thracian shore was at his back, the happier he would be.

Meanwhile, if truth were told, he was feeling damnably lonely. Menelaus was gone, banished somewhere over the eastern horizon, and the brothers might never see each other again. Grown gloomy and lugubrious since his son Antilochus had been killed only days before the city fell, garrulous old Nestor had sailed from Troy on the same day. Odysseus was now delayed in Thrace by the damage to Sinon's ship and was, in any case, no good company these days. Meanwhile Diomedes and Idomeneus had opted for a swifter route home, sailing southwards along the Asian coast before striking out for Argos and Crete.

It seemed that with the final triumph over Troy had come the breaking of the always uneasy Argive fellowship. Worse still, for all the treasure in the bellies of his ships, a curious, dispiriting emptiness had entered Agamemnon's heart. It baffled comprehension. Was he not now the most famous, powerful and wealthy monarch in the entire western world? Had he not led the largest army ever raised to the most complete of victories? He had achieved everything he had set out to do and thereby made himself into something closer to a god than to a mere mortal man. Was his name not immortal now? Heracles and Jason and Theseus had been great heroes in their day, but their day was done and this was the time of Agamemnon, Lion of Mycenae, Sacker of Cities, King of Men. Bards would sing of his deeds for ever. All of this was true and indisputable. Then why this sense of vacancy, as though his soul went hungry still? And how was it that he could find no consolation for that nameless deficiency except in the arms of Cassandra? The thought of it both alarmed and excited him, and all the more so because she had rebuffed his recent advances as though her pain was physical.

He was well aware that his men both wondered at the power the Trojan woman exercised over his moods and were dismayed by it, but none among them dared to speak of it within his hearing, and Agamemnon had taken to keeping his own counsel these days.

Meanwhile with every sea-mile that passed beneath the keel Cassandra's world was changing round her. As a princess of Troy she had rarely strayed outside the palace or the temple precinct. The air she breathed there was closeted within painted walls, heady with incense and the perfume of cut flowers. She had always been a child of the city, so when she first stepped aboard Agamemnon's ship, her heart had quailed at the prospect of a long exposure to the turbulent emptiness of sea and sky. She feared that her mind might dissolve in those volatile, windy spaces, for her prophetic spirit depended on her contact with the earth, and with such knowledge gone from her, what was she but a helpless woman like all the others who had been carried away from Troy to serve these coarse new masters with the labour of their flesh?

Her terror increased when they made landfall on the Thracian Chersonese and she realised that there were forces at work there that she had not foreseen. No prophetic pictures had prepared her mind for the horror of watching the murdered body of her brother Polydorus fetched up out of the sea. So she had stared at that poor corpse lying pallid and sodden on the deck of the ship, and knew herself overwhelmed less by grief for a brother she had hardly known than by the fear that her gift had left her forever.

It was her mother who had put her panicking spirit back inside her skin, for once Hecuba had accepted this latest and, as it turned out, final loss, a resolute calm had settled over her like a snow-field. All the women around her were awestruck by the change. The Trojan Queen was less a person now than an elemental force pursuing the line of least resistance as she set out to fulfil her own inexorable purposes. And as handmaid to the vengeful Fury that possessed her mother's soul, Cassandra had done everything that she was told to do. Strength had come with obedience. But she had known from the first that, one way or another, her mother must die for this. And she knew too that the choice to die was the only real freedom left to either of them now.

So she had come away from Cynossema with her clarity of mind restored. In spirit she already belonged to death, so there could be, she believed, nothing left in life to fear. Once she set foot on the earth again, her powers would return and she would be told exactly what the god required of her.

The tempest that struck as *The Fair Return* pulled away from the land of the Cicones was the worst the Aegean Sea had endured for years. In a tumult far more violent than the storm that had driven the Argive fleet back to Aulis a year earlier, bolt after bolt of lightning seared the sky, setting the spars alight so that the struck ships combusted like torches of oily tow. Awash among the billows, they foundered under a black sky thick with rain and loud with thunder. Men burned and drowned. Ships sank, taking their treasure to the bottom with them. By the time the seas subsided four days later, few of the surviving vessels were still in sight of one another, and fewer still knew where they were. Meanwhile, Poseidon and Athena had looked on with satisfaction.

Agamemnon was luckier than most of his fleet. Having a stronger ship and more oars at his command, he had made good headway since leaving Thrace and was able to take shelter in the lee of Mount Athos before the storm broke.

He fretted impatiently there but at least his weary oarsmen could rest rather than wasting their strength against the swell. But by the time his ship approached the dangerous promontory of Caphareus at the southernmost tip of Euboea he had begun to comprehend the full scale of the damage wreaked by the storm. All along the coast of Euboea smashed carcases of ships lay propped among the rocks. The waves were littered with wreckage and corpses, one of which lay floating on its back with an ankle tangled in the rigging of a spar. Though the flesh was puffy and discoloured, the features were still recognizable as those of Aias the Locrian, the man who had tried to ravish Cassandra as she clung to the Palladium in the temple of Athena at Troy. When one of the crew asked whether they should haul the body in and take it back to Locris for burial, Agamemnon merely scowled and shook his head. 'Divine Athena has taken her vengeance for his impiety,' he said. 'It would be unlucky to interfere.'

In any case, he had larger troubles on his mind. By the time they had doubled the cape he had counted the wreckage of at least sixty ships, and who knew how many more might have sunk without trace? He was appalled by the losses, and amazed by them too. Hadn't that brilliant young schemer Palamedes made sure that all the dangerous rocks and shoals of Euboea were marked by beacons? So how was it that so many ships had been driven aground?

With suspicions darkening his mind, Agamemnon considered

putting in at Eretria to demand an explanation of King Nauplius, but there would be time enough for that once he had disembarked at Aulis. Meanwhile his mind was fixed on the violent events more than a hundred miles to the north in Thessaly. Before he could allow his troops to disperse he needed to know whether or not they were urgently needed to halt the Dorian invasion.

As soon as he had docked at Aulis, he despatched Talthybius to Mycenae with instructions for the preparation of his triumphal return; then he summoned a council of the Boeotian and Locrian barons who had remained in Argos throughout the war. His intention was to gather as much information as he could about the struggle to throw back the Dorian invaders. In particular he wanted to find out whether it was truly the case that these barbarians were equipped with stronger weapons than any his own forces could command.

Almost all the news he received was bad. Neoptolemus and his Myrmidons had arrived too late to lift the siege of Iolcus, which was now firmly under Dorian control. Fortunately, Peleus had contrived to escape by sea as the city fell. Old and lame as he was, he had begun to organize a campaign of resistance to further incursions, and his depleted troops were greatly heartened by the return of the Myrmidons. Though the situation remained confused, as far as everyone knew, he and Neoptolemus were still holding the line in southern Thessaly.

Yet the mood among the Locrian contingent in Aulis was apprehensive. Their land would be the next to fall if the invasion was not halted and they were alarmed by many reports of the way bronze swords shattered against iron helmets and quickly broke in hand-to-hand fighting against iron blades. At the moment only the leaders of the Dorians were equipped with such invincible armour, but if the smiths forged enough of this weaponry to arm the entire Dorian horde then it could only be a question of time before all Argos fell.

'If they can make such weapons,' Agamemnon declared, 'then so can we.'

When he was reminded that the Argive smiths did not yet understand the magical processes by which iron was made, he demanded to know why no effort had been made to capture a Dorian smith and torment the secret out of him.

'That's easier said than done,' an old Locrian baron answered him. 'Their forges are behind their lines, far to the north of the fighting, and every smith who knows the secret is hamstrung to prevent him wandering off and selling his knowledge.'

'So at the end of the day we're fighting against cripples!' Agamemnon blustered.

'Yes,' the Locrian answered, 'but cripples who know how to make men of iron.'

Agamemnon came away from the council angry and frustrated. When he had first sailed from Aulis ten years earlier he had left behind him a strong, peaceful and united empire. With Priam defeated and his line extinct, only Hattusilis, Emperor of the Hittites, could compare with the Lion of Mycenae for strength and power, and his interests lay far to the east. Everything, therefore, should have been right with the world. Jubilation and acclaim should have been waiting for him here in Aulis. He should have found himself surrounded by crowds of dancing women and children, throwing flowers and singing paeans, not this worried bunch of old men muttering of trouble in the north. But the Dorians were clearly a formidable new foe. It couldn't be long before Neoptolemus called for his support in the struggle to keep them at bay; yet many of his own best fighting men had died under the walls of Troy and only the gods knew how many more had drowned in the storm. When the rest of his army got back home it would be in no mood for further fighting. Nor could Agamemnon be sure that, when all the losses were accounted for, there would be enough profit left from the war at Troy to finance another distant campaign.

In any case, he would have his hands full closer to home. With Menelaus banished, Sparta must be quickly placed in safe hands. Only trouble could be expected out of Euboea, and whichever of the sons of Theseus replaced Menestheus on the throne of Athens, Agamemnon now doubted that he could rely either on Acamas or Demophon for much support. They had not forgotten that Attica had been mighty in their father's time. Were Agamemnon to move his own forces northwards against the Dorians, Mycenae could soon be under threat at his rear. And somewhere amidst all this unanticipated turmoil, Aegisthus was still on the loose, harbouring his hatred for the sons of Atreus, eager to avenge his own father's death and to seize the Lion Throne for himself.

Agamemnon's anger wilted into gloom. He wanted Cassandra and the comfort of brief oblivion he had found in her embrace in the nights before the Thracian Chersonese. Yet even as the desire rose inside him, he recalled with a lurch of the heart, that there could only be more trouble when Clytaemnestra learned of her existence. The prospect of that imminent collision further darkened his mind.

The herald Talthybius travelled with as much speed as he could make along the muddy Isthmus road to Mycenae, breaking his journey for the night at a friend's house in a small town where men were shouting over a cock-fight in the square. Neleus had once been a herald himself, in service first to King Atreus, and then later, as a matter of expediency, to the usurper Thyestes; but he was among the early defectors to the cause of the Atreides when Agamemnon was fighting to regain the throne, and had been rewarded with a comfortable retirement in this farmhouse looking out across the Gulf of Corinth. These days he took more interest in tending his vines and groves than in the machinations of courtly life, but he had an ear for gossip and it was through him that Talthybius learned of the suspicious circumstances surrounding the death of the bard Pelagon.

After they had talked for a while of the degree to which King Nauplius of Euboea might be involved in conspiracies against Agamemnon, Neleus went on to warn Talthybius that it would be as well to warn his master that the son of Thyestes had also been seen travelling the Isthmus road.

'Aegisthus? You think he's up to something?'

'When was he ever not?'

'Does the Queen know of this?'

'Who knows what the Queen knows?' Neleus answered. 'She's always kept her own counsel. But her spies are all over Argos like lice on a mangy dog. If *I* know, then chances are that she does too.'

Talthybius withdrew into silence, pondering both what he had been told and the tone in which it was offered. As her loyal appointee – it was on the Queen's advice that Agamemnon had made him his chief herald many years earlier – he had secretly supplied Clytaemnestra with intelligence throughout the war; but the flow of information had been entirely one way. He had never received anything more than the occasional briefly worded demand in response. So he was now, he realised, entirely in the dark about recent developments in Mycenae, and the realisation left him more uneasy than he would have expected.

As soon as he arrived in the citadel late the following afternoon, Talthybius was admitted to Clytaemnestra's presence. This was the first time the herald had seen the Lion House for more than ten years and he was taken aback by the scale of the changes there. Though he was filled with admiration at the porphyry friezes and the gilded statuary and the stirring new frescoes with which the palace now commemorated some of the great deeds of the war, he could not help wondering how fully his master had been kept informed of the degree to which the hard-won booty of the Lydian campaign had been swallowed up by his wife's appetite for grandeur. He was more troubled, however, by the absence of familiar faces among the court officials, particularly in the busy secretariats that dealt with home security and foreign affairs. Admittedly he had been allowed only a brief glance around the humming chambers before he was conducted along the passages leading to the Queen's apartment. Nevertheless he was dismayed

to note that, if it had not been for the chamberlain's announce-
ment of his name, not one of those serious young men would
have known who he was.

Yet the Queen, when he came into her presence, welcomed
him as warmly as a long-missed friend. Though she was clearly
ruffled by his reports of the number of ships feared lost, she
contained her feelings, declaring that at least the war was over
and won at last, and nothing should be allowed to diminish the
scale of that triumph. Her questions showed a lively interest in
the part he had played in the more famous episodes of the war
– the embassies to Priam's court, the duel between Paris and
Menelaus, the dire problems posed by the quarrel between
Agamemnon and Achilles, the negotiations with the Trojan
defector Antenor. She listened with particular care to his account
of the fate of the Trojan women after the city had fallen, and if
she detected a certain delicate reserve when he came to speak
about Cassandra, she gave no sign of it.

Eventually Clytaemnestra declared that she was not unaware of
the streak of meanness in her husband and how it often left his
servants feeling undervalued. Talthybius need have no fear of such
treatment. The Queen would make certain that he was generously rewarded for all the loyal services he had rendered both to
the High King and, more discreetly, to herself. He could relax in
the knowledge that his future was assured.

More wine was served and the servant dismissed. Then the two
of them were alone together and therefore able – Clytaemnestra
insisted on it – to speak freely and in complete confidence.

'We are old friends, you and I,' she said, 'I know that I can
trust you.'

Talthybius warmed to her rueful smile. If the lines of her face
had grown more severe with the years, a rare intelligence was
evident everywhere in her grave eyes and the subtly understated
sensuality of her pursed lips. Not for the first time he felt his own
customary detachment yield to the brief touch of her hand.

'Agamemnon and I have seen each other only once in the past

ten years,' she said, 'and you will remember what happened on that occasion.' She took in the herald's uneasy nod and the movement in his throat. 'The truth is that my husband has become a stranger to me now. So tell me, Talthybius – you who have observed him more closely than anyone else for many years – is there anything further that I have to fear from him?'

Talthybius shifted in his seat. His eyes moved away from the disarming entreaty of her gaze to where the yellow blossoms dangling at her balcony glowed against the bruised blue of the evening sky. For the first time in all his years of double service he was unnervingly apprised of what it might mean to be caught in a narrow pass between the most powerful man in the western world and the most powerful woman.

It was not, for all the Queen's sympathetic assurances, the most comfortable place to be.

Clytaemnestra divined his difficulties. She smiled, soothed the back of his hand with the touch of her cool palm, and frankly admitted that after the atrocity at Aulis she could not pretend that there were any tender feelings left in her heart for Agamemnon. Her only interest was in the truth and, for that very reason, Talthybius should entertain no reservations about speaking his mind where her husband was concerned. She wanted to hear only the truth from his lips without any diplomatic hesitation about whether or not she would find it palatable.

A further silence ensued. 'I sense,' she said quietly, 'that you are keeping something from me. It will be better for us all if you share what you know.'

Talthybius released through a heavy sigh the tension in his chest.

'There is,' he said, 'the matter of Cassandra.'

At that moment Cassandra was standing alone in a chamber of the fort at Aulis in a state as close to complete mental derangement as she had experienced since the terrible moment, almost half her lifetime ago, of rejection by the god. Almost as soon as she set foot on firm ground in Argos she had felt her powers begin to return, cloudily at first, unresolved as a neuralgic ache that left her feeling giddy and light-headed; but then with greater force, like a sudden drop in atmospheric pressure presaging a storm. Then, on entering this private chamber, her heart had begun to beat more quickly, her breath came in quick, panting gasps, her whole body began to shake, and she knew that the oracular god had seized her.

When such fits had come upon her at home in Troy, her sisters and servants had always been at hand to care for her; but here, in this foreign land, she was alone apart from those women of Aulis who had been ordered to attend to her needs. To them she was no more than a captive daughter of the enemy — a haughty, distracted creature that, for reasons best known to himself, the High King had chosen as his concubine. They stared at her as though she was some exotic specimen from a zoo, remarking on the elaborate way she dressed her hair, and the muskiness of her perfume, with an impudence that failed to conceal their envy and contempt. And they had neither understanding nor sympathy for her plight when the prophetic spirit took possession of her.

To be surrounded by hostile, gawping strangers was a torment, but Cassandra held on just long enough to drive them from the room. As soon as they were gone, her consciousness dissolved into a stultifying sense of fear — not her own fear but the panic of a young girl whose shade was still inhabiting this chamber. Perhaps thirteen years old, she wore a saffron tunic with a coronet of flowers braided in her hair. The dappled skin of a fawn was tied about her shoulders. Her teeth were chattering. And her mind was seized by a terror so great that she could neither think nor speak. Until just a few moments ago this girl had believed that she had been brought here to prepare for her wedding; now she had learned that death was the only bridegroom she would meet that day. She was trying to remember exactly what she had been told; yet what had seemed to make sense when she was first told it had become incomprehensible to her now.

She was to be offered up as a sacrifice to an offended goddess. The man who had given that offence was her father, Agamemnon. It was he who would be waiting for her at the altar-stone. It would be he who wielded the knife.

Outside the chamber a mighty wind banged at the doors and windows. It gusted inside the girl's mind as she stared into the darkness that was waiting for her. She had been told that if she did not go consenting to the sacrifice then all her father's hopes would be wrecked and disaster must ensue. Yet she had always tried to be an obedient daughter. She had always tried to serve Divine Artemis with all her heart. So what had she done to deserve this fate? Why had the goddess turned her face against her? Terror was beating inside her like a bronze gong. Iphigenaia had never felt so utterly alone. Never had she been so afraid.

And that loneliness, that terror, overwhelmed Cassandra now. Even as she opened her eyes to find herself alone inside a silent chamber where no wind battered at the casement, the dread remained with her, helpless and hollow; intolerably, unappeasably her own. Her hands were shaking still. The commotion of her heart was the panic of a trapped bird.

If he was not yet in a state of mortal terror, Talthybius was fighting a rising tide of anxiety as he became increasingly aware of the isolation of his position.

With all the discretion he had acquired through a lifetime of court diplomacy, he had informed Clytaemnestra of her husband's incomprehensible passion for Cassandra. Watching the Queen's face harden as she listened, he had expected to become the hapless object of her rage; but it felt rather as if the temperature in the room had dropped. Clytaemnestra's eyes were as cold as her mind. When his account had faltered to its end, she merely nodded and said, 'And is this Trojan woman very beautiful?'

Talthybius glanced up and noticed how the skin around the Queen's eyes and at the corners of her mouth had begun to pucker and wrinkle with age.

'There are those who would say so,' he prevaricated.

'Are you among them?'

'Cassandra is . . .' He hesitated. 'She has a certain strange allure.'

'And does Agamemnon mean to make her his queen?'

The herald's mouth was dry after the wine. 'The High King entrusts me with many things,' he said, 'but the secrets of his heart are not among them.'

Clytaemnestra nodded. 'You were ever a loyal servant.' However she did not smile. 'The question is, to whom are you more loyal – my husband or myself?'

'I would like to think,' he answered quietly, 'that there need be no conflict there.'

'Do not,' she said, 'be disingenuous with me.'

He was about to protest but she silenced him with a raised finger. 'Tell me,' she demanded, 'what instructions did Agamemnon give you when he sent you here?'

Alarmed by the sudden frostiness of her manner, Talthybius saw that he could afford to make no assumptions about this woman's good will.

'I was sent,' he said, 'to inform you of his wishes concerning the triumphal ceremony that would await him in Mycenae. After the loss of so many ships, he is anxious that there be no needless extravagance. He has asked me to supervise the arrangements – in close consultation with your majesty, of course.'

Brushing that aside, Clytaemnestra said, 'And did he not also ask you to prepare a report on his Queen and on her management of affairs in Mycenae?'

Talthybius tried for a weary little smile. 'The High King is too concerned by developments in Thessaly to waste time worrying over his confidence in you.'

'Do you know,' Clytaemnestra said quietly, placing the palms of her hands together and raising the tips of her fingers to her chin, 'I'm not sure that I entirely believe you, Talthybius?'

She saw his eyes shift away. She observed the tip of his tongue dampening his lips. He said, 'Have I not always served you well?'

'To the best of my knowledge you have,' she conceded, smiling. 'But then I'm quite sure that my husband must think the same of you; and I greatly fear, old friend, that the time has come for you to choose.'

As they advanced to the acclaim of the crowds from Aulis to Thebes and Megara, and then through town after town along the Isthmus road towards Mycenae, Agamemnon's composure swiftly returned. Yes, he might have lost half his fleet to Poseidon's rage, and half the treasure of Troy might have sunk to the bottom with it, but he remained the mightiest monarch that Argos had ever seen. His noble grandfather Pelops was a mere provincial by comparison. The kingdoms he had ruled in the west were only a portion of the domains that acknowledged the High King of Mycenae as their suzerain; and not even Theseus or Jason, adventurous spirits though they were, had crossed the ocean to destroy a kingdom as wealthy and powerful as Troy.

And all these people gathered in the streets, strewing the path of his chariot with flowers and singing hymns of praise, or running down from their hillside farms and holding up their children to see him as he passed – all of them adored and feared him as the King of Men. Also the weather had cleared at last. Bright winter sunshine glittered off the harness of his team, dazzling the eyes of those who stared up at him in wonder. Had it not been for a baleful stomach, Agamemnon might almost have been in awe of his own magnificence.

Lines of armed infantrymen marched at either side of the procession, keeping the more importunate spectators at bay and guarding the ox-drawn wagons that carried Agamemnon's immense share of the plunder. Ahead of them, and far enough behind the High King's chariot not to be troubled by the dust rising from its wheels, Cassandra rode inside a litter that was carried on poles by slaves. Gauzy veils hung from its roof so that she could look out from where she reclined on cushions and see the Argive peasantry squinting at the litter through the sun's cold glare, but they could make out no more than a vague shadow of her form. She was remembering the day, many years earlier, when Paris had entered Troy in triumph with Helen carried behind him in much the same way. How strange the world was with its reversals of fortune! How comprehensive the imagination of the gods that all those reversals had been foreseen!

She had herself experienced such a strange, transfiguring reversal not long ago in that haunted chamber in Aulis. It had happened only moments after she had been inhabited by the shade of Iphigenaia, and the terror was still with her. She had been lying on the couch with her teeth chattering and her arms clutched across her breast, holding her shoulders for protection against the world, when she sensed a sudden change around her. Everything was silent, yet it was as though a deep-searching chord of music had been struck from a lyre. Now the air of the chamber was calm and filled with expectation. In an atmosphere so serene that it was impossible to sustain the fear, Cassandra understood that Iphigenaia had been standing in the presence of a god. Artemis, protector of virgins, on whose altar she was shortly to be sacrificed, had come to take the girl up in her kindly embrace. Even before Agamemnon offered his daughter up to the goddess, the goddess had already come to claim her. Iphigenaia had known herself under her protection. There could be, after all, nothing to fear.

Yet when Cassandra opened her eyes it was not the serene face of Artemis that smiled down at her, but the benevolent, far-sighted gaze of Divine Apollo, who was twin brother to the goddess. And she too knew in those moments that the god had no more abandoned her all those years ago in Thymbra than his sister, Divine Artemis, had ever turned her face away from Iphigenaia. He had always watched over her. He would be there, at her side, throughout the ordeal to come.

And with that knowledge the confusions that had darkened Cassandra's mind for more than half her young lifetime came through at last into clear solution.

How was it that she could ever have come to believe that she had been rejected by the god?

It was because, she remembered now, the high priest of Apollo at Thymbra had told everyone that Apollo had rejected her. The priest was an old man whom she had always held in awe and veneration. His name was Aesacus and it was to him that she turned for guidance when Far-sighted Apollo had visited her in a dream, asking her to become his sibyl. She had told her father of the dream and her father had sent her to Aesacus. The priest and the girl had spent many hours together while he instructed her in the mysteries of Apollo. And then, one hot afternoon – and it was this memory that had been distorted and erased by the shock of subsequent events – the old man had laid hands on her. They were alone together that day. She had been reclining with her eyes closed and her body entirely relaxed in the discipline of meditation when he loomed over her and put his hand to her breast. Shocked and dismayed by the expression on his face, she had tried to shrug his hand away. But he was stronger than she was. His weight moved over her body. She could feel him groping between her legs, tugging the skirt of her dress up around her thighs. He was making little shushing sounds as he murmured that the true service of the god required that she deliver herself over to him body and soul. She must understand, he said, that her body was no longer her own to command. As the servant of Apollo, Cassandra must do everything that the god required of her.

The thirteen-year-old girl had lain stiff as an effigy beneath the old priest. But the noises he made and the warm stink of his breath frightened and disgusted her. She could see the idol of Apollo staring into the still air of the temple. Then it was hidden as the priest lowered his face towards her. She saw the damp curl of his tongue. Her arms were trapped beneath his weight. Having no other means to protect herself, she spat into his open mouth.

When Aesacus recoiled in disgust, his body shifted just enough for her to slip out from under it. Cassandra ran out of the temple into the clean, dry air.

Later, when he was summoned to speak before her father, Aesacus would be grave and mournful. As King Priam could surely tell from her confused attempts to libel his own good name, he said, it must be clear that Cassandra was far too unstable to serve as priestess to Apollo. He regretted to have to report it, but in her incontinent desire to be made High Priestess to the god, the girl had desecrated his temple by offering her body as a bribe. When Aesacus rebuffed her, she had poured her execrations on him. But the god would not be mocked, nor would he see his priest abused. Cassandra's words could not be believed, Aesacus declared, because Apollo had spat into her mouth so that all the prophecies she uttered would prove false.

Confronted on the one hand by an austere old man of the highest reputation and on the other by a hysterical daughter, King Priam had made his judgement. Eventually, with no one to believe her, Cassandra began to doubt the truth of her own experience. All she knew for sure was that the world placed no trust in the visions that came to her. But in those redemptive moments in Aulis, the shade of a girl who had also been betrayed by a father, had visited her like a messenger from the gods. Having shared all the desolations of fear together, they had seen that fear must pass. And now, as she lay alone in the swaying litter making its slow way to Mycenae, Cassandra drew strength from the certain knowledge that the gods always remained true to those who served them well.

They passed the last night of their journey only a few miles from the city in the hall of an old baron whose son had been killed in the war. The man's grief darkened the triumphal air of their arrival. The women began to wail. Depressed by the misery around him, Agamemnon retired early from the feast. Too weary and morose to make demands on Cassandra, he fell asleep, grumbling that these people had no understanding of what had been endured at Troy.

Sure now that this would be the last night they would pass on the face of the earth, Cassandra looked down where the recumbent figure of Agamemnon, King of Men, Sacker of Troy, lay snoring at her side. And if her heart was heavy, it was not only with an uneasy mingling of pity and contempt, but with an overwhelming sense of the pathos of all human circumstance.

Death in the Lion House

They entered Mycenae late the following afternoon. On their approach to the city, Agamemnon had proudly instructed Cassandra to peer out through the veils of her litter. She looked up and saw the grim bastions crouched on their crag. She heard the shouting of the crowd long before they passed under the gaze of the stone lions guarding the gateway to the citadel. She saw the light gleaming off the bronze plates of the high double doors and, though those doors remained wide open to admit the rest of Agamemnon's train, she felt as helplessly trapped inside the city as if the huge masonry blocks of which the walls were built had collapsed behind her. Sharp sunlight glinted everywhere, cold as the light off a winter stream, yet after the airy elegance of Troy, Mycenae shadowed her mind. Her heart quailed when her eyes fell on the ancestral graves inside those walls. She caught, like the hot stench rising off an abattoir, her first close sense of the obscene history of this city.

At the top of the steps beneath the entrance to the palace, Clytaemnestra stood waiting to greet her husband. Talthybius stood at her right, holding his herald's staff; on her left, Idas and Doricleus, counsellors who had both served Atreus well in the old days and had known Agamemnon since he was a boy, smiled to receive the returning king. But, as yet, Agamemnon had not allowed his eyes to alight on his wife. Even as he acknowledged the acclaim of the crowd on his approach to the palace, his eyes were taking in the prodigious scale of her expenditure on the city. Yes, Clytaemnestra had certainly made Mycenae a capital fit for a homecoming king of kings, but he was wondering how much of the wealth shipped back from the sacked cities of Asia could be left in his treasury after the bills had been met for the huge number of architects, quarry-masters, masons, sculptors and artists it must have taken to create this magnificence, let alone for all the materials, many of them precious and rare, used in the building? Also, despite his specific instructions to Talthybius that there should be no extravagant arrangements made for his return, richly woven cloths of purple and scarlet had been draped along the streets all the way from the Lion Gate to the palace steps. The hooves of his chariot team had trampled on them.

As his driver reined in the horses, Agamemnon glanced quickly across the crowd of ministers and officials who were cheering and applauding him where they stood behind the Queen. Gorgeously robed, they crowded the steps and portico, loudly proclaiming their allegiance. Yet he was surprised how few of those faces he immediately recognized.

Agamemnon reminded himself that he had been away from the city for ten years; everyone he knew must have changed in that time, and old retainers who had perished from disease and accidents would have been replaced. In any case, his true friends were behind him now, the veterans of the long war, those who had paid in wounds and endurance for the luxurious lives of these young stay-at-homes. Well, they would have their reward. He would see they profited from the changes he made now that he was back in control of the city's affairs. In the meantime, to a tumultuous roar, he raised his right hand in acknowledgement of his people's adulation. The Lion of Mycenae had come home.

From where she still cowered behind the veils of her litter some distance behind the High King's chariot, Cassandra heard the roar go up. Drums were beating. When she peered through a chink in the veils she saw a flock of startled doves rise from the roof of the palace in a clatter of wings. Then her eyes settled on the lean figure of the queen where she stood with her strong chin tilted, smiling up at Agamemnon in his chariot. She was smaller than Cassandra had expected, yet nevertheless imperious in her long, flounced gown, with gold flashing from her neck-laces and bangles, its lustre brightened by contrast with the dark sheen of her hair.

And then, as if drawn by the intensity of Cassandra's gaze, Clytaemnestra turned her eyes on the litter as the carriers lowered it to the ground.

Reflexively Cassandra pulled back into the shade.

What was she to do? To draw the curtains and step out into the sunlight would be to attract the ferocity of that queenly stare. She could not bring herself to move. The shouts of the crowd became a roaring in her head. She huddled inside the veiled litter and watched a delirium of pictures forming in her mind. The scarlet cloths covering the steps to the Lion House turned to a torrent of blood. Someone had put out the sun. Mycenae became a city of ghosts and night. Cassandra's mind was in flight, moving swiftly along dark corridors. Murder and malice, hatred and vengeance polluted this city's sky. The air was thick and toxic. This palace was a butcher's cave, the streets runnels of blood. From generation to generation no one was safe. In Mycenae only the dead survived.

Cassandra recoiled back against the cushions, squinting against a sudden crash of light. Then a suave voice was saying, 'Come, lady, your presence will shortly be required.' When she opened her eyes she was looking into the tense face of Talthybius who was offering his hand.

Calling on Apollo to defend her and the Earth Mother to support her, Cassandra stepped into her fate.

He had postponed the moment for as long as he could – making dispositions for his retinue, receiving the greetings and congrat-ulations of old friends, quietly ordering Talthybius to look to

Cassandra's welfare, then making a long and solemn show of his ritual offering of thanks to the gods; but now they were alone together in the private apartment of the palace. Recalling how the last time he had seen his wife she had been transformed into a demented Fury by her hatred for what he was about to do, Agamemnon was still uncertain what to say to her. He knew she was watching him now as he took off his helmet and began to undo the buckles of his leathers. It seemed she had no intention of making this easy for him. There had always been a severe edge to Clytaemnestra's high-boned features and the years had done nothing to soften it. He found it hard even to look at her directly now.

Agamemnon heaved a weary sigh. For centuries to come the bards would remember him as the conqueror of Troy, but in this private apartment of the Lion House he would forever remain the monster who had sacrificed his daughter. And that terrible business at Aulis might have won him a fair wind back to the war but it had left deep lesions on his mind; and it made everything impossible back here in Argos. Above all, as far as he and his wife were concerned, it had abolished any possibility of truth.

Taking in the unfamiliar, sweetish odour of the incense burning in this chamber, he said, 'I see you've spared no expense on improving the city.'

If there was criticism in his tone, she chose to ignore it.

'I thought,' she said, 'that Mycenae should properly reflect your glory.'

'It feels more like your city than mine,' he muttered a little peevishly. 'I shall have to do something about that.'

'You are the King.'

'Yes,' he answered, fumbling with a stiff buckle at his hip, 'I am the King.'

A vault of silence closed down round them, from which, it seemed for a time, there might be no escape. Then she surprised him by sighing as a wife will who despairs of her husband's ham-fistedness.

'Here,' she took a step towards him. 'Let me help you with that.'

He hesitated for a moment, wondering whether he would prefer to call for his body-servant; then he relaxed his shoulders and turned into her reach. A moment later she was lifting the heavy corselet from his back.

Sighing again, he sat down, reached for the wine that had been poured and took a swig. 'It feels as though I've been locked in armour for the last ten years.'

'Then it will be good to put it down. The slaves are heating water for you in the bath-house. You have done well,' she conceded. 'It's time to take your ease.'

But he did not entirely trust this muted benevolence.

'Not for long,' he said. 'Not if there's any substance in the reports I've been getting from the north.'

'The Myrmidons are holding the Dorian advance,' she quietly replied. 'The son of Achilles will not let them pass.'

'You are confident of that?'

'The Dorians invaded only because they thought the Lion of Mycenae had his hands full at Troy. But Troy is finished. After the destruction you've made, your name is feared everywhere. Now that you are home they will withdraw.'

'I hope you're right.' He glanced across at her, reluctant to reveal the anxiety behind his question. 'Have you heard about these new weapons they wield?'

'Agents have already been placed behind their lines. Sooner or later they will find out the secret. Then we too shall have such weapons.'

Impressed by the quiet authority of her tone, he studied his wife with an involuntary surge of the admiration that this formidable woman always inspired in him. Surely other men must feel it too. So had she taken a lover from among them while he was away? The reports from Pelagon had always assured him of her fidelity; but Pelagon had died and Agamemnon had heard nothing since. And ten years was a damnably long time for any woman to nurse her virtue. He would make discreet enquiries of Idas and Doricleus. If there was cause for concern they would have caught wind of it.

But he glanced away wondering whether such suspicious thoughts demeaned him. Could the earth have a stronger or more resourceful queen to show than this one had proved herself to be? Agamemnon very much doubted it. And in any case Clytaemnestra was Queen here only because he was King, and it was evident that she enjoyed that queenly power too much to surrender it lightly. With a little cunning it ought to be possible, therefore, to retain her invaluable services while looking to Cassandra to supply his more intimate needs. Like harnessing a new pair of horses to the chariot, he thought, it was all a question of handling.

'If I was able to give all my thought to winning the war at Troy,' he began, 'it was only because I could rest in the knowledge that Mycenae was in safe hands.'

Clytaemnestra nodded her acknowledgement. The nuances of movement about her lips might almost have suggested a smile.

Agamemnon also nodded. 'There'll be time enough for you to give me a full report tomorrow. But you too have done well. Come and sit down with me.' He sighed as she chose a seat by the window some distance across the floor from him. Something further was required. With a loose hand he gestured towards the frescoes on the chamber walls. 'I even approve of some of these changes you've made.' Though in truth he did not at all care for the painting on which his eyes fell at that moment. As far as he could make out, it showed the occasion on which Zeus had been bound with rawhide thongs by his wife Hera and the other Olympian gods. It would be wiser, however, not to reveal his distaste for it. Not yet at least.

Then another thought occurred to him. 'Where are the children? Why is Orestes not here to witness his father's triumph?' Only after the words were out did he recognize how close they brought him to perilous ground. Was she hiding her children from him out of some irrational fear that he might do them harm?

But she answered him calmly enough. 'They are with King Strophius in Phocis. Orestes is greatly attached to the king's son Pylades. He is safe enough there.'

'He would be safer still with me here in Mycenae.'

'I know.' Clytaemnestra glanced away, and back again. 'And he is disappointed to miss your triumph. But I had reason to leave him in Phocis for the time being.' She did not flinch from the interrogative glare in his narrowed eyes. 'Consider this,' she said, '– it is all of ten years since you and I were alone in each other's company. The truth is we are little more than strangers to each other now. I felt that we needed time to renew our life together. Time to try to heal the harm that has been done. There will be time enough for the children when that is accomplished.' She drew in her breath. He saw the effort that this declaration had required. He respected her truth when she added, 'It will not be easily done.'

Almost grateful that she had decided to breach the silence between them before it became impassable, he said, a little hoarsely, 'I do not forget the grief I have given you.'

Where she sat in her chair by the window, Clytaemnestra closed her eyes like a woman in pain. She shook her head, not evidently in refusal of his appeasing gesture, but as an indication of the gravity of that pain. With the long fingers of her left hand she stroked her cheek.

'I even concede,' he said, 'that I may have given you cause to hate me.'

He had left an opportunity for her to offer some answering word of demurral. When no word came he flushed and looked away. Already he was regretting this rash impulse of conciliation. But having said so much he must say more.

'We were all in the hands of the gods.' He tapped his clenched fist against the arm of his chair. 'I had no desire to do what I did . . . How could any man? But you must understand that I was left with no choice. I had no choice at all.'

Clytaemnestra gazed out of the window at where the sky had reddened above the mountains, casting a hectic glow on the high slopes of snow. Soon those clouds would be ferrying dusk across the plain. Sounds of revelry rose from the streets below. The air was savoury with the smell of an ox roasting on a spit.

'Yes,' she quietly averred, 'sometimes the gods leave us with no choice.'

A silence settled between them. He took a measure of satisfaction in it. Were there to be no recriminations then? Had the passage of time taught her some philosophy; or was her pragmatic spirit sufficiently appeased by the fact of his victory and the wealth that came with it?

'And look,' he risked after a time, 'evil it may have been, but see what good has come of it. Haven't we done what we set out to do? The treasure of Troy is ours.'

'Yes,' she concurred, 'we have done what we set out to do.'

'And the past is the past. We cannot change it; but need it haunt us for ever?'

He looked across at her with the mild urgency of a man appealing to reason. 'Can we not put a stop to it?'

As though impelled by a residual impulse of affection, she smiled at him wanly.

'Yes,' she whispered to the evening air, 'I believe we can put a stop to it.'

'Good,' he said simply, pouring himself more wine. And again, 'Good.'

He took a drink and felt his head swim a little. This wine was strongly mixed. When he looked up from the goblet he saw that she was watching as he wiped the back of his hand across his beard. Evidently she had not yet finished with him. Some other issue was pressing on her mind. Then it occurred to him that if she had spies in place behind the Dorian lines, then she might also have kept spies behind his own. Did she already know something about Cassandra? If so, it might be better to have it out now while this air of truce prevailed.

'Well?' he demanded.

'I was wondering,' she said, 'do you have news of my sister?'

Relieved to find himself on easier ground, Agamemnon sniffed and grunted. 'Not a word. Not since she and my brother sailed from Troy.'

'You decided to let her live then?'

'It was his choice. If it had been left to me . . .' Agamemnon stared into his wine, shaking his head. 'I don't understand the man . . . To take her back like that, after all the humiliation and pain she's caused him.'

He looked up and caught a wry, ironic glint in Clytaemnestra's eyes.

'Perhaps Menelaus has also decided that the past is the past,' she said.

For a moment he thought she might be mocking him.

But she got to her feet and said. 'You must be weary. Come, your bath is prepared. Let me help to soothe your limbs.' She took the golden combs from her hair so that the piled coiffure fell in a black cascade about her shoulders. Then she held out her hands to raise him from his chair. 'The war is won. You have shown yourself for what you truly are. The world knows it and all your troubles will soon be at an end. From today,' she smiled, 'everything will be different. I promise you.'

Astonished and mollified by the alteration in her manner, he got up and followed her through to the bath-house where steam was rising from the sunken bath that had been heated for him. Nereids and dolphins danced together against the azure blue of the walls. The humid air was fragrant with perfumes and scented oils. His own body-servant stood waiting there along with three women from the palace, but Clytaemnestra dismissed them all. 'The King desires to be alone with his Queen,' she declared. 'I will attend to his needs myself.'

As the servants left by the door leading to their quarters, Agamemnon pursed his lips in a smile of gratified surprise. He had not fucked this woman for more than ten years and in all that time she had lacked the consolations that had been available to him. This lioness must be on heat. And once she was replete and satisfied, he thought, it might be much easier to raise the matter of Cassandra.

He moved to take her into his embrace but Clytaemnestra placed the palm of her hand at his chest and pushed him, smiling, towards the bench of white marble that stood beside the pool. 'First,' she said, 'you must take your bath.'

Already erect, he opened his hands in appeal.

'Go,' she reprimanded him lightly. 'Disrobe.'

Like an obedient boy, he turned to do as he was bidden, shuffling off his sandals and pulling his dark red linen robe over his head and shoulders. Admiring the lines of her figure where she bent over to gather towels from a chest, he slipped out of his kilt and drawers and stood naked in the steam from the bath, suddenly conscious of the aches and pains locked into his limbs. He flexed the sinews of his arms and pushed his hands back through the mane of his loosened hair. Though he had put on weight since Clytaemnestra had last seen him this way, he was still, he thought, a handsome figure of a man; and if his skin was etched like a butcher's block with the many wounds he had taken, they were all honourable scars, the signature of his valour and virility.

'Look,' he said, displaying his body, arms outstretched, as she came towards the massage table with a bundle of soft towels in her arms, 'here is a map of the war at Troy. I have good tales to tell about each of these scars.' With the tip of a stubby finger he traced the white ridge that ran along his upper right arm, almost from the elbow to the shoulder. 'This is the gash I got from a Trojan spear on the day they drove us back to the ships. The host panicked when they saw me bleeding. Odysseus and Diomedes also took wounds that day, and Achilles was out of the fight, sulking in his lodge. For a time I thought it was all up with us.'

But she had, it seemed, discouragingly little interest in his story. 'Get into the bath,' she urged. 'You can brag of your valour to me while you soak.'

In mock offence he pouted his lips at her. She answered with a haughty toss of her head and laid the heaped towels carefully on the table. Turning away from her, Agamemnon walked across the tiles towards the bath. He was about to step down into its soothing heat when he was struck by another thought. He looked back to share it just in time to see her standing as a fisherman stands at the prow of his boat when he casts a net. Then something swooped in a widening loop towards him. It came at him through the air like a silent cloud of bees, and before he had time to understand what was happening, the meshes fell in a gauzy shower over his head and shoulders, and then dropped down across his arms and thighs. Perplexed and shocked, he was raising his arms to push the coarse grey blur away from his body when she tugged with both hands on the slender length of rope she held and the net tightened around his limbs.

He was shouting now. Still able to keep his balance on his bare feet, but tangled like a maddened bear inside the trammels of the net and scarcely able to move his arms and legs, Agamemnon twisted his body round to confront his wife. He saw Clytaemnestra walking towards him with a sword gripped in both hands. Its pommel trembled close to her chin; the blade angled down in front of her breasts; but his eyes were fixed on the pallid mask of hatred that was her face.

In the moment when Agamemnon saw that his wife was about to murder him, she raised her arms above her head and brought the blade down with all her might, through the toils of the net, into the broad target of his chest where he felt the breast-bone shatter.

He might have fallen then from the force of the thrust, but his ribs were caught on the blade and the pressure of her grip on the hilt supported him. For a few seconds they stood together, face to face, conjoined by the sword, staring into each other's eyes as the steam rose round them. Both were sweating in the moist air, though neither was now entirely in this world.

Agamemnon coughed, choking on something deep in his throat

that should not be there. Harm had been done to his breathing. The channels of his ears were loud with noise. Each part of his body had begun to panic like a routed army. He knew that he could no longer count on the strength of his legs.

Leaning forward, with a twist of her wrists Clytaemnestra tugged the sword free; and felt the frisky spatter of blood across her face.

He staggered as his head went down. Now he was spluttering on the froth of blood and spittle bubbling in his mouth. Agamemnon raised his chin and saw, through the mesh of the net, an unsightly red smear staining her cheek as she wiped the back of her wrist across her eyes. Was she wounded too? Was the blood his or hers? No matter, for he was trying to spit his throat clear of obstructions so that he could breathe again when the sword came back at him.

The blade swung in lower this time, held in only one hand, yet entering his naked belly with alarming ease. The force of it winded him. Sodden air gushed upwards from his punctured lung. As the sword slid out again terrible things had already begun to happen in places he couldn't see. Nor could he even raise his arms to hug himself. A huge tidal wave of self-pity pushed Agamemnon down to his knees. Blood had splashed on the tiles. He knelt in a gathering pool of it, gasping and wheezing there. This was no way for the King of Men to die. There was neither justice nor glory in it. He refused to die like this.

Summoning his failing reserves of strength, Agamemnon lifted his head; but his eyes were bleary with tears when he looked up again.

He saw the figure of a woman standing near him and, in a quick flurry of relief, thought that he recognized Cassandra. Yes, she would come to help him now when help was needed. She would comfort and succour him. She would wipe this mess from his mouth and take him to her breasts where her nipples stood dark and sweet as figs. He tried to hold out his hand to her but the toils of the net prevented him. In a sputtering of blood he whispered her name.

'Have patience,' the woman hissed, 'your Trojan whore will lie beside you soon enough.' And he heard the hatred there and saw that he was mistaken, for the face that stared at him was the face of Clytaemnestra after all.

And there are two figures standing before him now, neither of them clear, neither of them quite stable. They are looking not at him but at each other and both their mouths are agape. They might be shouting, both at the same time, but he cannot be sure because of the hollow roar gusting through his ears. One of them is his wife wearing a blood-stained gown; but the other? A man, yes, but who among his subjects could stand and look on and do nothing while this dreadful harm was done to him?

Before Agamemnon can make out the features of that face, his own head droops on his neck and he is vomiting blood and bile and the wine he has drunk. His beard stinks of his dying. He wants to lie down. That's all he wants, and it's little enough to ask when he is in such pain, but someone has crouched down in front of him and is holding up his chin in the tight pluck of a finger and thumb. Through the trammels of the net a man's face sneers into his own. As if against a strong gale, a voice is asking, 'Do you know me, cousin?'

Agamemnon knows only that time and breath and light are running out on him.

When he shakes his head he is merely trying to clear the thick, obstructing slobber from his throat, but the man takes it for an answer.

'I am Aegisthus,' he hisses, 'son of Thyestes. Now do you know me?' He holds up the bronze blade before Agamemnon's bewildered eyes. 'This is the sword with which my mother killed herself. This is the sword with which I took righteous vengeance for my father by slaying yours. And this, dear brother in treachery, is the sword with which I mean to cleanse the world of you.'

But Agamemnon is no longer present to feel the blade intruding on his flesh. He has been watching Troy burn again; he has seen Menelaus and Odysseus, Ajax and Diomedes laughing at his side, and his mighty fleet of ships flexing their oars against the glitter of the sea; and here now is his father, King Atreus, grim-faced and resolute as he watches his wife drowning in the Bay of Argos. And then, only a moment or two later, after a little, clumsy fall over which he has no control at all, Agamemnon is down there in the water with his mother, feeling the warmth beneath the surface, letting it enter him, becoming it, as Poseidon grips him by the hair and tugs him down into green shadows and the last light spins away.

PART TWO

THE BOOK OF
Athena

The World Turned Upside Down

Of all these things we Ithacans remained in ignorance for some considerable time after the fall of Troy. A brand from the burning city had been used to light the beacon fire on Mount Ida. Within minutes it was spotted by the picket of Argive scouts camped on a mountain peak sacred to Hermes on the island of Lemnos. From there the fanfare of flame leapt across the Aegean to the rock of Zeus on Mount Athos, and thence down the mainland, from summit to summit, through Thessaly to Locris, from there into Boeotia and Attica, and on across the Saronic Gulf until at last a beacon was lit on Mount Arachne. That blaze was seen by the watcher on the crag at Mycenae, and there the fiery signals stopped.

Having all the information she needed, Queen Clytaemnestra was possessed by no urgent desire to share it further. So the western kingdoms of Argos would have to wait for runners to bring the news; and Ithaca must wait still longer, for the Ionian Sea was tormented by gales throughout that wintry month, no ships were putting out, and we might have been as distant from the Peloponnesian mainland as we were from Troy itself.

Then the winds abated and the seas calmed down. A Phoenician merchantman, damaged by the gales and blown off course for the island of Sicily, put in for repairs at a haven on Zacynthos. Two days later an Ithacan fisherman who had been stranded there returned to our island with the news that the Phoenician captain had heard about the fall of Troy just as he was putting to sea again from Crete. It was rumoured that the Trojans had been completely wiped out and that the Argive host had taken a stupendous quantity of plunder.

Telemachus and I were in town on the morning that the excited fisherman pulled his boat up on the strand, so we were among the first to hear the news. I jumped up and down in the sand and gave a little skip; then I turned and punched Telemachus in the shoulder. 'Did you hear that?' I shouted, amazed that he was not more excited. 'We've won. It's over. Troy's done for. It can't be long before they all come home.'

'Be quiet, Phemius,' he said, and he turned to the fisherman — his name was Dolon — asking whether there was any news of his father. Unfortunately, Dolon was not the brightest of men, and he was passing on what he had learned at third or fourth hand, so none of us could make much sense of what he had to say about the crucial role played in the fall of Troy by a cunning horse belonging to Odysseus. It wasn't long before Antinous and Leodes, two of the young men of the island who had been drawn down to the strand by Dolon's shouts as he drew his boat ashore, accused him of spreading fanciful gossip.

'No, no, it's true,' Dolon protested. 'They were dancing on Zacynthos when I sailed. Already they are feasting in Same. It's true, I tell you. It's all true.'

'But my father's alive?' Telemachus pressed. 'They said he was alive.'

'Oh yes, Odysseus is alive,' Dolon answered with a grin that exposed his few remaining teeth, 'he's alive all right and no doubt covered in gold these days. We shan't know him when he comes back. He'll be chiming like a herd of goats with all the gold dangling about his person.'

Antinous, who had been drinking wine, sneered at Telemachus, saying, 'I can't think why you're so excited. You won't know him anyway. And I can't see Odysseus being at all happy about sharing your mother's bed with you.'

Telemachus glared up at Antinous with his mouth open and his fists clenched, but this handsome lout was well over a foot taller and more than ten years his senior. If it came to a fight, there was no doubt which of them would win, and both of them knew it, which was why, in the absence of Odysseus, Antinous took malicious pleasure in keeping warm the bad blood between their two families.

Antinous was the son of a prosperous baron called Eupeithes who kept court in the north of the island on the far side of Mount Neriton. He was a distant kinsman of King Laertes, but there was little warmth between them, and Odysseus had not been surprised when Eupeithes contributed two small ships to the Ionian fleet but declined to go to the war himself on the grounds of ill health. Some years earlier the man had revealed a cowardly and duplicitous side to his nature when he came sweating into the palace late one afternoon seeking refuge from the wrath of his own people. Soon afterwards a band of shepherds were hammering at the outer gate demanding that he be handed over to them.

Things only came clear when a spokesman for the shepherds was admitted to the palace. He claimed that Eupeithes was in league with a gang of Taphian pirates who had recently despoiled several villages on the coast of Thesprotia. Some kinsmen of the northern Ithacans who had settled there a generation earlier had refused to pay these pirates for protection. Days later they had seen their crops and houses burned and their cattle and sheep run off. Three men who tried to resist the pillaging had been cut down. And when King Laertes demanded to know what any of this had to do with his cousin, the shepherd answered that cattle bearing the brand of one of the Thesprotian farmers had been found among Eupeithes' herd.

Though Eupeithes at once denied the charge, his guilt had been immediately evident to Laertes and Odysseus. They were unconvinced, however, that he deserved to die for his unsavoury part in the affair. 'Let me reason with him,' Odysseus suggested, and Eupeithes soon found himself entangled in the devices of a subtle mind. Beguiled by his kinsman's understanding manner and mistaking it for sympathy, he ended up confessing that he had been a fool to get mixed up with the pirates in the first place. Moments later, he saw the sense of it when Odysseus muttered that the only way that Eupeithes could now save his skin was by paying generous compensation.

Relations between the two men had been uneasy ever since, and when he was recruiting warriors for the fleet he would take to Troy, Odysseus had been in no doubt that he would rather leave such an unreliable character at home than have him fighting at his side. Briefly he considered drafting Eupeithes' eldest son Antinous, but the boy was not yet twelve at the start of the war and Odysseus guessed that he would probably turn out to be more trouble than he was worth. So Antinous had stayed at home, where at every opportunity he took pleasure in humiliating Telemachus.

The two of them stared at one another now, Telemachus quivering where he stood, Antinous smirking down at him. Beside them Leodes gave a little snigger of contempt. Flushing, Telemachus turned on his heel and walked away. I was about to follow him when I saw our friend Peiraeus among the people hurrying down to the strand where the fishwives had begun to sing and dance. Anxious to divert attention from what had just happened, I called out the news.

'Now you'll really have something to sing about,' he said as we caught up with Telemachus. 'You'd better start working on a song for when Odysseus gets back. It can't be long now.' Then he took in the taciturn frown with which Telemachus was staring at the sea. 'You don't seem too cheerful about it. Why the long face?'

But though Telemachus flushed again, he failed to answer.

'Antinous is a fool,' I said. 'Take no notice of him.'

'What did he say this time?' Peiraeus asked.

When Telemachus still said nothing, I muttered 'It was nothing. Just some stupid remark about our not recognizing Odysseus when he gets back.'

'But he's right,' Telemachus snapped. 'I won't know him, will I? I've no idea what he looks like. He'll be nothing more to me than a glorious stranger.'

Again he turned away and walked on ahead of us, taking the path that led around the hill towards the southerly shore where the pale glare of a wintry sun shimmered across the sea. Peiraeus and I looked at one another, wondering whether to follow him, both of us aware that in his injured pride the boy might stay glum and sullen for hours now, even with us, his friends.

'Aren't you going to the palace to tell your mother?' Peiraeus called after him.

'She'll find out soon enough,' he said without looking back. 'You can tell her.'

'But she'll want to share the joy with you,' I protested. 'What shall I say you're doing?'

Telemachus stopped in his tracks for a moment. I watched him struggling with his feelings, a turbulent eleven-year old with a fearsome frown, who eventually pushed back the shock of tawny hair that fell across his brow and said, 'Tell her I've gone down to the Cave of the Nymphs. Tell her I'm making an offering for my father's speedy return. Tell her what you like. I don't care.'

In the event, I discovered later, he did neither. Instead he walked to Arethusa's Spring where he stood scratching the back of a fat sow that the swineherd Eumaeus had penned away from the rest of the herd while she suckled an early litter. From there he could gaze southwards across the sheer fall of Crow Rock to where the island of Zacynthos lifted its blue-grey blur on the horizon. A strait of water separated the island from the mainland, and it was through that strait that his father's fleet of ships would sail on the day of their return.

Telemachus had been looking forward to that day for as long as he could remember; yet now that it was at hand he was filled with unexpected trepidation. What if he didn't like the man? After all the marvellous things he had been encouraged to believe about him, wasn't he bound to be a disappointment? Still worse, what if his father should take a critical look at him and form the same low opinion of his son as Antinous held? Again Telemachus flushed at the thought. Big as Antinous was, he should have bloodied his nose down on the strand and taken the punishment it brought, rather than turning away and saying nothing. What would Odysseus, sacker of cities, the hero of the war at Troy, make of a son who backed down before a bully's jibes?

With her farrow beginning to snatch at her teats, the sow snorted and waddled away across the grass towards the shade of a holm-oak, where she dropped her hind legs and collapsed, grunting, onto her side. Squealing, the piglets clambered over one another in their haste to plug their small snouts to her belly.

Telemachus was staring at them, wishing he was older, wishing he was bigger, when a voice behind him said, 'Niobe's a good old sow. Farrowed a dozen she did, and she's still suckling the lot.' He turned and saw Eumaeus standing there with his grandfather, old King Laertes, leaning on his staff at his side.

In his rough smock and tattered straw hat, Laertes looked more like a peasant farmer than the lord of all the islands. 'It's good to see you taking an interest, Telemachus,' he smiled at his grandson. 'Your father's head was always full of ships and the sea when he was a boy. He loved the island well enough, but he was restless – thinking more about what lay over the next horizon than what was here in his own back yard.' Shaking his head, Laertes squinted into the glare of light off the sea. 'Odysseus wasn't like you – he never had the patience to make a good farmer.'

Telemachus had heard this complaint a number of times before. Each time it was uttered he noticed the only half-suppressed note of admiration – of envy almost – in the old man's voice – as if the old king loved, and missed, his errant son a great deal more than he cared to admit.

Eumaeus said, 'There'll be time enough for him to learn patience when this war is over and done with.'

'It's finished,' Telemachus said, almost dully. 'Troy's fallen. We've won.'

The two men looked at him in some bewilderment. The news, if it was true, was tremendous, but it had been announced with so little excitement that they thought the boy must be imagining things. Seeing their uncertainty, Telemachus allowed himself to smile. 'It's true,' he said with more elation. 'Dolon the fisherman got back from Zacynthus an hour ago. He heard the news there. He's telling everybody. Troy's beaten. They're singing and dancing down in the town.'

'You're sure of this, boy?' Laertes demanded.

But the swineherd was frowning dubiously as he said, 'Dolon's got fewer wits than he has teeth.'

'I know,' Telemachus replied, 'but he seems certain of it. He heard it from a Phoenician trader who'd put in on Zacynthos for repairs. I think the fighting's been over for weeks but nobody told us.'

Laertes and Eumaeus looked at each other, scarcely daring to believe. 'What about your father, boy?' the old king asked. 'Was there news of him?'

'Dolon said he was the great hero of the hour. He said something about a clever horse that my father brought to the fight . . . It seems to have made all the difference, but I'm not sure how.'

'A clever horse?'

'That's what he said. But I may have got it wrong. I couldn't really make head or tail of what he was saying. Anyway, it seems my father's definitely alive. And Dolon says he's going to come back very rich.'

'Rich?' Laertes hand was trembling at his staff. To his amazement, Telemachus saw that tears had started at the rims of his eyes. 'If he still has all his limbs about him he'll be rich enough for me.' The old man lifted his staff and shook it in the air. A laugh cracked out of his throat, and another that turned into a shout of triumph at the sky; then he and Eumaeus were jumping up and down together, hugging each other by the shoulders and laughing and shouting as they wept.

Laertes turned his head to see his grandson staring up at him in wonder. 'I must share this news with the Queen,' he exclaimed, 'and there are grateful offerings to be made to the gods. And what does your mother have to say about it, boy? Has she ordered up a feast already? It must be attended to immediately. Back to your sties, Eumaeus. Pick out some good porkers. And tell Philoetius to choose a bull for the sacrifice.' Only then did he arrest the flowing torrent of his pleasure long enough to observe the almost sickly flush of distress on his grandson's face. 'What is it?' he asked, his concern only slightly tinged with impatience. 'And what are you doing up here on your own here anyway? Why aren't you celebrating with the others? Why aren't you at your mother's side, sharing her joy?'

Telemachus stood frowning at the recumbent sow and her tussling litter, not wanting to cloud his grandfather's happiness yet unable to disguise the turmoil of his feelings.

'What's the matter with you, boy?' Eumaeus asked.

Telemachus had been biting his lip but now the words burst out of him. 'What if he doesn't like me?' Heated and angry, he looked up at the two perplexed old men. 'Sometimes I think everybody knows him but me. And I'm his son. His only son. But I don't even know what he looks like. If he stepped off a ship tomorrow I wouldn't know who he was. And he doesn't know me either, and he's a great hero, isn't he? The whole world knows about him. He's famous everywhere from here to Troy and probably further than that by now. And what am I? I've done nothing. No one knows who I am outside this island. And even here . . .'

Uncertain whether he was more amused or perturbed by this untypically verbal spate of emotion, his grandfather said, 'What about here, boy? You're the royal prince of this island and don't you forget it. You're the scion of a noble line that goes back through me to my father Acrisius, and his father Abas, who was grandson to Lynceus and great-grandson to King Danaus himself. There's no better blood in all Argos than runs in your veins.' He frowned down at Telemachus, shaking his head. 'Your father will be as proud of you as you should be of him. It's my belief that for these last ten years he's been pining for nothing more than the moment when he gets back home and holds his wife and son in his arms again. So let's hear no more of this sorry nonsense. Now I'm going back to my farm to tell your grandmother this news, and you should hasten to share it with your mother. This is a great day for Ithaca, boy, a great day!'

Laertes tousled his grandson's hair, then turned away and hurried off through the glade, making for his lodge where Anticleia would be busying herself about the garden or the farm. Telemachus watched him go, feeling the weight of his ancestry about his young shoulders more closely than the reassurance that Laertes had sought to give him. When he looked round, he saw Eumaeus scratching his beard as he studied him with shrewd eyes.

'So what's brought this on?' the old swineherd asked. 'T'was only two days ago you were jumping up and down to have your father back.' When he saw that Telemachus was reluctant to speak, he said, 'What is it, lad? Has somebody been goading you?'

Again Telemachus flushed. 'Why do you ask that?'

'Because I don't only keep my eyes out for my pigs, you know. I've been watching Antinous and his cronies throw their weight about. Phemius tells me they've been giving you a hard time.'

'Phemius should mind his own business.'

'Phemius cares about you. We all do. And as for you – you don't want to take any notice of those layabouts – especially Antinous. He was too young to go to the war when Odysseus first set out and he didn't answer when the call went out from Aulis for more men last year. Strutting about on Ithaca making a nuisance of himself is all he's good for.' The swineherd gathered the spittle in his mouth and spat onto a fern. 'I blame his father for it. Eupeithes never amounted to much himself, and 'tis like enough his son will go the same way.'

'I should have struck him,' Telemachus said. 'I should have tried to knock him down.'

'And got a bloody nose for your pains? Believe you me, your father wouldn't have seen much sense in that! That Antinous is twice your size, boy. And he's old enough to know better. Just hold your water till the master gets home. He'll teach him respect soon enough. Now on your way. Do as your grandfather says. Your mother'll be looking for you, and there's feasting tonight. So put a cheerful face on. And be grateful to the gods you've got a father to admire.'

Not for a long time had anyone on the island seen the lady Penelope look as blithe and beautiful as she did at the feast that night. True, there were a few moments when Laertes and Queen Anticleia first came into the hall wearing all their finery and with garlands in their hair, and the three of them embraced one another in a small squall of tears; but there was more relief and gratitude in their weeping than regret for all the lost years of the war, and those moments were quickly over. Soon the old king was to be seen tripping featly in the dance as though twice that number of years had fallen from his shoulders and his heart was young and strong again. All the old men of the court danced with him — Mentor first among them, stamping his feet and clapping his hands, while the women called out, laughing as the pace quickened. The eyes of Telemachus brightened with excitement, and once the hall grew quieter, I struck my lyre and opened my voice in the song of praise to Lord Odysseus which I had been harbouring for many weeks, waiting for just such an exalted time as this.

The hall must have fallen silent around me but I was conscious of no one and of nothing there. As though I had taken a deep draught of wine, the god came into me and in those rare moments I was left with no sense of my body's boundaries; with no sense of my self at all, if truth were told, for I was as much an instrument in the god's service as was the lyre in my hands. Nor was there any space left in which to be astonished that such a thing should have happened in the company of others, even though the god had only visited me before when I sang alone in the high places of the island, looking down across the empty acres of the sea. And so, for a time that might have been no time at all, but a kindly gesture of eternity towards my mortal life, I and the god and the song were one; and I knew that my fate had come upon me and I could never again be quite the same.

The applause rang loud and long when the song was ended. I saw tears in the eyes of Eurycleia, the old woman who had nursed Odysseus when he was a boy. Mentor and the other lords of the island were beaming with approval. For a time my heart swelled with the pride and pleasure of that moment. Then the god went out of me as swiftly as he had come, and I was left empty and disarrayed like a soiled garment when the hot night's dance is over and done.

I saw Telemachus looking at me with a kind of wonder from where he sat, fondling the ears of the dog Argus, but I could not hold his gaze. Only later when, with her customary tact and grace, Lady Penelope sought me out, not merely to commend but also to counsel me, did I begin to recover my senses.

'Your song was a good song, Phemius,' she said quietly. 'The Lord Odysseus will be proud to hear it on his return, and your father will be prouder still . . . if the sea-gods have spared him.' Then she crouched down beside me, right there at the edge of the hearth, and studied me with such tender concern that I scarcely knew where to put myself. Stammering out an awkward phrase or two of thanks, I made to stand, but was stopped by the gentle pressure of her hand. 'I see what has been given to you,' she said, 'but there is always a price to pay for such gifts. I think you should go alone from the hall soon and make an offering to the god. And you would be wise to ask for his mercy as well as his strength.' Rising gracefully to her feet, she rested the tips of her fingers on my head and added, 'I feel sure that this is what your father would tell you if he was here.'

I was still not much more than a boy in those days, and I see now that I had less understanding of her words than I believed at the time. But I had a youth's impatience to be taken seriously, and that, above all else, was the gift that those words conferred on me. I had loved Penelope before, as all the island did, with warm affection and regard; now I was lost in adoration of her. And so, as I stood alone under the night sky, making my solemn offering to the god as she had bidden, I truly had nothing more to ask of life than the right to sit for the rest of my days at my lady's feet in the great hall at Ithaca and serve her with my gift.

Telemachus and I quarrelled around that time. Four years divided us, so his behaviour sometimes felt petulant and childish to me. For his part, he took my lapdog devotion to his mother as a rebuke to his own, sometimes cruel efforts to detach himself from her care. I suppose he was trying to accelerate his growth into manhood in order to ready himself for his father's return, but the effect was to turn him into a cross-grained prig whose fractious moods drove his mother close to distraction. One day our exchanges became so vehement that I told him I would have nothing more to do with him until he apologized both to his mother and to me. But he was too proud and intransigent for that, so Telemachus withdrew into a tight-lipped solitude on which only the patient old swineherd Eumaeus was sometimes permitted to intrude.

The loss, as it turned out, was as much mine as his. I tried for a time to get along with Antinous, Eurymachus and the other young men who hung about the taverns of the town, but they were all older than me, and too much idle comfort had made them sophisticated in ways which left me feeling uneasy and gauche. By contrast, there had always been a bond of kinship between Telemachus and myself; our tastes were similar, our imaginations were fired by the same stories, we were both happier listening to the chime of goat-bells in the hills or the sound of the wind working off the sea than to the prattle of the town. So

I missed my friend in those difficult days. Probably more than he missed me.

Yet if Telemachus and I were despondent, so too, as the weeks dragged by, was everybody else. Even though we knew our hopes unreasonable, the feast had generated an expectation that Odysseus would come sailing home with his fleet within a matter of days. Old men whose sons had gone off to the war, and boys much younger than Telemachus, began to gather on the cliffs to see which of them would first spot the mastheads crossing the horizon. There were dawns when I woke filled with the irrational conviction that this was the day when the ships would make port and my father Terpis would be there at the prow, alive and well, singing his vessel ashore. So I would run all the way out to Crow Rock and stand staring out across the blue-green swell with the birds lurching on the wind above my head. But there was nothing to be seen through the haze where sea became sky and the great world lay beyond our own small clutch of islands.

Late one afternoon, when all the others had long since lost interest in the vigil, I heard a sound among the rocks behind me. I turned expecting to find nothing more than a sheep tugging at the rough grass, and saw Telemachus staring at me, his mouth tightly drawn, his eyes uncertain. We both remained silent, neither quite ready to make the first conciliatory move. The wind bustled about our ears. The concussions of a stiff swell against the cliff shook the air.

'There's been news,' he said at last, as if to the stones.

'Of the war, you mean? Of the fleet?'

'Does any other kind matter these days?'

'But how?' I demanded. 'I've been here all day and I haven't seen any ships.'

'You were looking the wrong way,' Telemachus scowled. 'Amphinomus put in from Dulichion two hours ago. One of his merchantmen got back from a voyage into the Gulf of Corinth the day before yesterday. He says that more than half the Argive fleet was wrecked in a tempest sailing back from Troy. Hundreds of men were drowned. He says that King Agamemnon has been murdered in Mycenae and the son of Thyestes rules there now. He says that there's fighting all over Thessaly. A new people with magic weapons have invaded. He says that the whole world has been turned upside down.'

I stood listening to this news dumbfounded. The last we'd heard was that Troy had fallen and the fleet must soon be sailing home in triumph. If the gods had granted us a glorious victory after ten years of war, surely they would spare the host the ravages of a storm? And Agamemnon was the King of Men – how could anyone possibly wrest his throne from him? So when Telemachus began to talk of magical weapons, I became convinced that he was out to make a fool of me.

'Yes,' I said, 'and doubtless the sea will run dry tomorrow and these invaders will walk across the strait and we shall all be struck down by their magic.'

'It's true,' he retorted. 'It's all true – not like your stupid songs.'

He turned away and would have left me there on the cliff but I had seen the distress on his face before the anger displaced it. 'Telemachus, wait,' I shouted after him. He stopped at my call, a scrawny figure in the fading light with the wind ruffling his hair. 'Was there any word of your father?'

For a few moments longer he stood in silence; then without turning he said, 'Nobody knows where he is. Nobody knows whether he's alive or dead. The fishes might be eating him for all I know.'

King Laertes and all the elders of the island gathered the next day to hear what Amphinomus had to report, and the more we heard the more it seemed that the world had been turned upside down. We learned that the northern reaches of Thessaly and Magnesia had indeed been invaded by a foreign horde armed with weapons stronger than bronze; and that, even though Neoptolemus and his Myrmidons were fighting at his side, King Peleus had been pushed out of Iolcus and was hard-pressed to withstand the Dorian incursions. We learned that Menestheus was no longer king in Athens, having been defeated by Demophon, the son of Theseus, who had now reclaimed his father's throne. We learned that Agamemnon had indeed been assassinated by his wife and her paramour and that Mycenae was not the only scene of unexpected revolution. Apparently Lord Diomedes had returned to Argos after surviving shipwreck on the Lycian coast only to discover that his wife and her lover had seized the throne of Tiryns; while a similar illicit conspiracy had unseated King Idomeneus in Crete

Being as shrewd as she was wise, Lady Penelope quickly divined the hand of King Nauplius behind this repeated pattern of betrayals. 'But surely those ill-used lords could combine their powers to help each other,' she said. 'Diomedes and Idomeneus are heroes of Troy. Who could stand against them?'

'They gathered at Corinth with precisely that intention,' Amphinomus answered. 'I was there. I heard them planning to join forces and launch a campaign to retake Tiryns first, then to advance against Mycenae, and lastly to mount an expedition into Crete. But the truth is that the war and the storm have left their forces so depleted that they could do none of these things without help; and where were they to turn? Neoptolemus already has his hands full in the north. As yet' – he cast a rueful glance towards Penelope – 'they had heard no word of my Lord Odysseus, and Menelaus is rumoured to be far away in Egypt. Of all the warlords, it seems that only old Nestor has returned safely to his throne.'

'And would he not help them?' King Laertes asked.

Amphinomus shook his head. 'He declined their invitation to come to Corinth. He said that, much as he loved his comrades, he was old and weary and still stricken with grief over the death of his son Antilochus in the last days of the war. But he also said what may be true – that it would be unwise to plunge all Argos into a civil conflict which could only leave it weakened against the Dorian threat. Nestor intends to see out his days in peace in sandy Pylos. Should they wish to do so, Diomedes and Idomeneus are welcome to join him at his hearth.'

Yet Amphinomus had not come to the island only to report on events in Argos. It was also his intention to prepare Penelope as best he could for the possibility that her husband might never return. Things he had heard in Corinth left him in no doubt that the Aegean Sea had been hit by a disastrous storm. The coast of Euboea had seen many shipwrecks. Hundreds of men had drowned. As was shown by the case of Diomedes, vessels blown eastwards by the storm had fared little better, and since he had got back, no other survivors had appeared. Amphinomus feared that these unhappy facts offered no good omens for the safe and speedy return of Lord Odysseus.

'Yet Nestor's ships all seem to have survived the voyage,' Penelope countered. 'And their passage required them to double Cape Malea where the waters can be more treacherous than Euboean kings and faithless wives.'

'Lord Nestor made an early departure from Troy after the death of his son,' Amphinomus answered, glancing away. 'He would have been well across the Aegean before the worst of the storm blew up. He was among the first to return.'

Penelope sat in silence for a time, staring into the hearth where the brands collapsed with a sigh amid a scattering of sparks. For a moment I thought that she too had given up hope; then she shook her head and gave a little smile. 'But tell me, Amphinomus,' she said, 'does the world know of a better seaman than the Lord of Ithaca?'

The young prince of Dulichion shook his finely boned head. 'There is none, lady,' he replied, 'or if there is I never heard tell of him. And yet . . .'

'Yet what?' she defied his frown.

'I am anxious only that you do not entertain false hopes.'

'Nor you either,' Telemachus put in from the shadowy corner where he sat.

The hostile edge to his voice was unmistakable. Mentor and

the older men around the table stirred uncomfortably at his petulant breach of hospitality.

'I try not to do so,' Amphinomus answered, 'even though the fate of my kinsman Meges also remains uncertain. I merely seek to be realistic.'

'As I do myself,' Penelope intervened, frowning at her son.

'Yet the fact remains,' Amphinomus said quietly, 'that Odysseus was last seen turning back to rescue Sinon and his crew from their sinking ship.'

Penelope smiled. 'I would expect nothing less of him.'

'Nor I, my lady, but such care for his friends will have left him far behind the rest of the fleet. He will have been given less time than them to run for shelter. His ship must have taken the brunt of the storm.'

'Odysseus has run before many storms and lived to tell tales of them. And if I read what you say aright, Amphinomus, then the false beacons that Nauplius lit around Cape Caphareus will have burned themselves out before my husband could be confused by them as others were.'

'Yes,' Amphinomus conceded doubtfully, 'it is certainly possible. Of course I pray, as we all do, that you are right.'

'Then pray louder and longer,' Telemachus muttered beside me, 'and trouble our hearts less.'

But his mother had already raised her indomitable voice. 'I am quite sure that my husband lives,' she declared, 'for I am certain that I would know if he did not.' Penelope was smiling with the confidence of a woman assured of her own truth. 'Some difficulty has delayed his return. Shipwreck perhaps . . . yes, it is possible in so severe a storm; yet even if he has suffered such mischance, he may have survived only to be frustrated by unfavourable winds, or confined by some enemy looking to ransom him. But that Odysseus is alive I have no doubt. My husband has always been among the bravest and most resourceful men in the Argive host. I know that the same courage and ingenuity that took him into Troy when everyone else had begun to believe that city unassailable, will bring him home safely to his wife and son.'

Telemachus led the cheers that greeted her words. I joined in roundly; but so close was the attention I paid to the nuances of my lady's face these days that I could not miss the pensive shadows that settled briefly about Penelope's eyes and mouth moments later when she thought herself unobserved.

Zarzis

The Thracian shore vanished in the unnatural brown gloom of the light from the thunderheads just as the skies were torn open by a ferocious strike of lightning. The mast and rigging of a nearby ship combusted into flame. A moan went up from the oarsmen of the struck ship when the mast cracked and the scorching yard-arm fell among them. Oars clattered together in the swell as the rowers leapt in panic from the benches. The vessel lost way, yawed and turned broadside on to the waves. Only moments later, it was pushed over onto its side like a tipped bucket, hurling men into the clamour of the seas.

Two hundred yards away, scarcely able to hold their own against the might of the billows breaking over their prow, Odysseus and his crew were forced to watch their comrades drown while the exposed keel of the capsized ship rose and fell. Another pang of lightning flashed across the sky. The flames from the blazing spar guttered for a time with an eerie glare, and were extinguished in a sizzling of smoke and steam.

Odysseus caught a last glimpse of a man shouting through the froth of a crest before the sea dragged both him and his stricken ship down into the advancing hollow. The day thickened prematurely into night, and with the darkness came the rain.

Odysseus led the three great shouts for the drowned men who

would never now receive proper burial. Some of his crew were already retching as the rain and spray smacked against their faces. With the prow and cutwater mounting the tall wave at his back, Odysseus staggered down the slope towards the stern where Baius was struggling to control the steering oar. He just had time to clutch the sternpost with both hands before his ship took the steep plunge over the crest.

A torrent of water fracturing into spume as hard as hailstones scattered across the decks and benches. Closing his eyes against the tempest, Odysseus felt the whole world lurching under him. The clamour of thunder merged with the clash of waves in a great collapsing roar. When he opened his eyes the deck-boards were awash and it seemed that *The Fair Return* was hurtling through a green-black passage twisting into foam, where sky was indistinguishable from sea and both were inimical to the survival of his ship.

Baius, who had sailed with Odysseus many times, had already divined his intention. The two men braced themselves together at the steering oar, looking to keep their vessel from being taken aback or swept broadside by the strength of the swell. A green light glittered about the masthead as lightning seared the sky. Over the noise of thunder Odysseus shouted to his men to ship their oars before they were snatched from their grasp. Then *The Fair Return* was running before the wind and there was nothing to be done but hang on to the straps and thole-pins while the cutwater of the frail craft plunged and climbed across tremendous seas.

He woke to the sound of palm fronds rattling in a breeze off the sea. Swallows scudded through the high blue zone beyond the fringes of a thatched awning above his head. He could hear the sigh of surf breaking on the shore and, somewhere closer, the laughter of men and women chatting together over the reedy sound of a flute. The tune seemed to wobble on the hot, dry air. When Odysseus lifted himself on to his elbows to look around, his eyes were dazzled by the flash of sunlight off white sand. Then he made out the sinewy body of Eurylochus stretched out on a dune, wearing only his breech-clout, while a woman whose skin was black as grapes leaned her long breasts across his chest. Beyond them, more members of his crew clapped their hands as a drum struck up. Another woman began to sway to the tune of the flute while, further down the strand, a small boy carrying a catch of sponges smiled and stared. Odysseus closed his eyes, shook his head, looked round again, and only then did he see a small town with shining buildings and terraces and date-palms — all as it should be, in perfect detail, except that it was hanging upside down in the sky. After a moment it began to shimmer like the haze above a fire.

He thought to himself, 'I am surely dead and in the Land of Shades.'

A voice behind him, thickly accented and throaty, said, 'So you are awake at last,' and Odysseus turned to see a neatly bearded man reclining in the shade. He wore a finely woven robe of deep-blue linen. His skin was as swarthy as his voice, an oily chestnut-brown, wrinkling under the high, turbaned overhang of his brow. His nose curved like a kestrel's beak.

Odysseus said, 'Have I been sleeping long?'

'For two nights and the better part of three days,' the stranger nodded. 'You were, I think, a truly exhausted man.'

Remembering the long struggle with the worst seas he could recall ever having encountered, Odysseus merely nodded and sighed.

'That town,' he remarked vaguely, 'appears to be upside down.'

'Yes,' the foreigner answered, 'it appears so. In fact it is not there at all.'

'Then my eyes are deceiving me.'

'Not your eyes but the light. I know the place. It is perhaps forty miles from here. The desert air works such trickery. In a little while it will be gone again.'

'In my island,' Odysseus replied, 'buildings prefer to remain where we put them.'

'But then Ithaca is not Zarzis.'

'Zarzis?'

'You are in Libya, my friend, in the land of the Gindanes.'

Odysseus frowned. 'We were blown right across the Cretan Sea?'

'So your men tell me. Your three ships are beached over there.'

'Only three?'

'In such a storm perhaps the sea was merciful to spare so many?'

Odysseus tried to get to his feet, but his head swirled with a dizziness that was not entirely unpleasant. Like a drunkard puzzled by his condition, he sat back down again. Despite the calamitous news he was strangely untroubled. In fact, he felt oddly serene, with a degree of acceptance that was more dream-like than philosophical. Life came and went, men lived and died, ships floated for a time then sank, and if a town saw fit to shift itself forty miles across the desert air and then hang head-down like a bat as it snoozed in the afternoon sun, well that was fine by him. And the music too was mildly narcotic. In fact the more he thought about it, this languid country, of which, if truth were told, he had never previously heard, was a pleasant enough place to fetch up.

'The Land of the Gindanes, you say?' Odysseus studied the smiling, magisterial figure across from him. For the first time he noticed two dark patches at his temples where the skin might have been scorched by fire a long time ago. 'And you are a king among these people?'

'By no means,' the Libyan smiled, 'I am a king nowhere. Merely a wanderer filled with curiosity about the world.' Relaxing back against a pile of fringe cushions, he told Odysseus that his name was Hanno, that he came from a peace-loving people called the Garamantes, who lived to the south of Lake Tritonis, and that he liked to travel wherever the desert winds blew him.'

'Have you sailed to Argos then,' Odysseus asked, 'that you speak our language?'

'You are not the first Argives to come to these parts,' Hanno answered. 'Your hero Jason was blown to Libya once. His ship became landlocked in Lake Tritonis a hundred miles from here. The goddess released him when he dedicated a silver tripod at her shrine in offering for his safe return. But some of his men chose to remain in Libya. I learned your language from their sons.'

The music writhed like a snake on the sultry air. Odysseus looked back where his crew were loudly applauding the dancer. One of them, a stout-bellied fellow called Grinus, leapt to his feet and began wiggling his hips beside her.

Hanno laced his fingers together at his chest. 'They are happy, I think, to find themselves in a place where they are welcome – as they were not, I understand, in Phrygia and Thrace.'

'They've told you about that?'

'I had heard rumours of the war before you came. Now I know more, Lord Odysseus.' He opened his hands in a mildly ironic gesture of obeisance. 'I know, for instance, that your men love you fiercely. It has been hard to persuade them that you were merely sleeping from sheer exhaustion and should not be disturbed. They will be glad to find you awake when the dance is done. In the meantime, is there something more I can do for you?'

'I am,' Odysseus realized, 'immensely hungry. If you have an ox to roast, I have room to devour it. Perhaps two even.' He looked up, smiling, and was surprised to meet an expression of dismay on the other man's face.

'When you know Libya better,' Hanno said, 'you will see that none of the wandering tribes between Egypt and the Pillar of Heaven ever taste the flesh of cows. The beast is held sacred to the goddess.' He rose to his gorgeously slippered feet. 'In any case, it will be wiser if you do not eat too much too soon. Come, take more wine. It will help restore your strength. And you must try the local fruit. I think you will find it much to your taste.'

His companions were overjoyed to find their captain recovered from his long ordeal at the steering oar of *The Fair Return*. Already exhausted from the long battle with high seas during the southward voyage around Euboea and Sounion Head, Odysseus had tried again and again to double the steep eastern bluff of Cape Malea. Once through that rough passage, they could make the home run for Ithaca. But both wind and current has been against him and the waves were riding higher than his masthead. At each attempt to round the cape the ship was forced back; yet he had given up the effort only when Baias, equally exhausted at his side, cried out, 'Poseidon is against us, lord! Better to run with the wind than be driven onto the cliff.'

With tears of rage and frustration mingling with the rain in his face, Odysseus had watched the savage headland fade into the flashing grey blur of the blizzard. Cythera became a ragged shadow drifting past his port bow and vanished. By the time the western coast of Crete smudged the horizon he was sleeping where he stood at the stern of the scudding ship.

Vaguely he remembered Eurylochus relieving him at the steering oar; then, so cold and stiff that he could scarcely bend his joints, he had been led to the foot of the mast and lashed there for safety while the ship hurtled on through the night.

The storm had finally cleared not long after a lurid dawn. The ship idled at last in a calmer swell. Eurylochus could make out two other vessels some distance away, but of the rest of the little fleet there was no sign. When land was sighted and the crew found the strength to row their battered vessel ashore, they had no idea where they were.

'But I think we've discovered the Happy Isles,' Eurylochus grinned at him now.

'Certainly we've been lucky,' said Baius, who had recovered more quickly than his captain, 'and I thank the gods for it.'

'And for the pleasures of this place,' added Demonax, who was captain of the *Swordfish*.

Odysseus glanced at the half-naked dancer who sat glistening in her sweat with her thighs protruding from the fringed folds of her vermilion skirt. A number of brightly coloured leather bands were fastened about her legs.

He said, 'The women, you mean?'

'The women, yes,' fat Grinus smiled, 'the women are very good, but . . .'

'And you can tell which are the best at making love,' put in young Elpenor, 'by the number of anklets they wear.'

'Each of them is a tribute from a satisfied lover,' Demonax explained. 'So the more she has, the better!'

'As long as you like your women well-used,' Odysseus said. 'However, my own thoughts incline more towards food right now, and this fruit of theirs . . .'

'The lotus,' Eurylochus supplied.

'Well, whatever it's called, I find it a touch sweet on my tongue. I gather that beef isn't eaten hereabouts, but I was hoping that Procles might roast me a sucking pig.'

'They don't eat pork either, I'm afraid.' Eurylochus was grinning as he spoke.

'Yet you call this the Happy Isles! Is there nothing to eat but this cloying apology for a fruit?'

The men smiled at each other in amused conspiracy. 'You mustn't speak ill of the Lady Lotus, Captain,' said Eurybates, whose black head was still bandaged from the wound he had taken at Ismarus. 'We've all become her devotees.'

It had been a long time since Odysseus had seen his crew in so mellow and benevolent a mood. A little perplexed by it, aware that he was being teased, he said, 'Then you all have even coarser palates than I thought.'

'Not at all,' Demonax tapped a finger at his pursed lips. 'It's an acquired taste.'

'But it's what happens when it's made into wine,' Grinus offered in explanation. 'You've already tasted quite a lot of it, Captain, but perhaps you were too sleepy to remember. Here, let me pour you some more.'

An hour or two later, having eaten well on squid and barbecued goat's flesh and a sticky dish made from the lotus fruit, Odysseus was sitting with his companions watching a huge sun sizzle like molten metal where it sank into the western sea. To the north a pale moon lay on its back with a single star hung in attendance. *The Fair Return,* the *Nereid* and the *Swordfish* lay side by side on the strand, all in need of repair, their holds only lightly guarded by a dozy watch of sailors. Egrets flashed their white wings in the evening sky. Not far away a string of camels recently arrived from a desert journey coughed and snorted as they lapped at a spring, while a solemn-eyed boy wearing goatskins soothed them with his pipes. In the distance, where the olive groves gave way to a rocky scrubland of juniper and tamarisk, they could hear a jackal yapping to the moon.

Not since they had been at home on Ithaca had the men known such a blessed time of peace. Strangely, however, none of them were thinking of home, not even Odysseus who had thought of almost nothing else in the last days of the war. The lotus had quietly worked its spell on him. Time had collapsed into a passive sequence of moments on which the past had no pressing claims, and where the future, with its prospects of anxiety and desire, was a matter of no enduring interest. And the war itself seemed to have dissolved into a wry anthology of stories that were, by this serene Libyan moonlight, curiously painless and often downright funny.

When Glaucus, the captain of the *Nereid*, dryly remarked that the yapping of the jackal put him in mind of that scurrilous dog Thersites, his words occasioned more hilarity than they merited. They led on to a happy remembrance of the way Odysseus had silenced Thersites' foul-mouthed rant against him. Then they found they could laugh at the ridiculous quarrel between the insufferable Achilles and that vacillating bullfrog Agamemnon, and they were all helpless with mirth after fat Grinus reminded them of the truly awful stink of Philoctetes' wound.

'I see that the Lady Lotus has made you merry this evening,' Hanno smiled as he came up beside them.

Odysseus made a wide gesture of welcome. 'Come and join

us. We've got plenty more in these rather handsome jars we lifted from Priam's palace.' But when Hanno politely declined the offer, his presence had a subduing effect on their jollity. Glaucus began to hum a song that was dear to him. Young Elpenor, whose head of blond curls now rested in a young woman's lap, made only a poor effort to suppress an attack of giggles. Otherwise the group was silent for a time beneath the moon.

That casual reference to the sack of Troy had briefly lent a gloomy cast to Odysseus' mind; yet he had no sooner observed the change than he seemed to float off into a more tranquil zone some distance away from his still weary body.

And it was not at all the same experience as being drunk with wine, for there was a startling clarity that came with it – a heightened sensitivity to every small sound chivvying the quiet air: the high-pitched shrilling of the cicadas, the choral belch of bullfrogs, the swishing murmur of the surf. He could also pick out the quite distinct scents of the salt-breeze off the sea, the sweet smell of the lotus and the nocturnal fragrance of jasmine and moonflowers. Then he became fascinated by the burn-marks scarring the skin of Hanno's temples as though the man had once been branded there. With uncharacteristic forwardness he asked about them.

'The marks are customary among my people,' Hanno diffidently replied.

'As a sign of dedication to a god?' Odysseus pressed.

'Nothing so mysterious, I'm afraid. Our mothers burn their infants here and here,' Hanno indicated the marks on his own head, 'with a smouldering piece of flock from a sheep's fleece. We believe that it induces clarity of mind in later life.'

'A pity that Agamemnon wasn't born in Libya,' Demonax muttered. 'The war might have been over years ago.'

'It might never have begun at all,' said Odysseus. Then to stave off the shadow once more, he asked Hanno to tell them more about the various peoples among whom he had travelled and the customs that distinguished them.

And so, as the moon mounted the sky, he was taken on a voyage of the imagination across the wide regions of Libya, through countries where the women wore bronze leg rings, where men had mastered the art of harnessing four horses to their chariots, and where the dead were buried seated upright in their tombs. Hanno told him about his own people, the Garamantes, who took no interest in the arts of war, and of another tribe who were defeated in a war with the south wind which left them buried deep beneath the sands.

'Meanwhile, to the west,' he said, 'around Lake Tritonis, can be found a cult of warrior maidens who serve the one you call Athena. She has her shrine and oracle there.'

Among the many marvels he listed, Hanno spoke of a spring called the Fountain of the Sun that was known to run both hot and cold according to the time of day; of oxen which walked backwards as they grazed because otherwise their long horns would get stuck in the earth; of an obscure race of troglodytes who fed mostly on serpents and spoke a language like the screeching of bats; and of a tribe of bee-keepers who painted their skins bright red and feasted on monkeys. He spoke also of a city he had seen that was built from blocks of salt – some white, some purple – by a people who were never visited by dreams.

'Their land stretches to what you Argives call the Pillars of Heracles,' Hanno declared, 'but beyond that realm I have not travelled myself. Yet I have heard stories of dense forests to the south where elephants and horned asses abound; and two-legged creatures with the faces of dogs, and people without heads who bear their eyes in their bosoms; but apart from elephants, I have never seen such things myself. Also those traders who follow the sun around the coast tell of a land where gold is plentiful. Because its people speak no language that can be understood, the Phoenicians do business by leaving their goods on display at the shore and then withdrawing until the local people have determined the value of those goods in gold. Then they too withdraw so that the visitors can consider what is offered. If the Phoenicians think the measure of gold insufficient, they withdraw again until more gold is brought. The goods change hands only when both sides are satisfied. They call this honourable custom *the silent trade*.'

Listening to the Libyan's stories under a black night thick with stars, Odysseus felt the universe expand around him. On Ithaca he had always been the one who returned with tales to make his kinsmen marvel. His reputation as an adventurer ran right across Argos to Thessaly and beyond. He had sailed eastwards as far as Sidon. People in Cyprus and Egypt spoke admiringly of him. Yet here in Zarzis, at the northern margin of a continent that stretched southwards, if Hanno was to be believed, for many hundreds of miles across deserts and forests and snow-crowned mountains and lush plains haunted by curious beasts, he felt as though he had been no more than a village pedlar bragging that his name was well-known in nearby towns. And the longer he listened, the more his heart stirred with the aching thrill of wanderlust that had fired him in his youth.

The night shimmered around and inside him. His mind became a map of unknown regions. He remembered a time, many years earlier when he had talked with Theseus of voyaging out past the Pillars of Hercules and on around that exotic coastline just to see what was there. Surely that was the spirit in which life ought to be lived? That was how Jason and his Argonauts had unlocked the secrets of the Black Sea trade in gold. That was how Theseus had dared the ancient might of Crete and brought it under his subjection. Let the crass Agamemnons of this world destroy and plunder as they wished. Henceforth it would be his mission to enlarge the world of men, to bring light to dark places, to foster trade and the profitable exchange of culture, to kindle the imagination.

His own imagination was scintillating with that very thought when, as abruptly and noiselessly as his companions around him, Odysseus dropped like a bull at an altar into a sleep as crowded with wonders as the huge Libyan night.

★ ★ ★

He woke late the next morning feeling a stiff twinge in his old thigh wound. Elsewhere, his headache might have put him in a foul mood for the rest of the day; here in Zarzis he felt surprisingly mellow – as though the pain provided an excuse, were any excuse needed, to laze in the shade with his indolent friends. At their encouragement he broke his fast on goat's milk and a dish of the sticky lotus mashed with oatmeal that was served to him in a calabash by a woman with a benevolent, gap-toothed smile. Later in the day he would find that food was not all she had to offer and only a residual qualm of conscience reminded him that he was on his way home to Ithaca where his wife faithfully awaited him.

Yet the greater temptation was to sleep, for here in Libya, sleep had proved to be a banquet of the senses in which an endlessly intriguing landscape unfolded round him, where curious beasts and monsters flourished, and everything made a bizarre kind of sense. Deciding that his ambitious vision of the previous night would take time to plan, he soon turned over on his side beneath the awning and closed his eyes against the light.

Afterwards, Odysseus would have difficulty recalling how much time had passed while he and his men lay about the shore of Zarzis, eating, drinking, fondling the women who made themselves available, and smiling with contentment at the complaisant men of the region, who appeared to have as little sense of urgency as they did themselves.

One morning they woke to find a huge grey fish stranded on the beach. It had a fronded mouth and its ribbed body was much larger than that of any fish they had seen before. They strolled about it for a while, gazing into the sad jelly of its eye and listening to the remote, failing thunder of its heart. But none of them could work up sufficient energy either to kill the monster or refloat it; so the great fish was left gasping in the sunlight till it died. After a time, when its flesh began to stink, they merely moved their mats downwind into a sheltered place and waited for a higher wave than usual to reclaim the rotting carcass and draw it out to sea.

Around that time Odysseus discovered that the lotus was not always benign. There were deranging moments when he was revisited without warning by images that had been seared on his memory at the fall of Troy. The lotus allowed ample time to inspect the gaudy colours erupting from the fat belly of a Trojan citizen he had slaughtered. He found himself staring at the white, pulpy texture, stained with pink, that he had seen in the brains of a boy whose head someone had smashed against a garden wall. He could hear the sounds of screaming women almost as clearly as the cries of the fish-eagles dawdling in the sky; and there was a bald-headed man with jewels in his ears who kept begging him for mercy, over and over again, as he lay pissing himself with fear on the steps of King Priam's palace.

At other times the shade of Hecuba was everywhere, barking and jeering, as she clutched the eyes of Polymnestor in her hands.

After one such visitation, Odysseus sat up groaning and beating his head with his fists, only to find Hanno looking down at him with mild concern. When the Libyan asked the cause of his distress, he tried to explain what had happened on the night that Troy fell and in the days that followed. His account was rambling and fragmentary, articulate only in its pain.

Hanno said, 'So you blame yourself for all the destruction that was done at Troy?'

'Who else can I blame?' he growled. 'It was me who thought up the means to get us inside the city. It was me who gave the false promises that persuaded Antenor to come over to our side.'

'I know nothing of war,' Hanno answered. 'But from what you have said it seems you had no knowledge that the promises were false?'

Unwilling to accept such glib absolution, Odysseus said, 'The truth is, I might still have given them even if I'd known how false they were. And perhaps I knew it all along – not consciously, but in my secret heart, you understand?'

Hanno nodded his dark head and sighed. 'In any case, my friend, each of us must follow his fate. The gods gave you a quick mind and a plausible tongue. You have merely made use of them.'

'But I can't seem to think straight these days. And I find it hard to talk as well.'

'Sometimes the lotus darkens our thoughts. It is the price we pay for the illumination it also brings.'

Odysseus turned away. 'I'll not blame my troubles on a fruit. Nor do I expect the gods to look kindly on the desolation I've caused.'

The two men sat together in silence for a while watching some members of Odysseus' crew at a dice-game along the shore. Sighing Hanno said, 'I remember discussing such matters once with a teacher out of India whom I encountered in Egyptian Thebes. He was a very old man and as wise as he was old. He told me that the secret of life is to float on its surface as the flower of the lotus floats on water, without sinking and without wetting its leaves. I believe the teaching to be sound.'

Dryly Odysseus said, 'Was he ever present at the sacking of a city?'

'That I do not know,' Hanno conceded, 'though I believe him to have been a man of peace.'

'Then what could he know of a warrior's suffering?'

'As to that,' Hanno smiled, 'he told me the story of a warrior-prince among his people who came to a field of battle and was appalled to find kinsmen and friends armed against him on the opposing side. His mind was thrown in turmoil at the prospect of killing people whom he loved and admired; but in his confusion the hero was visited by a god whom he held sacred. The god told him that it was the warrior's duty to devote himself to battle in a righteous cause, and that he should be strengthened by the knowledge that the soul outlives the body, and that those who fall in battle do so only to be refunded into the great cycle of life.'

Odysseus studied the darkly smiling eyes. 'A very satisfactory story,' he said, 'if you believe your cause to be righteous and that we are permitted more than one sojourn on this sorry earth.'

'But how can we know that we are not?' Hanno asked mildly.

'I'm certain only of the here and now,' Odysseus answered. 'Life may be very pleasant here among the Lotus Eaters, but I've seen enough to know it's often wretched elsewhere. I too have had dealings with the gods in my time. As far as I can tell, we're nothing but their playthings.'

Hanno nodded undismayed, and glanced across at where two of the dice-players were now caught up in a torpid quarrel. 'You must allow the lotus more time,' he smiled. 'Come, my friend, take some wine.'

More weeks drifted by. Some desultory repair work was done on the ships; then the men relapsed into idleness again.

Late one afternoon, with a pang of self-disgust Odysseus disentangled himself from the sinuous black limbs of a woman whose name he could not pronounce. For the past half hour she had been employing the skills which had already won her many anklets to coax fresh life into his sluggish member; but suddenly he could abide her no more. He sat up, shook his head, and saw the oars of a warship flashing in the sunlight as the galley entered the quiet waters of the bay.

The captain of the ship turned out to be a Thessalian named Guneus whom Odysseus had vaguely known at Troy as a friend of Achilles and Patroclus. He splashed ashore from his beached vessel, exclaiming with surprise when he recognized Odysseus, burly and good-natured, the smile on his face cracked by the white ridge of a scar.

'I'd heard rumours of a party of Argives camped in these parts,' he said, 'but I didn't think to find you here. I'd given you up for dead, like everybody else. I should have guessed it would take more than a bad blow to finish off Odysseus. But there were so many ships lost in that storm, I assumed yours must have been among them.'

Enlivened by this reminder of a world that had almost receded over his horizon, Odysseus invited the man to come and eat with him. They sat down on the mats outside the lodge while a woman served them calabashes filled with lotus-meal. Explaining how he had been driven south by the storm as he tried to double Cape Malea, Odysseus caught the leathery face of Guneus frowning at the scene around him. As though looking through the newcomer's eyes, Odysseus saw his men lying about their ramshackle lodges, lax, bleary and unkempt. Many of them were too far gone in their lotus dreams to take much interest in the new arrivals. Embarrassed by the sight, he was suddenly at a loss to explain how it was that they had remained here for so long.

'We've been taking it easy here,' he muttered. 'After the long strain of the war, I mean . . . and one of the worst voyages I can recall.' He took in his visitor's polite but uncertain nod. 'Anyway, what brings a Thessalian as far south as this?' he added with forced good humour. 'The last I heard you northerners had your hands full fighting some new invader. Is it all over? Have you driven them back to whatever nameless wastes they came from?'

Guneus frowned and drew in his breath. 'The Dorians won't be driven back. They're too strong for that. There's too many of them and some of them carry weapons superior to ours. Neoptolemus and the Myrmidons are holding the line by sheer bloody-minded grit and obstinacy. With luck they might retake Iolcus next year; but the lands to the north are gone for ever – my own estates among them. I got back from Troy to learn that my father and young sons had been killed in the Dorian advance, and my wife and daughters taken into slavery.'

Offering his awkward condolences, Odysseus gazed into the man's grim face with sympathy; yet it was like listening to news from another, harsher world than the one he now inhabited. He struggled a little to connect with it.

'But surely Agamemnon won't let things stay that way?' he said. 'He needs Thessaly too much to let it go without a fight. He won't risk letting the Dorians advance any further south.'

Guneus looked up from the handful of food he had just scooped from the calabash he had been given. 'You haven't heard? I thought the whole world must know of it!' He took in the perplexity in Odysseus's eyes. 'Agamemnon's dead and buried, man. There's been revolution in Mycenae. Clytaemnestra murdered him as soon as he got back. Stabbed him to death in his own bath-house, they say.' The Thessalian's face wrinkled into a sour smile at the other man's shocked gape. 'It's true,' he declared. 'True as I'm sitting here in Libya. The King of Men got even less profit from his war than I did. At least I've come away with my skin intact – even if I've lost everything else apart from my ship.' Guneus wiped the back of his hand across his beard. 'I'm looking to rebuild here in Libya. I hear there's good country over to the west by the River Cinyps, and no one to claim it but a few beggarly nomads. It's there for the taking.' He scowled down at the mess of pottage in his bowl. 'What is this sticky pap you've given me? It's too sweet. Sets my teeth on edge.'

'It's an acquired taste,' Odysseus said without thinking. 'But what you said . . . it makes no sense to me. Agamemnon was coming home in triumph. He'd achieved everything he and Clytaemnestra planned together.'

And then, with a sickening lurch in his stomach, like that of a man waking from thick sleep to face the prospect of a dreaded day, he remembered the death of Iphigenaia.

'Clytaemnestra hated his guts,' Guneus said dryly, pushing his calabash aside. 'Always had done, if you ask me, long before he cut the windpipe of that pretty child of theirs in Aulis. So she got the King of Men to do what she wanted him to do – bring home the treasure of Troy. And once it was in her grasp, she got rid of him.' Grimacing, he licked his sticky fingers clean and wiped his hands on his kilt. 'Is there no meat in this camp of yours? Don't you Ithacans go hunting ever?'

'There's goat,' Odysseus answered with a hot darkness swirling in his mind. 'We'll get some skinned and roasted in a minute . . . but I'm still trying to make sense of what you're telling me.'

'If you can make sense of this world,' Guneus shrugged, 'you're a better man than I am.'

'But I can't believe the Mycenaeans would let a woman sit on the Lion Throne again – not even one as clever as Clytaemnestra.'

'They don't have to. She's taken a lover. Aegisthus son of Thyestes, would you believe? Yes, he's back in Mycenae again, and nominally king there now – though Clytaemnestra wields all the power of course. The two of them had the whole thing planned. They murdered the High King and Cassandra together, and the palace guard finished off any commanders who stayed loyal to Agamemnon.'

'Surely it can't have been that easy?'

'Well, a couple of the leading citizens did try to organize resistance, but when they were put to death Clytaemnestra had absolute control of the city. There's unrest in the army, of course, and in the hill country around Mycenae; and none of the other kings look likely to accept Aegisthus as suzerain. After all, who wants to pay tribute to a man who can't keep the peace in his own backyard?'

'But no one's raising a force against him?'

'There's talk of it. Agamemnon's son Orestes is still alive and he won't have anything to do with his mother now. I hear he's taken refuge with King Strophius in Phocis. Some of Agamemnon's men are rallying around him.'

Astounded to learn that the bloody history of Mycenae had taken a further malevolent and vengeful twist, Odysseus asked, 'What about Menelaus? Does he know what's happened?'

'There's been no sign of him. He's out east somewhere – Cyprus or Egypt, I don't know. Cuddled up with Helen, I suppose, and staying out of trouble.'

Odysseus sat in incredulous silence. How could the world have undergone such changes while he lounged on this uneventful beach in a stupor of ignorance? How long must he have been stuck here that such drama could have unfolded while he dozed? And what were its consequences for the lesser kingdoms of Argos? How might Ithaca be affected?

He looked up to see Guneus frowning at him, shaking his head.

'I'm sorry to have shocked you this way,' the Thessalian said. 'I thought you must know what kind of turmoil all Argos is in these days. I thought that's why you were holed up here.'

'What do you mean?' Odysseus demanded with a further lurch of apprehension. 'What else has happened?'

He listened in disbelief as Guneus informed him how Diomedes had returned to Tiryns after being shipwrecked in Lycia only to find that his wife and her lover had locked the gates of his city against him. Then he was shocked again to learn that Idomeneus had suffered the same humiliating fate on coming home to Crete.

'The last I heard,' Guneus said, 'they were in council together at Corinth, hoping to enlist old Nestor's help in regaining their lost kingdoms. But that would mean civil war right across Argos and, as you can imagine, there's no appetite for that. Either way,' he sighed, 'it looks as though the poor bloody Thessalians can't expect much help from the south right now.'

Struck by the cruel irony of it all, Odysseus said, 'You mean that Agamemnon and the others fought for all those years to bring home another man's faithless wife, only to find themselves betrayed by their own wives while they were gone?'

A touch uneasily, Guneus kept his gaze on the place where his crew were gathering eagerly around Eurylochus who was pouring wine into their gourds. 'That's about the size of it, I suppose.'

'But that all three of them should have done it . . . ?' Odysseus puzzled aloud to himself, becoming aware of a dull throbbing at the crown of his head and of pressure building at his temples. 'Clytaemnestra. Agialeia. Meda. And all around the same time, you say? It couldn't just have happened by chance. Surely they must have been in conspiracy?'

'The rumour is,' Guneus muttered, 'that King Nauplius of Euboea was behind it.'

'Nauplius? But he was one of Agamemnon's principal

backers. He put up a huge amount of capital for the war. Without him . . .'

Odysseus faltered there. He caught the knowing glint in the other man's eyes. A long-suppressed memory broke through the troubled surface of his mind.

'Palamedes!' he whispered.

'That's right,' Guneus nodded and spat into the sand, 'Palamedes. Old Nauplius never forgave Agamemnon for having his son stoned to death as a traitor. And who can blame him? It always struck me as a dubious business. Palamedes was too popular with the troops for Agamemnon's liking. Anyway, it must certainly have been Nauplius who ordered the lighting of the false beacons that wrecked the Argive fleet off Euboea. It could never have happened without his consent.' The Thessalian hesitated, glanced uncertainly at his friend, remembering too late how closely Odysseus had been implicated in the death of Palamedes; then he decided to proceed, though with less of the bluff confidence in his voice. 'There's a rumour that Nauplius had been travelling through the kingdoms of Argos long before that, trying to persuade the queens to betray their husbands. He wasn't strong enough to avenge his son's death any other way, so he turned himself into a viper pouring poison in their ears. He was definitely seen in Tiryns and Mycenae. It seems fairly clear he was in Knossos too.'

Sensing now that more was withheld, Odysseus said, 'And Ithaca?'

The leathery, scarred face of the Thessalian looked up at him.

'Yes,' Guneus said, 'in Ithaca too.'

'Tell me,' Odysseus said, and tightened his lips.

'It's all rumour,' Guneus answered uncomfortably. 'Ithaca's a long way off and . . . I don't know. We go away to fight a war and while we're gone, while all our backs are turned . . .' He smacked at a fly that was buzzing about his cheek. 'Anyway, ten years is a long time, I suppose, but . . . who knows what's to be believed?'

'Tell me,' Odysseus said again.

Guneus studied his friend grimly for a moment. 'It's only hearsay,' he said, twisting the bronze-plated wrist-guard he wore. 'It's probably not true at all, but the word is that there's some young prince out of Dulichion – Amphinomus I think his name was – who's been . . . Well, he's been spending a lot of time on Ithaca . . .'

Odysseus gave a small laugh of relief. 'Amphinomus? I know the boy. I know him well. He's the youngest son of old King Nisus. We lost his brother in Thrace. Amphinomus is harmless enough. He was too young to come to Troy with us and nearly broke his heart over it.'

Guneus cleared his throat. 'That was more than ten years ago, Odysseus.'

'Yes, but . . .' Odysseus faltered again. He watched the man's eyes shift away.

A burst of coarse laughter rose from where the two crews were drinking together.

Odysseus narrowed his eyes. 'What are you saying, Guneus?'

The Thessalian lifted the palms of his hands. 'I'm not saying anything . . . not for certain. But times change and the world changes with them. As I said a minute ago, ten years is a long time . . . Boys turn into men. Women can get restless . . . And no one knows what's happened to you, remember. By the time I left Argos everybody had pretty much given you up for dead.'

In a voice low with menace, Odysseus declared, 'Not Penelope.'

Guneus shrugged. 'Perhaps not. Perhaps she's different from the rest.'

'You don't know her. There's no perhaps about it.'

Sensing the heat in the man, Guneus made to withdraw. 'I'm sure you're in the right of it. Like I said, it's only hearsay.'

'Then you shouldn't go spreading it about.'

But the voice was so malignant now that Guneus got to his feet, reflexively checking the dagger at his belt.

'This is unjust,' he said. 'I spoke only because you forced me to speak. Left to myself I would have said nothing.'

Odysseus glared at him through hot eyes. 'You would have done better to keep silent sooner.'

Guneus grunted as a man will who feels himself badly done by. 'If my words have troubled you, Lord Odysseus, I'm sorry for it.' Adjusting the strap of the leather corselet he wore, he looked up, expecting some acknowledgment of his apology. When none came he grunted again, stared out to sea a moment, and then looked back to where Odysseus sat glowering with one fist tightly clenched. A fine trickle of sand was falling from it, down onto the fringes of his mat, as though he had ground a stone to dust in his bare hand.

'Well, I don't care to leave a man gnawing on his own vitals,' Guneus said, 'but I think it best if I withdraw.'

'Do as you like,' Odysseus snapped back, 'it makes no difference to me.'

Guneus looked down at him for a moment with an uneasy mixture of pity and contempt in his scarred face. Deciding to call his crew together and drag his ship back into the surf, he turned away, but he had taken no more than a dozen strides when Odysseus shouted after him, 'If you value your life, Guneus, you'll keep this slander to yourself.'

Guneus stopped in his tracks. When he turned to face Odysseus again there was something closer to mockery in his eyes. 'I'll defend my own honour before any man,' he said quietly, 'and I'll keep silent as and when I choose. But for the sake of the respect I once had for you, I'll say this much: take a look around you, Odysseus. I don't know what's been going on here and I don't want to know; but this camp's a pigsty and there isn't one of your crew who's in a fit condition to stand up against mine. Take a good look at yourself while you're at it. You've got a belly on you like an Aulis tavern-keeper. If I wanted to, I could knock you down as soon as spit at you. You'd better start shaping up and get out of this squalid hole if you're to stand any chance of winning your wife and island back again.'

He had turned on his heel and started walking back towards

his men when he heard Odysseus running across the sand towards him. With no difficulty at all he dodged the first blow that came at him and merely leaned the other way to avoid the loosely swinging second. Then, being a taller man than Odysseus, with a longer reach, he pushed the palm of his hand into the Ithacan's chest and stiffened his arm to hold him at bay.

'That's enough,' he hissed so that the men watching in dismay down the beach should not hear him. 'Stop it now or I'll humiliate you.' His fierce, imperative stare was fixed on Odysseus's bewildered grey eyes. A moment later, to his immense consternation and surprise, he saw tears starting there.

The Young Lions

In my later travels across Argos I encountered a chronicler who insisted that more than eight hundred thousand people had died in the war for Troy. Though his estimate strikes me as more blood-thirsty than accurate, many thousands of men and women must have lost their lives in what proved, in the end, to be a wholly destructive enterprise. Countless more came back with injuries that disfigured them for the rest of their days. But what of its effects on those other, unsung casualties of the war – those who were too young to fight?

Having grown up without a father's guidance, they were forced either to endure the wretched silence of those who could not bring themselves to talk about the war at all, or to listen again and again to stories which left them feeling that real life had passed them by. This is what Odysseus came to recognize as the dreadful patrimony of war. Even as he identified its corrosive power, he was aware of the shadow that his own glorious repu-tation cast across the life of his son; but I know that he was also thinking about Neoptolemus and Agamemnon's tragic son, Orestes.

The fierce young son of Achilles – his true name was Pyrrhus – was of a different order than other boys who had been left behind at home. Though he was only twelve years old in the final year of the war, he had been summoned to the fight by an oracle. It was prophesied that Troy would not fall until he came to the city, and so, against the will of his mother Deidameia and his grandmother Thetis, who were both devastated by the news of Achilles' death, he was fetched out of Skyros. No one expected him to take an active part in the fighting. He was seen merely as a kind of mascot, a talismanic presence required by the gods; one who might rouse the flagging morale of the host by reviving the memory of his father. Yet he was given the name Neoptolemus – the new warrior – and quickly astounded them all. It seemed that he put on his father's intrepid spirit with his gilded suit of armour, and the Myrmidons guarded his young life with a loyalty that encouraged him to such fearless acts that some said his soul was possessed by his father's ghost.

Odysseus believed the boy to be possessed rather by the idea of what his father's ghost demanded of him, for Neoptolemus was a child whose sense of manhood was shaped by the desire both to avenge the death of Achilles and to equal him in glory. It was a consuming appetite, unqualified by such tenderness as Achilles had known in his love for Patroclus and Briseis, and perhaps also for Polyxena. And so, long before he left Troy without a wound on his young body, Neoptolemus was a casualty of the war.

What could Andromache have made of him as she was forced to submit to his embraces on board his father's black ship? Here was a woman who had lain in Hector's arms. She had known the devotion of a man for whom warfare was not the chief goal and glory of a man's existence but a violent fate forced on him by other men. She in turn was forced to watch as Hector fell under Achilles' spear. She had seen her husband's body dragged around the walls of Troy. The son of Achilles had hurled her child from a balcony onto the stones below; and now she must endure the thrust of his callow hips as Neoptolemus strove to plant his seed in her loins.

Yet if her body was captive, her spirit was not, and the boy can have found little pleasure in her bed. After a time, he began to leave her alone; and though his Myrmidons may have guessed that she emerged the victor from those loveless encounters, those grim men were too loyal to reveal their amusement and contempt. But Neoptolemus knew what had happened, and the knowledge made him all that more furious a fighter. Returning from Troy to recover his father's lost lands, he was unable to land in Iolcus, which remained in Dorian hands; so he navigated the straits between Euboea and southern Thessaly and then marched inland in search of glory. The march brought him to the Orthris Mountains, where his grandfather Peleus — an old man aged further by the death of his son — had withdrawn his forces to make his stand against the alien invasion.

Before the day when his grandson marched the advance-guard of Myrmidons up into the mountains, Peleus and Neoptolemus had never met. The boy had been raised on the island of Skyros, in thrall to his formidable grandmother Thetis, from whom Peleus had been estranged for many years. Through her influence, Neoptolemus had developed a profound attachment to his heritage among the Dolopian people, some of whom had long since migrated from Epirus in the far west, through Thessaly, and on to Skyros. In these circumstances, Neoptolemus might have felt little attachment to Peleus, who was, for him, a remote and dubious figure, one who had long outlived the noble achievements of his youth. But the Myrmidons belonged to Peleus, and he had given them to Achilles; and since Neoptolemus had acquired an appetite for blood at Troy he had begun to think of himself as a Myrmidon first above all things. So now he was eager to make a stand beside his grandfather, and swear on his father's shade that the soldier-ants of Thessaly would not rest until they saw King Peleus seated again on his rightful throne in Iolcus.

The old man gazed at the armoured youth with tears in his eyes. He recognized more of his wife's features in the humour-less yet unexpectedly soft young face than he did his own. The hair blowing about the boy's head had the same reddish tinge to it as hers; the eyes were the same grey-green: and Peleus wondered

whether something of her rage still ran through his veins. But
there was a colder edge about him too – the coldness of a blade
in winter – as if the things he had done at Troy had cancelled all
feeling from his heart and left only ambition there.

Standing on the windy mountainside Peleus knew that when
this boy fought on his behalf, it would not be for love of him,
but merely out of a voracious appetite for battle. He shook his
head, remembering the disastrous quarrel among the goddesses at
his wedding feast at Mount Pelion all those years ago. There were
those who claimed that the seeds of the war at Troy had been
sown that day. Well, here was its harvest now – an unsmiling boy
who had lopped off King Priam's head and led a murderous assault
on his beautiful city. And the dreadful truth was that Peleus had
need of such warriors now.

'Did you come here directly from Troy?' he asked. 'You must
be weary.'

'I am rested well enough,' Neoptolemus answered stiffly.

Peleus nodded. 'Did you not put in at Skyros?'

The youth glanced away. 'For one night only. Iolcus had already
fallen, so one night could make no difference.' He hesitated a
moment before adding, 'Also I wished to speak with my mother.'

Peleus nodded. 'And with your grandmother no doubt?'

'Yes, with my grandmother also.'

So he had guessed right. Thetis had dropped some of her old
poison in the boy's ears. Yet she had not been able to prevent him
from coming at his call. Loyalty to his father's Myrmidon heritage
had brought Neoptolemus to the fight for Thessaly. Peleus could
build on that. Somehow he must find a way to win his love and
respect as well as his cold service.

Smiling into those calculating eyes, he said, 'May I see the spear
you carry?'

Neoptolemus considered a moment before relinquishing his
weapon. 'This was my father's spear,' he said.

'I know it was,' Peleus answered, feeling the familiar weight in
his hand, and balancing it there as if for the throw. 'And it was

his father's before him. This spear was given to me by the gods as a wedding gift. The head was forged in the smithy of Hephaistus. This ash-wood shaft was carved by Divine Athena.'

Unable quite to conceal his boyish awe, Neoptolemus said, 'You truly stood in the presence of the gods?'

'As we all do, all the time,' answered Peleus, 'though not all of us are privileged to see them. Your father once took down this spear from the hooks where it hung beside my hearth. He was no more than a restless boy at the time, younger than you are now. I found him hurling it at a tree for target-practice and was angry with him because he had taken my spear without seeking my consent. But it was on that day that Achilles declared his desire to become a Myrmidon.' Peleus smiled at the memory. 'I told him that he should have his wish but that I would keep my spear until I could be sure that I had a son who was fit to wield it.'

As stiffly as if some insult had been intended, Neoptolemus declared, 'No man was ever worthier than my father.'

'I know that,' Peleus answered him, unsmiling, 'and no father was ever prouder than myself. And now this spear is yours.'

The youth narrowed his eyes against the wind. The beardless jut of his chin was held high as he said, 'My hand shall never dishonour it.'

'I trust not, Son of Achilles.' Gravely, Peleus handed back the ash-wood spear. 'I am proud to have you at my side,' he said. 'I hope to be made prouder still. Now come, let us make our offerings to the gods and to your father's shade.'

Many weeks later, some fifty miles to the south, at the city of Crisa in Phocis, another son of the war – a sandy-haired youth with truculent eyes, some two or three years older than Neoptolemus – was practising sword-play with his friend. They wielded only wooden swords and carried light duelling shields, but both of them sweated from the length of the bout even though a cold wind was gusting off the rugged slopes of Mount Parnassus.

Growing suddenly impatient of his failure to break through his opponent's guard, the sandy-haired youth came at him with a swift series of swingeing blows that drove him back on the defensive; but the vigour of his assault left his shield-arm swinging almost as widely as his sword. Just as he was about to deliver what must be the winning stroke, he felt the blunt point of his opponent's weapon nudging at his ribs.

'Ha, you're dead, Orestes!' cried the darker youth. He gave a gay, slightly mocking laugh that was picked up by the four girls wrapped in brightly coloured shawls who had been watching them from the balcony above. Their clapping set the doves whirring their wings across the court.

Orestes glowered briefly up at them and flushed.

'Take no notice of them,' said Pylades, who was the king's son in Phocis and the most intimate friend to the youth he had just stabbed with his wooden sword. 'Their applause is as empty as their heads. In any case, it's you they fancy!'

'It was a lucky stroke,' Orestes scowled.

Smiling still, Pylades arched his brow. 'Even if that were so, you would still be dead. But I was waiting for you to lose control and that's just what you did.' Putting down his sword and shield, he wiped the back of his arm across his brow. 'You're still far too hot-headed. It's part of your passionate nature, and I love you for it. But if you want to live long enough to take your vengeance, you're going to have to rein in that temper of yours.'

'That's easy enough for you to say.' Doing his best to ignore the tittering of the girls, Orestes threw down his sword. 'The gods have always been kind to you. What complaint can you possibly have against this life?'

'None,' Pylades answered, 'except that it has treated my friend very ill.' He took a towel from the heap on the bench beside him and tossed it across to Orestes. 'Come, let's take a bath together. Then I'll give you a game of knucklebones before we eat.'

The two youths were cousins and had been friends since they were children, though it was not a friendship of which Clytaemnestra had recently approved. Even before the death of his sister Iphigenaia at Aulis, Orestes had become a major source of concern to his mother. His temperament was pugnacious and impatient, his manner verging on the insolent. In a court where everyone else went in fear of her power, Orestes had begun to take liberties, trying her patience in ways that he would not have dared to risk with his father. Yet Clytaemnestra found it hard to be firm with her son, even though she often devastated others with her cruel reproofs.

From the first, she had always entertained such hopes of him. One day he would marry his cousin Hermione and unite the thrones of Mycenae and Sparta, thus confirming the hegemony of their royal house across all Argos. And he would become the kind of king that her first husband might have been had Agamemnon not murdered him. A king who ruled supreme over a world of artistic beauty and intellectual excellence, a world such as she would have chosen for herself if a strong fate had not willed otherwise.

Yet with her mind preoccupied with the cares of state, Clytaemnestra had found it impossible to give her son the quality of attention that such ambitions required. She had recruited the best mentors she could find to teach him eloquence and music, to cultivate his aesthetic sensibility and encourage him in philosophical enquiry as well as instructing him in the elements of politics and statecraft. But the plain fact was that Orestes wanted to be at the war. More than that, he wanted to be fighting alongside Achilles — to serve as his cup-bearer or humble armour-polisher if no more glorious role was available. Anything to be close to the man whom he idolized above all others. While Troy still stood and there were deeds of glory waiting to be done, what interest could he have in poring over old clay tablets and the finer points of sophistry?

And then when Clytaemnestra returned to Mycenae with the bitter news that his father had put Iphigenaia to death on the altar of Artemis at Aulis, the mind of Orestes had taken a darker turn. What was he to make of this — that his sister, whose beautiful face and exquisite singing voice had always been sources of wonder and delight to him, should have been murdered by his father? How could such a thing make sense unless the gods themselves were mad? In his confusion, he raged against his mother. How could she have permitted this to happen? Why had he not been informed of what his father intended so that he could have offered himself up in Iphigenaia's place? But Clytaemnestra seemed remote and frozen inside her grief, and where Orestes looked to find maternal understanding, he met only silence or the impatient snarl of an injured lioness.

Eventually he found consolation in the company of his friend Pylades, who had been brought from Phocis to Mycenae in the hope that his companionship might make Orestes' hours of study less solitary. The two boys had always been fond of one another, but now their imaginations were ignited by the same hopes and dreams. At last Orestes had found someone willing to play Patroclus to his own Achilles; and the cheerful modesty of his friend elicited a greater generosity of spirit from the spoiled prince. The two boys became inseparable. They swore the same oaths of undying love for one another as their heroes had sworn. Secretly they began to sleep in each other's arms.

Then the news reached Mycenae that both Achilles and Patroclus were dead.

For a time Orestes was inconsolable. Not only did victory seem inconceivable now, but life itself seemed a vain and empty thing. How was it that everything he loved was taken from him? How was it that Achilles could have been slain by treachery while his father – a man he barely knew, who had callously put his own daughter to death – lived on and did nothing with all the power at his command?

Cooler-headed, more pragmatic in temperament, Pylades consoled his friend as best he could. Surely, he said, the best way to honour the shades of their heroes was to become greater heroes still. Together they would make good the loss. Let the war drag on, for soon the two of them must be called to the front. They were the young lions who would carry on the fight. Agamemnon would look on with pride as his son Orestes did what even Achilles had failed to do and led his forces through the Scaean Gate into the very heart of Troy.

Yet before any of that could happen, changes began to take place in Mycenae itself. Pelagon, the court bard who had sung for years of the deeds at Troy, mysteriously died. Familiar figures about the palace were relieved of their posts. Less approachable young men replaced them. Then Aegisthus appeared.

When his father first left for the war, Orestes had been too young to hear a full account of his family's history, so the name of Aegisthus meant nothing to him. Nor did he take against the man at first. Handsome and charming, the newcomer appeared to be no more than a further addition to his mother's ever-growing staff of ministers and officials, though one with whom she spent an unusual amount of time closeted in private. Only on the day when he remarked on the man's lively wit to Pylades, and he saw his friend glance uneasily away, did Orestes become conscious that something might be amiss.

'What is it?' Orestes demanded. 'Don't you like him?'

Pylades merely shrugged and carried on oiling his bow.

'I agree he seems a bit full of himself,' Orestes said, 'and I resent the way he tries to speak to me sometimes as if he thought he was my father. But he's better company than those other drones that hang about my mother. I mean, which of them ever stops to pass the time of day with us?'

'I don't trust him,' Pylades muttered almost below his breath.

Orestes blinked in surprise. 'Why not?'

'I don't know.' And then, two seconds later. 'I'd rather not say.'

'What do you mean?'

Pylades flushed. 'You must have noticed,' he murmured, 'how much time he spends alone with your mother.'

'They work together,' Orestes countered, but the back of his neck was suddenly hot. He wanted to demand what his friend meant by that mumbled remark but he couldn't do it without losing his temper. His mind started to lurch as he watched Pylades put more oil onto the kidskin. Could it be that the friend he loved was imputing his mother's honour? And why would he choose to do that unless he had good reason?

'I think,' he said quietly, 'you had better explain yourself.'

Pylades turned his honest face towards him, 'Do you trust me?' he asked.

'Are we not sworn to one another?'

'Whatever might happen? Whatever I might say?'

Orestes saw that they were both trembling a little.

'Now you're alarming me,' he gasped.

'Then perhaps silence is better.'

'It's too late for that. Tell me what you know.'

Pylades looked down at his feet. His knuckles were gripped tight about his bow. 'Do you remember some time ago when you were ill with a fever and you asked me to bring your mother to you? It was quite late one night.'

'I remember.'

Pylades swallowed before continuing. 'I went to the Queen's private apartment and saw her serving-woman Marpessa admitting Aegisthus to her bed-chamber.'

He watched the colours changing in Orestes' face. He saw the anger rising in his eyes, but he pressed on, forestalling interruption. 'I withdrew at once, of course, and came back wondering what reason I could give for not bringing your mother with me. Fortunately you'd already fallen asleep so I didn't have to explain.'

'Is that all?' Orestes demanded hotly. 'What's so terrible about that? Doesn't it occur to you that he might have needed to speak to her urgently? Some matter of state business must have come up. Anyway, if Marpessa was there, they weren't alone. There need have been no wrong in it.'

But his boyish heart was floundering.

'That's what I told myself,' Pylades answered. 'I would have put it out of my mind but Marpessa must have spotted me leaving the apartment because the next day Aegisthus came up to me and . . .' Pylades faltered there. He glanced away from his friend's fierce regard, uncertain but not abashed.

'What?' Orestes demanded.

'He threatened me.'

'How? How did he threaten you?'

Still not looking at his friend, Pylades drew in his breath a little shakily before answering. 'He said that he knew very well what the Queen did not yet know – that you and I have taken to sleeping in each other's arms. He said that if the Queen got to learn of it I would certainly be sent away from Mycenae.'

'How?' Orestes protested. 'How could he have known that?'

'He must have spied on us while we slept. He or some minion in his pay. I don't know, but he said that he would say nothing to the Queen about it so long as I too agreed to say nothing to anyone of what I thought I might have seen. He said that if we failed to reach such an agreement, he and I, then the consequences would be very unpleasant for you.'

'I'll kill him,' Orestes said.

'I don't think so,' his friend answered quietly.

'I'll go to the armoury and take a sword and plunge it in his traitor's heart.'

'Think about it, Orestes, Even if you got close to him – which I very much doubt – what would your mother do? How would you explain yourself without disgracing her? And who would believe you anyway? Pylades put a hand to his friend's trembling shoulder. 'I wouldn't have said anything, but you asked me and . . . I don't know, but there's something going on in this city that I don't understand.'

'What do you mean?'

'Why have so many of the old ministers gone from the palace? And haven't you noticed how hard it's become for ordinary people to petition the Queen? The whole feel of the place is different. Nobody seems to speak their mind any more. I may be quite wrong about it, but,' Pylades glanced around to make sure they were still unobserved, 'the only person I trust right now is you.'

Orestes listened to his friend with growing trepidation, for everything he said corresponded to vague feelings that had crossed his mind without ever becoming clear. Yet the implications were so worrying that his heart jumped about his chest and his mind refused to keep still long enough to think.

Pylades looked up and saw the agitation in Orestes' face. 'I'm sorry,' he said. 'I didn't mean to upset you. But it seems to me that the only thing for us to do is keep our eyes and ears open and our mouths shut till things come clearer.'

And that's what they did for a time in an anxious conspiracy against the world. Orestes found it hard to conceal his newfound feelings of revulsion for Aegisthus. Clytaemnestra felt ever more frustrated by her son's behaviour, and her daughter Electra resented the way that her brother and his friend excluded her from the secrets they shared. Then the boys' apprehensions were allayed in the excitement that burst across Mycenae with the news that Troy had fallen and Agamemnon must soon return to the city in triumph.

Yet Orestes found it still harder to sleep in his bed at night. How should he receive his father? Should he greet him, like everybody else, as the great hero of the age, the conqueror of Troy and King of Men? That was what he wanted to do; but he couldn't free his mind of the sickening thought that this was the man who had put his sister to death in order to further his ambitions. Orestes told himself that the thread of a man's fate was spun at his birth and there was no avoiding the ordeals that the gods devised for him. Yet that thought brought him no peace for it seemed to turn life into a prison where no one was free to choose for himself. Victory and defeat, courage and cowardice, fidelity and betrayal — all blurred to insignificance in a world ruled by capricious gods.

Lost in such dark contemplation, Orestes lay uneasily awake night after night, or jumped into darkness out of terrifying dreams.

One afternoon he returned from a long, uncomfortable conversation with his mother to find that Pylades had already gone from the city. All his things had been hastily packed and not a trace of his presence remained. Orestes was simply told that King Strophius had required that his son return home at short notice and that the herald who had brought the message would brook no delay.

On the following day Orestes and his sister Electra were despatched into the care of Lord Podargus in Midea. When Orestes complained that, as well as being denied the company of his only friend, he would not even be permitted to witness his father's triumphant return into Mycenae, he was told, incomprehensibly, that such was Agamemnon's express wish. No further explanation was forthcoming.

Some days later Orestes and Electra were sitting miserably together in the draughty hall at Midea when Podargus came up to them wringing his mottled hands. Something terrible had happened in Mycenae, he declared. They must brace themselves for a shock, for he could see no gentle way of breaking the news that their father had been assassinated.

Electra's face whitened as though she was about to faint. She uttered a little strangled cry, tried to stifle it further, and then burst into tears. Orestes sat in shock. He felt as if someone had struck him a blow on the back of his head.

Then he demanded, 'Who has killed him?'

But Podargus merely shook his gaunt head, grim-lipped. The situation in Mycenae remained confused, he said. He had told them the little that he knew. When more information became available he would share it. Now they must prepare to mourn and make their offerings for their father's shade.

Some time would pass, therefore, before Agamemnon's children learned that their father's assassin was their mother. The source of that information was a serving-woman called Geilissa, who was one of the small band of guards and retainers who had accompanied the children on their journey from Mycenae to Midea. She had known Orestes and Iphigenaia since infancy and had been wet-nurse to Electra, but she and Clytaemnestra had often been at odds over the Queen's cold way with her children. Geilissa never doubted where her own warm loyalties lay, and she had been included in the party against Clytaemnestra's better judgement only because Electra declared that she would refuse to go without her. Geilissa herself was glad enough to put Mycenae behind her and take care of her charges once more during their sojourn in Midea.

A cheerful soul, she had quickly made friends with the servants of the house, and it was from them that she learned the truth about the death of Agamemnon. With her own secret suspicions now confirmed, Geilissa saw how grave a threat these circumstances must pose to the welfare of the two children. Yet sooner or later the truth must come out. Better that they heard it from her than from some careless stranger.

So once again Orestes was forced to listen while a person he trusted told him things so terrible that he could hardly bear to hear them. Already distraught from the news that her father was dead – a grief that was as instinctive as it was emotional, for the girl had no retrievable memories of Agamemnon – Electra was devastated by this further revelation. She sat with her hand across her mouth, trying to suppress her wailing. Orestes sat beside her, gripping her shoulders as she rocked in his arms.

'It is Aegisthus,' he shouted suddenly. 'The villain has poisoned her mind. It must be his foul hand behind this thing. I should have killed him long ago.'

Anxiously Geilissa hissed, 'You must keep your voice down, master. Lord Podargus is not of your father's party.'

Orestes looked across at the nurse in bewilderment as he pieced together the long, manipulative process by which he had been separated from his friend, cut off from contact with his returning father, and sent to a place where he could be held in check. His mind was working quickly now. He was not a guest in Midea: he was a prisoner. His mother would send for him when she was ready. She would tell him that he had a new father and must learn to love and respect him. And if he failed to obey? Orestes remembered what Aegisthus had said to Pylades. He remembered the hostility he had glimpsed in the man's eyes when he had made his own mistrust for him plain. Aegisthus had no love for him. As far as Aegisthus was concerned, he was Agamemnon's brat. The man must be living in fear that a day must come when Orestes would seek to avenge his murdered father.

And he was right to fear it.

But for the moment Aegisthus held all the power. Only Clytaemnestra stood between Orestes and death, and Clytaemnestra had already killed her husband. Was she capable also of killing her son?

In an insane world where fathers killed their daughters, it was entirely possible.

For the first time in his young life, Orestes felt consumed by fear. Somehow he must get away from Midea. He must go to Pylades. His friend would take care of him in Phocis. He would know what to do.

It was Geilissa who arranged for his escape. On her way through the market-place, she observed a Sicilian merchant dealing in slaves who appeared to take reasonable care of his valuable human stock. When she learned that he would soon be moving on, it occurred to her that Orestes might be smuggled out of the city among his train. Geilissa discussed the idea with a friend she trusted from the old days in Mycenae – a grizzled warrior who had lost an eye serving at Troy with Agamemnon. When neither of them could come up with a less risky plan, she approached the merchant and quickly discovered that his venal soul had no loyalties in Argos other than to his desire for profit. Once sure of her ground, she set about persuading him that his desire would be well served if he delivered safely to the court of King Strophius in Phocis a certain person whose identity must not be disclosed in Midea or any other city through which they might pass.

'Including Mycenae?' the merchant shrewdly asked.

'Mycenae, above all, is to be avoided,' Geilissa said.

The Sicilian opened his hands. 'I look to do good business in Mycenae.'

'And doubtless you will,' Geilissa answered, 'on your return from Phocis. King Strophius is a wealthy man. He will compensate you well for the delay.'

'And what assurances do I have of this?'

Geilissa unwrapped from a cloth the casket in which were gathered all the jewels and golden ornaments that Electra had insisted on bringing to Midea. 'These are already worth more than all your slaves. You shall have the casket when you leave the city with my friend safely concealed in your train.'

'Let me think about this a little.' Smiling, the Sicilian made a self-deprecatory gesture with his hands. 'I am a timid man.'

Geilissa watched him stroke his beard. 'Think too long,' she said, 'and you may begin to wonder what there is to prevent you from taking the casket and then betraying my friend to those who mean him harm. You should be aware, therefore, that were you to do such a thing, there are those who will not rest till they have hunted you down and cut your tongue out of your throat and divided your manhood from your loins.'

The merchant studied her for a long moment with a ringed hand at his mouth. Then he lowered the hand to reveal a sour smile. 'You reason like a Sicilian,' he said. 'But I will do this thing for you. Pray tell your friend that this humble merchant is at his service.'

That evening they untied the long hair that Orestes wore clubbed at his neck, dressed him in one of Electra's gowns and wrapped around his head and shoulders a shawl that she had embroidered with figures of prowling lions and winged griffins. Geilissa started with shock when she looked at the finished effect, for in the unsteady light of the oil-lamps, it might have been his dead sister, Iphigenaia, standing demurely there.

So Orestes escaped from Midea early the next morning as one among a coffle of slaves. Unaware that the son of Agamemnon was slipping through their guard with a kitchen knife clutched under the folds of his pretty shawl, the sentinels at the gate paid scant attention to the train. Almost a month later he was welcomed to safety by Pylades with tears and open arms. Denied their chance of glory in Troy, and with the world at home turned hostile round them, the young lions began preparing themselves for the day when they too would play a significant part in the continuing drama of the long catastrophe that was the Trojan War.

As the reader will recall from my account of the day when Dolon the fisherman brought us the news that the war had ended, Ithaca also had a number of young lions frisking about the streets, and even before Troy fell, they had already begun to make a nuisance of themselves. That's how we thought of it at first – as no more than a nuisance, for we Ithacans might have our feuds and quarrels and grudges, and blood might even be shed at times, but murder was rare on the island and we lacked any talent for evil on the grand scale with which it flourished in Mycenae and the other great cities of the world. So King Laertes and his ministers did little more than sigh over the noise of drunken revelry in the streets of the town at night. But out of small neglected troubles larger problems grow, and soon there were signs that Antinous and the gang of young men who followed his lead were getting out of hand.

The first of the truly bruising encounters between Telemachus and Antinous took place at the Feast of Pan in the spring of the year after the war had ended. At that time the mood of the island was gloomy and apprehensive. Diotima, who had been priestess of Mother Dia's shrine on the island for longer than anyone could remember, had died during the course of a hard winter. Because she was already very old, her death came as no surprise, but she had outlived all the women who knew the ways of the snake well enough to succeed her, so the power of the shrine itself began to wane.

No one took her death harder than King Laertes and his wife Anticleia. They too were old, and each day that failed to bring news of their son increased their grief and anxiety. Laertes had been eager to lay down the burdens of kingship for many years, and the business of exacting tribute from men younger and more ambitious than himself, and of giving justice among quarrelsome islanders, was increasingly a trial to his soul. So to Queen Anticleia's concern for her son was added the further strain of watching her husband's strength fail. Her nights were sleepless and her appetite poor. Never a large woman, she began to shrink visibly, both in weight and stature. Soon people began to mutter that if her son did not return she might simply die from grief.

In these circumstances, Penelope had to be strong for everyone and her faith did not fail. Whatever private anxieties troubled her nights, she remained ever hopeful, refusing to allow any other possibility but that her husband was alive and on his way home. Yet she had not seen Odysseus for more than ten years, and there must have been times when she had difficulty remembering what he had looked like then, let alone imagining how he might have been changed by war.

For a time, everyone's spirits were lifted by the news that a Zacynthian sailor called Axylus had returned to his island, having walked hundreds of miles overland from Euboea where he had been cast ashore after his ship went down. Summoned to Ithaca, he reported that he had been among the survivors of a disastrous raid on Ismarus in which many men, including the brother of Prince Amphinomus, had been killed. He was certain, however, that Odysseus had managed to escape from the skirmish on the Ciconian shore, though how he had fared in the storm that had wrecked his own ship, Axylus was unable to say.

This was the first definite news that Penelope had received and she preferred to let it strengthen her hopes rather than darken her fears. Telemachus chose to share her optimism and draw strength from it; but when Amphinomus returned to Ithaca after his time of mourning was complete, and the boy watched his mother receive her friend, weeping, with open arms, his mood turned sullen again.

Though he tried to elicit my sympathy, I saw nothing wrong in the friendship. Sitting side by side at the high table or walking together on the cliffs above the expansive glitter of the sea, Amphinomus and Penelope might have been taken for a brother and sister who shared a lively affection and were always sensitive to each other's shifts of mood and feeling. So it seemed to me there was something excessive in the way Telemachus kept watch, like a prick-eared dog, over his absent father's wife. Only after a time did I come to see that his heart was riven with a kind of jealousy. Perhaps he couldn't bear it that anyone – least of all this handsome prince out of Dulichion – should be more intimate with his mother than he was himself? Whatever the case, sooner or later his anger was going to turn violent. It happened at the Festival of Pan.

The Spring Feast is always a bawdy and boisterous affair. Shepherds come from all over the island and, once the sacred offerings have been made, there is much eating and drinking and many hours of dancing and singing of songs. Commonly enough, a fair proportion of the children born each year are sired during the course of that night, not all of them in wedlock. Because the winter had been bitter and everyone had been miserable for so long, the revelry was wild that year. The heat of the sun lay heavy on the afternoon, the wine was strongly mixed, and fathers looked to their daughters as Antinous and a gang of randy young men paraded around the awnings with long leather phalluses protruding from the goatskin clouts they wore.

I was in luck myself that day – a plump young woman from a village over by Mount Neriton sat near me as I sang. She had honey-brown skin and thick hair, and an encouraging way of dipping her eyes. Later we found our way to a sunlit glade beneath the trees. She was my first, and it wounded my heart to discover a day or two later that she was already pledged to a prosperous shepherd in her own part of the world; but I have sometimes wondered whether his firstborn son has the gift of singing verses too. In any case, being so pleasantly occupied, I didn't learn what had happened elsewhere until Peiraeus told me after the event.

Waiting till late in the day when all the royal party apart from the prince had retired, Antinous asked Telemachus if he would judge the merit of a satyr play that he and Eurymachus were improvising for the people's entertainment. To my friend's astonishment, Antinous took the part of a woman overwhelmed by the blandishments of her lover, who was played by Eurymachus. Speaking in a high-pitched voice and fluttering his eyelids, Antinous allowed his hand to stray towards the grotesque codpiece protruding from between Eurymachus's thighs. Only when he released an amorous sigh and squeaked, 'But what if my husband should return, Amphinomus?' did the true nature of the game become apparent.

Before anyone realized what was happening, Telemachus had thrown himself at Antinous, knocked him off the wine-stained trestle-table where the young man reclined like a whore on a couch, and fastened his hands about his throat.

By the time Eurymachus and Leodes pulled the boy away, Antinous was choking and retching for air. Telemachus was still much smaller than the man he had attacked, and left to his own malevolent devices, Antinous might have inflicted a terrible beating on him. But some of the less drunken shepherds had been disgusted by the play, and many of them had no love for the family of Eupeithes. Three stood up from their benches making it plain that no harm would come to their prince as long as they were there to prevent it. Two of them were very burly. The other, an older man with a broken nose, thoughtfully weighed the curve of his crook in his hand.

Taking stock of the menace in their faces, Antinous glanced for support to Eurymachus who released Telemachus and stood uncertainly beside his friend with the ridiculous phallus knocked askew at his waist. Sensing that neither Eurymachus nor Leodes had the stomach for a fight, Antinous gasped, 'What's the matter with the brat? Can't he take a joke?'

'There's jokes and there's jokes,' said the grizzled old shepherd with the crook, 'and if you think that one was funny then you'll be even more amused when this ash-plant comes down across your ear – which it would have done by now if I wasn't making allowances for the belly-load of wine you're carrying.' Then he turned to Telemachus. 'And you'd better run along, young sir. If your father was home, he'd tell you that it's wise to pick a fight only when the odds are with you.'

Flustered and abashed, Telemachus turned on his heel, shouting, 'If my father doesn't kill you when he gets back, Antinous, I promise I'll do it myself.'

'Wake up, donzel!' Antinous shouted after him. 'Your father's not coming back, and you're going to have to answer for those words one day.'

Peiraeus told me that the shepherds would certainly have beaten Antinous in that moment had not Eurymachus had the good sense to hustle him away.

When I learned what had happened, I set out to look for Telemachus. Last seen heading for the palace, he wasn't to be found in his chamber and no one in the hall knew where he was. By now darkness had fallen, so there was no point wandering the hillsides in search of him, and I was about to give up and join Penelope and the others in the hall when I heard voices in Eurycleia's chamber.

Putting my ear to the door, I heard the hoarse croak of the old nurse's voice reassuring Telemachus that he was just like his father – too proud and too brave not to put himself at risk. 'He was about your age when he went hunting boar with his grand-father Autolycus in the woods around Mount Parnassus,' she was saying, 'Couldn't wait for the huntsmen to lay the nets – not him. Couldn't wait for the boar to come rushing at him neither. He has to leap straight at it with his spear, leaving his grandsire standing aghast behind him. He got his boar sure enough, but not before the great beast gored his thigh. He took such a gash that men wondered whether he'd ever walk straight again, which he did of course, though he bears the scar of it about him still. He was too proud for patience, you see – just like you – though he learned more sense in later years.'

I was about to walk away and leave them to it when I heard the shaky voice of Telemachus protest, 'But I've been patient. I've waited patiently for years and years and it feels like he's never coming back. I think he must be dead.'

'He's no deader than I am,' Eurycleia said. 'He's far too good a sailor to get wrecked by any storm, if that's what you're thinking. And he's too crafty to be kept down for long by any villains who may cross him. Believe you me, my boy, your father's the rarest of men. The gods have a care for a man like that.'

'Then why hasn't he come back?'

'I don't know,' Eurycleia answered, a little flustered now. 'Perhaps the fancy's taken him to go adventuring again. I wouldn't put it past him. Perhaps he's taken the Black Sea passage like Jason before him and come up against the Clashing Rocks, or got himself enchanted by the Sirens' song, or hasn't yet found the narrow way between Scylla and Charybdis. He always loved those old stories. He loved them just as much as you do. Perhaps he's gone to find out if there's any truth to them, and when he comes home he'll bring back something magical and splendid like the Golden Fleece. That's just the kind of thing Odysseus would do if he took a mind to it.'

I don't know what effect this fanciful gesture of consolation had on the mind of Telemachus but Eurycleia's words ignited my own imagination. I began to see how my *Lay of Lord Odysseus* might be embellished by motifs from those stories. I imagined his ship picking its way through the blue ice floes that came drifting across its bows out of the freezing fog of the Black Sea. I knew that if there was any chance of hearing the Sirens' song, then Odysseus would want to hear it. Like Jason, he would have himself strapped to the mast with cables while his crew rowed past the enchanted island with their ears stopped up with wax. With my mind already racing, I persuaded myself that if anyone could steer a ship between the many-headed monster Scylla, keeping watch from her cave on the cliff, and the fearful whirlpool of Charybdis, then Odysseus certainly could. So I hurried away down the passage with the song of the Sirens thrilling through my mind, and when I went to bed I lay there yearning for the day when my lay was done and I would be crowned with laurels as the greatest of all bards.

Then, in the small hours, I was jolted back to my senses by the miserable thought that all those songs had already been written. Everybody knew them. Those marvellous adventures belonged to the story of Jason: anywhere outside Ithaca, I would be laughed out of court if I tried to claim them for Odysseus.

Yet my mind would not rest and, before dawn broke, another thought struck me. There was a story belonging to our island that might still be turned into a noble song. It was a crude enough tale of the encounter between our ancient folk hero Oulixos and a one-eyed cannibal giant that devoured some of his men when they landed on his island. Trapped in the giant's cave, Oulixos and his men blinded the Cyclops and made their escape. But wasn't it possible that on his voyage home Odysseus had chanced on that same island? With all his resourcefulness, surely he would think up some ingenious way of outwitting that dull monster?

And so it was that, because I heard an old nurse comforting my friend with stories, I conceived the first lines of a song that would not be completed till after Odysseus' return and is sung across Argos by bards who claim it for their own. As is well-known, the song tells how Odysseus and his men escaped from the island of the Cyclopes by fooling Polyphemus into the belief that a man called 'Nobody' had put out his eye. But with Odysseus now long dead, I feel free to tell how there was once a time when his strong sense of identity was so reduced by his ordeals that Odysseus truly believed that he had become Nobody indeed.

Nobodysseus

The sight of their leader collapsed and weeping in the arms of Guneus shocked the crew of *The Fair Return* into a state of dumb bewilderment. This was Odysseus, their lord and captain, the most endlessly resourceful of men and among the most eloquent. What news could be so bad as to wreck him like this?

And Guneus himself scarcely knew what to say or do in that moment because the whole weight of Odysseus' upper body had slumped against his chest as if all the power had drained from his legs and he was left with strength only to gasp and shudder as he wept.

'I meant no harm,' Guneus heard himself saying after a time. 'The gods are just, Odysseus. I'm sure all will be well.' But Odysseus had passed beyond reach, beyond hearing and each word was of small account against the force of the blizzard gathering inside his mind. The tears running down his face and the sobs shaking his body were no longer marks of grief or loss or any other emotion with a known name: simply the outward signs of a suddenly accelerated process of dissolution over which he had no control, and which was as impersonal in its power as a flash-flood crashing through a forest and on into the chambers of a well-built house.

Guneus turned his head towards the dumbstruck men along

the beach and shouted, 'Give me a hand here, someone. This man needs help.' Then Baius came running, and Demonax, and Eurybates who now wore a vermilion cloth wrapped about his wounded temple in the Libyan fashion. But Odysseus fended them all off as though they were Furies coming at him like bats out of the dark. He pushed Guneus away, staggered in the sand, and stood swaying with his head in his hands and the sobs juddering through him and a hoarse, protracted noise, like the creaking of a door, breaking from his mouth.

Eurymachus came up alongside Guneus, demanding to know what was happening and was astounded to see Odysseus stare at him with a grimace of horror across his face, almost as though he was covered in blood, before turning away and making for his lodge with one hand still pressed to his head.

'What happened between you?' Eurymachus demanded of the armoured man across from him, who was tugging in puzzlement at his beard. 'What did you say to him?'

Guneus opened his hands as if to demonstrate his harmlessness. 'I just told him what's been happening at home. The news isn't good. It's given him a shock, I'm afraid. He'll be all right again when he gets over it.'

Yet the man's voice lacked the confidence of the opinion, and as the hours passed, the condition of Odysseus deteriorated further. He sat inside his lodge, rocking backwards and forwards, groaning and holding his head, and would accept no comfort from anyone – not the women who were used to serving him, nor from any of the friends who approached him. He either stared at them aghast without responding or snarled like an injured dog, demanding that they let him be. They muttered together outside the lodge, all of them dismayed by what they too had now learned of events back home in Ithaca and across all Argos, yet still unable to comprehend why Odysseus had been so unmanned by the news.

Arguments broke out as to what best should be done to help him, and the situation became further confused when Guneus decided that he had no wish to see his own crew contaminated by the febrile atmosphere of this camp. There were a couple of hours of light left in the day and he decided to use them to make progress towards the mouth of the river Cinyps rather than allowing his crew to sink into a stupor with this demoralised bunch of Ithacans. Not all his men were happy at being ordered back to sea but he forced his will on them, and climbed aboard his ship shouting to the Ithacans watching from the shore that if any of them were of the mind to shape up, he could always use good men.

Glaucus, captain of the *Nereid*, and Demonax of the *Swordfish* glanced uneasily at one another as they watched the Thessalian pentekonter pull out into the bay.

A rosy glow of sunlight glanced off her sail as it billowed from the yard. The oars were shipped, spindrift scattered from the prow, and a white wake glistened behind the vessel as she scudded westwards on the breeze. For the landlocked Ithacans it was like watching their own lives recede.

Some time after the sun had gone down Eurylochus decided to try to speak to his leader again. A good sailor, cautious and pragmatic, always with a keen eye for the run of the weather, he was never gifted with the sharpest of wits but had a feeling heart and could not bear to think of his old friend lying wretchedly alone. Prepared for a further angry dismissal, he went into the lodge with an oil-lamp in one hand and a bowl of food in the other, and found his captain lying on his bed in a dishevelled state.

'I've brought you some food,' he said gently. 'You should try to eat something.' When no answer came, he put down the lamp and bowl, stood uncertainly for a moment, then said, 'It's me – your old shipmate Eurylochus. You can talk to me.'

By the dim light of the lamp he saw Odysseus turn over on the bed. A haggard face looked up at him.

'Eurylochus?'

'That's right, sir,' the man answered, encouraged, 'Eurylochus, as ever was.' He took the hand that Odysseus reached out to him and felt the strength of its grip.

'I keep seeing her,' Odysseus said, 'again and again. I can't get my head clear.'

Eurylochus nodded his head in sympathy, certain now that he understood the cause of the man's grief. 'I'm sure you there's no need to trouble your head over Penelope, lord. Your wife has always loved you and she always will. You've got nothing to fear there, whatever foul lies Guneus was spreading.'

But Odysseus frowned and shook his head. 'No, it's not her' he said. 'You don't understand.'

Eurylochus furrowed his brow. 'Then who, sir? Who do you see?'

Odysseus lifted his stricken face. 'Polyxena,' he whispered. 'Even in the dark, she's there, looking back at me.'

Bewildered by the response, Eurylochus said, 'King Priam's daughter, you mean? The one that young Neoptolemus took in vengeance for his father? She's long dead and in the Land of Shades, lord. You don't have to worry about her.'

Tightening his grip on his friend's wrist, Odysseus said, 'We never atoned for her. That's why she won't let me go. Don't you see it? She was innocent and not one of us atoned for her death. We shan't ever be free of her now, not unless . . .'

Swallowing, calling silently on the gods for protection, Eurylochus said, 'Unless what, sir?'

'The thing is, I keep seeing her – even when I close my eyes she's there across from me. I see her baring her breasts on Achilles' tomb, lifting her chin before the sword, defying us, knowing that she'll always be there.'

'But you didn't kill her, lord,' Eurylochus tried to reason with him. 'If there's still blood-guilt there, it's none of yours. It lies with Neoptolemus.'

'I should have prevented him. I knew what he was going to do and I should have stopped it. He was only a boy. A boy possessed by what he thought was his father's shade. But he was too young. He should never have been at Troy. And neither should Achilles before him. And it was me who brought him there.'

'Indeed it was,' his friend encouraged him, 'and because you brought Achilles to Troy, Hector was killed, and it was because of that we won.'

But his bluff attempt at confirmation and reassurance sparked only anger. 'Did we, Eurylochus?' Odysseus demanded. 'Tell me, what did we win? Yes, we burned Troy and killed men in their thousands, but if Agamemnon and the others lost everything when they got back, and men like Guneus and hundreds of others like him are counting themselves lucky just to get out of the war alive, what did we win that's worth all that suffering, all those deaths?'

'You can't start to think that way,' Eurylochus protested. 'Madness lies that way.'

'But so does the truth,' Odysseus returned, 'and Polyxena knows that. That's why she won't let me go. She's always there, tilting her neck to show me her wound as if to say, "It was you, Odysseus. You were the cause of all of this." '

Eurylochus looked down in perplexity as his captain's body began to shake again. The hairs at the back of his neck were prickling. In the flickering lamp-light he sensed a presence that should not be there and the knowledge chilled his heart. He glanced around the gloomy lodge as though expecting to see the ghost of the dead girl standing in the shadows with the blood of a sword-wound flowing from her neck. He wanted to get out of there but how could he leave his lord to tremble on that desolate bed? Outside the notes of a flute haunted the evening air with their yearning for home.

Eurylochus said, 'This is only an evil dream. I think you must have taken some kind of a fever, lord. It will pass. Soon it will pass.'

'You don't understand,' Odysseus snapped back at him. 'This isn't the first and it won't be the last. There are others who come. I see all the others too – the ones we cut down like cattle in the streets of Troy. Sometimes in broad daylight I turn round and there they are, still lying in their blood and piss – the old men with their guts hanging out in gaudy rags, the boys with smashed heads – boys who'd never lifted a weapon . . . lying in piles in the streets where we burned them.'

'But we've killed men before,' Eurylochus said. 'We've taken other towns and men died there, and you weren't like this afterwards. If we won the victory, lord, it's because the gods gave it to us. Divine Athena spoke to you in your dream. It was she who showed you how to give us victory. And if the gods were with you, why should you reproach yourself?'

'Because I gave my word,' Odysseus snarled. 'It was never meant to be that way. All the blood of Troy is on my head.'

'It's done, lord,' Eurylochus urged him, almost impatiently now. 'It's done and it's over and you must put these things from your mind.'

But it was as if Odysseus had not heard him. 'That child never hurt anyone in all her days,' he said. 'She was innocent. Achilles saw it well enough. She was an innocent caught up in all the violence of our pride and fury. And it's as if . . . as if . . . It's as if she sees every terrible thing I've done and it's all fixed in her eyes like a frieze carved in marble, and none of it can ever be forgotten or forgiven now . . .'

'I think it's time we got you home, sir,' Eurylochus said. 'Guneus is right. We've stayed too long in this place and it's started to rot the bottom of our minds. Let's put back out to sea tomorrow and get the clean wind filling our sail . . . You'll soon start to feel better then, you'll see. The good salt-wind will blow these dreams away, and once you're home . . .'

'I can't,' Odysseus snapped at him. 'I can't go home.'

'Course you can, sir. With a favouring wind we can be there inside the week. And your lady is waiting for you. She's been waiting for ten long years. And that boy of yours – Telemachus – you've said it often enough yourself – he must be capering like a wild young horse for want of a father's hand.'

'I can't.' Odysseus freed his friend's wrist from his grip and sat up with his hands clutching at his head, saying over and over again, 'I can't, I can't.'

'Why not, lord? I don't understand. Why can't you go home?'

'Because I'm not fit.' The sobbing shook his whole frame again.

'Not right now you're not,' Eurylochus put a hand to his shoulder. 'I can see that clear enough. But we'll soon have you well again.'

Angrily Odysseus pulled the hand away. 'I'm not fit to touch her. Not with these hands. Don't you see? There's too much blood on them. So much blood and so much death that I'm not fit to be among decent people any more. Penelope wouldn't want me near our son like this. She wouldn't even know me because I don't know who I am myself. I don't know what I'm for. I don't know what to do.' He looked up at his friend with a pang of appeal in his eyes. 'Tell me, Eurylochus,' he pleaded, 'what do you do when you don't know what to do?'

But the worried seaman had no answer. He looked down at this ruin of the man he had known and loved and admired since he was a boy, and he too had no idea what to do except take his lord's weeping head into his arms and hold it against his chest and pray to all the gods he could think of to have mercy on them both.

That night Odysseus woke from a brief hour or two of troubled sleep with a headache so violent that he thought his brain must be bursting inside his skull. He had been wounded many times in his life but never had he known pain such as this. The hand of a god might have been twisting a stick inside a leather strap made fast about his temples. He might have been bleeding inside his head.

His groans woke Eurylochus, who had fallen asleep on the floor at his side. 'What is it, lord?' he cried.

But Odysseus could scarcely speak for the strength of the storm inside his head. 'My head,' he groaned. 'My head feels as though it must split apart.'

Eurylochus looked helplessly down at him. 'What can I do for you?' he asked, clenching and unclenching his fists.

'I don't know, I don't know,' Odysseus gasped. 'In the name of all the gods, you could take a sword to my head and put me from this pain.'

'I think some god is angry with you, lord,' Eurylochus muttered grimly. 'Shall I go out and make the offerings?'

But Odysseus had the strength only to nod his vague assent before he turned to the wall moaning with his head clutched between his hands.

By the morning the intensity of the pain had eased a little, though Odysseus still lay inside his lodge, white-faced and red-eyed, like a shipwrecked mariner barely clinging on to life. He drank some water but refused all food and asked only to be left alone. So he was angry at first when Eurylochus came back into the lodge saying that he had brought Hanno with him, for the Libyan claimed to have some understanding of physic and believed he might be able to offer help.

'I told you to leave me alone,' Odysseus growled.

But Hanno stood before him unruffled. 'Your friend thinks only to ease your suffering,' he said quietly. 'I have mixed something with this water that may ease the pain a little. Come, drink it. Then you will sleep for a time and I will come and see you again when you awake.'

Several hours later Hanno returned alone to the lodge. As the Libyan entered, Odysseus jumped up as if he had been startled and turned to see who was there, one hand already feeling about the bed for a weapon and finding none.

'Be calm, friend,' the Libyan said. 'No one means you harm.' He crouched beside Odysseus, laid a hand across his brow, then lifted the lid of each eye in turn and looked inside. 'How is the pain inside your head now?' he asked.

'It's still there,' Odysseus frowned, 'still bad, but duller than it was.'

'Tell me how it was.'

'I've never known pain like it. I think it was like the pain that Zeus himself must have felt when Divine Athena was labouring to be born inside his head.'

Frowning, Hanno was pondering that remark when Odysseus added, 'I wanted Eurylochus to smash my head open. Anything to stop the pain.'

Hanno nodded and said, 'Your friend tells me that your mind has become like our desert air and is showing things that are not truly there.'

'I see what I see.' Odysseus turned his face towards the mud wall of his hut. 'Eurylochus shouldn't have spoken to anyone about it.'

'How could he not when his friends saw him making offerings on your behalf in the night? You inspire great love in your men, Lord Odysseus. Everyone is concerned for you.' But when he smiled down into the haggard face he saw that his words had started tears at the man's eyes and that his hands were trembling again. 'I think your friend spoke wiser than he knew,' Hanno said. 'This is more than bodily sickness. It seems some god is indeed at work on you.'

'If I learned anything at Troy,' Odysseus snapped back, 'it's that men are too quick to blame the gods for the troubles that afflict them.'

'Perhaps so,' Hanno smiled, 'but pain is sometimes the only way the gods can find to make us face the truth of things. And because it is pain we fail to see it as their gift to us.'

'It's a gift I can live without.'

'No doubt you will.' Hanno took a small flask from the goatskin bag slung at his side and measured a few drops of liquid into a gourd of water. As he did so, he added, 'But first you must find the cause of your suffering.'

'I know the cause. I know what I've done. I know it can never be undone and that this is the price I have to pay.'

'So you presume to know the will of the gods without consulting them?'

'Leave me be,' Odysseus groaned. 'My head hurts too much to argue with you.'

'I seek no argument, but I will let you rest some more. Drink this. It may ease the pain further.' The Libyan returned the flask to the bag, gathered his robe at his shoulders and made to leave. 'In the meantime,' he said as he reached the door, 'perhaps you should think more about what you said to me a few moments ago.'

'What? What did I say?'

'That your head ached like that of Zeus in the time before Athena sprang from his head. Perhaps it is she who rages inside you. Perhaps she is trying to be born again in you.' And even as Odysseus gasped at what he took to be the impiety of the remark, Hanno was gone into the ruddy glow of the evening light.

Odysseus lay awake for a long time afterwards, brooding on how heavily the hands of the gods had come down against him since he had sailed from Troy. That Poseidon should oppose him with storms at sea was to be expected – the blue-haired god of the deeps had favoured Troy throughout the war. But that Divine Athena, the goddess he had always revered, should permit his wife and child and island to be taken from him – the thought of that was more than he could bear. Yet how could any Argive warrior expect favour of her when, in the scramble to plunder Troy, not one of them had made atonement for the way her temple had been violated? His own mind had been in such turmoil at that time that he too had neglected to make offerings to the goddess who had singled him out for special favour. Athena had visited him in the dream through which he had conceived the stratagem of the wooden horse, and by doing so she had made him the instrument of her victory; and if it was she who was causing him such anguish now that he could hardly hold his head up on his shoulders, then he need look no further for the cause than in the blindness of his heart.

He did not wait for Hanno to come to him again but sent for him late that night, and then insisted that they be left alone. His head was still aching as though he had been struck there by a hand-axe, but he gritted his teeth to speak civilly to the Libyan who was discomfited from having been disturbed in his sleep.

'I was thinking of what you said of Divine Athena,' he said. 'I see now that I have neglected to make my offerings to her. I need to do her proper honour.'

'I'm sure that would be wise,' Hanno answered, 'but what has it to do with me?'

'I seem to recall you saying that she has a shrine somewhere near here at Lake Tritonis – the place where she first sprang from her father's head?'

Hanno pulled down the corners of his mouth. Had he been woken just for this? The hour was late and he was in no mood for listening to this foreigner's ravings.

'That is not the story of her birth as they tell it at the shrine,' he said, 'nor do they call her by that name.'

'Then what name does she go by and what story do they tell?'

'Her sacred name is Neith. It was so long before you Argives claimed her for the daughter of Zeus.'

'Then why did you call her Athena?'

'Because it was the name by which Jason called her when he dedicated a tripod at the shrine.'

'So Athena and this Neith – they are one and the same?'

Hanno stirred uncomfortably. 'There is only one Goddess, though she has many aspects. And there is none greater than she who bore the aegis long before Zeus claimed it for himself.'

Odysseus frowned impatiently. 'I'm not about to argue theology with you. Just tell me straight – is the shrine sacred to Athena or not?'

'If you insist on calling her so, then yes.'

'Then I will go there.'

Hanno opened his hands. 'I wish you well of your journey.' He got up as if to leave but Odysseus reached out a hand to stop him.

'Wait,' he said. 'I need to know more. Can I get to the shrine by ship?'

The Libyan's shrug expressed no great interest. 'Perhaps. I am no sailor. All I know is that Jason's ship got landlocked there.'

'Why?' Odysseus demanded. 'How did that happen?'

Hanno shrugged. 'Sometimes there are movements in the salt that covers the land in those parts. Jason was stranded when the river leading to the lake became thick with salt behind him. That was why he made his offerings to the goddess – that she might free his vessel from the grip of her lake.'

Struggling against the pain pounding in his head, Odysseus said, 'But there must be an overland route from here?'

'Of course. But it has dangers.'

'What dangers?'

'As you come close to the lake the land is covered with a crust of salt. In places the crust is thin and the mud lies deep beneath it. It is said that whole caravans have been swallowed up without trace because they did not know the safe way.'

'Then we shall take a guide who knows that way.'

Hanno gave a little laugh. 'First you must find one. The lake is more than a hundred miles away across the plain. As you have seen, the people here are lazy. Why should they stir themselves for a foreigner in trouble with the gods?'

Odysseus glowered at the complacent face across from him. 'Didn't you say that your own people live somewhere near the lake?'

Hanno stood up, looking away as he wrapped the folds of his robe around his shoulders against the chill of the night outside. But Odysseus saw that he had remembered aright. Quietly he said, 'You will be my guide, Hanno.'

'Me?' Again the Libyan gave a mirthless laugh. 'Why should I trouble myself to go with you?'

Dismayed to find the Libyan unresponsive to his needs, Odysseus drew on the cold spring of ruthlessness that had sustained him through the thick of many battles. 'Because,' he replied, and his voice was deadly serious, 'either I or one of my men will kill you if you do not.'

★ ★ ★

High on the western horizon soared the snow-draped crests of mountains that changed colour subtly with each hour of the day, but their route lay across a low-lying basin of flat scrubland where every few miles a mud-brick hamlet, shaded by date-palms and olive-trees, huddled like a beggar above its spring.

With his head in pain and his sense of actuality still unhinged, Odysseus rode the swaying hump of his camel, shielding his eyes against the glare of the sun like a man at the mercy of a delirious dream. Wrapped in linen robes against the dust that rose in sharp flurries around his mouth and eyes, Eurylochus rode ahead of him, grumbling at his mount. Behind Odysseus came the various servants and carriers who had been conscripted for the journey, leading pack-laden camels and mules. A small boy in a dirty smock drove along a few scrawny goats with a switch. Hanno headed the procession, closely accompanied by young Elpenor who was under strict instructions to keep watch over their guide and make sure that he did not abandon them in the night.

The rest of the men had remained behind at Zarzis under the command of their captains Glaucus and Demonax. Already unsettled by the encounter with Guneus and the unaccountable behaviour of Odysseus, they watched their leader ride off into the hazy shimmer of light over the scrub, wondering whether they would ever see him again. After what they had learned of the changes in Argos and Ithaca, some of them — mostly from the crew of the *Nereid* — were wondering whether it might not have been wiser to throw in their lot with Guneus and make a fresh start along the coast in Libya. It was they who decided to set to work on repairing the ships at last. Others were too far gone in their taste for the lotus to care either way.

Meanwhile, with each day that passed, Odysseus felt himself growing ever more lost in an alien region where the phantasms still haunting his mind were sometimes exceeded in strangeness by the shifting phenomena of light in this unstable world. The green fronds of palm-groves beckoned him on across the dusty plain only to vanish as the air quivered and erased them before his eyes. When the caravan rested at one hill-crest town larger than others along the way, the Ithacans were amazed by the sight waiting for them there. A ring of excited men were jumping and shouting to a clattering of drums and rattles as they watched two bull-camels wrestling together. White froth sputtered from the nostrils of the great beasts as they butted at one another with powerful necks. Uttering doleful groans, each animal strove to lock a knobbly foreleg round that of his opponent and push him off balance – a spectacle which seemed as improbable to Odysseus as it was grotesque. Yet his own warrior heart stirred with recognition both of victory and defeat when one of the camels – a shaggy, boastful beast with fearsome yellow teeth – leaned its full weight on the other and forced it to the ground. Then the shouting men were pulling the beasts apart.

The noises of the journey too fell strangely on Odysseus' ears. In the expanses of the night, the barks and yelps of unidentifiable creatures echoed among the rocks; and as the camels picked their delicate way through the scrub by day, one of the drivers sang for much of the time – a tuneless, droning dirge that began to drive Odysseus to distraction. He frightened the fellow into silence for a while, but not long afterwards the chanting was resumed.

Late one day, they were passing through a patch of scrub relieved only by pink oleanders, when the small boy spotted a horned viper slithering away at their approach. If he had not cried out a warning, Eurylochus, who had been easing himself among the rocks, might have stepped onto the snake.

The episode prompted Hanno to recall the story of how one of Jason's followers, a man called Mopsus, had taken a bite from the fangs of such a snake. Mopsus had apparently died for a time, only to rise again and discover that he was now possessed of mantic powers. An oracle had been dedicated to him near the shrine of Neith. With a wry smile, Hanno suggested that the oracle might furnish Odysseus with an answer to the questions troubling his mind.

Eurylochus declared that he, for one, was glad enough to remain unbitten, just as he was, and proceeded to strike up a lively friendship with the Libyan boy.

After they had been travelling for five days, Hanno pointed ahead to where the land shone with a fierce white sheen as if snow had fallen and frozen to an ice-sheet across the land. As they came closer the glare became so intense that Odysseus could not bear to fix his eyes on it. He wrapped a scarf about his face and rocked back and forth blindly to the sway of his mount, listening to the dry crunch of salt beneath the camel's feet.

Late one afternoon, feeling the heat go out of the day, Odysseus peered out from his scarf and saw how the light off the salt was softening to an ochreous golden-brown as the sun declined. Moments later, the weight of a laden beast broke through the salt-crust into the ooze beneath. The camel fell to its knees and the crust splintered again in a splash of mud. Yelping and shouting, the drivers tugged at the harness of the fallen animal, pushing at its haunches till its hooves staggered free of the mud and it was chivvied with a switch back onto firmer ground. The next day, after another chilly night beneath the stars, the sky was full of birds, and they were travelling round the marshy, reed-fringed edge of Lake Tritonis.

That evening Hanno chose to pitch camp in a place where they could wash the dust from their skins and bathe their aching bodies in the soothing bubbles of a hot spring near the margin of the lake. Tranquil flocks of stilt-legged fowl waded among the reeds under a blue-mauve sky. A huge moon was already gathering radiance as, for the first time in many weeks, Odysseus let himself relax in the sulphurous smell of tepid water. He felt his mind dispersing into peace. He had done the right thing in making this pilgrimage into Libya. Triton-born Athena was waiting for him here. She would offer guidance to his soul.

But the brawny body of Eurylochus leapt into the spring at that moment, splashing the water over his head, cleansing the dust from his hair and beard. 'The god be thanked that blessed this patch of land with springs,' he whooped. 'I was beginning to think I'd crumble into salt before this trek was over.' He grinned at Odysseus, sliced his hand into the water and sent a warm wave splashing across his companion's face. 'What stories we'll have to tell when we get back to Ithaca,' he shouted. 'What stories we'll have to tell!'

Odysseus nodded, trying to smile; but the moment's peace had passed. He thought of his wife crying out with pleasure in the arms of a younger man. He thought of how he would be a stranger to his son when he returned to the island. Both thoughts intensified his pain. Lacking all confidence that he would ever see the shores of Ithaca again, he felt his heart turn hard inside him.

The temple, when they came to it, was like no important shrine he had ever seen. During the arduous haul across the hot Libyan plain, he had allowed himself to dream of something stupendous and graceful like Athena's sanctuary on the Parthenon rock at Athens, or the even grander colonnades of the Palladian temple in the citadel at Troy, which was no more than ash and rubble now. Athena was accustomed to such state. So how could the Libyans imagine that she would be content with a thatched hut of mustard-coloured brick on which nothing more decorous than geometrical patterns had been inscribed? And the reed-hurdles marking off the boundary of the sacred precinct might have kept a herd of goats from straying into corn, but such crude handi-work inspired no awe.

Odysseus turned in a misery of disappointment to Hanno, demanding to know whether this mud-built hovel was the best the Libyans could offer to the Daughter of Zeus.

Hanno, who had been standing before the entrance to the precinct with a clenched fist held to his forehead and his head bowed low, studied him for a long moment before speaking. 'This temple was old before Troy was built,' he answered quietly. 'The Goddess has dwelt among these springs beside this lake since the sun first rose and the moon first crossed the sky. The Pharaohs of

Egypt acknowledged the sanctity of this place long before Minos ruled in Crete. Great Kings of Ethiopia have come to make obeisance here. Others have travelled from the forests of the south. You would do well to remember that your Argive hero Jason was once forced to bow before its power. And if you are wise, my friend, you will not speak of the Triple Goddess as the daughter of Zeus when you stand before the temple-maidens. Now come, you must be washed clean of the blood you bring with you from all the killing you have done. And you must try to empty your heart of all vainglorious pride. Only then will you be fit to discover whether your offerings will be found acceptable at the sacred shrine of Neith.'

The rites to which Odysseus submitted in the sanctuary at Lake Tritonis lasted a day and a night and then another day; and he was left with plenty of time to think about them as he made the long journey back to his ships at Zarzis. Not that he found it possible to think clearly even then, for all of the rites except one had been conducted in a language he did not understand. They were performed by dark-skinned temple-maidens, wearing goatskin garments fringed with thongs, who smelled of sweat and curd and the medicinal herbs they burned about his head. While some of them chastised his flesh with scourges, others danced to the beat of drums and gongs and cymbals, singing songs of invocation. Step by step, hour by hour in the heat of the day, he was brought closer to the inner sanctum of the shrine, and as each stage of the rite was completed, they raised their voices in ululating shrieks of triumph such as he had once heard the Amazon warriors utter on the battlefield at Troy.

But Odysseus had eaten nothing since cock-crow on the previous day, and he was given only a strong, milky-coloured wine to drink, so his head was swimming in a trance-like condition by the time Hanno, who had been called upon to act as his interpreter throughout, informed him that it was time to make his offering.

Less was required of him than he expected. Apart from the initial payment of fees to the temple-guardians, all that the goddess asked was that he sacrifice a black ram and offer up its fleece to her. In his time Odysseus had killed more sheep than he could recall. He had grown up on Ithaca knowing the knack of it; so he was surprised and irritated when the fat ram he had purchased from the temple stockyard would not quietly bend to his strength. The animal wrestled in his grip, trying to butt away the hand that held the knife. Only with difficulty did he wrench it over on to its haunches and pull back its head. As he drew the blade across its throat, the animal was staring up at him through the slots of its eyes, still bleating refusal. Even then, with the life passing out of it, the beast struggled between his knees.

Odysseus was trembling and sweating as he sheared the fleece from its back. When he looked up to make the offering, he saw a figure standing over him at the threshold of the shrine. She too wore goat-skins, but where the robes of the maidens had been fringed with thongs, this tall priestess was draped in a heavy leather aegis fringed with vipers' heads. Two snakes were entwined around the buckle at her belly. The face gazing down at him was a black gorgon mask with ram's horns curling into serpents in its hair. Its bulging eyes were pierced by narrow slits. Cowry shells shone like teeth in the hideous gaping mouth.

From out of the mask came an incomprehensible screech that Odysseus recognized as a demand. He looked round for Hanno but the Libyan had vanished. Only the temple-maidens stood about him with expressions of dismay. The screech came again. Uncertain what else to do, Odysseus lifted the fleece from the ram's carcass and offered it with a lowered head. Two of the maidens stepped towards him, took the fleece from his grasp and gave it into the hands of the priestess, who raised her masked face and held up the fleece as if showing it in evidence to the moon. Uttering a few words in her archaic tongue, she turned with the snakeheads swinging at her skirts, and entered into the darkness of the shrine.

To Odysseus it seemed that he was kept standing for a very long time. A wicker hurdle stood immediately inside the entrance to the hut, so he could see nothing in the gloom. All he could hear was a prolonged low chanting, almost like the drone of bees. The event had begun to feel meaningless and primitive. His head was throbbing. He was swaying where he stood. He told himself that any trepidation he felt before that rudimentary shrine was only the fear of old night that lurks in all men's hearts and is easily stirred by superstitious practices. What seemed certain was that Divine Athena, Daughter of Sky-Father Zeus, in all her graceful, athletic radiance, was not to be found among these Libyan savages. He should never have come.

But having offered himself up before this Neith, this goddess of the Libyans, it would be unlucky to disrupt the ritual. So Odysseus of Ithaca stood and waited, weeping at what he had become. The dark fell round him. He was hungry and weary and drunk, and the fierce moonlight crashed like a gong inside his head. When he closed his eyes he saw Polyxena staring at him with her bloody throat.

He was all but ready to faint by the time he became aware of two temple-maidens standing at his side. One of them took him by the arm and led him across the dusty ground of the precinct and through a grove of palm trees to where a round hovel built of wattle and daub stood beside a spring. The other maiden had followed them, carrying the fleece which she now spread out on the dirt floor in there. Then she pointed to a gourd filled with water from the spring. Otherwise the hut was quite empty.

Odysseus was looking around in dismay when the maiden who had brought him there spoke in a thickly accented version of his own language. 'Here you sleep,' she said pointing to the fleece. 'In the night a dream comes. When the sun comes in the sky you speak the dream to us.'

He did dream that night but the women of the temple seemed unable to make much sense of it. They merely shook their heads and muttered in worried tones when Hanno tried to translate the images of a dream that was shaped by an old story unknown to all of them except Odysseus.

In the dream his ship had made landfall on a fertile island where meadows ran down the cliffs to the shore. At the head of his men, he set out to explore and came upon a cave hung with laurel boughs where two kid-goats were penned. Only when, as is the way with dreams, time shifted suddenly and he saw the one-eyed monster entering the cave, did he know that he was dreaming the story of the Ithacan folk-hero Oulixos and the Cyclops Polyphemus. But the story got confused in the dreaming. He and his men contrived to put out the ogre's eye and to escape from the cave by clinging under the fleeces of his flock of sheep; but when Odysseus stared into the face of the Cyclops with its burned-out ruin of a single eye, it seemed to be his own face that he saw. And when he tried to shout out in triumph as the doer of this deed, he could not remember his name.

He had woken from the dream with the deranging sense of not knowing who he was, and that his name was Nobody.

So bleakly did the dream mirror back to him the dark cave of his despair that Odysseus stood in no need of interpreters. Nor did he expect to take comfort from the women who muttered round him. Hanno, however, listened intently. After what seemed like an endless disquisition from an old crone with withered breasts, who rocked and chanted as she spoke, he turned to confront Odysseus.

'She says that in her wisdom the Goddess has turned the dark side of her face towards you,' he said, 'but you are not yet willing to look on it. She says that your mind is sharp like the edge of a sword but that the sword has turned its edge against itself. She says that your heart is so full of blood that it will burst inside you if you do not find a way to open it again. She says that she is sorry but at this season of your soul she can find no way into your darkness. She says that you will speak to the Goddess again in another place at another time but she fears that many years must pass before your soul stands up inside your skin again.'

Though he had expected nothing of this consultation, Odysseus's heart was stricken by this bleak confirmation of his desperate state. He got up and turned away, neglecting even to thank the priestess in his misery.

Narrowing his eyes against the blazing dazzle of light off Lake Tritonis, he felt bereft of everything that was Odysseus. His wit, intelligence, eloquence, courage, inventiveness – all were gone. All that remained to him was an ageing body and a grizzled head in which he could still feel the thunder of his pain. He was without a ship even – at least until that body had been dragged back to where his men were guzzling the lotus fruit. His limbs flooded with weariness at the thought.

'There is still the oracle,' Hanno was saying. 'If you have questions to ask, its priest may know better how to address an Argive's heart.'

Though they arrived at the place of the oracle before noon, the queue of people waiting with questions to ask was so long that it was nearly sundown before Odysseus paid his dues and presented himself before the scrawny, caramel-coloured figure wrapped in a sky-blue robe, who sat beneath a thatched awning at the edge of the lake. Crude pictures of birds were carved into the wooden poles supporting his pavilion. A black woman crouched behind him, flicking the flies from her face with a horsehair whisk. A horned viper, presumably with drawn fangs, lay coiled beside her in the shadow of a stone.

The man gave a cheerful, wall-eyed grin as Odysseus approached. 'It's a long time since we saw an Argive,' he said. 'Where are you from?'

'Ask the oracle,' Odysseus replied.

The man's face fell at once. When he spoke again, the friendliness had gone from his voice. 'The Oracle of Mopsus welcomes all who seek its aid, but the god answers only either *yes* or *no*. Tell me, is there blood on your hands?'

With a wry grimace, Odysseus said, 'More than you would believe.'

The man shrugged. 'But you have made your offering at the shrine of Neith? You have been cleansed there?'

'If you can call it cleansing, yes.'

'Very well. We shall proceed.' He studied Odysseus for a moment with his mouth down-turned. 'You would be wise to choose your question with great care.'

'I've already chosen it,' Odysseus said. 'Must I speak it aloud?'

Again the man shrugged. 'It is between you and the god.'

'Then I will keep it that way.'

The man grunted, turned his head and snapped his fingers at the woman who picked up an object wrapped in folds of blue linen from the ground at her side.

Then he reached for Odysseus's hand, opened it, and studied the lines inscribed there for a few seconds before placing a smooth pearly-white pebble in his palm. He touched the stone with the tip of his finger, saying, 'Yes.' Then he opened the other hand, placed a shiny black pebble inside it and said, 'No.'

Nodding sagely, as if some great mystery had been revealed, he moved to one side and the woman shuffled forward, chanting quietly, and crouched before Odysseus to unwrap the folds of linen. The Ithacan smiled grimly at what was revealed. She was holding a bronze war-helmet cast in the old Lapith fashion, plain but for its dents and scratches, and without a plume. One of its leather cheek-guards had gone and the other dangled dry and frayed from its rings. Presumably this antique object had once adorned the prophetic head of Mopsus.

This type of oracle was well-known to him. He told Hanno to leave, took the helmet from the woman's hands, dropped the pebbles inside it and sat for a time with his eyes closed, concentrating his mind on the question he wished to ask. Then he began to move his hands in a circular motion until the stones rattled inside the bronze. Grimly aware of his own absurdity, he swayed his shoulders, swivelling the helmet faster and faster until one of the stones jumped over the rim and fell to the ground before him. It was blacker than the woman's skin. She raised the whites of her eyes, sighed impassively, and took the helmet from his hands to wrap it in the linen folds. The oracle had spoken. It was time to go.

The disaster of this whole inauspicious expedition felt complete to Odysseus when he discovered the next morning that Hanno had slipped away from their camp in the night. Young Elpenor, who was supposed to keep watch over the Libyan, had drunk too much throughout the heat of the afternoon and fallen into a stupor of sleep.

Furious with the contrite young man, Eurylochus clouted him round the ears, while Odysseus looked on in a trance of dismay.

Their camels and pack-mules still stood tethered in the shade of a spring, but when the three Ithacans pooled their resources, they realized they had only the vaguest picture of the landscape through which they had passed on their way to the shrine. They could take their general orientation from the sun, and knew to keep the lake at their backs and the snow-clad range of mountains to the north; but not one of them was confident that he could guide the others across the salt-flats and on into the almost featureless waste of scrubland beyond.

An uneasy silence fell between them. Odysseus sat staring into the dazzle of the lake, thinking of the violets that must soon be flowering in Ithaca.

Then the voice of the small Libyan boy piped up from where he sat in his dirty smock, solemnly watching Eurylochus berating Elpenor for his stupidity.

'You want go Zarzis,' he said. 'I take you Zarzis.'

To pass the time on the journey there, Eurylochus had taught the boy a few words of his own language, and he must have picked up more by listening to the Argives chatting by the fire at night.

Dubiously Eurylochus said, 'You know the way?'

'I know it.'

'How do we know you know?'

The boy wagged his head from side to side and looked up at Eurylochus with widened eyes that were as black as olives. 'I come three time here.'

Eurylochus turned to his companions in amazement and delight. A smile broke across his grizzled face. 'I think this boy was sent to us by a god,' he said. Then he swung the little mule-driver up in his brawny arms. 'Hermes,' he shouted. 'That's what we'll call you. You're promoted, boy. Your name is Hermes now.'

But the boy, it turned out, was not always certain of the way, and the journey back to Zarzis took longer than the journey out. In the heat of one afternoon, they were running low on water and might have got lost for ever had Hermes not approached the hillside lairs of a reclusive tribe of cave-dwellers. A scrawny man in a loin cloth, with decorative scars etched into his cheeks, glowered at the boy for a time, saying nothing. But Hermes persisted, gesturing with impatient hands, until the man put them back on the right track through a wilderness of rocks.

Odysseus' mood grew grimmer with every mile they travelled. He could not dispute the answer that the oracle had given to his question, but to accept it consigned him to despair. He knew that if he was not careful he might die in this condition and he was not yet ready to die. So as he drove his camel onwards through the glare of heat, hour by hour he summoned the vestiges of his will. He imagined himself strapping and buckling it around the muscles of his heart. He enclosed his head inside it like a helmet of bronze, and he made up his mind that if the world was going to take everything from him, then he would make sure that he took something back.

Odysseus, Prince of Ithaca, Lord to Lady Penelope and father of Telemachus, might have died in the arid reaches of this Libyan desert; but Nobody the Rover still lived. His ships were waiting for him on the beach at Zarzis, and there was a whole unknown world to the west, out beyond the Pillars of Heracles, where a new life might be found.

Yet when they finally arrived, exhausted, on the strand at Zarzis, they found only two ships waiting for them there. Having almost made up his mind that his leader would never return, Demonax greeted them with joy and relief; but his face darkened as he explained that Glaucus and the crew of the *Nereid* had given up on Odysseus five days earlier. They had sailed westwards in search of Guneus and the Cinyps River where they were looking to mend their fortunes.

Only later did it emerge that many of the *Swordfish*'s crew were also restless. They too might have sailed, hoping to get safely back to Ithaca, had Odysseus' return been delayed by another day. Nor had the decision to put the *Nereid* to sea passed without furious disputes among the men. Most of the crew of *The Fair Return* had remained fiercely loyal to Odysseus. His helmsman Baius had even sworn that he would cut Glaucus' throat if their ships ever beached on the same strand again. There was, however, one encouraging piece of news: most of the men had been so shamed by the encounter with Guneus and his still-vigorous crew that they had resolved to pull themselves together. Apart from a few now chronic addicts for whom there was little hope, almost all of them had sworn off taking the lotus, though it had been a miserable time for those whose stomachs had convulsed in violent reaction to the sudden stoppage of the drug.

Odysseus took stock that night. He had two ships and around seventy men left to him. It was enough. If they rounded up a few sheep and goats from the local herdsmen, they could put to sea adequately equipped to make their way back into the sea-lanes around Sicily. There were islands he had heard of there.

Then he would hand over the *Swordfish* to any of his men who wanted to return to Ithaca, and turn his own prow westwards to discover what fate the gods might have in store for him beyond the known margins of the world.

The Wind-callers

A warm wind blowing off the mainland eased their passage north along the coast; then they struck eastwards hoping to make land-fall in Sicily. But an anxious time passed before the man at the masthead sighted a pale plume of smoke drifting from the summit of a cone-shaped island on the horizon. Recalling reports he had heard from navigators who had sailed westwards out of Argos, Odysseus surmised that this might be Aeolia, the island of the wind-callers.

His guess was confirmed when they approached the well-built harbour of a prosperous town and saw the banners flying from the bastions of the citadel. After the sultry heat of Zarzis, the sailors' hearts were lifted and refreshed by the airy music reaching their ears as they pulled in towards the marble wharf. Only when they docked did they realize that they were listening to the sound of the breeze strumming through countless wind-harps and chiming among webs and lattices of translucent shell. It felt as though the wind that had blown them there was now celebrating their arrival.

Odysseus soon discovered that his reputation had preceded him, although the crowd gathered at the wharf was surprised to learn that the Ithacans were little better informed about recent events in the wider world than they were themselves. The Aeolians knew that Troy had fallen and had heard rumours both of Agamemnon's assassination and the Dorian invasion. What they could not know – and he did all he could to keep them in ignorance of the fact – was that Odysseus was a different man to the one whose valour and resourcefulness they had heard lauded in stories told by earlier visitors to the island.

He had not been standing long on the wharf when a herald approached from the direction of the palace parting the crowd before one of the most handsome young couples that Odysseus had seen for a long time, and his first assumption was that this must be the king and queen of the island. But the tall young man with ardent blue eyes and bird-like features introduced himself as Macareus, the son of King Aeolus, and it emerged that the young woman at his side was not his wife but his sister Canace. They were delighted to welcome Odysseus to their island in the name of Zeus of the Strangers, and to inform him that their father was eager to receive him and hear at first-hand the stories he must have to tell about the glorious war that had been fought at Troy.

Charmed by the king's hospitality but reluctant to confess that he had been reduced to the role of a roving pirate, Odysseus sat a little uneasily beside Aeolus at the banquet that night. A man of austere bearing with the same intense eyes as his son and long white hair falling about his shoulders, the king would eventually prove to be both an astute questioner and a patient listener; but he was also discreet, and far too well-bred to importune his guest with immediate demands for information. So Odysseus was able to keep him at bay for a time by expressing his own desire to learn more about the life and customs of Aeolia.

His host, he learned, was the third king to bear the name Aeolus. Some eighty years earlier, and for time immemorial before that, it had been the custom for the island's king to die each year as the rite of the Great Goddess demanded. But sensing that the power of the Goddess was on the wane, the grandfather of the present king had refused to consent to death when his time came.

Under the aegis of Sky-Father Zeus, he had installed himself as permanent sovereign, taken the name of the island to himself, and securely established both his throne and his line. His son had consolidated the new regime, yet Aeolus confessed to Odysseus that the memory of the old religion still remained strong among the common people of the island. 'How could it be otherwise,' he conceded with a dry smile, 'when they believe that the power to call the wind is in her gift?'

When Odysseus asked by what name the Goddess was worshipped in those parts, Aeolus informed him that her sacred name was Cardea. 'They say that she lives at the back of the North Wind at the hinge of the year,' he said, 'and that it remains in her power to open what is shut and to shut what is open. For many years now my priests and I have dedicated the wind-rites in the name of Zeus the Cloud-gatherer, as my father and grandsire did before me. But the ancient practices remain much the same.' He looked back at Odysseus, shaking his head. 'Regrettably, my people are less changeable than the wind.'

With almost unseemly eagerness, Odysseus made plain his desire to learn more of those rites. 'I can imagine no more useful knowledge for one of my rootless trade,' he smiled in reparation. But Aeolus merely answered his smile with the suggestion – it was not quite a promise – that Odysseus might hear more of their art before he left the island.

'Meanwhile,' he added, 'the wind tells us many things and the Phoenician traders tell us more, but with such grave unrest in the world, I find it hard to keep abreast of the times. So I look to you for guidance, friend.'

Odysseus glanced away from the interrogative tilt of the old man's head and saw Macareus and Canace laughing together a little further down the table. Their evident pleasure in each other's company brought a sudden painful reminder of how things had once been on Ithaca, when he and Penelope had presided over many such feasts as this, each always taking pride in the other's talent for hospitality – gracious in her case, ebullient in his – and life had seemed to offer no larger ambition than the increase of their mutual happiness. The thought came hard to him now, and when it flashed on the dream image of his wife recoiling from him as a man of blood, it became pure pain. The convivial chatter of the feast turned to noise inside his head. Sweat broke at his brow. When he glanced across at Canace, the king's finely boned daughter, he saw the young body of Iphigenaia lying dead in her place. Her face was white. There was blood at her mouth and neck.

A little perplexed by his guest's absence of attention, Aeolus was saying, 'I feel sure that the war will have altered the balance of power in ways which sooner or later must affect us even here on our remote fastness. There must already be signs of it on your own island?'

Odysseus turned to stare at his royal host with the abstracted air of a man addressed by a stranger in the street. It felt as though the words had been impeded in their progress across his mind and were only now reaching him. 'Forgive me,' he said, struggling for coherence. 'You are a king with the power to call the winds, while I . . . these days I am a straw blown about by them. If you are in need of guidance, you would do well to look elsewhere.'

For a moment Aeolus mistook the response for a light gesture of modesty.

'Come, come, Lord Odysseus,' he smiled, 'your skill at guileful speech is well known, but we are plain-speaking folk on Aeolia. You may be frank with us here.'

Aware that he was in gross breach of all civility, Odysseus snapped back, 'You don't understand me. I don't mean to be indirect with you. The truth is I know nothing about the balance of power.' He looked up and saw the dismay in the older man's eyes. Making to stand, he put down his wine-cup carefully as though uncertain where the edge of the table lay. 'Forgive me,' he said again. 'I'm no longer fit to keep company with decent men. I should return to my ship.'

But Aeolus laid his own hand gently across the one with which

Odysseus supported himself against the table. The two men were arrested there for a moment, gazing into each other's eyes, and Odysseus felt himself under the scrutiny of an intelligence that was at once astute and sympathetic.

'Some shadow lies across your heart,' Aeolus said in a discreetly lowered voice. 'Come aside with me, away from this din. We will talk quietly together.'

At a word from their father, Macareus and Canace gladly undertook the hosting of the feast. Aeolus led his uneasy guest out of the banqueting hall into a comfortably appointed side-chamber where an open balcony looked out on the shifting radiance of the moon across the sea. Aeolus dismissed the serving-woman who brought them wine, saying that he would do the mixing himself. Once the wine was going quietly about its work, the king eased the occasion by telling Odysseus that he himself had never fully recovered from the time, some eighteen years earlier, when his island was visited by pestilence. All his children had been taken from him except Macareus, and he had lost his wife to an incurable malady of the heart soon after the infant Canace was born. 'I tell you this,' he said, 'only because I recognize suffering when I see it. Now you must speak to me of yours.'

Because this was the first time that Odysseus had confessed the full scale of his misery to anyone, the words did not come easily at first, and when they came he was more articulate in denouncing the way that he and his comrades had been corrupted by the war than in speaking his most secret fear, which was that the whole brutal adventure must have cost him the love of his wife and child.

'Yet you have no certain evidence of that,' Aeolus firmly reminded him when that difficult truth emerged.

'No,' Odysseus conceded, 'but I know that I have thrown away ten years of my life, and I know that the wives of my comrades have turned against them in that time. If there is justice in the world, I can see no reason why Penelope should not have done the same.'

'The inconstancy of others does not make your own wife inconstant,' Aeolus countered. 'She may be waiting faithfully even now.'

'She may or she may not,' Odysseus answered grimly. 'If she is wise – and I believe her to be so – then she will have come to see that I was never worthy of her love.'

'Come, man,' Aeolus reproved him. 'I cannot believe that to be the case. Once wretchedness begins to make us feel sorry for ourselves we no longer see things clearly. I do not know your wife and cannot speak of her, but one thing is clear to me and you would do well to remember it. Whatever may be happening on Ithaca, you are the island's rightful lord. If you're a true man, you will return as speedily as the wind will take you and reclaim what is your own. Should you find your wife has betrayed you, then make her pay for it. But secure your kingdom – by force if need be.'

Odysseus muttered something which Aeolus could not hear, so the king leaned forward, asking him to repeat it.

'The omens are against me,' Odysseus said more loudly and with a bitter edge to his voice. 'I consulted an oracle at the shrine of Athena Tritogeneia in Libya. I was told in no uncertain terms that I am unfit to return.'

Aeolus grunted with the corners of his mouth sourly down-turned. 'I have heard that they still serve the Mother before Father Zeus in that part of Libya.'

'They do. Yet the omens were clear enough. And they were confirmed by my own dream. But I can see it for myself without the need for oracles and omens. I'm no more than the shell of the man I was. I cannot cleanse myself of the blood I've shed. My dreams are dreams of blood as my life has been a life of blood. That blood dims my sight even.' Hearing the small noise of demurral in his host's throat, Odysseus stared fiercely up at him. 'It is true. Believe me. When I looked at your daughter at the feast just now, I saw her not living but dead. Dead as the daughter that Agamemnon sacrificed to the wind at Aulis. There was blood at her neck and mouth.' Seeing Aeolus make the sign to ward off evil, he added quickly, 'Yet clearly she is more vivid with life than any young woman I have looked on for a long time. It is a curse that travels with me since the things that were done at Troy. I cannot allow it to pollute the lives of my wife and son.'

'Why should it?' Aeolus answered. 'We have cleansing rites here on Aeolia. The days of the Goddess's ascendancy are gone. You should not permit her primitive darkness to oppress your heart. As a guest here you are under the protection of Sky-Father Zeus. Let me purge you of this guilt before his altar.' Opening his hands, he smiled warmly, supremely confident of his own powers. 'Then we'll see if we can't whistle up a wind to take you home.'

With an effort to restrain the tears rising inside him, Odysseus turned his face to the night outside. There could be no doubting this king's authority and benevolence, but he had no great experience of warfare and the harm it could work on a man's mind. In these tranquil moments Aeolus was aware of no other sounds than the hushed murmur of the surf and the song of the breeze through the strings of the wind-harps, but Odysseus could hear the screaming in the streets of Troy. He saw the people dying around him. He watched the sword in his own hand rise and fall. The smell of blood was in his nostrils still.

He shook his head in a vain attempt to clear the phantasm. Seizing control of his voice, he said, 'As we approached your island I saw smoke rising from the mountain that overlooks your citadel.'

With a smile, Aeolus said, 'We say that it rises from the smithy of Hephaistus.'

'I hear that they said the same thing on Kalliste before Poseidon shook the earth, and fire broke from the mountain and plunged that island beneath the sea.'

The smile faded from the king's face. 'Perhaps those people had offended the god.'

'Has fire ever broken from your mountain here?'

'The last time was a long time ago,' Aeolus frowned. 'To our knowledge the mountain has never raged with such violence as on Kalliste.'

'Yet the fire may come again.'

'If the gods will it, which I pray they do not.' Aeolus shifted uneasily in his chair. 'But why do you ask these things?'

'Because there are times when I feel to be like such a mountain.' Odysseus turned his haggard eyes towards the king. 'There are depths inside us into which we cannot see. Who knows what may be lurking there? I know only that more violence than I thought myself capable of broke out of me that night in Troy. Such fury might burst from me again. Can your rites purge me of that risk?'

'Submit to them,' Aeolus answered firmly, 'and we shall see.'

So the ships lay docked in the harbour at Aeolia for many days longer than Odysseus had intended. Again he endured long rites of sacrifice and purgation. He fasted and prayed. His body was scourged. Blood was poured over him and washed from him. And this time the power of Zeus invoked by the strong masculine will of Aeolus seemed to achieve what the Libyan priestesses of Neith had failed to accomplish.

The worried Ithacans quickly sensed the change in their captain's mood and temper. His heart felt lighter, his sense of value and purpose returned. When the king declared that the time had come to summon a wind that would speed his passage back to Ithaca, Odysseus gladly assented. His mind was clear, his confidence was high. He felt certain once more that his life – his true life – was waiting for him there.

Heralds went out from the palace and all of the three hundred people who lived on the island assembled for the great rite by which the wind was called. With King Aeolus and his white-robed priests at their head, they marched the sacred way around the smoking mountain, waving quince boughs as they walked, and with clay whistles slung on lengths of twine about their necks. They sang as they made their way towards a place on the northern strand where a narrow cave had been carved out of the cliff, and the air chimed with the sound of the warm south wind plucking at the harps.

With Macareus as his guide and companion, Odysseus stood a little apart from the sacred precinct where King Aeolus raised his arms towards the cloudless sky. Turning to each of the four points of the compass, the king cried out invocations in some ancient language unknown to Odysseus. At each cardinal station the assembled multitude cried out in response while an acolyte poured out libations of wine. Aeolus turned to face northwards last of all. An altar stone stood there with a herd of goats tethered beside it. A second acolyte covered the king's robes with a goatskin apron; a third handed him a bronze knife. After a further, longer invocation in which Odysseus recognized the names of Cloud-gathering Zeus and Boreas, son of Astraeus, Lord of the North Wind, the goats were offered up, one by one, in sacrifice.

There came a pause in the solemn proceedings while Aeolus was divested of the bloodied apron. Water was brought for him to cleanse himself. In the stillness of those moments Odysseus became aware that only faint ripples of sound now passed through the strings of the harps. The dangling nets of shell seemed muted in their chiming. When he looked up towards the summit of the mountain he saw that the plume of smoke which had been drifting north-eastwards on the breeze since the time of his arrival was almost vertical now. All around him the people of the island stood in rapt attention. At his side, Macareus fingered the clay whistle moulded in the shape of a coiled serpent that hung about his neck.

Standing with his back to the congregation once more, Aeolus raised his hands and head towards the sky as he chanted out a further invocation. At the climax of his call he turned and beckoned to a veiled figure in white robes who stepped forward out of the chorus of women and stood before him. He lifted her veil and Odysseus saw that her face was whitened with chalk so that she looked more like some ethereal shade than a creature of flesh and blood. Only after a moment did he discern the delicate young features of Canace.

Quietly, with her hands clasped at her breast, the princess began to sing. At first Odysseus took her song for a wordless ululation – less a hymn than a voiced accompaniment to the stillness of the moment; but then the music lifted into a paean of praise in which the sacred name of Cardea was distinctively uttered, and it felt as though the whole world had stopped to listen. Never in his life had Odysseus felt his soul searched so deeply by a voice. Its naked beauty thrilled on his senses and exalted his heart. So deep-reaching was its summons that it made him think of the song of the Sirens that the hero Jason claimed to have heard when he tied himself to the mast of his ship and made his crew stop up their ears with wax so that they should not be drawn to destruction. And suddenly his heart was beating faster as he discerned how the airy upper registers of her voice were answered by a profound harmonic resonance that seemed to rise upwards from the bare soles of her feet, through the cavern of her slender chest, and out into the open air. The breath of her body and the breath of the wind were one and identical; and for the duration of those timeless moments – Odysseus understood it as he felt the hairs rising at his neck – Canace and the Goddess had become one and the same.

The song eddied like a breeze into silence. Odysseus became aware of a light sobbing sound beside him. When he turned his head he saw tears of joy and exultation pouring down the cheeks of Macareus, whose eager eyes were fixed so intently on the now silent figure of his sister that he was entirely unaware he was observed.

Meanwhile, as his daughter gave verse to the final quiet cadences of her song, Aeolus and his acolytes had made their way towards the mouth of the cave. Now the king turned to the congregation and uttered a great shout. Again he raised his arms. As though they were a single person, all the islanders lifted their whistles to their lips and blew a piercing blast of sound towards the north.

Three times, like the mewing of some titanic hawk, the

whistling pierced the air. Each shrill blast set up such a vibration that it seemed to quiver in Odysseus' ears long after the actual sound had passed, and so intense was the pain that he closed his eyes against it.

When he opened them again, Aeolus and his priests had disappeared into the dark cleft of the cave. As out of nowhere, a gust of wind lifted off the sea and swirled across the strand. Odysseus felt it tugging at his hair, pulling the skirts of his kilt. His eyes watered as the gust passed over them. It touched his ears with cold. Then it had moved on, ruffling the corn-gold hair of Macareus, who stood with his face raised and his eyes closed as if savouring the fragrance of the wind.

The tension of the crowd relaxed in a deep, contented sigh. Someone laughed out loud, another man released a cheer; and then everyone was chattering and applauding as music struck up and the people began to dance with the kind of joy that comes only from experiencing the seamless mystery of things.

After a time, Odysseus turned solemnly to Macareus. 'Your sister is possessed of the most marvellous singing voice it has ever been my privilege to hear,' he said. But the young man was so overwhelmed by emotion that he could only nod in response with the tears still running down across his cheeks. He lifted the back of his hand to his nostrils and drew in his breath, striving to regain control of it. Unable quite to do so, he glanced upwards and away.

Sensitive to his embarrassment, Odysseus was about to avert his attention elsewhere when he felt the young man's hand grip tightly at his wrist.

'Look,' Macareus whispered, and pointed upwards with his other hand.

Lifting his gaze, Odysseus drew his breath in a gasp. The white smoke rising from the mountain had shifted, point by point, and was drifting towards the south-west. The wind, which had brought them northwards to Aeolia out of Libya, was now set fair for Ithaca and home.

*   *   *

The *Swordfish* had already put to sea and young Elpenor was at the prow of *The Fair Return* ready to cast off, when King Aeolus and his son and daughter came to say their farewells to Odysseus on the wharf. The king motioned to one of his attendants who stepped forward holding a large and very full goatskin bag that was carefully bound at its mouth with silver wire. 'This is the gift I promised you,' Aeolus said. 'Remember to handle it with great care.'

'Have no fears,' Odysseus smiled. 'This precious cargo will be stowed safely away below decks. I have your instructions by heart.'

'Then I wish you a truly fair return to your homeland,' Aeolus said, opening his arms in a parting embrace. Odysseus held his friend for a long time before turning to embrace Macareus and the delicate shoulders of Canace. Then he took the goatskin bag from the attendant and climbed aboard his ship with a shout to Elpenor to cast off. Carefully he put down his burden on an oar-bench and stood by the rail, waving to the diminishing figures on the wharf as his vessel pulled out into the clear waters of the bay.

At Eurylochus' command, the sail was unfurled. Quickly it billowed in the wind so that the sign of the ram's head painted on the sheet seemed to run for home. Dolphins leapt in bright splashes of silver from the waves, keeping pace with the ship's gathering speed. Water gurgled around the keel. A spray of spindrift lifted on the breeze. Homeward bound at last and with a fair wind at their backs, the crew began to sing an old seaman's chant that was dear to their Ithacan hearts. Meanwhile, balancing himself against the sway, Odysseus carried the bag along the benches under the curious eyes of all his crew, and ducked his head into the gloom beneath the afterdeck where Baius stood at the helm.

Elpenor glanced up at Eurylochus from where he was making the painter fast to its cleats. 'What do you suppose the old man's got there?' he asked.

'I've no idea,' Eurylochus glowered back, 'but whatever it is

I'm sure it's none of your damned business. Now look lively with that hawser and get your arse out of my way.'

They were making good progress along the northern coast of Sicily when a keen-eyed sailor on the *Swordfish* spotted a small fleet of ships emerging through the haze on the horizon.

'It looks as though there are two them,' he called up to his captain on the afterdeck. 'If we stay on this course we'll shave their bows.'

Demonax pushed his helm over to heave closer to *The Fair Return* and shouted the news across the water between.

'Let me know as soon as you can make them out,' Odysseus ordered, aware that the vessels could be either pirates or peaceful merchantmen who might have news of the latest developments in Argos and Ithaca. 'Keep her steady as she goes. We've got the weather-gauge of them whoever they turn out to be.'

Around an hour later the ships came into clearer view, and Odysseus saw that there were in fact three of them, all Argive built. Two of them were pentekonters, probably refitted after the war, while the third, bringing up the rear some distance away, was a small coastal trader making heavy weather of the light seas. None of the vessels carried any mark by which they could be identified, so Odysseus guessed they must be pirates.

He turned to Eurylochus, 'We're in better shape than they look to be,' he said. 'Do we want a fight or not?' But before his mate could answer, Demonax shouted from the *Swordfish*. 'They're shortening sail, Captain. It looks as though they're waiting for us.'

'All right,' Odysseus called back, 'let's find out who they are.'

To his astonishment, as they bore down on the first of the ships, he heard a voice call out across the water, 'Ahoy *The Fair Return*! Do you still have Odysseus of Ithaca aboard?'

Gripping a halyard, Odysseus mounted the rail. 'And if we do?' he shouted.

'Then his old friend Diomedes, son of Tydeus, would like to drink to his survival.'

Equally amazed to have encountered one another in these strange waters, the two comrades greeted one another with delight from ship to ship, but as their conversation developed the mood swiftly darkened. Diomedes was rankling with bitterness that he should have fought for so long abroad only to find his city and kingdom stolen from him on his return.

'I can live happily enough without that bitch of a wife,' he growled. 'But having struggled home after war and wounds and shipwreck, that I should be reduced to this . . .' He gestured at the little, weather-battered fleet that he and his followers had managed to scrape together from the shipyards of Argos. 'And what irks me most is that when we gathered at Corinth we couldn't rally enough support to reclaim what we'd lost. Even Nestor was too old and war-weary to help us out.'

Feeling the breath tighten in his chest, Odysseus said, 'Was there no one there from Ithaca?'

Diomedes shook his head. 'If you ask me, you've done the right thing in not trying to get back. That bastard Nauplius did a good job of shafting all of us. Agamemnon dead, Idomeneus and me deposed . . . At least you've been spared the humiliation of going back and finding a younger man in your bed.'

'How do you know that's happening?' Odysseus demanded. 'Do you know it for certain?'

'Not for certain, no. But the word at Corinth was that the centre of power in the Ionian Islands has shifted from Ithaca to Dulichion. They're all sure you're dead by now, and your father isn't strong enough to hold the kingdom together. I heard there's some ambitious young prince over there . . . I can't remember his name . . .'

'Amphinomus.'

'Yes, that's him. Well, there's a strong rumour abroad that he and Penelope . . .' Seeing the pain on his old comrade's face, Diomedes brought his fist down on the rail where he stood. 'In the name of all the gods, what's happening in the world? I could hardly believe my ears ten years ago when I was told that Helen had deserted Menelaus for that Trojan dandy, and now look. Clytaemnestra in bed with Aegisthus, Idomeneus' wife sporting with her lover in Crete, my own accursed slut Agialeia . . . It curdles my bowels just to think of it. Aphrodite has taken her vengeance on us all.' He looked across at his friend's grim face. 'So where are you bound?' he asked. 'Have you taken to roving again or are you looking for some place to settle, like we are?'

In a low voice, hoarse with feeling, Odysseus said, 'I was making for Ithaca.'

Only then did Diomedes understand the full savage impact of his words on his friend's heart. 'Well, it's up to you,' he said, 'but think how much time's gone by. Someone's sure to have made a bid for power by now. Penelope's a good woman, I know, but so was Helen and think what happened there.' He sniffed and scowled. 'It seems there's a whore inside every one of them just aching to break out. Go back if you like, but I very much doubt you'll fare any better than the rest of us.'

Odysseus was staring down into the blue-green swell between the two ships, thinking of the great bed he had built for his wife and himself. He had carved its posts from the bole of the olive tree around which their whole private apartment had been raised. He had known so many hours of joy there; and so much grief too as Penelope miscarried twice before his infant son Telemachus was brought to term. And then, after Menelaus and Palamedes had come to demand that he honour the oath he had sworn at Sparta and follow them to the war at Troy, Penelope had lain listening to him on that bed for hour after hour. He had known that she no more wanted him to go to Troy than he truly wanted to go himself; yet neither would she seek to manipulate him, fairly or otherwise, into compromising his honour. Ever since those anguished hours, he had tried to think the thing through again and again, and had always ended with the only conclusion that was tolerable to him – that he had been left with no choice. But after all the waste and horror of those years, after all the losses and deaths, he knew now that it simply wasn't true. He had always had a choice. Penelope had been quietly waiting for him to make the right choice, and he had chosen wrongly.

So what right did he have to expect her to wait for him year after year, wasting her youth and beauty as she pined over the memory of the husband who had betrayed their love? He had no right. No right at all. Or if he had ever done so, he had surely forfeited it by becoming the man of blood that he was.

This chance encounter with Diomedes on the high seas had quite extinguished whatever confidence had been briefly restored to him by the rites on Aeolia. Odysseus heard himself utter a little bitter laugh. Only a god so cruel and capricious that he lacked all compassion for the vulnerable human heart could have arranged for such a meeting to happen. Or perhaps after all there were no gods to preside over the affairs of men, perhaps only the fierce, impersonal forces of wind, weather and the unstable earth governed a universe in which human beings coupled with the lust of animals and devoured each other the same way.

'Why not join forces with us?' Diomedes was calling across the water. 'We're heading northwards up the coast of Italy. I'm told the people are still tribal there – a patchwork of small chiefdoms living a hundred years behind the times, and either quarrelling with one another or holing up out of harm's way. We could build a new empire there together, you and me. What do you say?'

Odysseus stared across at where the familiar figure of his old comrade bobbed and swayed with the motion of his ship. 'I've heard enough talk of empires.' The wind picked up his words and scattered them. 'I'll take my chances at sea.'

But the encounter had an unsettling effect on the crews of both Odysseus's ships, many of whom were disgruntled by the realization that their leader no longer intended to make the run home for Ithaca. That afternoon they made landfall on the coast of Sicily. The two ships tied up side by side among the rocks of a gloomy cove that was sheltered from both wind and sun by the high cliffs all around. While scouts went out to survey the surrounding terrain, Odysseus and Demonax conferred together and agreed that the most sensible course was to sort the men into two groups – those still eager to go home, who would put to sea in the *Swordfish* the next day, and those who, for one reason or another, preferred to sign on for the roving life with Odysseus.

The scouts returned with the news that they had landed in the country of the Laestrygonians, a primitive, sheep-rearing people who, as far as they could gather from the halting exchanges with the woman they had interrogated, were descended from an aboriginal race of giants.

'How big was this woman?' Odysseus asked.

'She was big enough,' his chief scout answered.

'To eat you?' Demonax joshed him.

'Well, I don't know about that. But she was big.'

'She was probably just trying to scare you off,' Odysseus said. 'But it sounds as if there's nothing to keep us here anyway. We'll take as many of their sheep as we need and the two ships can go their separate ways tomorrow.' He looked across at his other captain. 'What about you, Demonax? Will you stay with me or take the *Swordfish* home?'

Demonax pensively stroked his beard. 'I wish I didn't have to choose,' he said.

'But you do,' Odysseus answered. 'I'm not going back to Ithaca.'

Demonax considered the discomfited group of men who were missing their wives and families and farms back home, or had simply grown tired of war and wandering. 'There isn't a decent navigator among that lot,' he grunted. 'If I'm not there to pilot them, they'll end up back in Libya or run aground on a lee shore. It looks like we've come to the parting of the ways, old friend. I think we should get very drunk tonight.'

And that, after they had rustled the sheep they needed from the grazing flocks, was exactly what they did. There were many sore heads and a lot of heavy hearts when they woke next day in the chilly light of the cove and prepared themselves for parting. The narrow strand was so rugged that most of the men had decided to sleep on board ship, and they were still there, stowing away their bedding and making ready to row out to sea when the first of the rocks came hurtling over the edge of the cliff.

It was so large a boulder that it must have been prised loose with levers. Colliding with the rocks below, it smashed into the *Swordfish*, splintering her planks, breaking through the rail and cracking the mast. The morning was loud with the screams of injured men and the great booming shouts of triumph that came from the top of the cliff. Odysseus looked up and saw a gang of huge figures up there carrying what looked like a tree-trunk to the next boulder, while others began pelting the stricken *Swordfish* with smaller rocks. He was ordering his own crew to push off as quickly as they could when he saw Demonax fall to the deck with his skull shattered by a stone. A moment later the damaged mast of the *Swordfish* creaked and swayed for a moment; then it collapsed over the ship in a tangle of sailcloth, spar, pulley-blocks and ropes.

Odysseus joined his bewildered men in the struggle to get *The Fair Return* out into deeper water before the next boulder fell. He could hear men crying out to him for help as his cutwater crunched clear of the strand. With no need for orders, Baius was working the steering oar to turn her head out to sea, but as Odysseus stared back up the cliff he saw the next rock topple over the edge and hurtle towards him. He heard the Laestrygonian giants give another great shout, but half-way down the cliff-face, the boulder was deflected from its course by a protruding neck of rock. It plunged into the water three yards wide of *The Fair Return* yet close enough to drench him with the great fountain of water it raised. Then his crew were at the oars, pulling away from the strand with all their might.

Odysseus lay in his hammock aboard ship that night wondering whether a man had ever been so cursed by misfortune. Fearful of venturing ashore again in those parts, they had dropped a stone anchor some distance offshore in a sheltered bay and he had given orders for two men to be on watch at all times. The ship lazed in quiet waters making barely a sound, and he could hear some of his men muttering together further forward of where he lay.

Not for the first time that day, young Elpenor was remarking on the good luck that had brought him back to *The Fair Return* to collect a bag he'd forgotten when otherwise he might have been crushed under the stone that smashed into the *Swordfish*. But most of the crew were shocked and demoralised by the loss of their comrades. Someone growled that Elpenor should stop going on about his luck and there was an uneasy silence before the muttering began again.

Though not all their words were distinct, it came clear to Odysseus that some of his men were now questioning his judgement. Such a thing had never happened before in all his years of command, but who could blame them for it? Each time he took a decision it seemed only to invoke a hostile fate, and the wind that had blown them from Aeolia was more constant than his own tormented mind. His heart stretched like a drum-skin inside him each time he remembered that the men killed aboard the *Swordfish* were the ones who most dearly wanted to go home. Better that his own ship had been sunk, for he and his crew were already dead to their homeland. But that was not the way of things in this universe of storms and monsters. And he, who had always prided himself on the strength of his mind, could no longer trust it.

Eventually Odysseus fell into a thick and troubled sleep. When he woke again, hours later, the ship had swung about on its anchor. The wind had veered in the night and a stiff gale was buffeting his ship out of the south. So much, he thought, for Aeolus and his magic.

Only when he went under the afterdeck to take a change of clothes from his sea-chest did he see the goatskin bag lying beside it with the silver twine unloosed around its neck.

White-faced with rage, he picked it up and ducked his head back into the light.

'Who in the name of Zeus has dared to lay hands on this?' he demanded. The crew stared back at him, most of them bewildered, a few of the others shame-faced and shifty.

'Grinus,' he shouted to the nearest man, 'what do you know about this?'

Fat Grinus shrugged his shoulders and shook his head, but Odysseus did not miss the baleful glance he cast at Elpenor.

Eurylochus said, 'If you don't own up, Elpenor, I'll throw you overboard myself.'

Sickly-faced and stammering, Elpenor stared down at his feet as he confessed to having got drunk and taken a peak inside the captain's bag.

'It was only out of curiosity,' he pleaded. 'I never meant to take nothing. Anyway, there's no great harm done, is there, sir? I mean, there was nothing in there but air, which struck me as an empty sort of gift for a king to give a guest.'

Odysseus stood shaking before the frightened young man. Had he not known and loved Elpenor's father all his days he might have struck the young fool down there and then on the spot. But what was the point? No point at all. No point even in explaining the harm that had been done, for his own decision not to sail home had already refused the magic by which Aeolus and his priests had confined all the countervailing winds inside that goatskin bag.

Rather than row against the strength of the gale, Odysseus decided to let it blow him northwards and, as if by an ironical reversal of the magic that had brought him from that place, the wind blew his ship back to Aeolia. But the island had changed almost beyond recognition in his absence. Not physically so, for the smoke still drifted from the fire-mountain and the marble quay glinted as brightly as ever; but the faces of the people were so stricken by grief that pestilence might have returned to the island. Yet he could find no one willing to speak of the cause of their sorrow till he came to the palace and found his wish for an audience with the king blocked by the herald who rose from his seat at the door to the royal apartment. Having expressed his surprise at seeing Odysseus again, the herald declared gravely that it was a time of mourning on Aeolia. 'We have been visited by great tragedy,' he said, 'and my lord the King has made it plain that he wishes to see no one until he has come to terms with his loss.'

Wanting at least to leave some appropriate message of condolence, Odysseus tried to persuade him to say more about the nature of that loss, but the herald glanced away, saying that he preferred not to speak of it.

'Is it the king's son?' Odysseus pressed. 'Has he lost his heir?'

Uneasily, the herald shook his head. 'No, Macareus still lives.'

'Then his daughter? Has some mischance befallen Canace?'

'No mischance,' the herald answered. 'Yet Canace is dead.'

Odysseus recalled the young woman, vivid with life – he had used those very words of her – uttering the wondrous strains of her song before all the people. There had been no indication of illness anywhere about her. He simply could not conceive how anything other than a terrible accident could have taken her life.

'But how?' he protested as if this diligent officer of the court was responsible for an offence against all reason. 'How could it have happened?' When the herald grimly shook his head and turned away once again, Odysseus raised his voice with all the royal authority he could command. 'King Aeolus is my friend. He was there beside me in my own hour of need, and I will not leave this place till I have been given the chance to offer him such comfort as I can.'

'The King will see no one,' the herald said, but at that moment the doors of the apartment opened and Aeolus was standing there, his robes torn, his long white hair dishevelled, his face a mask of fury and grief. He raised a quivering hand and pointed it at Odysseus. 'Get your accursed presence from my land,' he cried. 'I sent you once from here with a fair wind at your back, little knowing what evil omen you had laid on me when you saw my daughter in her blood. If you are here again, Odysseus of Ithaca, it can only be because the gods have turned their faces against you as they have done against me. Get you from my sight.'

Shocked by the vehemence of the assault, Odysseus stared at him aghast.

'I have done nothing to wish your majesty harm,' he protested. 'If I am here on Aeolia again it is only because an ignorant fool among my crew meddled with the gift you gave me.'

'It is through our folly that the gods work justice on us,' Aeolus retorted.

'It may be so, but I swear that I had no hand in your daughter's death.'

'This,' – Aeolus held up his trembling right hand – 'this is the hand that struck my whore of a daughter down. I found them together on the night that you sailed. They were plotting in their lust, waiting for me to die so they could bring the goddess back into her power and rule in the Egyptian manner – king and queen, brother and sister, equal on their thrones as in the foulness of their bed.' Aeolus looked up, panting, from the diseased vision that possessed his mind. 'And in my love for them,' he gasped, 'I was too blind to see it.'

Tears were pouring from his eyes, but the only love evident there was the insane, contraverted love of an old man who had endured too much grief and found himself overwhelmed by more primitive emotions he could not control.

'Your vision of blood spoke true, Odysseus of Ithaca,' he snarled at the dumbstruck man across from him. 'Now get you gone from my island lest the gods find other ways to infect me with the curses that you bring.'

Before Odysseus could speak, Aeolus had turned away and slammed shut the doors behind him. Odysseus glanced helplessly at the herald, who merely shook his troubled head and averted his eyes. An appalling silence filled the hall.

When he returned, still reeling from the shock, to his ship,

Odysseus found his crew still puzzled and dismayed by the desolation of the island. Eurylochus was playing knucklebones with the Libyan boy Hermes who had insisted on coming with him out of Zarzis. Others lounged about the deck, grumbling over their fate. Odysseus was about to climb aboard when a figure wrapped in a dirty white robe came running from an alley-way between two buildings off the quay, threw himself at his feet on the marble wharf, and grasped him by the legs.

Odysseus scarcely recognized him at first because his corn-gold hair had turned quite white, and the ardent, handsome features were crumpled in pain.

'I beg you,' Macareus beseeched him in an agonized whisper, 'there is no life for me here now. Take me away with you from this place.'

Aware of his crew watching in astonishment, Odysseus said. 'What of your sister?'

'I loved her,' Macareus answered. 'I loved her more than my life.'

'Yet she is dead, and you are here, clutching my knees.'

'Yes,' the response came back at once, fierce and unashamed. 'It would be too easy to die. It is my curse to live.'

When Odysseus looked down again it was into anguish as truthful as any he had seen since he looked into the face of Queen Hecuba at Troy.

'Very well,' he said after a time, torn between his pity for the man and revulsion for what he had done. 'Follow me if you wish. It will make no difference. We are all cursed aboard this ship.'

A Game of Shadows

Blown northwards by the wind, they found themselves following the coastline of a moist, green land where thick forests of oak, myrtle and laurel reached inland for mile upon mile. Only an occasional thin spiral of smoke rose among the trees.

Watching the virgin landscape drift past, some of the crew began to wonder whether Diomedes had not been in the right of it after all. A man could chance on worse places to settle down. But most of them were still demoralised by the loss of their comrades under the assault from the Laestrygonians. If people of such monstrous size and savage temper were to be found in one place, why not in others? Who knew what kind of men might lurk among those green shades? They were an awful long way from home, and might there not be truth in the old traveller's tales of the Cyclops and the even more fearsome creatures with many arms and legs and mouths?

Yet they could not beat along this coast for ever without pulling in to replenish supplies of food and water. When Odysseus saw what he took for a wooded offshore island with a sheltered bay where he could harbour *The Fair Return,* he decided to hunt for some fresh meat and see what else this land might have to offer. So the sail was hauled in and the crew took to the oars to scull the ship ashore.

They were met only by the cries of sea-birds and the calling of doves among the myrtle boughs. The sun was high and the land pleasantly warm. When nothing in the tranquil air of the place gave any cause for concern, Odysseus reached for his spear and splashed ashore at the head of a small hunting-party. They advanced quietly through the trees and had not gone far before they came to a place where the land rose before them on one side and fell away to a damp fen on the other. A large, antlered stag was stepping delicately through the water in the hollow.

Having whispered to his lieutenant Polites to climb the rise and get a wider view of the island, Odysseus crept stealthily down-wind of the stag, making his way under the cover of the brakes till he could get a clear shot. His spear struck cleanly into the lungs of the great beast. He saw its eyes roll and heard it cough. He watched it try to rear free of the spear; then he was leaping through the boggy water as the animal slumped back among the reeds. When the hooves had stopped kicking at the air, he tied them together with withies and slung the stag across his shoulders. He was staggering out of the fen under the dead weight of the beast when he saw Polites hastening back down the rise towards him.

'I can't see a lot because of the trees,' he reported, 'but there's smoke rising over in that direction, a mile or so away. It must be a settlement of some kind. And there's another wooded hill, quite a bit higher than this one, just beyond it. Kites and ravens are circling and swooping round the summit, so it looks as though there's something – or someone – dead up there.'

That evening, after they had all dined well on roast venison, Odysseus called his men together into council. He told them that he liked the look of this country. There was plenty of fresh water and game and no sign of a hostile response to their arrival, so he intended to explore further inland the next day and see what manner of people lived there. Immediately the council divided into two parties: the few who thought this the right thing to do and the more faint-hearted crew-members who had been disturbed by what Polites had said about the birds of prey circling the island's highest hill. Having already made up their minds that the carrion was human, they neither wanted to accompany Odysseus into this unknown land nor let him put his own life at risk.

'Send a shore party to investigate, if you like, captain,' Grinus suggested, 'but if you lead it yourself and come to harm, how shall the rest of us navigate our way home? Better that you stay here with us anchored offshore so that we don't get surprised again as happened among them giants in Sicily. Then, when the shore-party gets back, we can think again. And if they don't come back . . . well, we shall know we're not welcome in these parts.'

When this cautious position proved to be as close as the crew could get to agreement, Odysseus turned to Eurylochus. The second-in-command felt less confident than he had done before the discussion, but he agreed to lead the mission to the interior of the island. Instantly the Libyan boy Hermes said that if Eurylochus was going then he would go too, and Polites, who was among the coolest-headed of the men volunteered to go back ashore with them. A couple of the other braver souls – Clitus and Mastor – also put up their hands. Then Macareus, who had been a gloomy and, for the most part, taciturn presence aboard the ship since they had left Aeolia behind them, also spoke up.

'It no longer much matters what becomes of me,' he said, pushing his hand through the white locks of his hair. 'If I can be some use to you all, then I'm ready to go along too.'

Odysseus was about to settle for the worryingly small size of this party when, to everyone's surprise, young Elpenor declared that he too was willing to join the little band of explorers.

'I'm not altogether sure I want you under my feet,' Eurylochus snorted at him. 'You've caused trouble enough already.'

'That's just it,' Elpenor acknowledged ruefully. 'It's my fault we're here at all, so it's only fair I should do my bit.' He turned his young face in appeal to Odysseus, who studied him dubiously for a moment and then nodded his head in assent.

'Just don't go dipping your head into the wine-jar looking for courage tonight,' he said, and the council ended in uneasy laughter.

The night passed without event under a moon that was nearly at full. Early the next day, Odysseus stood by the anchor-rope at the prow of his ship, watching the small party disappear into the damp mist rising from the line of trees beyond the strand. As the sun climbed across a hot blue sky the mist dissolved. A couple of men idly fished over the side of the ship. Sea-birds dawdled above the masthead. Only the breeze off the sea disturbed the green trance of the trees. When high noon came and went, Odysseus began to worry. Even if Polites had underestimated the distance, or the terrain had proved more difficult than anticipated, the shore party could easily have been there in an hour's walk. Allowing an hour to look round, and another hour to return, they should have been back before noon. So where were they? What was happening? Should he abandon them and cast off with the rest of his crew? Or should he land a larger rescue mission under his own command? The alternative was simply to wait – yet delay might mean that an attempt to recover any survivors would come too late.

The shadows were already beginning to lengthen across the island when two figures, one large and one small, broke out of the trees and came running down the strand. They were not shouting and there was no sign of anyone in pursuit. Odysseus ordered the ship pulled in nearer to the shore, and a few moments later, panting and dripping with sweat, Eurylochus was telling his story with Hermes sitting beside him confirming what he had to say. Both of them seemed shaken by what they had seen.

Though Eurylochus was as brave as any man when confronting an enemy he understood, like most sailors he was superstitious. Nor was he the most eloquent or the most intelligent of men. So for a time Odysseus had some difficulty making sense of his garbled account of people being turned into animals by a witch with a poisonous brew. But when he got his frightened friend to tell the story in more detail, he learned that the shore-party had travelled a mile or more inland when they fell in with two young men who were drinking wine together in the shade of an oak tree. Macareus had approached them and told them that he and his friends were strangers in these parts and wanted to know more about the name and customs of the place in which they found themselves. Already tipsy, the young men seemed friendly enough. They offered to share their wine with the newcomers and happily informed Macareus that he was on Aiaia, the Island of the Dead, where they declared that the sun could be seen shining at midnight. They explained that they were on their way to the Feast of the Wolf, which would be held that night – the night of the full moon. If Macareus and his friends wished to learn more of the customs of the place, they should come along and join in the festivities.

During a brief consultation with the others, Macareus declared that the young men seemed trustworthy enough, if a little the worse for drink. He saw no reason why they should not accompany them and try to learn more about the people of the island. Eurylochus pointed out that Aiaia – the Island of Wailing – was not encouragingly named. If they were not to cross the threshold into the Land of the Dead themselves, they should remain on their guard. So the shore-party followed their guides through the forest to a wide track where they joined a large number of festive men and women who were making their way across the island.

As they walked along the track they heard the sound of a woodpecker yaffling somewhere deep among the glades. One of the young men laughed and said that it must be Picus, who had been a handsome king in those parts once but had been transformed into a woodpecker by a great sorceress because he had refused to forsake his true love Canens for her. But it was only when the other young man cheerfully announced to Elpenor that he expected to be turned into a wolf by the festive rites that Eurylochus became convinced that witchcraft was afoot. He became more alarmed by the thought when he learned that a powerful priestess called Circe, who was skilled in the art of working with magic herbs and potions, would preside over those rites. By now, however, they had arrived at the sacred grove where the feast was already in full swing, and the shore-party was warmly drawn into the revelry by the garlanded young women who attended on the tables with wine-jars in their hands. Only Eurylochus, with Hermes at his side, had hung back, worriedly taking in the scene, though at first he saw nothing out of the ordinary there.

The people seemed to be a simple sort of peasantry, much like the shepherds who would be gathering for the Spring Festival on Ithaca about this time. The songs they sang to the accompaniment of harps and pipes were bucolic ditties. Small children and dogs ran between the trestle-tables on which there was plenty to eat – roast lamb and goat, venison, fish, sea-food, strong cheese, olives, and bowls filled with fruit. And almost all the buildings Eurylochus could see were of crude wattle and daub construction, the reddish walls painted with geometrical designs and the roofs thatched with reeds. Only the temple or palace – he was unsure which it was – overlooking the site from a raised terrace suggested a more sophisticated world, built as it was out of dressed marble with a portico of columns and roofed with terracotta tiles. Near the foot of the steps a spring poured into a cistern through a lion's mouth carved into the stone, and from there it ran in a clear stream through the clearing. Both the water and the marble from which it flowed gleamed in the sunlight with a cool, refreshing radiance. The warm woodland air was heady with the scent of cooked thyme and rosemary. Above the noise of the people, Eurylochus could hear the splashing of the spring, and though he had drunk much less than his comrades, and resisted the allure of the women dancing attendance on them, he felt the sultry heat of the day tugging at his senses. He was, he admitted, kept from joining in the revelry only by his duty as leader of the shore-party, answerable to Odysseus.

'And it was just as well,' he said, 'because after a time things began to turn very strange. A man came out of the temple or palace – whatever it was – or at least I would have said it was a man but he had the head of a lion and was covered in a tawny lion-skin with long talons on his hands, and he gave a great roar at which all the people squealed and shouted as if they were in terror. Then more figures came out after him, but these were wolves – or men turned into wolves, for they still walked on two legs – and they ran among the people, chasing the women in particular and whipping them with thongs. And I couldn't tell then whether they were frightened or not because they were all drunk and some of them seemed to be laughing as the wolf-men ran among them. But there was a mad sort of feel to the place by now and I didn't much care for it. But when I called to the others they wouldn't come away. I don't know what drug was in that wine but they were as drunk as everybody else and wouldn't come away when I called. So Hermes and I withdrew into the cover of the trees to see what happened next, and after a time this strange music struck up inside the palace and we heard the sound of a woman's voice singing. Then the young women in the crowd took the young men by the arms and led them up the steps into the palace, and when I looked I saw that Macareus was going with them. He stood out from the crowd because of his white hair. A half-naked young woman with long black curls had him tight by the arm and she was leading him up the steps. Elpenor and Clitus were following on along behind, each with a woman on his arm. I think that Polites and Mastor seemed to be hanging back at first, not sure what to do; but half-way up the steps Macareus looked back and called something to them. I couldn't make out what he said, but the next thing I knew even those two were on their feet and being led up the steps and through the portico. That was the last I saw them of them except that . . .' Faltering there, Eurylochus glanced askance back into the stillness of the trees.

'Except what?' Odysseus demanded.

'Like I said,' Eurylochus was trembling a little as he spoke, 'I think she turned them into pigs – the witch, I mean. Circe. I think she turned them into pigs.'

'Why would you think that?'

'Because I saw them,' Eurylochus gasped, '– in the shadows of the portico. These figures . . . they were standing up on their hind legs like people, but they had the heads of pigs.'

Several hours later, Odysseus stood concealed among the trees, looking into the clearing where some people were singing and dancing still, while others lay with their heads flopped on the tables. Again he told himself that Eurylochus had been muddled by the loose talk of the young men that the shore party had met in the wood. It had combined with the wine and the heat of the day to work on his imagination when he saw men wearing wolf-skins and lion-skins as the ritual gear of some cult celebration different from any he had ever seen on Ithaca. But the pigs were less easily explained, which was why Odysseus surveyed the harmless throng of merry-makers uneasily. Eurylochus himself had been so unnerved that he had refused to show his captain the way to the clearing. Nor were any of the rest of the crew eager to go with him, so he had been guided by the Libyan boy on the strict understanding that Hermes would be allowed to return to the ship as soon as he had taken Odysseus to the palace of Circe. Yet he was still standing by his master in the shadow of a laurel tree as they peered into the glade. A huge moon hung in the sky like a gong.

As yet Odysseus was uncertain what he intended to do. If his men had gone into the temple freely, it was possible that they might return the same way. But Eurylochus had been certain that the wine they had drunk had been doctored with a dizzy-making drug, so they might be under the spell of witchcraft after all. And Odysseus had heard too many sailors' tales of strangers having been put to death as sacrifices in this primitive part of the world not to be worried for them.

Somehow he must establish the facts of the case, and then contrive a means of rescuing his men if they were still alive – or if they were still men, for that matter! And if they were being held by force or enchantment, he had no hope of freeing them unless he could overpower the priestess of this shrine. For that purpose he had concealed a long-bladed knife beneath his robe. That blade and his wits were all that now stood between him and death or – what might be worse –transformation into a pig.

He drew in his breath and was about to step out into the moonlit clearing when he felt a hand tugging at his arm. Looking down, he saw Hermes raise a cautionary finger as he whispered, 'Wait.'

The boy slipped out of the cover of the trees and crossed stealthily to a table where a bearded man in a red linen smock lay on his back with his mouth wide open. Hermes stood beside the man for a moment, making sure that he was sound asleep. Then he leaned across his chest to take something from him. He returned to the shadow of the laurel, clutching the slender stem of a plant with a bulbous root and a starry cluster of flowers that emitted a strong scent of garlic.

'I see all these men here wear this,' he said. 'Put it to your robe – in this place.' Hermes tapped his master's chest. 'Then you will be like them.' He looked up into Odysseus's puzzled gaze. 'Maybe it keeps you safe, like them.'

Thinking that at the very least it might help him to be mistaken for a reveller, Odysseus fixed the flower to his robe, and smiled down at the boy. 'I wonder if you aren't possessed by Hermes after all,' he said. 'Now on your way with you, back to the ship.'

Swaying slightly, pretending to be drunk, Odysseus stepped unremarked among the merry-makers. He took in each of the faces around him but could see no sign of his missing men anywhere among the dancers or those still feasting at the tables; so he made his way towards the marble steps of Circe's palace. A couple sat embracing by the mouth of the spring but they were too absorbed in one another's bodies to take any notice of him.

Expecting to be challenged at any moment, he began to climb the steps.

Leaning against the wall in one corner of the portico sat a figure he might have mistaken for a wolf had he been able to see only the sleek fanged head with its pricked ears; but a very human pair of legs protruded from a kilt beneath the wolf-skin and Odysseus knew that the fears of Eurylochus were unfounded. This might even be one of the young men he had met earlier in the day, now initiated into the wolf-cult and looking forward in his dreams to a time when he too might prey on the women with his thong. Putting a hand to the hilt of his long knife, Odysseus stepped through into the ante-chamber of a torch-lit hall.

Three figures were in conference there. An athletic young man clad in a tawny leather kilt stood beside two women. The lion-pelt that he wore as a cloak now had the beast's roughly maned head thrown back across his shoulders like a hood. The taller woman, robed in a richly embroidered blue gown of many flounces wore a jewelled diadem shaped in the head of a falcon with its curved beak protruding from her forehead. The thick hair hanging sleek and black at either side of her face was cut short at the line of her jaw. She was talking to the shorter woman beside her, who wore a plain white dress that hung in folds to her sandalled feet and was tied at her hips with a girdle that sparkled in the fitful light from the torches. Her face was completely covered by a mask that had only narrow slits for the eyes and was as silvery-white in its sheen as the full moon in the night outside.

None of the three saw Odysseus enter the room. He would have remained perfectly still, trying to overhear them, but at that moment one of the wolf-men stepped out of the shadows beside him saying, 'The hour is late to make your offering, friend. Come, leave the Lady in peace.'

Immediately the three figures fell silent and turned to look his way. When the wolf-man put his hand to Odysseus's arm, seeking to turn him away, the Ithacan stood his ground, demanding to know whether he was in the presence of Circe, the mistress of this place.

For a moment no one answered. The man in the lion-skin stepped forward, seeking to interpose himself between this intruder and the two women, but he was stopped in his tracks by a clipped word of command at his back. The taller woman gestured to the woman in the moon-mask, who turned away and disappeared through the doorway into the inner hall; then the beak of the falcon was pointing directly at Odysseus and he saw that the eyes beneath it were dramatically painted in black and glittering green.

'I see you wear the sign;' she said in a clear, dry voice, 'yet you do not know the Lady when you see her. This is very strange. But yes, you do indeed stand in her presence. What business do you have with her?'

Odysseus said, 'I have come to seek the release of my friends.'

'Release?' The falcon-head seemed to look about the place as though in some bemusement. 'We keep no prisoners in Aiaia.'

'Then am I to assume they are dead?'

'Why should you assume that? Do you think we are savages here?'

'Lady, I don't know who or what you are – whether you are the queen of these people or their sacred priestess, or,' Odysseus made the sign to ward off evil, 'as some men seem to think, a witch.'

'Then you are ignorant indeed!'

Again he refused to be thrown by the cool authority of her voice. 'Perhaps. But certain men about whom I care came here in peace and friendship today and they have not yet returned to my ship.'

'Perhaps,' she echoed him dryly, 'they have no wish to return.'

'I will believe that when I hear it from their own lips.'

Again the man in the lion-skin stepped forward with the claws of its great pads swinging at his side. 'Do you accuse the Lady of lying?'

'Peace,' the woman commanded sharply. 'Leave us now.' And

when the man hesitated, glancing first at Odysseus and then back at the Lady Circe, she repeated more firmly, 'Leave us, I say.'

Glancing balefully at Odysseus once more, the man bowed his head to the woman, touched his fingers to his forehead, and then backed away. The intense eyes beneath the falcon-beak held Odysseus under their scrutiny for what felt like a long time before the woman said, 'You and I will speak together, Odysseus of Ithaca.' Without waiting for him to answer, Circe turned on her heel and stepped through into the inner hall. The marble floor rang beneath the high-soled shoes she wore.

Checking that they had indeed been left unattended, Odysseus followed her through into a chamber where a fire blazed on the central hearth. By the light of oil-lamps burning in bronze sconces he made out the paintings on the walls – deer and wild boar prancing through woodland, with hawks circling overhead and owls and woodpeckers flying through the trees. An upright loom on which an unfinished tapestry was warped stood beside a low throne that was little more than an elaborately carved stool with the seat shaped like a crescent moon. The tall, graceful figures of three goddesses were painted on the wall behind it with two groups of attendant maidens dancing beside them. Only as the light shifted did he realise with a shock that the maidens had the heads of sows.

Circe had crossed to a table on which stood a silver mixing-bowl of wine and was pouring some of the dark liquid into a goblet.

Odysseus said quietly, 'One of my comrades tasted some of your wine and I hear that it is mixed with more than water. I prefer to keep my head clear.'

'I see,' she smiled. 'As you wish. What else did your comrade tell you?'

'That his friends were so intoxicated by your wine that they were easily seduced into your palace where he believes that something very strange became of them.'

Circe turned to look at him intently again. He saw that she

was older than he had first thought, a woman in her forties, whose strong features were heightened by the skilful use of cosmetics around her angled eyes and sensuous lips; but her poised presence emanated much the same kind of unquestionable power he had felt in the hieratic figures he had once seen on a papyrus brought out of Egypt by the captain of a ship he had plundered in his youth.

'Tell me,' she said, 'what manner of strangeness did your comrade see?'

Odysseus hesitated a moment before answering. 'I didn't want to believe him but I've just looked at this painting here, and now I am not so sure. My friend was afraid that your magic had transformed my men into pigs.'

Circe's scoffing laugh echoed in the silence of the hall. 'Why should I trouble to do that,' she said, 'when they were already eager to make pigs of themselves?'

The disdainful edge to her voice reminded Odysseus of his encounter with Thetis, the wife of Peleus, when he visited Skyros to bring their son Achilles to the war. She too had commanded the dark, residual powers of the old religion and had possessed something of this same impersonal asperity which conceded nothing to men in the realms of either spiritual or political authority.

Odysseus had never been at ease among such women. Even Clytaemnestra had unnerved him at times with the icy, insidious power she wielded over the men around her, though she was, for all practical purposes, subject to Agamemnon's rule. Yet Agamemnon was dead, he reminded himself, and by Clytaemnestra's hand. And Peleus, who had once been numbered among the greatest Argive heroes, had been reduced to a shadow of himself by a wife he had never learned to control. It would not do to dally with this woman too long.

'Nevertheless, the men are mine, madam,' he said, 'and I demand to see them.'

Again she laughed. 'By what authority do you make demands

here in Aiaia where you and your men are no more than vagabonds?'

'Zeus of the Strangers requires that all travellers be afforded proper hospitality,' he declared quietly, 'though I fear you are some-times less civil with them in these parts.'

'Do not think you can shame me, Odysseus of Ithaca.' As if to demonstrate that his fears had been groundless, she drank some of the wine she had poured. 'I answer to One older and greater than your Zeus.'

'Then it seems you live behind the times.'

'The Goddess knows nothing of time.'

Odysseus drew in his breath. 'I ask you again, madam, in the name of Zeus and his daughter Athena, yield up my men to me.'

'And if I choose not to do so?'

Faintly aware of the garlicky scent of the flower he wore, he took four steps forward to stand more closely beside her. 'You asked by what authority I make my demand,' he answered, slip-ping his hand inside the folds of his robe. 'Here is my authority.' The blade of the long knife was now pointed at her breast.

Unflinching she looked down at its bronze point, and up again into his narrowed eyes. Then she took a step backwards, smoothing the folds of her gown behind her, and calmly sat down in the crescent-curve of the stool. Her chin was tilted upwards, presenting the bare length of her neck to the blade. When its point came no closer, she shifted her gaze so that their eyes met. With a jolt that shocked invisibly through him, Odysseus sensed her entering his mind.

'You have seen such a moment before,' she said after a time. 'You saw Agamemnon stand this way above his daughter on the altar at Aulis. You saw one who is little more than a boy stand like this over a girl at his father's tomb. And there was another time — a man you know well, a friend, who stood with a sword in his hand over his wife on a bed of blood. You have seen this many times because this is how men always stand over women when they are confronted by a darkness inside themselves that they can neither understand nor control. So is this how you will stand over your wife when you return to her? Will you tell her she must do as you say or you will cut the breath out of her throat?'

It was as though she had looked directly through into the shadows of his mind. Swallowing, he sought to obliterate each of the pictures she had examined there, but they would not go away. The point of the knife was now trembling in his grip. He heard the shrieking of women inside the breached walls of Troy. Sweat broke at his brow and at the back of his neck. He saw Hecuba lying dead before him. He remembered how Aeolus had told him to return to Ithaca and take his life back by force if necessary – Aeolus who now had his own daughter's blood on his hands. Again he saw his wife Penelope running to meet him down the strand on Ithaca. Again he watched her face fall as she saw that he was drenched in blood. He forced open his eyes and saw that he was looking into the face of a woman who wore a falcon's beak that seemed poised to tear his liver out.

'What can you know about what happened at Troy, sitting here in this remote place where men still grovel at your command? You can know nothing about me. Nothing at all.'

Circe heaved a sigh. 'I know a man who is in trouble with his soul when I see one. Put down that knife, and come and drink some wine with me.'

Odysseus raised the blade of the sword towards her throat. 'Give me back my men and let us go.'

'Your men are safe,' she replied, untroubled. 'Nor do I think they would thank you for disturbing them right now.' He caught the wry smile in her eyes. 'No, they have not been turned into pigs. Your friend must have glimpsed the masks of the moon-maidens and his imagination did the rest.' Circe lifted the falcon-diadem from her head, placed it beside her and shook out her hair. 'The morning will be soon enough for you to meet with them again. Now why not sheathe this weapon? Or are you still thinking of using it?' With the silvered fingernails of her right hand she pushed the knife aside. 'Come,' she said, 'you need have no fear of my magic, you who already carry the sign of my initiation. Let me see if I can't help you to be worthy of the Moly flower before this night is done.'

Circe was smiling – a smile that spoke more of compassion than contempt. It seemed to imply that what was unfolding between them was a kind of game – a game of shadows; a serious game, but a game nonetheless; and one in which he would be wiser to rely on his intelligence than his strength.

To his astonishment, he found it difficult to resist that smile.

And so, as quickly and easily as that, Odysseus of Ithaca, Sacker of Cities, most resourceful and ingenious of men, found himself outflanked.

Not knowing what to expect when he entered the marble palace, he had believed himself prepared for all contingencies; but Circe was, it turned out, unlike any woman he had encountered before – with the possible exception of his wife, who always seemed to be waiting for him at every turn of his thought and feeling. But Penelope had never laid claim to any power other than that which came from her loving heart, so the two women were of a quite different order. And where Thetis had remained imperious and unyielding, the Lady of Aiaia seemed ready to abandon hostility for friendship as soon as the occasion warranted it.

Odysseus put aside the knife as he was bidden, and sat down on the couch at which she gestured. After a moment's hesitation, he drank from the cup that she put into his hand.

Seeing him taste the wine with more wariness than delectation, she said, 'Your friend was correct in his suspicions. The wine he drank earlier today was more than wine. It is our custom on feast days to open our hearts to visions other than those Dionysus brings. But what you have is only wine – although I think you'll find it mellower on the tongue than any from your Argive vineyards.'

'You are familiar with Argos then?'

'I know Asia better,' she said. 'I lived in Colchis when I was a small girl. My mother was Circe there before me, and her mother in the time before her. It was she who encountered your Argive hero Jason on his quest for the Golden Fleece and cleansed him and Medea of the murder they had done – though she foresaw that only disaster could come from their passion.' She stood up, saying, 'Would you mind if I worked at my loom as we talk?'

'Please,' he said, thinking with a pang of homesickness that she might have taken the words out of his wife's mouth. When Circe had settled at the loom, he said, 'But if you are Asian-born, how is it that you are here, so far away?'

Passing her shuttle through the warp, she said, 'We came because my mother foresaw that the rule of the Goddess was ending in that part of the world. Like Argos, Troy was already delivered over to the Olympian gods, and the Scythians were invading from the north. It was time to move our cult-centre to a safer place; so we sailed westwards till we came to this country and founded a new island of Aiaia. This is a gentler, more peaceful place, and we found that the people here worshipped the Goddess above all others still. I far prefer it.' Biting off a length of yarn between her teeth, she smiled across at him. 'And in answer to the question you have been too delicate to ask – yes, I have many husbands, all of whom are dear to me; but sadly I have no children. There, I have told you my story; now you must tell me yours.'

He began reluctantly at first, staring gloomily down into his wine-cup, admitting that this was the second shrine of the old religion he had visited since leaving Troy.

'At the temple of Neith-Athena at Lake Tritonis in Libya,' he said, 'the priestess declared that the goddess had turned her dark face towards me. She said there was so much darkness in me that she could see no way through it.'

Circe lifted her eyes from the tapestry. 'Was that all she said?'

Odysseus cast his mind back to that dismal shack by the salt-lake where it seemed that the world had finally closed down round him. 'She conceded that things might go better when I came to another shrine of the goddess.' He saw the quick lift of her brows. 'But this can't be the place she meant,' he added. 'Not if she spoke truly.'

'Why so?'

'Because she said that many years must pass before I would be at one with my soul again.'

'It seems you agree with her judgement. It seems you've grown attached to your darkness.'

'It is a curse, like blindness,' he frowned.

'There are blind men who see what others cannot see.'

'But a man is a fool if he pretends to more light than he has.'

'All pretence is vain,' she answered. 'The Goddess is patient with everything but the wilful obscuring of the truth.'

'But what if the truth is too painful to be disclosed? Isn't it best that we keep our wounds covered?'

'And let them fester? I think not. Aiaia is a place of healing.'

'Yet Aiaia is also an Island of the Dead,' he countered.

Her hands were busy with her shuttle as she said, 'Sometimes we must die to ourselves before we can be healed.'

Odysseus said, 'I don't believe I understand that.'

'Because it is a mystery on which you've not yet entered, for all that you wear my flower.' She glanced back at her loom. 'I wonder how you came by it.'

Half-ashamed of his answer, Odysseus said, 'It was stolen from one of your people by a serving-boy who came with me out of Libya. He thought it might protect me from your magic.'

'He stole it, you say?' Circe was smiling. 'Is this the boy Hermes of whom Macareus speaks?' And, when Odysseus nodded, 'He is well-named. Perhaps the god travels with him; and if Hermes is with you there may be hope for your soul after all. So why are you here, I wonder? Why have you not gone home?'

Odysseus did not speak for a long time, and once he began to speak, his answer soon became long and involved, sometimes hesitant, and not always coherent in its attempt to gather together all the ravelled tangles of his distress. By the time he ended the lamps were guttering on their sconces and the full moon had travelled far across the sky.

He had spoken almost entirely without interruption. Listening intently as she worked at her loom, Circe only occasionally asked for more detail about some event he had reported skimpily or for a fuller account of the dreams to which he referred. Intuiting his need, she had kept silent during those long moments when he too was silent, staring fixedly into space as the pictures of death and devastation returned to his mind and left him trembling.

'So you see,' he ended at last, 'this is what I have become.'

'But your story has not ended yet,' Circe responded. 'And even the tale you tell might be told another way.'

'I've given you the truth I have,' he glowered. 'No one has been given more.'

'I don't doubt it,' she smiled, 'and clearly you are not as blind as you led me to believe. But you see your life as the Cyclops of your dream might see it – with only a single eye; and that way it is impossible to see how things relate in depth to one another. If you wish to become Odysseus again, then we must talk more. And talk alone will not be enough to recover your self for yourself. There are things that must also be seen and done and undergone.' Again she looked up at him sharply. 'You must earn that flower that you wear above your heart. I warn you, it is not won without suffering.'

'I'm no stranger to suffering,' he answered.

'No,' she nodded as if in agreement, 'you have suffered much in your travels. But they were journeys out across the world. There is another kind of voyage a man might make. Are you ready for its risks, I wonder?'

It was not decided at once. All that was agreed was that Odysseus would sleep in the palace for what remained of the night, and that a messenger would be sent to *The Fair Return* to let his crew know that he and his men were safe and well. The next morning he would meet those of his friends who were already in the palace, and he and Circe would talk again. If he decided that he had no wish to remain on Aiaia, then there was nothing to prevent him leaving,

When Odysseus met his missing men the next day he found them unharmed. Most of them, like Elpenor who greeted his captain with an apologetic grin, were simply content to have passed the night in a heightened state of sexual pleasure; but Polites seemed to have experienced something deeper, of which he professed himself unable yet to speak, and Macareus was evidently transformed by whatever had happened to him during the course of the rites. The eager light which had been banished from his face by the death of his sister had returned to his eyes, and where he had been almost speechless on the voyage out of Aeolia, he was now voluble in his desire to remain in Aiaia.

'It is what Canace and I always dreamed of,' he said to Odysseus when they were alone together, 'a realm where the Goddess is revered as the very portal of life itself. But there is more, far more . . . a true mystery . . . something I would never have believed possible, and that is the real reason why I won't keep company with you if you decide to leave today.'

'Are you able to say what it is?' Odysseus asked.

'It is a secret thing,' Macareus said below his breath. 'You must swear to keep it so.'

Reflecting that this eager man was making a poor job of keeping the secret himself, Odysseus said, 'You have my word.'

Macareus ran a hand through his white hair, trembling with excitement as he spoke. 'The woman who accompanied me yesterday . . . we talked intimately together . . . she searched out the causes of my grief, and when I told her my story . . . of my love for my sister and the manner of her death . . . she said that there were rites known to her people by which I might speak with Canace again.'

Odysseus studied the fervour in the young man's face with dismay. Gravely he said, 'Your sister is dead, Macareus.'

'But what does that mean?' Macareus answered. 'And are the dead necessarily beyond our reach? This is the Island of the Dead, Odysseus. Those birds flying over the Hill of Silence are feeding on the flesh of one who died the day before we came here. To those who can see only that, death must seem to be the end of everything. But it's the law of the Goddess that everything inherits everything else; and nothing that is real and true can die for ever.' Macareus rested his hands on his friend's shoulders. 'Believe me, Odysseus, the people of Aiaia understand these things. They can show me how to live again.'

At once sceptical of these claims and strangely elated by them, Odysseus decided to remain for a time in Aiaia. When he spoke to Circe again the next day his sense of purpose and commitment grew. The length of the stay was extended, and though many of his crew were content to spend time ashore in a place where they could eat well and drink well and sport with the women of the island, by no means all of them understood why they were kicking their heels in this backwater when there were ships to be taken on the high seas, or towns to plunder and, if all of that grew tiresome, then a home awaited them in Ithaca. But when they tried to raise these issues, they found only that their captain seemed unduly preoccupied with the Lady of the island.

Not that he got to spend all his time with her. As Queen and Priestess, Healer of the Sick, Keeper of the Mysteries, and Guardian to the Gate of the Dead, Circe had many duties, and Odysseus watched with increasing admiration as she performed the public rites of her role. Clearly the people from many miles around Aiaia loved, respected and feared her in equal measure. She and her helpers treated the sick and dying with great care. She listened attentively to disputes and gave judgement fairly, without prejudice and often with good humour. Her lively presence could be felt everywhere as the intelligent genius of the place, yet her individuality was entirely subsumed when she wore the mask and robes of the priestess who conducted the dead to the Hill of

Silence and later consecrated their bones in the island's ancient ossuary.

When he met alone with Circe, their conversations often lasted for hours and were intense, exhausting affairs. Other meetings were cut short, however – insensitively so, it sometimes seemed to him, and not always for reasons that were made clear. Then came several, frustrating days when he did not see her at all, and during that time Odysseus found that his feelings towards Circe were undergoing turbulent changes.

Even when she had removed the elaborate ritual cosmetics she had worn at their first meeting, he saw that Circe was a woman of striking appearance. The angled eyes, the high cheekbones, and the aquiline nose above her almost Ethiopian mouth could be as impassive as a statue of Apollo at times; but at others they were quickened by her bright laughter at some of their more absurd misprisions, and he found that he had come to love the sound of that laughter. It wasn't long before he began to believe that he was in love with its source.

When he first confessed this evolution in his feelings, Circe studied him gravely for a time as though he had advanced a mildly interesting business proposition. Then she said, 'You mean you wish to make love to me?'

'Yes, I do,' he said, delighted that she had come so quickly to the point, though a little dismayed by her absence of excitement.

'Very well,' she assented. 'You may come to my chamber tonight.' And before he could say anything else, she returned him to the place where they had left matters in their unresolved exchange of the previous day.

By the end of that morning's conversation his feelings were no longer quite as ardent as when he had first woken; but it had been a long time since he had lain in a woman's arms, and Odysseus was not a man to give offence by failing to keep an assignation once it was made.

Wondering whether he had embarked on a huge mistake, he entered her chamber that night feeling like an untried boy. But the oil-lamps were discreetly placed, and the air of the room was fragrant with blossom and aromatic herbs, and she lay smiling in her great bed as though the half-naked man standing awkwardly across from her was a familiar and dear friend on whom she was glad to lavish her favours. A raised hand beckoned him towards her.

She revealed herself to be a tender, skilful and generous lover. So much so that Odysseus, who had been armoured against intimacy for ten long years, was overwhelmed by the generosity and refinement of her passion. His scarred body accomplished its climax in a torrent of tears, and he lay in her quiet arms for a long time afterwards, sobbing from the sheer joy of release at first, and later with the stress of conflicting emotions he endured.

Once his breathing subsided, they lay talking far into the night. Strangely, with no sense of embarrassment or indiscretion, he spoke of his love for Penelope and the exquisite pain he felt each time he confronted the thought that he might never see her again. He spoke too of the son he had never seen, and of his own parents, and their love for one another and for himself as their only child. And soon he felt so large a yearning for Ithaca in his heart that he could contemplate no other possibility than that of taking ship next day and making speed for home.

But then he became conscious again of the woman lying at his side.

Falling silent, he reached for her again; but she raised a hand to his chest as he lifted his weight across her. 'Be aware that we can give only this single night to Aphrodite,' she whispered. 'A time will soon come when your feelings for me will change into their opposite.'

'Never,' he protested; but she raised the tips of her fingers to his lips. 'Believe me,' she whispered, 'in this as in other things.'

Though he was determined to prove her wrong, things turned out much as Circe had said. The ardour of that night proved transient. The next day she was cool and reserved with him, and he experienced the rebuff less as disappointment than as humiliation.

Thinking his manhood rejected by her, he rejected her in turn, comparing her severity with the less exacting charms of younger women. As she probed more deeply he began to fight fiercely over ground he might have conceded earlier. Yet even as he did so, he felt the ground slipping away.

Coming out of an abrasive encounter in which her dispassionate control contrasted with his own infuriated turmoil, his eyes fell on a small clay figure of the pregnant Goddess standing in its alcove in the hall. Circe had told him that it was very ancient and also very precious to her because she had discovered it when they were digging the foundations of her house. But someone must have picked the figure up to examine or clean it and then carelessly replaced it, for it now stood perilously close to the alcove's edge. Wilfully, Odysseus brushed past it with his cloak and heard the clay shatter as it fell to the marble floor.

He winced at the sound and bit his lip. For a moment he might have walked on, but he turned and saw the thing in pieces.

With tears starting at his eyes, he dropped to his knees and began to gather together the broken bits. When he rose to his feet again he saw a young woman staring at him. She had been crossing the hall towards Circe's apartment when the sound of the fall stopped her in her tracks. She stood in dismay now, lifting the fingers of one hand to the cleft of her chin.

'It was an accident,' he muttered. 'I was careless.' Concealing the tears, he glanced down at the fragments in his palm. 'It seems the thing can't be mended. What should I do with these?'

'Give them to me,' she said and came closer to take the painted terracotta from his hand. 'This was very dear to the Lady.'

'I know,' he replied hoarsely.

But when he looked up again it was into a face of such poignant beauty that he could not understand how this girl had escaped his attention before. 'Yet she is full of forgiveness,' she said; 'and you are very dear to her too.' Then she blushed and turned away and was gone on silent feet across the marble floor.

★   ★   ★

When they were next together he confessed to Circe what he had done. She was feeding the house-snake as he entered and continued to do so as he spoke.

'It was deliberate,' he said. 'I wanted the figure to break. I wanted it because it sometimes feels as though you're trying to break me – breaking my heart, breaking my will. I wanted to smash something of yours.'

'The figure was only clay,' she reflected quietly, looking up from where the snake lay in her lap, 'but you and I are flesh and blood. This thing is painful for both of us.'

'I was stupid and brutal,' he said. 'Can you forgive me for that?'

Circe raised her eyes, reproaching not his crime but his doubt. 'If we cannot forgive one another,' she said, 'what hope can there be for change?'

After that it was as if they were free to move through into a space where there was neither anger nor sentiment; only the serious and concentrated diligence of two hearts and minds looking for mutual respect and understanding across what seemed at times an unbridgeable divide. Yet each time they parted he was left with two irreconcilable feelings: that his presentation of his own perspective of things had been both cogent and complete; and that behind each exchange there was always present a veiled and silent figure that vanished whenever he tried to identify her, and who consistently refused to share that valuation.

Again and again they returned to the subject of the war. Whatever he might affirm to the contrary, Circe insisted that Odysseus was as much a casualty of the war at Troy as Queen Hecuba had been.

'To suggest that the evil-doer and the victim of evil are as one in their suffering is to abrogate all standards of reason and conscience,' he protested. 'Hecuba is dead because King Priam and all her sons and daughters and grandchildren are dead; and if they are dead it is because I was the instrument of their murder.'

'Yes,' she cried, 'yes, and again yes. But can that be the end of it? Can that be the whole of it? Thousands of men behaved as you did on both sides of that catastrophe and many with more enthusiasm. What is required now is that you understand the deep roots of that violence and allow that understanding to become part of yourself. Doesn't the renewal of your life depend on it?'

'But how?' he demanded in frustration.

When she did not speak, he said, 'Why do I always feel you know the answers to the questions you ask, yet wilfully choose to withhold them from me?'

'Because those answers are my answers, earned from my experience. Were I to tell you these things you would only nod your head and forget them. You must see them for yourself. Otherwise they are nothing.'

'How?' he shouted. 'I ask you again: how?'

Circe studied his petulant frown, aware once more that he was on the point of walking away from her. 'You might begin,' she said, 'by thinking about the origins of the war.'

Impatiently he shook his head. 'The causes of the war are obvious. One needs look no further than Agamemnon's ambitions and the injury that was done to his brother Menelaus.'

'That is the tale as the Cyclops might tell it. Look deeper.'

'To what? To the madness of the gods themselves?'

'That might be closer,' she nodded. 'I believe your bards have something to say on that score.'

'The story of the quarrel over the golden apple, you mean, when Paris chose Aphrodite as the fairest of the goddesses because she promised him Helen?'

'An interesting moment, don't you think? But doesn't the drama begin earlier?'

Odysseus frowned, casting back his memory, wondering why she was troubling him with old stories that, in the exhausting violence of the war itself, had been considered seriously by no one but the poets.

'With the wedding of Peleus and Thetis,' he said. 'The last occasion when all the gods were present among us.'

'All except one,' she said.

'Eris,' he remembered.

'Yes. She who was not invited.'

He said, 'Who wants to have discord at a wedding-feast?'

'Yet she came anyway, and because she was uninvited she brought trouble.'

'In the form of the golden apple, yes.'

'And why should that have caused such trouble?'

'Because it was inscribed *For the Fairest,*' he answered impatiently. 'That was what started the goddesses quarrelling, and from that came the judgement of Paris, which led to the abduction of Helen, which was what started the war. Or so the stories say. But if the tale proves anything it's that the goddesses can drive the world mad if they are not kept firmly in hand by Zeus. I'm surprised that you would want to remind me of it.'

'Clever Cyclops!' she mocked him, smiling.

And met only his baleful glower.

'Your bards are men in the service of kings,' she said. 'That is how they choose to tell the story, as a competition among petulant females, each of whom behaves badly. But sometimes Truth also comes uninvited to the feast, though you have to listen hard for her amid all the noise the men are making.'

His eyes were averted from her, looking out across the green glade in the direction where his ship still idled in the harbour. There were better things for a man to do with his time than listen to old stories.

'I have a question for you,' she said. 'Who is Eris?'

He shrugged impatiently again. 'The answer is in her name. I've said it already. She is strife, discord, quarrelling.'

'War?' Circe added. 'Or at least the seed of it?'

'Yes, that too, if you like,' he said without thinking, wanting to be gone.

'And Eris was there right at the start of it all,' she said, 'before Paris gave his judgement, before the abduction of Helen, long before Agamemnon's ships set sail and Priam summoned his allies to the defence of Troy. She was present as the uninvited guest.'

She saw him frowning at her now, puzzled by the oblique line of her thought. 'Something was left out of consideration,' she said. 'She was ignored, rejected, perhaps repressed. And there the trouble began.'

'It might have ended there too,' he said, 'if each of the three goddesses had shown more maturity.'

Circe said, 'if you have learned anything while you have been here on Aiaia, you will know that the Goddess is one and single like the moon. And like the moon she has four aspects, not just three. Name them for me.'

'The new moon, the full moon, the waning moon, and . . .' He hesitated there, thinking beyond the answer.

She waited.

'The dark moon,' Odysseus said, feeling a glimmer of dark radiance inside him as he spoke. 'The moon we do not see.'

Circe nodded. 'And where was *she* at the judgement of Paris?'

His thoughts were moving quickly now. Was Eris also an aspect of the goddess, the turbulent dark shadow cast by Hera's bounty, Aphrodite's beauty, Athena's wisdom? But, 'How could Paris be expected to judge what he couldn't even see?' he demanded. And then another thought struck him. 'In any case the quarrel was among the goddesses. It was none of his choosing.' Odysseus faltered, frowning. 'At least, not until he was asked to choose.'

'And why should the immortal gods need a mortal to sort out their differences?'

'I don't know,' he admitted eventually. 'I've never understood that.'

'Perhaps the story isn't about the gods at all?' she suggested. 'Perhaps it's a story about men and the choices that men make for themselves? About who they deeply are, I mean, and how they intend to live their lives, and what values they mean to serve. And if that is so, why do you think the dark aspect of the Goddess should have been left out of count?'

'Isn't that obvious? The service of Hera offers us a house and home, power, dignity, wealth. Aphrodite brings beauty, passion love. Athena yields wisdom and strength. All these are desirable. Paris's folly was to make the choice at all – to serve only one of them to the exclusion of the others. But what does Eris have to offer a man? Discord, bickering and argument. Who in his right mind would choose to give his life over to that kind of strife?'

Circe said, 'You ask me that, who have just spent ten years of your life fighting a war?'

'That's a different matter,' he frowned.

'Is it so very different?' she pressed. 'Don't your poets tell you that Eris is sister to Ares, Lord of War? Perhaps her rage is the consequence of her exclusion? And might it not be as great a folly to split Eris off from the entire body of the Goddess by rejecting and ignoring her as it was for Paris to single out Aphrodite? She too is immortal. And once she is left out of consideration, what becomes of her power?' Circe brought her hands together. 'It is enough for now. You should think more on these things. And dream of them too.'

Then she stood up with an air of finality and withdrew.

But Odysseus was in no mood for thought. He was restless and irritable, annoyed once again by her sibylline manner; and by the implication that he was some kind of dunce for whom the obvious was too difficult to grasp.

He decided to go hunting, not because food was needed, but for the clean sport of tracking something down; for the pleasure of killing it.

No game came his way. Hot and frustrated, he put his spear down at a spring that broke out of a grassy mound. Lifting the severed goat's tail that some shepherd had fixed dangling over the source, he let water splash into his mouth.

Even as he drank he sensed a presence near him. He looked up at the sound of giggling and saw a broad-hipped woman smiling at him. Her name was Mopsa and he had often seen her laughing with his crew while she served them wine.

Ten minutes later he had mounted her from behind like a billy-goat in the sunlit glade. He was groaning to his climax with both hands grasping at her breasts when a movement in the afternoon dazzle of light and shadow caught his eye.

Glancing across the glade, he saw that the herb-gatherer with a withy-basket who had disturbed his concentration was the same young woman who had seen him smash the clay figure of the goddess some days earlier. Once again the expression on her exquisite young face was of mild dismay.

'Who was that who came into the glade?' he said afterwards to the woman who panted in the grass beside him with reddened cheeks.

'I didn't see anyone,' Mopsa replied.

'She was gathering herbs and simples, I think.'

'Oh' – Mopsa flapped a hand to shoo a bee that was buzzing near her curls – 'that must have been Calypso.'

He had bad dreams that night. He was out at sea at the steering oar of *The Fair Return* in uncertain waters under a dark sky heading for a narrow strait. Gloomy cliffs rose at either side of him, yet there were, he dimly sensed, graver dangers imminently present on both bows. On the starboard side the seas were twisting into a vortex that might suck him down if he drifted too close; so he pushed the oar hard over on a course that would take him away from that danger and closer to the portside cliff. He was congratulating himself on his skill when several arms like the tentacles of a giant octopus swooped down on the ship out of the crag. To his horror he saw six of his men plucked screaming from the oar-benches and lifted up to the many mouths of a hideous, dog-like monster who crouched on the head of the cliff screaming that she had been made that way by Circe's magic.

Odysseus jumped up on his bed sweating and shouting and did not sleep again. His anger grew as he tossed and turned on the bed. It was still broiling inside him when he went to see Circe early the next day. Before she could speak he said, 'Last night I was visited by a dream. It was made plain to me that if I'm not careful I'll be swallowed up by the maw of your Goddess or sucked down by it. Either way, I will no longer be a man.'

Circe looked up from the wax tablet on which she was inscribing a message. 'Tell me your dream,' she said.

He did so, sparing none of the revulsion it had aroused in him, and when he was done, she said, 'Did I not tell you that the dark aspect of the Goddess will not be excluded? If you don't admit her to the feast of your waking life, then expect to find her waiting in your sleep. Also I should point out that you burst in here without invitation. I have no time for you today. Perhaps you will find a warmer welcome in Mopsa's arms.' Then she returned her attention to the wax.

When Odysseus left her chamber, he found Macareus waiting in the ante-room with a warm smile of greeting on his face. 'Oh it's you, Odysseus,' he said. 'I heard voices, so I didn't knock, even though I can hardly contain myself today.' Swallowing his excitement, he added with an attempt at sobriety, 'If all goes well, the Lady has promised to admit me to the next initiation. I believe that means I'll shortly be taken to the Oracle of the Dead.'

A sickly wave of apprehension passed across Odysseus's mind. 'I wish you well of it,' he scowled. 'It seems the Lady no longer has time for me.'

'Tell me,' he demanded the next time he was admitted to Circe's presence, 'have you taken Macareus to your bed?'

She widened her eyes momentarily at this indiscretion and glanced away.

'Well?' he demanded.

'And if I have?'

'You say that as if it was a matter of no consequence,' he snapped.

'I do not see,' she said, 'how it can be of any consequence to you.'

'Have you forgotten who I am?' he demanded, outraged. 'I am Odysseus of Ithaca and as much a lord on my own island as you are Lady here. My name is known from Sicily to furthest Egypt as one of the great conquerors of Troy. On board my ship my power is as unquestionable as that of Zeus himself. Whereas that man . . . that man belongs nowhere now. He is merely a member of my crew, and because of that there are issues of discipline and respect . . . and confidence.'

Already he saw that his complaints were becoming more than faintly absurd. 'Besides,' he tried again, 'the man is . . .'

'Yes?'

'He is guilty of the crime of incest.'

'You mean that he loved his sister?'

'What foul kind of love is that?'

Circe left him treading water in a long silence before she said, 'Do you know, I cannot believe that any true love is foul. Why are you angry with me, Odysseus?'

'I'm not angry with you,' he snapped back. 'I'm just . . . appalled.'

'Oh dear,' Circe bit her lip to restrain a laugh he would have found intolerable, 'how fiercely she has you in her grip! It really is time you began to listen to her.'

'Who?' he frowned. When Circe merely shook her magnificent head, he said, 'This is entirely between you and me. It has always been so. I've listened to you and I've tried to learn from you; but how can I respect you if you let any man take you, however basely he may have behaved?'

'No man takes me,' she said, 'though I give myself to whom I choose.'

'Then I must think you as promiscuous a whore as the goddess you serve.'

She left a further silence before saying, 'Insult me if you must, but beware how you speak of the Goddess. She has had you in her power for a long time, even though you were scarcely aware of her existence when you first came to me. But now that you know of her and still won't let her in, she's turning you into a crabby sort of prude.' She looked at him coldly. 'And I'm afraid that makes you merely ridiculous!'

Circe had been seated when he came in and he was standing over her. He raised his hand now and was about to bring it down across her face when he saw that this was exactly what she had anticipated. Her cheek was tilted to receive the blow. Her eyes were open. 'If it will make you feel better,' she said, 'go ahead and hit me, Odysseus of Ithaca, Sacker of Cities, Striker of Women.'

It had already been late in the day when he came to her. Darkness had fallen outside. The evening was loud with the shrill friction of cicadas and the croak of bullfrogs in the distant fen. Somewhere across the house a woman was singing. The only other sound came in the creak of his breath as the unstable foundations of Odysseus' life shifted under this last, minimal exertion of pressure, and the collapse for which Circe had so patiently waited quietly began.

Telemachus

Late in the spring of the year after the war had ended, all of Ithaca was thrown into mourning by the death of Queen Anticleia. The daughter of that old rogue Autolycus, who ruled the lands around Mount Parnassus and claimed descent from Hermes himself, she had been a much-loved figure on the island ever since she first came there as bride to King Laertes more than forty years earlier. And if ever there has been a love-match on this troubled earth, it was between that shy and happy couple.

Laertes had been an adventurer in his youth, sailing with the Argonauts and taking part in the great hunt for the Calydonian boar, but once the two of them were wedded, neither had any larger ambition than to rule over the islands in peace and spend as much time as possible in each other's company. Once affairs of state were dealt with, they took most pleasure in tending their vineyards and gardens together, and encouraging the islanders by example in all the best practices of animal husbandry. But the greatest joy of their life was found in their love for their only child, Odysseus.

In his later life, Odysseus always maintained that such understanding of love as he possessed had been instilled into him at an early age by the knowledge that he was devoutly loved by two parents who shared an unquestioning love for each other. If it was a love that allowed him to rove freely across the world in his youth as his father had done before him, it was also one which demonstrated daily on each of his returns that true and lasting satisfaction would eventually be found only in such a life as his parents were now living together. So it was among the happiest times anyone had known on Ithaca when Odysseus came back one day with Penelope, daughter of Lord Icarius of Sparta, and announced their intention to live thereafter in quiet contentment on the island. By the same token, it was among the most grievous of times, when he was drawn away to the war at Troy, taking most of the young men of the islands with him. But by then, Odysseus and Penelope also had a son, and Laertes and Anticleia consoled themselves as best they could by keeping both Telemachus and his distraught mother in their care.

Though Odysseus had warned everyone of his conviction that the war must drag on for many years, no one had wanted to believe him. Yet his prediction proved true, and there was nothing to be done about it but endure the empty years, and make the offerings to the gods, and take measures to ensure that the kingdom which Odysseus would inherit on his eventual return remained in good order. Yet the stress of managing the often quarrelsome people of the islands without his son at his side, soon began to age Laertes beyond his years; and though she was never heard to mutter a word of complaint against her son, Anticleia's heart sometimes turned grey with grief as she worried over the fate of Odysseus and the growing signs of weariness in her husband's face.

Then the news came that the war had ended. For a time, like everyone else, Anticleia lived in the happy expectation that Odysseus must soon come home. But as the months passed and he did not return, it was as if some portion of her being without which life could no longer be supported, began to fail inside her. In many ways she remained more alert to the stresses at work in the life of the islands than was her husband. She was sensitive to the loneliness which led Penelope to take comfort in the friend-

ship of Amphinomus; and she was deeply troubled by the hostility
that the friendship stirred inside Telemachus. So each morning
Anticleia prayed to Athena for Odysseus' return; yet with the
passing of each day her heart was oppressed by the fear that her
prayers would not be answered. She began to lose weight. Gaunt
hollows appeared at her cheeks. Though no one knew it but her
old servant Eurycleia, she was in great pain.

Then, during the course of one night after a rancorous council
meeting which had left her husband exhausted and confused,
Queen Anticleia passed away.

Laertes was found weeping over her frail body the next morning
and it was a long time before he could be persuaded to leave her
side.

I remember being astounded that, alone of all the people present,
Telemachus shed no tears at his grandmother's funeral. He stood
stiffly upright beside the frail figure of his grandfather, with the
wind blowing through his hair. Staring out across the cliff into
the glare of the sea, he knew that he would never see his father's
ship cross that horizon. He must find the strength inside himself
to endure all the misfortunes that had fallen on his family.

And that, over the following five years, is precisely what he
did. Sometimes I looked on in wonder as he subjected himself
to a gruelling round of athletic exercises, running for miles across
the hills of Ithaca, practising hour after hour with the discus and
the spear, as though he was quite certain that one day another
war must come and it must not find him unprepared.

On one occasion, when he was not yet fourteen years old, I
found him fondling the great bow that his father had left behind
in Ithaca, a springy length of yew-wood fortified with ibex horn
and curved at either end to increase the tension when an arrow
was nocked at full stretch. No one had taken it from its protective wrappings since Odysseus left for Troy, and I doubted that
Telemachus had been given permission to do so either; so I
expected to see him reprimanded when Penelope chanced on us

sitting together in the armoury. But she looked down onto her son's defiant face with a fond and rueful smile.

'That bow has a tremendous history,' she said. 'It was given as a gift to your father by the hero Iphitus after Odysseus helped him to recover a string of mares he had lost in the mountains near Sparta. Iphitus had inherited the bow from his father, the great archer Eurytus, who claimed to have had it straight from the hand of Far-shooting Apollo himself, who is the greatest archer of all.'

Looking up from where he greased the bow with hot tallow, Telemachus said, 'Is it true that no one but my father can bend this bow far enough to string it?'

'No one else has ever dared to try,' she smiled. 'But your father told me as much and I've never known him lie to me. He used to practice with it all the time; and his hand grew so steady that I once saw him whistle an arrow through the handles of a whole line of axes he had set up out there in the courtyard. That was just before you were born.' She gave a little laugh. 'He was so happy at the prospect of your birth that he was quite sure he could do anything. And he inspired such confidence that everyone else thought so too.'

Penelope looked down at the bow again, biting her nether lip. Then she looked back earnestly at her son. 'Believe me, Telemachus, there has never been such a man as your father. One day, when you're older and strong enough, he'll teach you how to draw this bow.'

For a moment the boy's young heart was lifted by the eager light in his mother's eyes; but at that moment he heard Amphinomus call down the passage outside. 'Where have you got to, Penelope? What are you doing down there?'

Immediately the face of Telemachus darkened again. 'If he ever comes back,' he scowled.

'He will come back,' Penelope said sternly. 'Don't you ever dare to doubt it.'

'Your friend out there doesn't seem to think so.'

'I don't care what anybody else thinks,' she answered. 'Nobody knows Odysseus as I know him. Only death could keep him from us; and I'm quite sure he's not yet dead.'

'Where is he then?' the boy demanded.

'I don't know where he is and I've no idea what he's doing. But I do know that if his life-thread was strong enough not to break during all those years of the war, then nothing since will have broken it.' Crouching down, Penelope held her son by the shoulders and gazed steadily into his eyes. 'Your father will come home, Telemachus. I can't tell you when he will come or how long he will take about it, but he will return. So be careful how you handle that bow,' she smiled. 'Odysseus will want it when he gets back.'

Thereafter Telemachus took to waxing the bow more often, for he was greatly heartened in his resolve that day. It was as if he drew strength from the sturdy pliancy of the bow, and with it came a stronger sense of his father and a firmer conviction that he would indeed return. But few people across the islands shared that conviction and, when another year passed with no news of Odysseus' whereabouts, the issue of good governance became more problematic.

As tribute time approached, Eupeithes and his son Antinous sailed across to Cephallenian Same where they put their heads together with the local overlord Polytherses and his son Ctesippus, who was now looking for a wife. Together they decided that it was time that a Council of the Islands was called to discuss the future. In particular they agreed that serious thought should be given to the question of the succession now that Odysseus was dead. When they managed to rally support among a number of the other chieftains, including King Nisus of Dulichion, who had ambitions for his son Amphinomus, a formal petition was drawn up and addressed, with many signatories, to the attention of King Laertes.

The old herald Peisenor, accompanied by Medon his junior, delivered the petition to Laertes on his farm. With quivering hands the old king put away the skin on which it was written and looked up in dismay. 'I knew something of the sort must happen sooner or later. Why can't they leave me to die in peace?'

'That's what they're afraid of, lord,' Peisenor answered. 'You and I are old men these days, and Telemachus is too young to rule. If you were to die without naming a stronger heir, there would be a struggle for power across the islands, which would do no one any good.'

Stubbornly Laertes said, 'Odysseus is my heir.'

Peisenor nodded and glanced away. 'But his fate is uncertain, lord.'

Laertes sat in the porch of his farmstead staring out over his garden. 'Do you see that orchard over there?' he pointed. 'The pears, the apples, those forty fig trees? Odysseus and I planted them all when he was still a child. They were only saplings then, and look what loads they're bearing now. They belong to him, do you hear me? The fruit of their harvest is his.'

A younger man aware of the gravity of the mission, Medon shifted uneasily. 'But the concerns expressed here are not unfounded. How are we to answer them?'

'Don't answer them,' Laertes grunted after a time. 'Not yet. Call Lord Mentor and my old friend Aegyptius together at the palace. I'll come to them there and we'll deliberate on this tomorrow. And ask the Lady Penelope to attend on us too. Her counsel is always wise. Together we will see what is best to do.'

But even that meeting of friends was not without its difficulties. Having been given charge of his affairs by Odysseus, Mentor stood firmly with Penelope in guarding the interests of her son. 'If we let them come together in council,' he insisted, 'they'll draw strength from one another. Then it'll be hard to get them to disperse until some decision is made. Better to keep them separate on their own islands. They're more likely to stay patient that way.'

But Aegyptius was less certain. 'As far as we older men go, you may be right,' he conceded. 'But a whole new generation has grown up during the war – my son Eurynomus among them – and patience is not their strength. They missed the fighting at Troy and they need to make a name for themselves. It's my guess that Antinous and his friend Eurymachus are somewhere behind this petition. They want to feel their manhood has weight. If we don't let them come into a council where they can sound off a little, they're sure to find some other way of making trouble. Better to have it out in the open where we can see it.' He turned to where the old king sat stroking his cheek with the fingers of one hand. 'You're still the High King, Laertes,' he said. 'Use the council to assert your authority.'

Laertes winced at his friend. 'I know them all, Aegyptius,' he said. 'I've known them since they were tugging at their mother's paps. I've watched them grow till they have beards at their chins, and I know there's not one of them measures up to my son. Nor do any of them have a claim on the succession while Odysseus lives or while his son lives after him. I won't have them thinking I'd consider it.'

Mentor tapped the table in agreement.

A little peevishly, having listened to the absent-minded manner in which Laertes had failed to except his son Eurynomus from his general dismissal of the island's young men, Aegyptius said, 'Telemachus is a fine boy, but we all know that he's green still. And who can be sure that Odysseus lives?'

'He lives,' Penelope quietly interposed.

'So we all pray, my dear,' Aegyptius answered. 'Yet the years pass.'

'They have no claim, I say,' Laertes repeated.

Again Lord Mentor registered his agreement. 'Then let that be an end to it.'

'Yet there is talk of how a claim might be legitimised,' Aegyptius ventured. 'Not that I endorse it myself, but my son tells me he has heard Antinous say that a time must come when the Lady Penelope will take another husband. One who will act as regent till Telemachus comes of age. He wonders why a prince of

Dulichion should be preferred over an Ithacan when the choice is made.'

Taken by surprise, Penelope flushed. 'I have a husband already,' she declared, 'and will hear no talk of other marriages while my husband lives.'

Aegyptius raised his hands in a gesture of self-exculpation. 'Which is exactly what I said myself. However, people still talk.'

Turning to her father-in-law, Penelope laid her fingers across his mottled hand. 'I cannot control how people speak of me behind closed doors, but I will not have this question raised in public council.'

'Never fear it, my dear.' Laertes turned a reproachful glance at his friend. 'There will be no council. I will send my heralds out to all the islands with the message that I remain High King still and my royal writ still runs. It is my will that my son Odysseus succeeds me. If it is the will of the gods that he dies before me, then I shall live on until his son Telemachus is old enough to be king in my place.'

But the expenditure of moral energy had cost the old man in physical strength. He began to cough, patting his chest with the flat of his hand. Penelope had turned to him in concern when he drew in his breath with a noisy sniff. Sagging back on his throne, Laertes said, 'Now may I please go back to my farm?'

One by one, and then in increasing numbers, they began to present themselves at the palace. Each of them declared that he understood Penelope's grief over her absent husband and deeply sympathized with it; but they claimed that, with each passing year, it pained them more to watch her waste the sweetness of her prime in hopeless yearning for a man who must certainly now be dead. What else could explain his failure to return? Why would he not at least have sent a message explaining what kept him away? Odysseus had never been a wilfully cruel man. If he was alive he would surely have found some means of sparing her the distress of this uncertainty. And if, as they believed, he had passed away, then he would certainly not want her to grieve as a widow for the rest of her days. Had he not, like all the other husbands departing for the war, given his wife his blessing to remarry once she knew that he was dead? Many women had already done so, even though, in their case, there was none of the same responsibility for the continuing welfare of the state that devolved on Penelope's shoulders. So it was in that spirit of public service, as well as out of esteem for her own person, that they now humbly presented themselves before her as suitors for her hand.

At first Amphinomus was not among them. He had not been seen on Ithaca for some time, for when she learned how their names were abused in the gossip of the islands, Penelope decided to forgo the pleasure of his company in order to preserve her good name. Amphinomus was saddened and hurt by her decision, but as a gentleman he felt obliged to comply with her wishes.

Telemachus rejoiced at his departure, taking it as a further auspicious omen that his father must come home. At the same time, he tried to become more considerate of his mother's feelings, though on more than one occasion I heard him complain to me that she failed to respond as cheerily to his efforts as he would have liked. Certainly none of the royal household were pleased when Antinous and Eurymachus arrived at the palace, preening in their finery, each offering himself as the desirable solution to Penelope's troubles. Politely but firmly they were turned away, and we hoped that might be the end of the matter; but boat after boat put in during the weeks that followed, and more and more suitors came calling at the palace from every island in the archipelago.

'It's got to be some sort of conspiracy,' Telemachus growled when he saw Antinous and Eurymachus return to join the throng of contenders now gathered at the court, 'They've worked this up between them. They're trying to force her to declare my father dead. If I was a few years older I'd clear out this whole foul stable with my sword.'

With his grandfather permanently retired to his farm these

days, Telemachus turned for advice to Lord Mentor, demanding to know whether it was truly the royal family's responsibility, as the suitors seemed to think, to house them for as long as they chose to stay, and feed them, and keep them in good wine while they pledged their unwelcome suits.

'The law of hospitality requires it,' old Mentor sighed. 'It is a law your father would want us to respect.'

'Then my mother must learn to be shorter with them.'

'As always, your mother thinks only of the good name of your father's house.'

'As I do myself.'

'Then I presume,' Mentor reproved him gently, 'that you would not have it become a byword for meanness across the islands?'

'Rather that,' Telemachus retorted, 'than watch it turned into a tavern.'

Ctesippus of Same happened to pass at that moment, intending to join a party of suitors who were drinking wine on the balcony that overlooked the sea. 'Why the sour face, Telemachus?' he grinned. 'Has something disagreed with you?'

'This whole state of affairs disagrees with me,' Telemachus scowled.

'Then get your mother to put a stop to it by making up her mind.'

Flushed with anger, Telemachus spat back, 'She would die sooner than marry any of you.'

'That's not what *she* says,' Ctesippus grinned, and turned away. The boy might have thrown himself after him but Lord Mentor caught him with a restraining arm.

'I think you should talk with the Lady Penelope,' he said in a low, cautionary voice. 'She may be wiser in this matter than you think.'

Telemachus found his mother at her loom with Eurycleia and the other women about her and so was forced to restrain some of the heat he had brought with him. When they were alone, however, he gave vent to an intemperate assault on her for the humiliations he was suffering.

'Antinous swaggers about the court promising to teach me better manners as soon as he becomes my step-father, and the others are just as bad. I don't understand why you don't just throw them all out,' he said. 'You shame us all by entertaining their advances. If my father was here . . .'

'If your father was here there would be no problem,' she interrupted him sharply. 'But he's not here, and I have to think what he would advise me to do.'

'Whatever it was it wouldn't be this. I think he'd kill you sooner than watch you pander to these louts.'

'You will speak to me with respect,' Penelope reprimanded him, 'or we will not speak at all. What you've just shown me is that you have no understanding how shrewd a man your father is. You have a great deal to learn from him when he gets back.'

'If he ever bothers to come back!' Telemachus glanced back into his mother's reproving face. 'So what would he expect us to do?'

'Are you prepared to listen to me now?'

Staring out of the window at the restive sea, Telemachus nodded.

'Your father once dealt with a situation rather like this in Sparta a long time ago. All the most powerful princes of Argos had gathered there, vying for the hand of my cousin Helen. Her father King Tyndareus had been weakened by a stroke and he couldn't see how to choose any one of them without making enemies of all the rest. Odysseus showed him how to make use of them against each other. And that's precisely what I'm trying to do now. If I were to do what you want and send all these men packing, it would only be a question of time before one of them made a violent bid for the throne. There would be revolution here, as has already happened in Mycenae and Tiryns, and I doubt very much that you would be allowed to survive it. But if I can keep each of them in hopes of becoming my consort one day, then none of them will have reason to cause trouble.' She sighed with impatience at a fate that left her fighting even with her own son. 'Can't you see, Telemachus? We're just not strong enough to keep them at bay any other way. The gods know, I want nothing to do with any of them. I'm simply playing for time until your father comes home. Each day I pray to Athena for the strength to carry on. And it would help me a great deal if you could try not to make my life any more difficult than it already is.'

Telemachus told me of this conversation shortly afterwards, and we agreed that – hard as it came to both of us – we would do what we could to preserve the balance of Penelope's desperate strategy until Odysseus came home. While I made it my business to pacify the rowdy guests with my songs and stories, Telemachus overcame his revulsion and began to act the part of the genial host. Led by Antinous, a few of the suitors took advantage of this to make his life a misery, but most of them responded to the change with good humour. Even so, after weeks of hanging about the palace, each of them hoping for more time alone with Penelope than she ever granted, the contenders grew bored and impatient. Their behaviour became noisier and more insufferable, their demands more importunate. The strain of concealing her true feelings before men she despised began to show on Penelope's face. Yet when she reproached them, they merely reminded her that she was prolonging this unsatisfactory state of affairs by refusing to make up her mind.

'Choose one of us – preferably me, of course,' Antinous smiled, 'and all your troubles will be over.' He turned, smirking, to his friends before glancing back at the unhappy woman. 'I promise that your bed will be warmer too!'

To get out of that rancorous atmosphere, Telemachus and I used to take long walks around the cliffs of Ithaca with his father's grizzled old hunting-dog at our heels. We were returning late one hot afternoon when we saw Amphinomus walking up the slope to the palace from the harbour. A few minutes later Telemachus watched with a sickly scowl on his face as his mother fell into her friend's arms with a little cry of pleasure and relief.

'It's so good to see you again,' she said. 'Life has become impossible here. You must help me, Amphinomus.'

I confess that my own heart fell in that moment too. Yet if Penelope was looking to Amphinomus for unquestioning sympathy she was to be disappointed. He was permitted more time in her private company than anyone else, and there is no knowing exactly what was said between them; but he cannot have wasted the opportunity to remind her, however gently, that he had made strenuous efforts to get news of Odysseus without success, and now, more than four years since the war had ended, it was very unlikely that he would ever return.

One can be sure that he pressed his own claims on her affections. Amphinomus would have pointed out that he had been at pains to prove himself worthy of her. Though it had grieved him sorely at the time, he had stayed away from Ithaca at her request, and the moment she asked him to return he had done so. He stood ready and eager to marry her now. If Penelope would only consent to give herself to him, all her troubles would be at an end, for as heir to the only other large island in the archipelago still ruled by a single king, he was strong enough to protect both Penelope and Telemachus until her son was old enough to claim the High Kingship for himself.

For all her loyalty to Odysseus, Penelope must surely have been tempted by the prospect. Her fondness for Amphinomus was clear; his grasp of the political situation was sound; and his consideration for the rights of another man's son appeared sincere. And having seen the far from downcast expression on his face as he left her apartment, I would guess that her refusal to give him an immediate answer was less resolute than it had been when others pressed her.

Yet his disappointment was evident two days later when he called his rivals to order in the great hall of the palace. He announced that he too had asked for Penelope's hand in marriage and he too had been told that she would not consider remarriage until she was absolutely certain that her husband was dead.

'We've heard this before!' Antinous shouted. 'How are we supposed to prove he's dead? Without a body to show, she can keep us hanging on for as long as she likes.'

'No,' Amphinomus silenced him, 'for she has now agreed that a time limit be set, after which Penelope will accept that she is widowed and will reconsider the question of marriage.'

'So how long are we supposed to wait?' Ctesippus called out.

'King Laertes has asked her to begin work on weaving his funeral shroud. She has promised me that she will give her decision when the work is done.'

The scoffing voice of Antinous rose over the general murmur in the hall. 'Have you ever heard those women chattering at their looms? If she puts her mind to it, she could make that task last for ever.'

'I think,' Amphinomus retorted, 'that those who care for the lady's honour will trust her in this matter. Her own estimate is that the task will keep her occupied for the next two years.' He waited for the loud groans of complaint to die down a little before raising his voice again. 'Can I suggest that she is more likely to make progress with the work if she is not distracted by the demands of a large houseful of guests?' The hall fell silent at that point. 'I for one intend to return to Dulichion tomorrow,' Amphinomus declared. 'If you hope for success in contending for the lady's hand you would do well to respect her desire for peace, for when the prize is so precious, anyone who thinks the wait too long has already declared himself unworthy.' He let the words settle on the silence before ending. 'Come, gentlemen, let us leave this house in good order and agree to return at the Spring Festival in two years' time. We can fairly look for her answer then.'

Not everyone was happy with this judgement, but enough of them saw the sense of it to make it impossible for the rest to stay. By the end of the next day the hall was cleared of suitors, and it was generally agreed that though the prince of Dulichion might not have won the reward he thought he merited, he had done Penelope a great service. Even Telemachus expressed his thanks.

The customary quiet routine of life in the palace was resumed. Penelope drew up her design for the richly woven winding-sheet in which the body of Laertes would one day be buried, and began to dress her great loom with a fine warp. The feast days of one year came and went; another began; Laertes tended his vines and garden or spent time recalling the past with Eumaeus at his sties; and at all seasons, Telemachus practised the arts of war, sharpening his skills with sword and spear, strengthening his sinews and putting on height until, as a youth of seventeen, he was becoming a force to reckon with. By that time too, his confidence had grown from his success in loosening a girdle or two across the island; so he was no longer the same impetuous boy that his mother had worried over. But by then the violets were raising their heads in the glades of Ithaca once more; and still, despite all the efforts that Amphinomus claimed he had made to find him, there was no word of Odysseus.

Again the Spring Festival proved to be a boisterous affair and many of the suitors were already drunk by the time they presented themselves at the palace. Telemachus and I watched them roll into the courtyard with sinking hearts. As they set to, making the most of the feast that had been prepared for them, letting their hands stray round the buttocks of the serving-wenches, I tried to calm the air with some of my sadder songs, but they soon shouted me down, calling for livelier tunes with bawdy refrains that set them banging the tables with their cups. Penelope had wisely chosen to remain in her apartment. When Eurymachus demanded to know what was keeping her, Telemachus dryly replied that she was working late on his grandfather's shroud.

Amphinomus arrived the next day, having presided over the Spring Festival on Dulichion, and it was he who led the delegation that was allowed to inspect the progress of Penelope's work. Though they were all impressed by the wondrous complexity of her design, they were also dismayed to see how much of the warp remained unwoven. Amphinomus endorsed her unruffled plea that work of such fine quality could not be hurried, but he raised no objection when Antinous and Eurymachus maintained that an agreement was an agreement and that they at least intended to stay in the palace to see the work completed.

Eavesdropping on their conversation as they came away, Telemachus was forced to bite back his rage when he heard Ctessipus grumble that at this rate old Laertes' corpse would be well-rotted by the time his winding-sheet was done.

Yet by now, with the king fading into senility and Telemachus too young to rule men stronger than himself, the suitors had a reasonable case to make. The islands could not be allowed to drift for much longer without a firm hand on the steering-oar. Some of the barons claimed they were already finding it harder to collect tribute. For the first time in living memory beggars had begun to appear in the streets, and the Taphian pirates were lifting cattle again, safe in the knowledge that they would meet only disorganized local resistance.

Because no councils had been called, this was the first time in several years that all these lords had met to share their difficulties, and the longer they talked, the graver grew their concerns. Demands for action became more vociferous. The gathering shouted its assent when a Zacynthian lord moved that they should summon an embassy from Taphos to ask what that kingdom intended to do about the pirates. And once they had felt their concerted strength, they were ready to demand that, whether or not the shroud was finished, Penelope must agree to choose a new husband for herself by the time of Apollo's summer feast or they would choose one for her.

The Taphian ambassador was a man called Mentes who had been a friend of Odysseus in the old days. He was astounded, therefore, to arrive at the court of Ithaca only to be subjected to a bout of drunken barracking. Amphinomus tried to restrain his colleagues, but they had found a vent for their frustrations in the presence of this foreigner and it brought out the worst in them. At last, having endured their insults with offended dignity, Mentes rose to his feet, declaring that he had come of his own free will to consider the problems posed by a few unruly young men of his own land. It seemed, however, that Ithaca had fallen into the hands of its own disorderly rabble, and Taphos would have no further dealings with them until they brought themselves to order.

Mentes would have left the island immediately but he was stopped outside the hall by Telemachus who sought to apologize for the shameful way he had been treated. The ambassador would have shrugged him off, but when Telemachus announced himself as the son of Odysseus, he became more sympathetic.

'That loudmouth Antinous is dangerous,' he warned. 'Allow this state of affairs to carry on for much longer and you'll have real trouble on your hands.' Quickly he glanced around. 'Will you take a word of advice from your father's old friend?'

'Gladly,' Telemachus responded.

'It's clear to me that nobody here has any serious interest in seeing Odysseus return. I know for a fact that Amphinomus has been less than energetic in his efforts to look for him than he would have you believe. So if you want to find him, you're going to have to seek him out yourself. I know your father of old, boy. We've done some roving together in our time and I've seen him ease his way out of more scrapes than a greased cat. I'm pretty sure he's alive and kicking somewhere out there. Someone's sure to know where he is.'

'But who?' Telemachus asked. 'I don't know where to begin.'

Mentes thought for a moment. 'You could start with his old comrade Nestor in Pylos. If he knows nothing, move on to Sparta. I hear that Menelaus is back there now. He may have come across Odysseus somewhere out east. And while you're there, you should seek the aid of your grandfather Icarius.'

Telemachus frowned. 'I believe he's never had much love for my father.'

'But Penelope remains his daughter. He won't like to see her suffer. If all else fails, Icarius can invoke the power of Sparta to help find her a husband who'll have more care for your welfare than any of this gang will. And remember,' Mentes pressed, 'you're your father's son. You must have some of his fire in your blood. Assert yourself. Call a formal council and tell them what you intend to do. That'll give them something to think about.'

Tense with excitement and dread, Telemachus said, 'That's what I want to do, but my mother opposes it. She says I'm all she has these days. She doesn't want to lose me too.'

'A time comes when a boy has to stop listening to his mother,' Mentes said. 'I can see that you're still young, but you come from a proud line and young men can achieve great things when they put their minds to it. Look at what Orestes has done.' He took in the uncertain frown on the boy's face. 'You haven't heard about that yet? Orestes and Pylades made their way back into Mycenae a month ago. Agamemnon's son cut down the usurper Aegisthus, and then,' – Mentes made the sign to ward off evil – 'he did for his mother as well. They say his mind has been haunted by the Daughters of Night ever since, and only the gods know how he'll cleanse himself of Clytaemnestra's blood. But think about it, boy – if Orestes was ready to kill his own mother in order to avenge his father's shade, surely you've got balls enough to go against your mother's wishes and do what you have to do?' He shrugged and glanced away at where some of the suitors were watching him suspiciously. 'If I were you,' he said, 'I wouldn't even tell her about it. I'd just make my offerings to Grey-eyed Athena, then take ship and go.'

I was the first person that Telemachus took into his confidence. When I saw that he was resolved to go in search of his father, I offered to sail with him, but his thinking was ahead of mine. He said he needed someone he could trust to remain at court and reassure Penelope after he'd gone, and it was a request I couldn't refuse.

There remained the problem of how to get a ship without arousing suspicion. I offered to discuss the matter with my friend Peiraeus, who was now master of his own trading vessel. I knew that he was planning his next voyage and felt sure he would agree to time his departure to suit Telemachus' needs. So on the day that was named for the council meeting his ship stood ready in the harbour.

That council – the first in many years – turned into a rancorous affair from the moment that Telemachus outraged the suitors by appealing over their heads to the older members of the council. Complaining of the way his mother was being harassed and the resources of the royal household squandered, he called on them in the name of Themis, the divine mother of justice, to support him against the gang of self-seeking wastrels who were already shouting as he spoke.

Even before he had finished, Antinous was on his feet, reminding the council of the agreement that had been reached with Penelope two years earlier. Though he began reasonably enough it wasn't long before he was accusing Penelope of unravelling by night the work she had done on the funeral shroud by day in order to delay the moment when she must honour her promises.

'That's a foul lie!' Telemachus shouted and looked to Amphinomus for support – only to pay the price for all the oblique insults he had directed at the man over the years. Amphinomus said nothing, preferring to remain aloof from what was degenerating into an unseemly brawl.

Finding his confidence in his own case weakened by the sudden suspicion that his mother might indeed have been crafty enough to do exactly what Antinous had accused her of, Telemachus became ever more emotional in his responses. At one point he came perilously close to tears. I could see him gripping his hands so tightly that the knuckles blanched. Lord Mentor tried to speak up in his support but he was immediately shouted down by someone declaring that the old order was over and done with and it was time for fresh blood.

The row might have turned violent, but for a most unusual event. Above the noise of argument, the air was split by a piercing shriek. We all looked up and saw two eagles fighting against the brilliant blue of the sky. They seemed to hang there for a time, directly overhead, as if hooked to each other. Everyone stared in amazement until the birds swooped and curved away with talons flashing, spilling pinion feathers from their wings.

The old soothsayer Halitherses spoke up in the silence. It was he who used to attend the prophetess Diotima at the shrine of Earth-mother Dia, and over the years he had become proficient in bird-lore.

'This is a sign that bodes no good for evil-doers,' he cried. 'Mother Diotima foretold that Odysseus would be gone from Ithaca for many years, but she did not say that he would not return. His time is at hand. When he comes he will demand satisfaction of those who have wasted the substance of his kingdom.'

The whole episode had been so startling that everyone was speechless for a moment; but then Eurymachus – the coolest thinker among the suitors – was on his feet dismissing the soothsayer's reading of the sign with coarse humour.

'Had the eagles shat on our heads Halitherses might have had me worried,' he scoffed. As soon as the uneasy laughter died down, he turned to Leodes, who had just succeeded his father as guardian of the temple of Apollo and might have made a decent priest but for his weakness for wine. 'Tell us, Leodes, how does the priest of Apollo read this sign?'

Without great conviction, Leodes said, 'It could be that the eagles were showing us the way things fall apart when a country lacks a strong king.'

Amid the murmuring, Antinous leapt to his feet. 'Or it could be that they're just having a bad day like the rest of us. Either way, I'll trust my own judgement sooner than an old fool's superstitious rant.'

The other young men cheered and jeered in support. Telemachus, however, seemed to have drawn strength from the sign. 'Say what you like,' he shouted, 'but the gods are just and this island has a king who will come back to claim his own. I've heard enough of your impious wrangling. I mean to take ship this day and go in search of my father. If I hear certain word that Odysseus is dead, then my grandfather, the Lord Icarius of Sparta, will choose a new husband for my mother – one who will rule Ithaca till I'm of age to claim the kingship for myself.'

Then he swept away out of the courtyard, leaving them all open-mouthed in their stone seats. By the time that they had collected enough wits to try and stop him, Telemachus had boarded Peiraeus' ship and was putting out to sea.

The Mysteries

Darkness. A darkness so deep it leaves no place to stand. A darkness where all his dead lie in wait for him. He feels he is drowning in this darkness. Long ago, it had been the starting-point of his involuntary descent; it deepened throughout the long middle passage. Now, as he struggles to breathe on darkness and the struggle no longer seems worth the effort, it must also be his destination.

The dead are indeed assembling here.

Consciousness returns as the sound of Circe's voice. Later he is vaguely aware of someone else in the chamber – another, younger woman wearing a veil, who comes and goes, bringing water and wine and other things, the identity of which elude him. It is she, he realises, who is singing to him now. She is singing the words of a hymn he has never heard before, and it is as if the darkness turns to sound inside him. A sound that travels through his body with the circulation of his blood and breath.

What had for so long seemed a descent without hope or compass is converted by that voice into an onward journey of the heart.

Had the strains of the hymn lulled him into sleep or not? He is unsure. But he is certainly conscious again and somewhere close to the dead centre of things. He is a traveller resting by a tall stone herm on which only an open eye is carved. There is no moon, though the sky is full of stars, and it feels as though the whole world is circling round him in a slow and stately dance.

There comes the bronze reverberation of a softly struck gong. Quietly, like chords of water, a lyre strikes up.

Now Circe is chanting. The words sound ancient on her tongue. They might have been cast, long ago, in gold. 'The doors are swinging in the House of the Dead,' she chants. 'What was once open is now closed; that which was shut is open now. Sunlight enters the unlit house. The soul returns with its shadow.'

And with tremendous force something radiant comes into him like the strike of lightning at a mast. He can scarcely breathe for the power of it. His hair might be on fire, his whole skeleton is luminous; then he is staring into the dark dazzle round him. What he sees is the midnight sun.

Events that take place inside ritual space cannot be told in the annals of time. Nor could Odysseus himself remember everything that happened during those incubatory hours in Circe's chamber. But he recalled that many stages of the way were painful, for all the horrors of the war at Troy returned to him again that night. More vividly than at any time since he had seen the city fall, they flashed across his vision. They were written on his mind as indelibly as his wounds were written on his body. Each was a station on his way, all permanently him.

Also there were experiences that were neither dreams nor waking dreams, yet fluid with elements of both, so that he seemed to sink and float like an amphibian in those nocturnal waters – old Nobodysseus roving the seas in dirty weather, struggling with the steering-oar, again and again unable to double Cape Malea.

It was then that he saw Penelope, standing on the cliff at Ithaca, yet receding down the halls of time with a speed that frightened him.

Yet the terror of that moment was only the preliminary to the fear that seared across his nerves when he lay, strapped like Prometheus on his rock, watching the Goddess shifting shape through form after terrifying form: the Lady of Ruin and Despair, the Whore of Heaven, the Lady of the Lotus, the Lady of the Knife, the Lady of Flame, The Lady of Light, The Beggared Lady, The Lady of Strength, of Thunder, of Slaughter, of Splendour, the Lady of Death.

Image after image appeared before him, some so fearsome that he heard himself cry out loud; others so lambent with beauty that he wept with awe. There were times too when he felt that this display of air and fire must end in madness; and others when he was so oppressed by her presence that he sensed evil rise inside him like a sludge of asphalt from the sea.

Yet once the fear and the evil were expressed they seemed to pass out of him. He was lifted through into another place, a place of sensual exultation where everything appeared possible again and his breath passed freely through him like the calming balm of poppy in the wine.

The clearest memory of all came from the moment of waking. It might have been the morning of the next day or a week after he had entered the chamber. But it was light, a fresh dawn light, sweet with the fragrance of orange-blossom on the air, and he could hear the doves among the myrtle boughs outside. Yet his most prescient sensation as he lay with eyes closed was of his own lightness, as though a great weight had been lifted from him and he had been left as vacant and bouncy as a dandelion seed.

When Odysseus opened his eyes again, a vaguely familiar face was gazing down at him. Her eyes were an intense gentian blue, long-lashed; her black hair was braided in glossy coils; and there was such a startled expression at her lips when his eyes shot open that he wanted to laugh out loud.

It was, he thought, quite the most beautiful human face he had ever seen.

★ ★ ★

When he next woke he knew himself entirely rested, avid both for food and life. The air of the day had never tasted so fresh; the trees around the house were luminously green, and the sound of water at the spring almost shone upon his ears as he sat beside it with Circe later that day. Above all, he was seized by a sense of the seamlessness of things, for everything around him rejoiced in its individual existence, while nothing was finally separable from anything else. The world was entire, single and whole; and he himself no longer an abject, exiled consciousness, apart from that communion, but wholly at one with it. And as the kites swooping above the Hill of Silence reminded him, that unity was nowhere more evident than in the dependence on death for renewal.

He felt refashioned, stripped down, scoured out and remade – the old, exhausted Odysseus replaced by a more vigorous and wiser man; one more attuned to the deep mystery of things. Circe, however, seemed merely amused by his desire to make immediate love to her.

'I'm quite sure,' she said, lightly pushing him away, 'that you'll find plenty of women to help you ease that ache if it presses you so hard.'

'But it's you that I want,' he insisted.

'You and I have known our time with Aphrodite,' she smiled. 'Now you must look elsewhere.'

'There is, I admit,' Odysseus said with a teasing hint of hesitation in his voice, 'one young woman who's caught my eye. I saw her when I first awoke.'

Frowning, she said, 'While you were in my chamber?'

'Yes.'

'You looked on her face?'

When he nodded smiling, she glanced away. After the levity of her manner a moment earlier, he was surprised by the coldness in her voice as she said, 'It should not have been permitted.'

'But I've seen her before,' he protested lightly.

Circe's face grew sharper. 'Where?' she asked. 'Where did you see her?' And when Odysseus told her about the chance encounters, first in the hall of the palace and then in the woodland glade, her consternation was plain. Yet his spirits were riding so high that he failed to take the change in her quite seriously. Was it possible, he wondered, that she was envious of Calypso's beauty?

'I believe I've also heard her sing,' he smiled.

'She is not for you,' Circe answered. A moment later, with a self-reproachful sigh, she added, 'Nor for any man. She is vowed to the Goddess. Her person is sacred.' She rose to her feet, arranging the folds of her gown about her. 'You must look to other women for your sport.'

'Have I offended you?' he asked, dismayed.

Abstracted in thought, Circe shook her head. 'No,' she said, 'the fault does not lie with you. But you must excuse me now. We will talk again soon.'

He saw nothing of Calypso in the next few days. Nor did he see Circe herself apart from the single interview in which she instructed him to prepare for his admission to the Oracle of the Dead at Cuma.

'You have now seen everything that we can show you here on Aiaia,' she said. 'Soon you must leave, but whether the omens are yet favourable for your return to Ithaca is not in my power to see. For that you must consult Teiresias and be conducted into the House of Shades.'

'The Oracle of the Dead?'

'Yes.'

'Will Macareus be allowed to accompany me?' he asked.

'Macareus has gone before you.'

'Did Calypso go with him?'

'That is not your concern. In any case, the Oracle must be consulted alone.'

'But you will be there?'

'My place is here in Aiaia.'

'So I won't see you again?'

'You will go to Cuma by ship,' she said. 'The voyage will take two days and a night. I trust that you will return before you sail for Ithaca.'

He drew in his breath, looked around at the shining marble of Circe's house, at the green woods beyond and the high hill where the scavenger kites still flew. 'If that is indeed my destination,' he said. 'But I shall certainly come back.'

His departure was delayed by an incident that brought an inauspicious omen for his voyage. In the weeks they had spent on Aiaia, many of the crew of *The Fair Return* had grown bored and restive. Eurylochus, in particular, never overcame his initial mistrust of the place and gloomily foretold that no good would come of spending too long living in the shadow of the dead. For some time he had been itching to make sail for Ithaca and home, and could not understand what kept Odysseus loitering in this dismal spot. Having discovered that Aiaia was not an island after all, but a marshy promontory joined to the mainland, he spent most of his time leading hunting-parties into the hills where they found bears foraging the woods, as well as deer and wild boar. Others, however, had made themselves at home among the local peasantry, enjoying the weather and the easy pace of life. Among them, young Elpenor was almost permanently drunk on the local wine, and most of his afternoons were spent sprawled in the sun on the tiled roof of the palace with a wineskin at his side. He was lying there when Odysseus called his crew together to announce that they were taking ship the next day. Jumping up at the sound of the horn, he lost his footing, scrambled to hold on to the tiles, and fell to the ground, breaking his neck.

To the aggrieved consternation of his comrades, Odysseus insisted that they would not burn his body and raise a funeral mound in his name. Instead they would give him with all due reverence to the kites and ravens as was the custom of the place, and collect his bones for burial on their return. Again Eurylochus, who was beginning to despair of his master, could be heard muttering that no good would come of it. His mood was not lightened when the crew learned that they were bound, like Macareus before them, not for Ithaca, but for the Halls of the Hades, God of the Underworld, and his bride, Persephone.

Before the end of the first day's sailing, the sky seemed to darken early and there was a greenish tinge to the dim light of the setting sun. The next morning, as they were piloted along the coast, they realised that the light was obscured not merely by clouds but by a thick and acrid fog of black smoke drifting from the summit of a distant mountain. Darker and more baleful than the thin plume they had observed over Aeolia, it filled the crew with trepidation. Even Odysseus began to worry as he remembered his own words to Aeolus about the fate suffered by the island of Kalliste; but he could not believe that his life-thread would be cut so soon after his soul had been washed clean on Aiaia.

Around noon on the second day they passed through a narrow strait between an island and the mainland, and then doubled a sharply pointed cape into a craterous gulf. The shoreline steamed in its mantle of lush green vegetation. Under brighter sunlight the blue width of the gulf would have been quite dazzling, but the smoke gave the quiet waters a doleful air brightened only by the hectic yellow of the easterly cliffs. A stink of sulphur came drifting off the land.

They put in at a ramshackle township that had grown up at the sandy edge of a bay within the gulf. Here the pilot handed Odysseus over to a taciturn guide who said only that he would lead him and a small group of chosen companions on the trek across country to the Oracle of the Dead.

Polites immediately agreed to go with him. When no one else volunteered, Perimedes said he would go too. As they were about to leave Eurylochus discovered that his loyalty to his captain was stronger than his fear. Grumbling at the bleating of the two sheep that Circe had bidden them give in offering to the Oracle, he brought up the rear.

The track passed through a marshy plain of bamboo and reeds

where pools of boiling mud bubbled and simmered, emitting puffs of smoke, and bursting out here and there into hot blowholes that stank of rotten eggs. Insects tormented the sweat about their eyes and ears. At one point, through a fissure in the ground, a river of molten sludge oozed slowly by; and then came stretches where at every step they feared they might plunge through the earth's crust and plummet down into the vast inferno that must be burning beneath them. Even the air seemed hostile, for there was no wind in the heat of the day and, whichever way they turned their heads, a stagnant smell assailed their nostrils. Yet when they complained of the stink, their guide merely shrugged and, as if taking a perverse pleasure in adding to their unease, told them about a lake lying only a mile or so inland which emitted vapours so toxic that no bird would fly across its waters.

Then they were climbing up a wooded hill through ancient stands of holm-oak and white poplar. The air tasted fresher there and drifts of white and blue and brimstone-yellow wildflowers bloomed in the glades. Near the crest of the hill they came upon a grassy terrace where more trees had been felled and a tunnelled grotto with many doorways of an unusual, trapezoidal shape had been carved directly into the soft, whitish rock of the cliff. Dogs began to bark even before they stepped out of the trees. Undeterred, their guide walked on, pointing to where a snake slithered away into a clump of rocket as he passed. The air was fragrant with herbs. Below them, they could hear the sound of the sea.

The first people they met were two old women who proved to be officials of the oracle. They already knew Odysseus' name and purpose, which was not surprising, as he remarked afterwards to Eurylochus, given that Macareus had preceded them there, though as yet they had seen no sign of him. Having taken the fees that Odysseus had been warned he would have to pay − a sum large enough to cover the cost of sacrificial animals, the wine for the libations to be poured, and various administrative costs that remained unspecified – the women explained the procedures of the oracle. As it was late in the day, they said, he might remain with his friends that night. In the morning he could also seek their help in making his preliminary offerings. Thereafter he must submit to ritual cleansing before his first interview with Teiresias. If all was well-aspected, he would be admitted to the sacred precinct. Then, after a time of solitary fasting, the Sibyl would conduct him down into the Halls of Hades where the dead would rise in answer to his question.

Odysseus declared that he understood and accepted these terms. He and his friends were shown to the lodge where they would pass the night. Food and wine were brought to them and oil-lamps were lit. Then they were left alone.

Their conversation was uneasy, and when they fell silent their oppressive proximity to the dead reminded Eurylochus that Elpenor's corpse still lay, unburned without a mound, on the hill in Aiaia.

'What if his angry shade is waiting for us here?' he said.

'Elpenor died drunk and happy,' Odysseus replied. He gave a little laugh. 'If he's here already he'll only be working up another thirst for my libations!'

Perimedes and Polites both laughed in the darkness, but Eurylochus was still troubled. 'I've heard of places like this before,' he said. 'There's one such in Boeotia. The Cave of Trophonius they call it.' He lay in silence, wondering whether to say more; and could not stop himself. 'They say that once a man goes down into the underworld he never smiles again.'

'They also say that the Boeotians are the dullest-witted people in the world,' Odysseus silenced him, 'Now go to sleep, will you?'

But he lay unsleeping himself, encountering in his thoughts the many shades that still lay heavy on his conscience.

Not one of them got much sleep that night and they were up and about by dawn. As instructed, Eurylochus, Polites and Perimedes rounded up four of the bullocks that Odysseus had purchased for the sacrifice, and the first of them was brought to the altar. Making fervent prayers to Athena and Zeus, and craving favour of the Dark Lord and Lady of the Underworld, Odysseus put each of the animals to the slaughter. He was covered in blood by the time the rites of offering were complete. Most of the beasts had gone consenting to the sacrifice, but his companions did not conceal their anxiety as he said farewell and was led away.

After his ritual cleansing, Odysseus was blindfolded and led from the bath-house, wearing only a white smock he had been given. He walked for some distance with a guide at either side to prevent him from stumbling, and when the blindfold was removed, he found himself seated in an arched chamber cut out of a cliff. An old man with stringy white hair and curiously pallid skin sat across from him on a stone seat, fingering his beard.

Odysseus smiled in greeting, but met no response from the soft, almost feminine features of a lean, introverted face that seemed more interested in the natural patterns of the rock-face than in the appearance of the man standing before him. Only after a few moments did Odysseus realize that he was blind.

'You have come from Aiaia,' Teiresias said. 'I am informed that you underwent the initiation there.'

'I was afforded that privilege,' Odysseus answered, aware that he was in the presence of a man whose stillness was graver, and filled with more searching wisdom, than any he had encountered since his meeting with Cheiron the Centaur on Mount Pelion many years before.

'You will know then,' Teiresias said, 'where the sun has its home.'

Without thought or reflection, Odysseus heard himself reply, 'Where else but in the earth at the heart of darkness?'

From the depths of his own darkness, Teiresias smiled and nodded. 'Your fame travels before you, Odysseus of Ithaca. So tell me, what satisfaction do you take from having brought about the fall of Troy?'

The question was unexpected. For a time the Ithacan gave it thought.

'That was the achievement of another man,' he replied eventually, 'one who believed he was acting in the service of Athena. That man has since found the death he both deserved and desired.'

'And now?'

'I know that Athena is not her only name and she is greater than I thought.'

Again the seer nodded. 'Then what do you seek in the House of the Dead?'

'Guidance.'

'And who among the shades can give you that?'

Odysseus glanced away uncertainly. 'I know only that there are many among the dead who have no cause to love or aid me.'

'Then you must beg their forgiveness. There will be time for that before you are admitted to their house. Are you prepared for that ordeal?'

'I am no stranger to death,' Odysseus said.

'Yet death too may be greater than you think.'

'I would be disappointed,' Odysseus said, 'to find it otherwise.'

His smile went unseen and unanswered. Teiresias sat in silence for a long time. His white head was tilted slightly as though he was listening for some sound on the still air of the chamber. At last he drew in his breath, reached for the gilded staff that leaned against the wall at his side, and tapped it twice, sharply, on the stone flags of the floor. Immediately the two men who had led Odysseus into the chamber returned. Again he was blindfolded and led out into the day.

For three days he was left alone in a locked chamber which contained only a large jug of water, a cruse of oil to renew the lamp, a pallet for him to sleep on, and a hole in the floor for easing himself. It was from that last corner, furthest from his bed, that he could faintly hear the sound of running water. There were no windows in the chamber, though every inch of the walls was covered with paintings. It was like being shut inside a static theatre of dreams. But those dreams were the figments of an imagination obsessed, it seemed, both by the naked beauty of women and by the dreadful things that life can inflict on them.

Because the only source of light came from his lamp, the pictures seemed to move and flicker as he looked at them. He took the lamp to examine them more closely and believed he could name some of the figures depicted there. Many of them were of women ravished by the gods, and the skill of the painter made them appear lovelier even than he had conceived when listening to their stories. And the portrayal of those who had suffered darker fates was just as exquisite in its detail, so that Odysseus felt himself instantly oppressed once more by his own memories of Hecuba and Polyxena, of Cassandra and Andromache, and of all the women of Troy whose lives had been violated by the war.

Had he known from the first how long he would remain locked up alone with those pictures, he might immediately have hammered for release. Even so, he was soon angered by his confinement. Not very long ago he had dreamed of sailing across far horizons, through the fabled Pillars of Heracles and on around the unknown coast of Libya. Now he was imprisoned like a felon in a cell so small he could cross it in four strides. How arbitrary a fate was this? What was he supposed to do in here? What could he do but sleep and think? And despite his bad night, he was not yet tired, so he lay on his pallet-bed contemplating the pictures on the walls until he was forced to close his eyes against them.

He slept for a time and, when he woke, his sense of time was broken. There was a taste to the water he did not entirely trust. The pictures merged into his dreams. After only a few hours he was hallucinating with extraordinary clarity. Whenever he closed his eyes he became certain that he was no longer alone in the room; but when he snapped them open again the room was empty. He searched every inch of the wall for spy-holes and found none. The search merely left him with an even profounder sense of isolation and he fell into depression.

He tried to console himself by meditating on the names by which he had heard Teiresias addressed. On their journey to the

oracle their tight-lipped guide had referred to him once as
Iatromantis – one who heals by prophesy. That was a reassuring
thought. A man celebrated as a healer could surely have no evil
designs on him, just as the *pharmakopeia* Circe had turned out not
to be a sorceress after all but a curer of souls. Yet a second term
used by one of the women who had greeted them at the shrine
had a less friendly ring to it – *Pholarchos, the Lord of the Lair.* It
made Teiresias sound like a wild beast, which seemed odd for a
highly civilized man who had an elusive air of the feminine about
his face and posture. His birth-name would not have been Teiresias,
of course. Teiresias – *Delighter in Signs* – was a title, not a name.
The title had been born by many seers in Boeotian Thebes; and,
as Eurylochus had reminded him the night before, Boeotia also
had its Oracle of the Dead. So perhaps this man had crossed the
sea as Circe had done, to found an old cult in a new land? Yet
Odysseus sensed that this sacred precinct, situated as it was above
the boiling rivers of Hades, was already very ancient. Perhaps
Cuma too had known many generations of seers called Teiresias?

For the time being, these things were only puzzles that distracted
his mind. When he was free again, and had risen out of the underworld, he must remember to ask about them. But even as the
thought occurred to him, he doubted that the old seer would
encourage such enquiries. And it was followed by the further
thought that he might not, in any case, emerge with his mind
intact.

The hours dragged by. He dozed and woke again, then dozed
some more. Once when he woke, he saw the shadows shifting
round him and panicked when he saw his oil-lamp gutter. Quickly
he leapt up to replenish the oil from the cruse and realized that
he was panting as the flame revived. Now he had no knowledge
of whether it was day or night outside. Only the fierce pangs of
hunger quivering through his system informed him that it was a
very long time since he had eaten.

Hunger further lightened his head. Odysseus became certain

that something terrible was about to happen. He knocked on the door for a long time and no one answered. But the dread was hard to bear, so he tried to calm himself. He tried to calm himself by thinking of Penelope but that opened up a chasm in his heart. So he wrenched his thoughts away from Ithaca and began to think about Circe and the rites he had undergone during his time on Aiaia.

He remembered the frustration of their early conversations – how he had felt sure that she was in possession of insights that were at once so profound and obvious that only a dunce such as he could fail to grasp them. He tried to recall exactly what it was she had said. He tried to reconstruct the subtle labyrinth of questions she had raised around him.

He was gazing at the pictures as he thought. And then, quite suddenly, like an increase of light inside the room, his thoughts and the images began to coincide. Circe's questions were now urgently his own. Was it possible, he wondered, that if the dark aspect of the Goddess was admitted to the wedding-feast after all, then everything might change? Was it possible that if she was restored to an honoured place among the immortals, if an effort was made to see things through her eyes, to understand and inhabit her perspective, then she might prove to have healing powers? That instead of whirling the world down into a vortex of rage, she might make her true self manifest as its deep and fertile ground?

The questions came from a place so far outside the usual margins of his thought that Odysseus scarcely knew how to think them at all. Indeed, in those receptive moments, it felt less as though he was thinking *them* than that the thoughts were thinking him. And in the tranced space of that condition, three names began to chime like a riddle in his mind: Ares, Eris, Eros.

The divine names weaved a wild dance through his thoughts. Was it possible, he wondered, that the masculine predilection for violence might be converted into love by admitting the power of the dark goddess in the soul? Could this be the true source of compassion? Was it possible that Achilles had come to ask himself this kind of question in his final days when he released Briseis, the helpless captive of his spear, and sought out Priam's daughter as a friend? Was it possible that Menelaus had been moved by some obscure sense of what the question might mean when he stood over Helen with his sword in his hand and could not bring himself to kill her? Was any of this possible?

Yet how could it be? Such thoughts seemed to invert the common order of the world. Things simply didn't work that way.

Odysseus tried to shake his head clear. He reminded himself that he had been confined alone too long, that he was no longer in touch with his senses, that even his water might be doctored.

Outside this room there was a world where men went about their business untrammelled by such fantasies. That was the real world, a world in which he had always made his way by keeping his head clear and using his wits.

But hadn't the consequences of the long and bloody war already turned that world upside down from Troy to Mycenae and beyond? Perhaps it would take such unfamiliar thoughts to set it deeply right again?

Was it possible? Was any of it actually possible?

Excited, famished, dizzy, Odysseus stood alone inside the painted room and let the questions swell inside his heart. It felt as though his head was spinning.

The sound of the water in the drain below his cell became a sibilant whisper piping in his ears. It might, he thought, have been the hissing of a snake. It might have been the sound made by the motions of the stars.

Guided by an instinct older than his consciousness, Odysseus went to lie down on his pallet-bed. He lay there unsleeping, listening to that whisper in the silence, still as an animal lying in its lair.

At dawn on what was the morning after the third night two women came to fetch him. When he complained about having been left alone for so long, the older of the two merely shrugged and said, 'The ways of the Underworld are perfect and may not be questioned.' Then he was led out into the day.

He saw the first light breaking through the clouds. Birdsong rose with the mist among the trees. The early fragrance of rosemary, the murmur of the sea below the hill, all the ordinary gestures of each waking day blazed across his senses. The black ewe that he had brought from Aiaia was laid before him on the altar. A knife was put into his hand. He made the offering. The entrails were examined and pronounced well-aspected.

He was taken to a bath-house near the painted cell where he was allowed to lie for a long time in waters that bubbled up from a hot spring amidst a dizzying mist of fumes. These were, he was informed, the Waters of Forgetfulness by which he would be cleansed of all the residual traces of the world he was about to leave behind him.

From the bath-house he was conducted back into the painted chamber and left for a further period of prayer and meditation. A further bath followed at noon in the colder, fresher Waters of Memory. And then, throughout the long afternoon, when he was already weak from hunger and disoriented by weariness, he looked on as a conclave of priests and priestesses made ritual offerings to Hades and Persephone, the Lord and Lady of the Dead.

Not until sunset did the Sibyl appear. Odysseus had sacrificed a black lamb to the Mother of the Fates, to Dread Night and to her Sister the Earth. With the small animal lying dead at his feet, they dressed him in a white tunic and bound up his hair with white ribbons. A short bronze sword was fastened to a belt at his side. Estranged from himself, he was swaying where he stood in the torch-lit gloom when he looked up at the sound of low chanting and saw a procession of priests clad entirely in black passing in single file through a portal in the rock. Their faces were covered beneath high-pointed hoods. Only the hands carrying fronds of black cypress were visible. They might have been shades themselves.

Not until the last of them had vanished did Odysseus see the erect figure of a woman in a scarlet dress beckoning to him from where she stood at the entrance to what appeared to be a circular tomb. Her face too was concealed, but not by a hood. She wore a featureless mask that gleamed with an eerie white radiance.

As bidden, he approached her. Without a word, she handed him the bough of glistening mistletoe she held, and then turned on her heel and entered the tomb. With two attendants at his back urging him on, Odysseus followed and watched the Sibyl begin to climb down a ladder into a dark hole at the centre of the floor. Another push urged him to follow her.

His heart was beating very quickly now. Less than two feet wide, the shaft felt cramped about his shoulders. He couldn't see where he was going, but he had descended for rather more than his own length when his feet touched the earth and he saw that he was standing in a round underground chamber smokily lit by lamps. The black hooded priests were already gathering there through a different entrance. From a third doorway appeared another figure who dragged by a rope the bleating black ram that Odysseus had brought from Aiaia.

When all were assembled in the stuffy heat of the chamber, the Sibyl crossed to the entrance of a tunnel like the mouth of a narrow mine-shaft and began to descend. Quailing inwardly, Odysseus followed her down the dark slope, feeling a cold wind blow about his legs and smelling the fog of black smoke blown out of the tunnel from a descending line of lamps.

He was not a tall man yet he could feel the roof of the tunnel pressing down not far above his head. Without a guide he would have progressed far more slowly, feeling his way as he went, but the Sybil walked confidently ahead, approaching a turn to the right. Behind him, though there was now no room to turn, he could hear the chanting dirge of the priests at his back and the bleating of the sacrificial ram. Odysseus knew that he had long since passed the point where he could change his mind about this journey into the underworld, but now there was truly no way back. As he followed the Sybil around the dark turn, he felt sweat seeping from his body.

The passage descended more steeply now and was lit by more frequent lamps so that the light dazzled his eyes. They had not progressed far when a sudden alteration of the air-flow in the tunnel brought the smoke from hundreds of lamps billowing towards him. It seemed to coat his throat. Then his skin shrank at a wailing sound that echoed on the thick silence of the air.

Were there truly souls in torment then down there in deepest Tartarus? A priest pressed at his back. Ahead of him the Sybil descended steps cut into the rock. Around the next bend the tunnel widened. Priests began to file quickly past him at either side so that he was now walking through a passage of moving shades. When the tunnel turned again, he saw that the Sybil had halted with her priests lining the walls behind her. She was waiting at a low landing-stage that jutted out on timber piles into the warm black flow of an underground river. A bearded figure clothed in rags stood in a small boat by the jetty holding on to one of the wooden posts. From across the river echoed the fierce barking of dogs.

The bearded ferryman held up a hand to help the priestess down into a coracle made of basketwork and hides. Still clutching the bough of mistletoe, Odysseus stepped down into the little craft after her, and the two of them sat in the hot, vaporous gloom while the vessel was poled slowly across the dark flood. They could hear the sound of water bubbling upwards to break the surface from two hot springs. An acrid smell of sulphur tainted the air.

As they approached the opposite shore the barking grew louder and more ferocious. And then, in the fitful light cast from a torch in the wall, Odysseus made out the shadow of a dog with three heads, all of them snarling and barking.

At that point his courage might have failed entirely, but the Sybil stood up in the coracle and threw some sort of sop into an alcove in the rock. Immediately the barking ceased. Yet the silence chilled his heart almost as much as the savage din that preceded it, for in this dim, hot space under the earth, he had been confronted by the materialization of things he had encountered before only as figments of story. The wailing must have come from the mouth of Phlegyas, who was condemned to eternal torment in the underworld; Charon the boatman had ferried him across the River Styx; the three-headed hound Cerberus guarded the other shore. Other, darker terrors must lie in wait for him.

Despite his efforts to remind himself that these were mortal men and women who were conducting him on this journey into the earth, his mouth was dry and his breathing terse as he disembarked from the coracle and followed the Sibyl up a long, steep flight of stairs. At the top of the stairs the scarlet figure took a sharp turn to the right where Odysseus found her waiting for him in a small chamber. For the first time since they had entered the warren of tunnels the mask was turned to face him again – white and unnervingly featureless but for the eye-slits and the open hollow of the mouth. Still silent, she gestured for him to place the mistletoe into a low niche carved in the rock as his offering to Persephone.

When he had done so, she pointed to a stoup of water from which he might sprinkle himself. Then she stepped aside, revealing a door into what he knew must now be the most sacred, inner shrine, the House of Persephone, the dread Queen of Hades.

Odysseus followed her through into the dimly lit sanctum. To his astonishment he saw the black ram that had been following him through the passages already waiting there. By some enchantment it had arrived in this place before him and was lying on the altar with its legs trussed. A hooded priest stood over the silent animal holding a knife. In a language which Odysseus did not understand he called out a ritual chant of invocation and drew the knife across the ram's throat. For a moment Odysseus thought he had recognized the voice of Teiresias, but then the chamber was loud with the sound of moaning.

A smell of incense clouded the air. When the priest stepped

aside, the bare wall that had been at his back was suddenly crowded with shadowy faces that moved and swayed before Odysseus' astounded eyes.

Face after face appeared there, some howling, some grimacing with pain, others scarcely discernible at all; then he drew in his breath sharply for a face that he was sure he recognized was gazing back at him. A moment later a gust of wind blew out all the oil-lamps except the one illuminating the place behind veils of gauze in which the Sibyl stood with outspread arms like a figure of flame. Again Odysseus gasped, for the white mask had vanished. He was now staring into the bulging eyes and hideous, snake-wreathed features of a Gorgon's head.

So severe was the shock that for a moment he thought his heart had stopped. Then the figure began to tremble and shake, moaning like a woman possessed. The moans gave way to a faint hissing whisper which, only after it was repeated a third time, did he recognize as his own name – but his name spoken as a snake might speak it. Then the voice addressing him changed again. Though still hollow and hoarse, it was now distinctly a human voice, the voice of the shadowy face he had just recognized: the voice of his mother, Queen Anticleia.

My authority for this account of a journey into the Land of Shades is Odysseus himself. Though he was depleted by hunger and isolation, and his senses had been deranged by whatever drugs had tainted the water he drank in the Painted Room, and though he was, by his own admission, terrified half out of his wits by each, ever more disturbing stage of the ordeal, never-theless he retained, until the moment he had now reached, remarkably clear memories of everything he had undergone. But the sight of his mother's face, followed almost immediately by the sound of her voice, shocked him to the bottom of his soul.

As far as he knew, his mother was alive and well on Ithaca. So strong had that assumption been inside him that he had scarcely given her a moment's thought since leaving Troy. When he thought of home, it was primarily of his wife and small son, and then of his father. His mother was little more than an adjunct to his picture of their life, someone who had always been present, working quietly in the background and playing no part in the affairs of state other than through her many small acts of care for her husband. Her temperament had always been too shy and retiring for any larger role. So on those rare occasions when Odysseus gave thought to her, it was as an infinitely patient, always proud and almost entirely undemanding feature of his own life. Not since she had last scolded him as a boy had Anticleia exercised the least restraint on his lust for adventure. Then once he had decided to marry and settle down, she delighted in his choice of wife. Later, Odysseus had left for the war just as confident that she and Penelope would always be friends as he was sure that Anticleia would prove a doting grandmother to his son. Such was her nature – the modest, self-effacing manifestation of love as the deep and ordinary ground of things. His mother was simply, and always, there.

And now she was here, a shade in the Land of Shades.

The final shred of his composure frayed with the sudden understanding that his mother must be dead. Overwhelmed by the knowledge, he lost control of his will. For a time he was little more than a child again, unable to see or hear for his pain. Only gradually did he become conscious of the words that were trying to reach him as his mother's voice, speaking through the mouth of the Gorgon mask, reproached him for leaving Ithaca, for wasting all those long years in the terrible war at Troy, for failing to come home. He heard her bewail the way that his long absence had broken her heart and brought her to her grave. The voice was coming and going as though a dark wind gusted round it. He cried out urgent questions about his wife and tried to make sense of the reply. Dimly he heard the voice chant, 'Many lay claim to what once was yours.' When he demanded to know about his son, the voice said only, 'The child seeks to become the father that he lacks.' But the scarlet-gowned figure of the Sybil was shaking as if the words were forcing themselves out under tremendous pressure. Odysseus' eyes were blurred with tears. He tried to reach out to embrace the shaking figure, but his hands met only the gauzy veils. When he cried out at last, 'Tell me, has the time now come for my return?' the chamber fell silent as if holding its breath.

Again the Sybil began to sway and moan; then the voice issued low and hoarse from the lips of the mask: 'The life you knew has gone for ever.'

Odysseus stood trembling in his tears. As though pushed by invisible hands, the Sibyl was shaking before him like an epileptic. Uttering a few, quick pangs of breath, she gave a shriek of pain and collapsed on the ground before him.

He was about to reach down to the fallen figure, demanding to know more when he was overwhelmed by the confusion around him. Quickly the priest interposed his body between Odysseus and the Sibyl. Amid a murmured babble of voices, hooded figures grabbed Odysseus by the arms from behind. A door other than the one by which he had entered swung open. He was bustled out into another dark tunnel and hurried along through the swirl of smoke from the oil-lamps. They came to a door that shone with a cool ivory sheen. When it opened, he was urged through into an upward sloping passage.

Though his mind was in turmoil, he tried to take comfort from the thought that he must now be on the journey upwards, back into the world of men. They came to a place where a ladder climbed up through a trapdoor in the roof. One of the priests scaled the rungs first. Odysseus followed with two men coming after him. He was ushered through into a small chamber where he was made to take the only seat. Uncertain what else might happen, he waited there, distraught and confused. When he tried to speak to his guardians, demanding to know what was happening, not one of them would answer.

Eventually the door opened again. Another hooded figure

entered. 'Tell me, Odysseus of Ithaca,' he said, 'did the shades of the dead rise to meet you?'

Odysseus could only nod his head.

'And did they speak?' the figure asked.

'One of them did,' hc answered hoarsely.

'In whose voice did the shade speak?'

Trembling still, Odysseus said, 'In my mother's voice.'

'You are quite certain you heard the voice of your mother's shade?'

'Yes.'

'You would swear to it by the Gods of the Underworld?'

'Yes.'

The figure stood over him for a time. Odysseus heard the sound of breath drawn in. When he looked up, he saw his interrogator leaving the chamber. Another door opened. Odysseus was ushered out and along a short passage. Only a few moments later, bewildered by grief, emotionally exhausted, he found himself alone again inside the Painted Room.

For a long time the events of that night haunted his mind like shadows of a dream that had left him more shaken than enlightened. Once he was back in the light of day and returned to the company of his anxious friends, he might have taken ship for Ithaca at once, resolved to deal with whatever he found there and to reclaim what was his own; but two things delayed him.

Before he was permitted to leave the Oracle of the Dead, he was interviewed by Teiresias once more. As soon as the blind seer spoke, Odysseus felt certain that this was indeed the hooded figure of the priest he had encountered in the House of Persephone. He knew, therefore, that Teiresias had been present throughout the time when the shade of his mother was speaking through the Sibyl's mouth.

Neither pretending to know nothing of what had happened nor implying that his knowledge was supernatural, Teiresias sat across from Odysseus, an austere figure gazing blindly into space as he tapped his golden staff on the stone floor and began to utter his prophetic omens.

'Yours can still be no easy journey home, Odysseus of Ithaca,' he said, 'for neither the gods above nor the gods below are ready to ease your way. And the home that you find will not be the home that you left when you departed for the war at Troy.' Twice he rapped the tip of his staff. 'Neither will Ithaca prove to be your journey's end, for one day you must travel far inland to a place where men will not recognize for the thing it is, the oar that you will carry with you.'

Odysseus opened his mouth to question Teiresias further, but the seer's acute hearing must have heard the indrawn breath, for he raised an imperious finger, tapped the staff three times and began to speak again.

'Beware the Cattle of the Sun, for they are sacred and not to be harmed.' The pale skin of the seer's brow wrinkled in a frown. 'There are things I do not clearly see – perils of the heart, perils of the sword . . . your home in turmoil.' He opened his lips as if to add more, but then appeared to change his mind. Odysseus waited apprehensively. He was beginning to wonder whether the audience was at an end when Teiresias tapped his staff once more. 'Yet death, when it comes to you, will come easily,' he sighed, 'and it will come from the sea.'

Teiresias rose to his feet. 'I adjure you, as you care for your life, to say nothing of the rites you have undergone in this place. The Gods of the Underworld are always listening. They know how to claim those who would reveal their secrets.'

Then the audience was over. One acolyte stepped forward to lead Teiresias from the chamber; another ushered Odysseus out into the light of day by a different door. Eurylochus, Polites and Perimedes were waiting for him there. At their side stood Macareus with a comprehending smile of welcome on his face. Embracing Odysseus, he whispered in a low voice, 'The ways of the Underworld are perfect are they not?' And with a quick pang of the heart, Odysseus realized, that of all the people he knew, only this son of King Aeolus would understand him were he to ignore the adjuration of Teiresias and try to explain what it was like to enter the Halls of Hades and become one among the dead before one died.

The second, utterly unanticipated encounter of that day would delay his return to Ithaca for far longer than he could ever have guessed. By then he had left the Oracle of the Dead behind him and travelled back down through that volcanic landscape to the little town of Baia where his ship was beached. Word was sent out for his crew to return from the taverns and whorehouses that had sprung up on that shining shore, and he was about to climb aboard his vessel when he heard a woman's voice calling out his name. Turning his head in surprise, he saw a dishevelled figure hurrying along the strand towards him.

She was running with the muddied hem of her skirts raised above her shins. Bright hair streamed behind her as she ran. When she came to a halt, panting, before him, he recognized the distraught face of Calypso.

'You must take me with you,' she demanded, but her eyes were filled with helpless entreaty.

Astonished to see her at all, let alone in that condition, Odysseus said, 'I don't understand. What are you doing here?'

Calypso shook her head as though his questions were of no account. 'I can't go back down into that darkness,' she said. 'Never again. It terrifies me now.'

Odysseus stared at her in amazement. 'It was you,' he said. And when she nodded he frowned down into that beseeching gaze, remembering his earlier encounters with this young woman both on Aiaia and in the gloomy chambers of the dead. 'But surely you are in the service . . .' he began.

'No longer,' she cried, interrupting him before he could speak the name of either god or goddess. 'I have forsworn that service. I can bear it no longer. I want to live my life in the light. You must take me home.'

Already Odysseus shared her avidity for the light. Having spent so long enduring the dark mask of the Goddess – the Gorgon stare that had transfixed him in the House of Persephone – it brought a sense of exhilaration to look on the beautiful human face now gazing up at him. He saw, and recognized, the famished appetite for life blazing in her eyes.

'You wish to go back to Aiaia?' he frowned. Already he could imagine what kind of welcome this distraught fugitive would receive in Circe's palace.

But Calypso was urgently shaking her head.

'I cannot go back there,' she said. 'You will take me home to my own island of Ogygia. It lies south of here, to the west.' She looked up at him again, her chin raised, her breast rising and falling as she breathed. Her eyes fixed themselves on his with the absolute certainty of one who has chosen her fate.

Odysseus said, 'My course lies eastwards.'

'I was there for you at a time when you needed help,' Calypso declared. 'I know you to have a compassionate heart. Now it is your time to help me.'

Odysseus stood by his ship, aware of his men watching him, aware of what Circe had said about Calypso, aware of the utter impiety of what she had done and of what she now contemplated.

Then she said, 'If you leave me here I will certainly die.'

And as he looked down into the face of this young woman appealing to him for aid, he saw another frightened face looking hopelessly across at him as a boy wearing his father's golden armour led her away to her death on Achilles' tomb. Odysseus winced at the elision of those two young female faces, for he had done nothing to save Polyxena at Troy and he had been haunted by her desolate shade ever since. But it was Calypso who endured his silence now, watching the dark thoughts cross his face like the shadows of clouds passing across a hill.

'Did my mother truly speak through you?' he demanded. ·

'Truly,' she said, 'and with a power that frightened me. That is why you must take me from here.' Not for a moment had her eyes glanced away from his gaze. They held his attention with a power that astonished him now as she added, 'That is why you will take me home.'

Menelaus

Telemachus stood at the prow of Peiraeus's ship for much of the voyage to Pylos, taking the spray in his face and watching the spume flake from the dolphins' backs as they broke the glittering surface of the sea.

This was the first great adventure of his life.

Since he was a small boy he had been allowed the free run of his island-home, but having consigned her husband to the risks of war, Penelope was loath to let her only son adventure out to sea. So Telemachus had spent much time on the cliffs, watching the boats come and go, dreaming of the day when he too would set sail for far horizons. And now that day had come. The cutwater of this ship was taking him across the threshold into manhood. Holding onto the forestay while the ship's prow dipped and rose among the waves, Telemachus began to understand why his father had stayed away from Ithaca so long.

Always before, he had assumed that Odysseus must think of Ithaca as the true ground of his life, the homeland hearth from which he was kept only by the chance of war. Now Telemachus grasped how much freedom his father must have found beyond those cliffs and sheepfolds. Odysseus had sailed all the seas from Ithaca to Sidon. His name was known in the richest cities of the world. He could count the heroes of two generations as his friends and had numbered Troy's proudest warriors among his enemies. In all those years of wandering he must also have encountered many women who melted at his fame. But wasn't all of this what it truly meant to be a man?

Telemachus had always known that his father set the standard in these things; now he grasped that the true message of his long absence was that for a man to prove himself a man he must do more than wrangle in the council or brag over wine in a tavern with his friends. He had to go forth and take his place among the heroes of the age. And to do that he must put everything at risk for no other reason than an uncompromising love of glory. Only so might his name live on with honour after his ashes were interred.

And now that he had put the frustration and humiliations of boyhood behind him, Telemachus was resolved that the world should learn that Odysseus of Ithaca had a son worthy to bear his father's name.

As the ship approached the sandy beach at Pylos, they saw a large number of people gathered there. Evidently a festival in honour of Earth-shaker Poseidon was in progress, for smoke billowed from a number of fires along the strand and the salt air was savoury with the smell of roasting meat. Under countless banners snapping in the breeze above brightly coloured awnings, companies drawn from right across the kingdom were watching the sacred offering of black bulls.

Astounded by the size of the celebration, Telemachus gazed in awe at the multitude of richly dressed men and women with children running noisily among them, and at the sheer number of beasts bellowing as they waited their turn beneath the knife. Here was the great world assembled as if to greet him; and Pylos was by no means the largest of the Argive kingdoms. Yet its king, who must be somewhere at the centre of this immense feast, had been famous even before Odysseus was born. In his youth Nestor had fought wars against Elis and Arcadia; he had aided the Lapiths in their battle with the drunken Centaurs and he had taken part in the great hunt for the Calydonian boar. Later he had become a close friend and advisor to Agamemnon, and even though he was much older than the other Argive generals, his courage and sagacity had made him indispensable throughout the Trojan War. Across three generations, King Nestor incarnated the living history of the age; and when he thought of this, Telemachus felt daunted by the immediate prospect of appearing before him.

He said as much to Peiraeus, who merely smiled at his friend, told him to trust to the gods that had brought him there, and then made ready to run his keel ashore.

They were greeted by an open-faced young man who declared himself to be Peisistratus, the youngest son of King Nestor. Taken at once by his friendly manner, Telemachus guessed that there could be no more than a couple of years' difference in their ages, though the Prince of Pylos seemed altogether more accustomed to the courtly ways of the world. Without rudely enquiring who these visitors might be or where they had come from, Peisistratus invited them to take part in the general offering to Poseidon in thanks for a safe voyage and in hope of a successful return to their homeland. Then they must come and join the feast and be introduced to his father the King.

So it was that Telemachus was eventually brought before his father's old comrade. King Nestor was now well past his seventieth year. His white hair hung thin about his shoulders and his skin was wrinkled and dry as a walnut-shell. Sitting beneath a gorgeous parasol on a gilded throne that had been brought to the strand, he smiled amiably enough at all who passed before his gaze; but his grey eyes wandered as though no longer willing to contemplate anything for very long, and his ringed hands were quivering where they hung below the arms of the throne. At one side of him a young woman wafted an ostrich-feather fan, while at the other a bald-headed Libyan attended to his needs with all the fussy concern a grandmother might show for a helpless child.

As they approached the throne together, Peisistratus whispered to Telemachus, 'Pray don't mistake my father's manner for aloofness. He is the kindest of men but his strength is not what it was, and sometimes his thoughts seem to wander. He has never recovered from the way my brother Antilochus was killed so near to the end of the war. The grief of it distracts him still.' Then the young prince of Pylos advanced towards the throne and raised his voice over the noise of the throng. 'We have guests, father. They have made their thankful offerings to Divine Poseidon and wish to give you their greetings.'

Nestor lifted his head in a vague smile as Telemachus and Peiraeus bowed their heads in obeisance before him. 'They are welcome in Pylos,' he said, 'as are all men of good will, especially the young. Give them wine, give them wine.'

Comforted to find King Nestor a less formidable figure than he had anticipated, Telemachus drew in his breath. 'All Argos honours you, Lord Nestor. My friend Peiraeus and I bring you salutations and rejoice to find you in good health.'

Nestor nodded and dabbed his lips with a napkin that the Libyan handed to him. 'Where are you from, boy?' he asked, glancing away along the strand where, with a groan, yet another bull staggered and fell beneath the sacrificial knife.

'My land is Ithaca, where Laertes is king,' Telemachus answered. 'I believe my father is well known to you. I am Telemachus, son of Odysseus.'

Only after the last word was uttered did the old king's distracted glance drift back towards him. 'Odysseus, eh?' he smiled. He took a drink from the proffered goblet. 'Tell me, how is my old comrade? I dearly miss his company.'

'As do we all, sir,' Telemachus answered. 'I regret to say that my father has not yet returned to Ithaca. I have come here in the hope that you or one of your well-travelled subjects might have news of his present whereabouts, or knowledge of his fate if the gods have determined that he shall not come home.'

'Not yet come home, you say?' Nestor nodded as though pondering what such a thought might mean; then his face creased in a smile of admiration. 'It was he who thought up the idea of the wooden horse, you know. I was too old to ride in it myself, but one of my sons was in there with him . . . The one who's still here somewhere . . . Can't quite remember his name.'

'Thrasymedes, father,' Peisistratus supplied.

'Yes, that's him. Not half the man his brother was, but good enough in his way.' Nestor darted a confiding glance at Telemachus. 'Antilochus was killed, you know . . . not long before we breached their walls. I could better have spared the other son . . .' Shakily he drew in his breath, wiped his mouth with the napkin again. 'So many of them dead and gone at Troy . . . Young Achilles and his friend Patroclus, who were boys at Cheiron's school together once. Thysander before them, cut down in that clash at Clazomenae. And bluff old Ajax, Telamon's son . . . Ajax who lost his wits and threw himself on his own sword after Achilles was murdered by Paris. So many of them gone into the Land of Shades. And now,' his grey eyes blinked with doleful incredulity as he shook his white head, 'now they tell me that Agamemnon is dead . . . stabbed by his own wife as he went into his bath-house . . . What kind of world is this? And Diomedes . . . driven out of Tiryns . . . Idomeneus of Crete gone too. So many of them dead and gone, with only me left to remember them.' Sharply he sucked in his breath. His manner grew more agitated. 'Ten years we were there, freezing in the winters, driven half-crazy by the flies in the summer heat . . . And for what, I ask you, for what?' His mood seemed to darken with the demand. His eyes narrowed; he glanced up at Telemachus in accusation. 'Who did you say you are?'

'Telemachus, sir — son of Odysseus.'

Nestor grunted. 'So have you come to tell me that Odysseus is dead as well? Is that it? Have you come to tell me I must learn to grieve all over again?'

Hastily Peisistratus interposed himself between his father and the discomfited guest. 'Telemachus doesn't yet know his father's fate,' he explained softly. 'He's come here to Pylos hoping that someone has news of him.'

Nestor nodded at his youngest son, a little tetchily. 'I know, I know.' He frowned back at Telemachus. 'Listen to me, boy. You want to know about Odysseus – let me tell you this. Your father is the craftiest man I ever knew . . . No one will have caught him napping . . . not unless by treachery . . . and the gods know there's enough of that in the world. So when you find the villain who murdered him don't hesitate to cut him down. Cut him down without mercy. That way your father's shade will rest in peace and you'll make a name for yourself. Do you hear me, son of Odysseus? That's the way of this world. Blood cries out for blood. Do you hear me, boy? Do you hear?'

Telemachus nodded uncertainly. The old king spluttered on his wine and began to cough. The Libyan servant wiped his mouth and patted him on the back until he was pushed impatiently away. Nestor looked up at the sky with stricken eyes. 'We should never have done it, you know. We should never have offered up that child Iphigenaia on the altar in Aulis. That was a strong fate that Artemis inflicted on us then . . . Never have I done a harder thing . . . She was such a beautiful child. A child to charm the heart . . . I gave her a pony in Mycenae once, when she was just a little girl still. I was always soft with her . . . But that business at Aulis . . . It should never have happened . . . It was a terrible thing. A terrible, terrible thing.'

Speechless and dismayed, feeling the desolation of the world gather force, Telemachus watched the king's palsied hand shake uncontrollably at his side. There was a muttering among his attendants. A palanquin was summoned. Shaded by the parasol, with his hand-maiden fanning him, King Nestor was carried away along the strand, back to the royal comforts of his bed.

Anxious to explain that his father's mood was rarely so grim, Peisistratus apologized to Telemachus; and then, still eager to do what he could to help, he called his older brother Thrasymedes into council with them.

'Be grateful you have no brothers who were killed in the war,' Thrasymedes said wearily when he learned what had happened with his father. 'Believe me, they would always mean more to your father than you ever could, and there's nothing at all you could do about it.'

'I'm not even sure that I have a father still,' Telemachus replied.

Thrasymedes shook his head in gloomy sympathy. 'There's been no word of Odysseus here, I'm afraid. Nor did anyone know where he was when Diomedes called the council in Corinth. You understand now why I had to send word there that my father was in no shape to fight. But the truth is that none of us were. We'd all had our bellyful of fighting out there in Troy.' He glanced away to where the women were dancing along the strand. 'It's been nearly six years since the war ended. You have to face it, boy, there can't be much hope for Odysseus. So many men were drowned in the storm off Euboea.' He took in the grief and disappointment on the young face before him. 'Don't misunderstand me. I know it must come hard. He was a great man, your father. I admired him more than anyone else I met in the war at Troy. He was brave and resourceful and wise . . . and he was a funny man too. Even when things looked hopeless, he could still make us all laugh. That's how you should try to remember him.'

'You speak as though you know he's dead,' Peiraeus put in, dismayed that they had come so far to receive so little, 'but no one knows that for certain yet. And there's a lot of trouble on Ithaca right now. Telemachus stands in need of more than good advice.'

'The whole world is in trouble these days. I wish there was more we could do to help, but I don't see what it would be,' Thrasymedes answered with a touch of impatience that he immediately regretted.

'What about Menelaus?' It was Peisistratus who had spoken, having listened carefully to the previous exchanges. 'The word is that he's been back in Sparta for some time now. Perhaps he's heard something?'

Thrasymedes shrugged. 'I suppose it's possible. They say he's been out east in Egypt for years. I can't think why Odysseus would have gone that way, but you never know.'

Peisistratus directed an encouraging glance at Telemachus. 'If I were you I wouldn't give up either. Why don't you go on to Sparta? It has to be worth a try. In fact, I'll keep you company, if you like. I'm eager to see something more of the world and there's nothing to keep me here. What do you say?'

Menelaus had been at the court of King Proteus in Memphis when he was told that Agamemnon had been assassinated. Fully apprised by his agents of the terrible events in Mycenae, Proteus chose a moment when Helen was absent among her women, for he thought it best that her husband should inform her that her sister had murdered his brother and taken his principal enemy to her bed.

Yet Menelaus himself could scarcely comprehend the shock of what he was told. There must be some mistake, he insisted. The agents must be misinformed. Agamemnon had returned in triumph from Troy. He had accomplished everything his wife desired of him. Why would Clytaemnestra dream of doing such a thing? But even as he protested, Menelaus recalled how many reasons Clytaemnestra had been given to revile her husband. And such an unthinkable act was entirely consistent with the bloody history of Mycenae. It was, quite simply, the atrocious kind of thing that happened there.

Sick at heart, Menelaus sat recalling the night when he and his brother had cowered together in the damp darkness of the water-stair at Mycenae before making their escape through the postern gate. With their lives under immediate threat from the usurper Thyestes, they had vowed always to be true to each other. Embracing his younger brother so fiercely that Menelaus found it difficult to breathe, Agamemnon had sworn that no harm would ever come to him as long as he was alive to prevent it. But Agamemnon was dead now, and the longer Menelaus contemplated that fact, the more he became aware of a great weight lifting from his chest. He felt as though all his life had been spent in the clutches of that embrace. Now that those arms had fallen lax about him, he might begin to breathe freely again.

Just as astonishing to him was Helen's response when he found a way to tell his wife that her sister was now a murderer.

'So she has dared to do it at last,' she said; and he would have sworn that a wry smile passed across the shadowed beauty of her face.

He said, 'I thought you'd be horrified by the news.'

Helen held her needlework up to the light. 'I was horrified when I heard that Agamemnon had killed Clytaemnestra's first husband and their child. I was horrified again when reports reached Troy that he'd sacrificed his daughter in payment for his own impiety.' She turned her frank gaze towards Menelaus. 'But we both know he was a monster; and now he's met a monster's end.'

Taking in the shock on his gentle face, she added quietly, 'Perhaps I've seen too much horror. Perhaps my senses have been dulled by it.'

Dry-mouthed, Menelaus said, 'He was my brother still.'

Helen reached out a hand to cover his. 'Do you ask me to grieve for a man who would have had me killed if you hadn't stood in the way? Did he not threaten your own life too?' She took in the pain on his face. 'Nothing will cure this world of cruelty, but at least my sister has put an end to Agamemnon's part in it.' Sighing, she put down the little wooden frame. 'I would rejoice at what she's done if I could believe that anything other than more blood will come of it.'

Wondering whether he would ever understand this woman whom he loved more than his life, Menelaus made offerings alone to his brother's shade. Yet even as he poured the libations, he wondered whether the time had now come to return to Argos and reclaim the kingdom of Sparta. And with that achieved, he might even make a bid for the Lion Throne himself.

But when he broached the matter with Helen, he was dismayed by the strength of her resistance. Agamemnon's writ of banishment had forced them to fly east and, by the grace of some god whose mercy she scarcely deserved, Helen found herself at ease in the orient as she had never been among the rowdy princes of

Argos. Here her beauty was a matter for appreciation rather than the cause of strife. Here she was respected. Here at last she was at liberty to be herself.

'Yet there are things you must understand,' Menelaus protested. 'Aegisthus sits on a throne to which he has no lawful right. A long time ago, while he was still a boy, he slew my father. Now he has had a hand in my brother's death. What must the world think of a man who stands by and does nothing while the murderer of his closest kinsmen flourishes?'

Glancing away, Helen said, 'I no longer greatly care what the world thinks.'

'Then what must a man think of himself in such a case? What sort of man must he be?'

'A man who has already seen too much of war?' she answered. 'A man who understands that the lust for vengeance is the curse that destroyed his father and his father's house. A man who has learned to value love above everything else?' But she grew impatient then. 'Isn't it enough that our passions have already burned a great city and caused the deaths of many thousands who wanted only to live their lives in peace? Are you so restless with our life that you want my approval to start another war? Or do you imagine that my sister will give up what she has won for herself without a fight? I promise you she will not.'

Helen had been pacing the room as she spoke. She turned to look back at him. 'In all the Argive lands there is only one thing I want,' she declared. 'It is the one thing that you too should want more than anything else.'

'And what might that be?' he asked shortly, discomfited and unhappy to find himself so quickly at odds with her.

'Our daughter,' she answered.

And for several long seconds she let the silence stand between them.

So painful were their separate feelings of guilt over the child they had not seen for nearly twelve years that neither of them had yet dared to speak of her. Yet in all those years Hermione had never been far from Helen's thoughts; and at each returning thought of her daughter she was seared by a remorse so profound that there were hours at a time when she could scarcely breathe for the pain of it.

'Hermione is my child,' she said. 'I need to see her again. I need to hold her.'

'I understand,' Menelaus answered. 'But the girl has been well cared for. I made sure of that. Hermione will be waiting for us in Sparta.'

'There's too much darkness there, don't you see? Please, Menelaus,' Helen turned her abject eyes on him, 'let her come here to live with us in Egypt.'

Now almost sixteen years old, Hermione had seen neither of her parents since she was a child of four. She remembered them hardly at all — only that her mother had been a remote and anxious figure who had smelled like lilies and was suddenly gone; and that her father had changed from a kindly giant into a morose, short-tempered man who rarely looked at her. For a time she had been raised by her nurse in the house of her kinsman Icarius, who was boring and stiff-necked and mostly concerned that she should acquire at the earliest possible age an unshakably Spartan sense of modesty and virtue. Then, at the behest of Queen Clytaemnestra, she had been moved to Mycenae.

Once there, Hermione became utterly devoted to her cousin Orestes. Soon her admiration turned to adoration, though her feelings were coyly concealed when she realized, to her bitter disappointment, that he was only moderately interested in the fact that the two of them must eventually be married. Even when she shed her childhood gawkiness and revealed her share in her mother's beauty, Orestes remained more attached to his friend Pylades than to anyone else; but Hermione endured the pain of his rebuffs, confident in the knowledge that the dynastic interests of their two families would bring him one day to her bed.

About the time of her first offering to Artemis, the feel of life in the Lion House altered for ever. Without explanation, her cousin Iphigenaia disappeared. Her foster-mother Clytaemnestra, who had never been easily approachable, became still more formidable and cold. The friendship between Orestes and Pylades turned secretive. Then suddenly, for reasons Hermione did not understand, she was returned to Sparta.

Some time passed before she learned, through the gossip of servants, about the dreadful thing that had been done in Mycenae. And then it seemed for a time that the world had forgotten about her. In her isolation the girl grew introverted and self-willed. She took pleasure in nothing but being peevish with her servants and small acts of cruelty to the pets that were meant to distract her. With the adult strangers whose duty it was to care for her welfare, she was stubborn and petulant. Her single desire was to be reunited with Orestes, but as he was now forced to live in hiding somewhere a long way away, it seemed that her wish was doomed to frustration. Not without justice, Hermione came to believe the world did not care for her; and the world, she decided, must be made to pay for that.

Then, with all the shock and glamour of divine intervention, a herald had come from Egypt. Reconciled to each other once more, her parents wanted their daughter to join them there. They loved her and missed her and wanted her back. She was to gather together all her most treasured possessions and take ship for the east as soon as possible.

Hermione arrived at her parents' mansion in Canopus in a state of high excitement. After the tedium of Sparta, she loved the exotic feel of Egyptian life. But mostly she adored the unprecedented fact that both her parents were at her beck and call, eager to gratify her whims, to distract her at the first sign of dissatisfaction, to load her with gifts.

Yet no amount of exquisite jewellery, expensive perfumery, finely embroidered gowns, candied delicacies, attentive menials, talking parrots and ridiculous monkeys could ever quite appease the ache of abandonment inside her. Hermione's heart was afflicted with a profound grievance against life. Because that grievance left her as ill-tempered as she was insecure, she found ample opportunities for punishment; and its principal target was Helen.

The desire to hurt her mother was as incomprehensible to Hermione as it was uncontrollable. It yielded no lasting satisfaction and left them both distressed. Yet time after time it got the better of her, for as the girl now viewed things, the only reason why her whole life had not been the subject of such extravagant attention as she was now receiving was that Helen had forsaken her when she was too young to protest. And she had done it from no larger motive than the pursuit of her own pleasure. Already it was evident to Hermione how much pain and humiliation her father must have suffered; so where to put all the blame for the family's years of wretchedness except on her mother?

To add to the injury, Helen's entrance still consumed all the attention in a room, for by the simple, disastrous fact of her incomparable beauty, she relegated everyone else to dullness. This too was unforgivable.

If Hermione intuited that that her mother had long ago passed the same verdict on herself, it made no difference. Nothing Helen could do was ever quite right for her daughter. Her advice and opinions were dismissed, her jokes disdained, her gifts derided, her concern misconstrued. And so, over the next two years, by a slow insidious process of erosion, Hermione achieved what all the tribulations of her mother's life had so far failed to accomplish: she broke Helen's spirit.

Having believed that all the happiness he had originally conceived for his family in Sparta might soon be recovered here in Egypt, Menelaus found himself stretched between his wife and his daughter. When he discovered that Helen had begun to drown her pain in the poppy prepared for her by the serving-woman Polydamna, he felt angry at first; then, increasingly, he was inclined to join her.

★   ★   ★

Hermione had been in Egypt for three years and was almost nineteen years old when she at last heard word of Orestes.

Canopus is a great trading city standing on the Delta of the Nile, and not much stirs in the world without news of it reaching the waterfront there. That the son of Agamemnon had avenged his father's death by murdering his mother caused a buzz of horror to run throughout the taverns and bazaars within a week of its happening. Less than an hour later it had reached Menelaus. Instantly he felt all the old ghosts rising round his head.

Where other families loved and cherished one another, the House of Pelops feasted on each other's blood. Helen was right: they were monsters spawned by monsters. Of all of them, he alone was not guilty of slaughtering his own kin, though he had come within an inch of killing the wife he loved. So there was, Menelaus saw, a terrible inevitability about it all. And he had always been fond of Orestes. The boy's imaginative spirit had lightened the dour air of the Lion House, which was all the more reason why Menelaus had long entertained hopes that a marriage between Orestes and Hermione might initiate a new age across all Argos. One free from all the old curses. A golden age of prosperity and peace.

Well, so much, he thought now, for the dreams of an unworldly man!

And somehow, he must tell Helen that her sister, the murderess, had in turn been murdered, and by the hand of her child.

Yet this time it was his daughter's response that astounded him.

'I must go to him at once!' Hermione cried. 'He must be in terrible distress. I'm sure he needs me now.'

Half drowsy with poppy, Helen said, 'You would offer comfort to a man who has murdered his own mother?'

'I would do more than that,' Hermione answered.

Menelaus tried to intervene. 'This matter is not your concern, Hermione.'

But his daughter turned on him with outraged eyes. 'How can you say that? Orestes belongs to me. He has always belonged to me. You promised him to me a long time ago. We have always been meant for each other.'

Menelaus glanced away. 'As you say, that was all a long time ago. After what Orestes has done, things can never be the same.'

But the girl was not to be deterred. 'I understand well enough why he was driven to do what he has done,' she said. 'His suffering is my suffering. He needs our love not our judgement now. I will go to him and marry him.'

'You will do no such thing,' Helen gasped. 'The youth has passed beyond the protection of both men and gods. He belongs to the Daughters of Night now. Put him from your thoughts.'

'Your loyalty does you credit,' Menelaus said more gently, 'but no sane man can bear to contemplate what he has done. Orestes is not for you, Hermione. Let that be an end of it.'

But that was the beginning not the end of the harrowing encounter. It ended with Hermione smashing a delicately painted two-handled jar that she knew was dear to her mother's heart as she ran in a blizzard of rage and grief to her room.

Thereafter, life in Egypt became intolerable to all three of them. Hermione was beyond all reason, contemptuous of both her parents, trapped in her own fury.

Menelaus and Helen could see no way through the misery except to find a suitable husband for her as soon as possible. He would need to be a man strong enough to rule Sparta, but also, which might prove more difficult, to cope with their daughter's powerful will. So despite Helen's reservations, Menelaus wrote a long letter to Neoptolemus, son of Achilles, who had recently won a significant victory in his war with the Dorians.

The letter suggested that in uncertain times, with Mycenae in a state of confusion, it made sense for Thessaly and Sparta to enter into an alliance for their mutual protection and support. The future of Sparta would be secured that way, with Neoptolemus as the country's strong king. The combined forces of the two kingdoms might withstand any renewed incursion by the Dorians; and one day, if the gods looked with favour on their endeavours, the High

Kingship might be restored with Neoptolemus on the Lion Throne. The treaty would be sealed by his marriage to Hermione; and if this proposal proved acceptable to his young friend and comrade, Menelaus would return to Sparta with his family in the near future so that all the arrangements could be put in place.

On the afternoon after he had broken the news of her fate to his daughter, Menelaus sought to distract himself by putting in hand the commissioning of his ship. He was walking along the waterfront when he met a Phoenician trader called Hylax who had kept him supplied with luxuries from the east and news from the west in the early days of his arrival in Egypt. Throughout the war, Hylax had made a fat living by profiteering from the sale of necessary goods both to the beleaguered Trojans and the besieging Argives; but he was an engaging rogue and Menelaus had found him useful.

The two men had not met for some years, however, and there was much inconsequential chatter to be got through before Hylax bared his big teeth in a grin, and said, 'So what are we to make of your old friend Odysseus of Ithaca? Such a stir he has caused! May the gods spare him for his iniquities!'

When he saw that he had Menelaus at a disadvantage, Hylax made him wait for the kernel of his news. First his listener had to be assured of the veracity of its source – another Phoenician, a reliable man who plied his trade between Sidon and Sicily, calling in on smaller islands between. Then consideration had to be given as to what Menelaus might offer in return for an item of such interest, and only when he had agreed to use the ship's chandler that Hylax recommended, did the Phoenician reveal what he knew.

Having listened to his story, Menelaus was first left feeling that if Odysseus of all people could behave this way, then there was no loyalty left in the world. But after a time he was forced to recognize that he was envious of the freedom from care that his old comrade seemed to have won for himself. Agamemnon was dead; Diomedes and Idomeneus had been deposed; Neoptolemus was still struggling to defend his birthright; and old Nestor's life-thread must be running short by now. Out of all the surviving captains of the war at Troy, it seemed that only Odysseus had found much in the way of happiness.

Yet of all of them, Menelaus thought with a rueful smile, perhaps he was the one who most deserved it.

In the spring of the year that Menelaus and Helen returned to Sparta they were visited at different times by four young men.

Neoptolemus had recently strengthened his position in the north. Taking a small detachment from the forces with which he and Peleus had stalled the Dorian advance, he debouched westwards into the shadowy gorges and high, slate-blue mountains of Epirus. Once established there, he rallied the Dolopian tribesmen of the region, who were his own ancestral people, and then combined with Peleus' forces in the east to engage the Dorians on two fronts. Their fierce simultaneous attacks had forced the invaders to retreat, and Neoptolemus was now hopeful that the lost capital of Iolcus would soon be recovered. Nor did his plans end there, for his successes led him to foresee a time when he would become suzerain of all the northern kingdoms, with the little son whom he had sired on Hector's widow Andromache one day ruling Epirus on his behalf.

In this already exalted state, Neoptolemus received the letter from Egypt proposing a marriage alliance. It seemed that things were changing everywhere, for he had often heard Agamemnon and Menelaus talk of the day when their kingdoms would be united under the rule of Orestes and Hermione. Clearly such a union was out of the question now; and Mycenae, where Talthybius was struggling to control a gang of unruly barons, was in turmoil still. With Menelaus offering him the Spartan succession, a distinct possibility emerged that the son of Achilles might one day seize the Lion Throne as High King of all Argos.

It would also be good, he thought, to have a younger and more compliant partner in his bed than Andromache. Neoptolemus had found no comfort in the arms of a woman who detested him and, having proved his manhood by making her pregnant at last, he had been glad enough to leave her behind his lines and get on with the more profoundly satisfying business of war.

So, yes, Andromache could be disposed of without great loss, and he would take Hermione as his wife and future queen.

Menelaus received him warmly in Sparta as an old comrade; but never having met Helen before, Neoptolemus had come to the city filled with expectation and was disappointed by her remote and wary presence. Had ten years of war really been fought on account of this woman? If so, he found it hard to see what all the fuss had been about.

Hermione was another matter. If her mother lacked fire, this girl's eyes glowed with it, though it was, he thought, a sullen sort of fire that might prove petulant if not kept under strict control. Nor could he find much enthusiasm in her curt responses to his efforts to interest her in the new war he was fighting. It further occurred to him that, after the luxury of her life in Egypt and Sparta, this spoiled young woman might not take kindly to the spare and disciplined life awaiting her in Thessaly. Neoptolemus was obliged, in fact, to suppress a number of uneasy reservations he felt about this marriage in favour of the advantages it would bring. Just as well, he thought, that the need to love and to be loved had never ranked very high among his priorities.

Having spent time recalling stories of the war together, and giving thought to the effects of its turbulence on the world, Menelaus and Neoptolemus eventually got down to discussing the terms of the marriage settlement. Hermione, it seemed, would bring a generous dowry with her, but only on condition that Andromache's child be passed over in favour of any sons that Hermione might bear. The condition came hard to Neoptolemus who had grown fond of his little son Molossus in the few hours he had spent with him; but Menelaus would not shift on the point and eventually it was agreed. Satisfied with the business he had done, Neoptolemus returned to his mountain fastness in order to prepare for marriage later that year. And if Hermione behaved throughout this whole stiff occasion with a restraint that left her parents feeling pleasantly relieved, it was only because she was concealing quite different plans of her own.

Orestes had grown into his young manhood torn between two contradictory imperatives. The first was the duty to avenge his father's murder by taking the assassin's life; the second was the age-old taboo against matricide that made it unthinkable to kill his mother. In an attempt to resolve his intolerable dilemma, he consulted the oracle at Delphi as soon as he was of an age to do so. The answer he received was unequivocal: Agamemnon's death must be avenged.

And so, accompanied by his friend Pylades, whose love for him had remained constant throughout, he returned covertly to Mycenae, where he might work out a plan of action with his sister Electra. Certain only that he wanted to kill Aegisthus, Orestes was still hoping that the gods might contrive some other means to end his mother's life.

If Aegisthus had been allowed his way, Electra would have been dead some time ago, but Clytaemnestra had already lost too many children to yield to his ruthless will. Yet she understood very well that if Electra married and bore a son, the child would become a rallying point for all the disaffected barons of Mycenae. The Queen's solution was to marry her daughter to a commoner – a man from whom her aristocratic spirit would proudly shrink – so that there could be no issue from the marriage.

When he secretly met his sister and heard the story of her humiliations, Orestes wept. What kind of mother was it, Electra asked, who could pleasure herself with her husband's murderer, while inflicting shame on her daughter and leaving her son to be hunted down like a rabid dog? Her hatred had grown so powerful that she declared herself ready to kill Clytaemnestra herself if her brother's courage failed. She reassured him that there many people in the city who had no love for either the queen or her lover. They knew that blood must have blood. It was the law of things. Mycenae had become a city ruled only by fear. Once the deed was done, Orestes would be greeted with joy.

Even as he listened to his sister, Orestes could feel fate shutting down around him. He was being pushed into a dark place from which he might never escape. Yet he was the son of Agamemnon, the rightful Prince of Mycenae, and his father's blood was crying out for vengeance. So the moment arrived when Orestes resolved that the pollution of his mother's death could be allowed to fall on no head but his own. Together at their father's tomb, he and his sister prayed for the help of the gods. Electra made her sacred offerings to Persephone, asking the Queen of the Underworld to guide their actions, while Orestes prayed to Sky-Father Zeus for his support, to the Earth Mother for her mercy on him, and to the shade of Agamemnon for the strength to do what he must do.

Five years had passed since either he or Pylades was last seen in Mycenae, and both were bearded now. It was feasible, therefore, to present themselves at the gate to the Lion House disguised as emissaries from the King of Phocis with an urgent message to deliver. Even when they stood before Clytaemnestra in the private chamber where she received ambassadors and suppliants, they went unrecognized. Solemnly Pylades stepped forth holding an urn. It contained, he declared, the ashes of the queen's son Orestes, who had been killed in a chariot-race during a festival at Delphi.

Gripping a knife in the folds of his robe, Orestes watched the blood drain from his mother's face. He heard the sigh she released as one of her hands reached backwards for her chair.

Was it grief that overwhelmed her? Or merely exhausted relief that the threat of her son's vengeance was lifted from her head? It was impossible to say, for that impassive face had long grown used to concealing its secrets.

When Pylades stammered out his regret at bringing such unhappy news, Clytaemnestra wearily shook her head. 'If I had not heard it from you,' she said, 'someone else would have told me soon enough.' She lifted a weak hand, and got to her feet again. 'You will excuse me. I need to grieve alone.'

Unable to move, Orestes watched his mother walk out of the chamber. A roaring, like a big wind, gusted through his head.

As Pylades stared at him aghast, the lean-faced secretary who had shown them in to the chamber cleared his throat and stepped forward to usher them out.

They stood without moving, staring at each other.

'The Queen is understandably distracted,' the secretary offered. 'If you will wait outside for a time, I feel sure your patience will soon be rewarded.'

The seconds passed. Again the secretary cleared his throat.

Appalled that they had risked so much and accomplished nothing, the two young men were about to turn and follow him out when they heard voices in the next room. The inner door by which Clytaemnestra had left the chamber opened again and Aegisthus was there demanding that they wait. Casually dressed, he was dabbing barber's soap from his face with a towel.

'Leave us alone,' he dismissed the secretary, 'I wish to question these Phocians more closely.'

When they were alone, he addressed his visitors with a theatrically doleful smile. 'Forgive my appearance,' he said, 'but such tragic news demands immediate attention. Come closer, I pray you. Tell me what you know.'

He half turned to indicate a couch on which they might be seated. In the same moment, as though acting under urgent orders, Orestes strode quickly across the floor and thrust the knife into his side. Aegisthus stared down at the harm that had been done to him in disbelief. He opened his lips but only a gasp came out. Quickly, Pylades grabbed the towel and pressed it firmly over the gaping mouth.

Orestes pulled out the knife and took a step back. Then he pushed the blade into the man's ribcage and twisted it there. Blood splashed across his tunic as he stabbed again, and again, for a third and fourth time. By now he was desperate for this ruined body to die. When a red stain soaked the towel where the mouth must be, the dying man's grip on his killer's shoulders slackened. A moment later Aegisthus slid to the floor where his lean, athletic form shook and shook as in the throes of a fit. With the knife in his hand still, Orestes stood shaking over him.

Sensing his uncertainty, Pylades hissed, 'It has begun. Now it will be easier. Remember Apollo's command.' Then he crossed the room and threw open the inner door.

Even before he entered her apartment Orestes knew that what happened next would play itself out over and over again in the arena of his mind. Each time he took a knife to meat he would remember the blade entering his mother's breast. Each time he closed his eyes against the night he would see the hand lifted to her mouth as the blood sprayed from it. Whenever he slept – if he ever slept again – his dreams would be loud with her last, gasping whisper of his name. As he stepped through to where his mother looked up, suddenly weak and old and jaded, from the couch on which she lay with her hands in her hair, he knew that he was stepping into the darkness where the Furies live. He knew that they would pursue him from that place forever. And so great was the need to shift into his body the pain that seared his mind, a day would come – just one of the many intolerable days of which his life must now consist – when he would gnaw to the bone, and finally bite off, the index finger of the hand that held that knife.

And it would make no difference. Nothing would ever make any difference. No rite of cleansing. No word of understanding and consolation from a friend. No imprecation of the gods. Not a second of this horror could ever be undone.

And this was the haunted young man who burst into the palace at Sparta one humid afternoon many months later, demanding to have audience with Menelaus, wanting to know what treacherous dealings had led his uncle to forswear himself by giving away his promised bride Hermione to another man.

Still indomitably loyal to his friend, Pylades had travelled to Sparta at his side, and the two fugitives might never have gained admission to the palace had it not been for the iron laws of hospitality. The porter did not feel easy about these travel-worn desperados shaking dust from their hair as they dismounted from their chariots, but when one of them brusquely announced himself as Orestes, son of Agamemnon and nephew to the King of Sparta, and the other as Pylades, Prince of Phocis, he could not refuse them entry.

The chamberlain Eteoneus despatched a minion to warn Menelaus and Helen of their arrival, and they were at once thrown into consternation. Reports of his unpredictable behaviour had preceded Orestes along the roads of Argos. How best to receive this young madman? Should he be calmly entertained, as Menelaus believed, and then ushered away with a kindly word? Or was Helen wiser in her conviction that it was too risky to grant him an audience? They had just agreed that, whatever else happened, Hermione must be kept well apart from her cousin when they heard shouting in the hall below.

Stepping onto the inner balcony, Menelaus saw that two spearmen had already been summoned from the guardhouse. Orestes was growling at them with bared teeth like a distempered boar-hound while Pylades restrained him with a firm hand at his shoulder. Seeing Menelaus, Pylades demanded to know whether such an inhospitable show of force was the custom in Sparta these days.

'It certainly is not,' Menelaus called down as he descended the marble stairs. 'But neither is it customary for our guests to behave like unmuzzled dogs.' He stood before them with narrowed eyes, struggling for composure. 'First let me bid you welcome in the name of Zeus of the Strangers,' he said; 'then I think you should be seated, gentlemen, so that we may discuss your business here.'

'I'm no stranger, Menelaus of Sparta,' Orestes retorted. 'I am your kinsman Orestes, son of Agamemnon, lawful heir to Mycenae, and well you know it.'

With a dubious smile Menelaus said, 'Surely not? I remember my nephew Orestes as a well-bred young man.'

'So I was once, in the days when you gave me my first hunting knife as a gift. But that was before the curse on our house came home to me. And it has done so with a vengeance.' Orestes glanced at his friend with a sickly smile on his face. 'Did you hear that, Pylades? I said it has come home with a vengeance.' But then he turned savagely on his reluctant host. 'Don't toy with me, Uncle. I warn you, it would not be wise. I'm here only to claim what is rightly mine. Hermione has bid me come to claim her. We were promised to each other long ago. I will not leave this house without her.'

Stunned, Menelaus said, 'Hermione asked you to come here?'

'She did. I have the letter here.' Orestes fumbled with the straps of the wallet at his belt and took out a piece of Egyptian papyrus. 'See for yourself.'

Menelaus looked down at the misspelled scrawl with which Hermione had summoned this mad young man to rescue her from the unwanted marriage to Neoptolemus. He looked up from it, flushed and angry. 'My daughter had no leave to send this letter. She has transgressed the bounds of obedience and modesty. I regret that she has brought you here on a fool's errand, but I am a man of my word and she is promised to another.'

'And if I meet with Neoptolemus I will surely kill him,' Orestes snarled. 'A man of your word, you say? A man of your word! Believe me, Uncle, I will kill you too sooner than let you break the solemn pledge you made to my father that Hermione and I should wed.'

At that moment more spearmen rattled into the hall. Raising a hand to prevent them from entirely surrounding Orestes, Menelaus studied the angry young face across from him, aware how dangerous was the unstable mind behind it.

Yet still he hoped to reason with him. 'That pledge was made many years ago,' he tried, 'in a different world. Everything has changed since then. We have all been forced to rebuild our lives.'

'Some of us have been forced to do more,' Orestes glowered at him. 'Yet some things remain constant. The gods know that Mycenae is mine though I have been banished the city. Hermione is mine though you seek to give her elsewhere. Do not add to the storm in my mind, Uncle. Give me what belongs to me in Sparta. The rest I will reclaim for myself.'

'I cannot do that, Orestes,' Menelaus sighed.

'If you are a man of honour you can do nothing else.'

'Surely you must see that your own actions have made it impossible?'

'I see only a double-dealing villain who promised me the throne of Sparta once. I mean to make him keep his promises.'

Helen, who had been standing in the shadows of the balcony since Menelaus began to descend the stairs, stepped forward now. 'And I see only a mad boy who has murdered his own mother and my sister.' Her voice had echoed through the hall. Orestes stared up at her, wincing, as if into bright sunlight. 'I see you, son of Agamemnon,' she cried. 'I see that you have no love for my daughter. There is nothing left in your heart but guilt and hatred. You would have to kill me too before I let you take her.'

'Is that the whore of Troy I hear accusing me?' Orestes shouted. 'I have two deaths on my conscience. How many thousands lie on yours?'

'None by my own hand,' Helen retorted, flushed with passion now, 'nor any by my wish. I am not answerable for the madness of the world. No, and not for your madness either. That you got from your father. Only a fiend willing to murder his own daughter could father a son capable of taking his own mother's life.' She heard Menelaus call up to silence her, but she was not to be stopped. 'You spring from the same rotten seed as him, Orestes of Mycenae,' she cried. 'I will never permit that seed to pollute my daughter's loins.'

In that moment the crazed young man might have sprung up the stairs towards her if the spearmen had not been there to prevent him. As it was, Menelaus looked on astounded as Orestes released a violent shriek of pain and clutched his head with his hands. Then he was down on his knees, crumpled upon himself, rocking and gasping, as though he was being kicked by a hostile crowd. Pylades bent over him only to be pushed away unrecognized. When Orestes looked up there were flecks of white foam at his lips. His eyes bristled with terror. Raising the mutilated hand before his face, he tried with the other to fight off something that only he could see. He was groaning as he did so, and uttering frenzied pleas to Apollo for his aid.

The spearmen fell back, blanching to look at him. Some of them made the sign to ward off evil. Pylades cast an anguished glance up at Menelaus; then turned back to Orestes, whispering his name, trying to reach him down whatever chasm had opened up inside him.

'It is my sister's ghost that haunts him,' Helen cried.

'No,' Pylades shouted up at her, 'his own Furies torment his mind. Because he loved his mother they will not let him go.' He bent down over his friend again but Orestes recoiled from his touch as though an asp had stung him. He slumped to the marble floor, drawing his knees up to his chest and covering his head with his hands and arms.

And that was how Hermione saw him when she joined her mother on the balcony, drawn there by the terrible noises rising from the hall.

When he heard the frightened gasp that broke from her, Menelaus looked up and shouted, 'Get away from there, Hermione. Return to your chamber now.'

But Helen grabbed her daughter by the arm. 'No,' she cried, 'let her stay. Let her see just what manner of man it is she wants to marry.' She turned to confront Hermione. 'Look at him well. This is the man with whom you've conspired behind our backs. This is what you've chosen for yourself. And don't imagine that Orestes has any love for you. What he wants is Sparta. But go to him if you want him still. Take the curses of his house upon yourself. Go to him. I won't stop you.'

For a time Hermione stood frozen on the balcony, looking not at the man she had once believed she loved, but at the hostile fire in her mother's eyes. She wanted to run from the hall but her legs felt faint beneath her. She was no longer a nineteen year old woman trying to seize control of her life, but a dumb animal petrified by the cruelty of a world she could not understand. All the years of unshed tears rose inside her and shook her where she stood.

Knowing that she had been much the same age as this frightened girl when Paris came to claim her, that she had been younger still when Theseus had come, driven by nothing nobler than his lust, to carry her away, and that she too had wept for a vanished mother when she was only a child, it seemed to Helen as if the universe was no more than a cruel wheel on which generation after generation was born to be broken. For such a world there was no remedy but human tenderness. Blinded by tears, she reached out and pulled her daughter to her breast.

Below them, in a hall now silent but for the muffled whimpers of a tormented boy, Menelaus looked down at his nephew's trembling form. 'There is nothing for you here, Orestes,' he whispered as gently as he could. Exhausted by grief and pity, he too was weeping as he said, 'You do right to pray to the god that drove you to your vengeance. Only he can help you now.'

Some memory of this wretched invasion of the palace at Sparta must have been troubling Eteoneus when the chamberlain treated with suspicion two other young men who arrived uninvited at its gates not long afterwards.

Earlier that day Menelaus and Helen had bidden farewell to their daughter as Hermione set off with a long train of attendants on the journey to the recaptured city of Iolcus where she had consented to wed Neoptolemus. In an effort to lift his wife's spirits, Menelaus had commanded that there be a feast that night; so when Eteoneus came to him with the news that there were strangers at the gate, he sharply reminded him of the obligation of hospitality and ordered that the guests be given an opportunity to refresh themselves before joining the banquet.

If Telemachus had been impressed by the splendour of Nestor's citadel at Pylos, when he entered the palace at Sparta he felt as though he was being admitted to the Olympian hall of Zeus himself. Gazing at the profusion of gold, silver, amber and ivory on display around him, he whispered as much to Peisistratus, but Menelaus overheard him and gave a little laugh. 'I confess myself fortunate in my wealth, young man,' he said, 'but I'm far from being a god, believe me. Merely a mortal who has had the rare luck to survive the mischance of war and return with something to show for his pains. But come, sit down while we wait for my queen to join us, and tell me what brings the two of you to Sparta.'

Less awed by the magnificence of the palace than his companion, Peisistratus immediately announced that he was the youngest son of King Nestor; and when they had talked about his father's ailing condition for a while, he introduced his friend Telemachus as the son of Odysseus of Ithaca.

'When I last saw you,' he said with a rueful smile, 'you were still mewling in your mother's arms, no more than a few weeks old. And look at you now. Your father would be proud of you, young man.'

Telemachus was about to say that he had come in search of news of his father when their attention was distracted by the arrival of Helen and her ladies in the hall. Menelaus called out to his wife at once. 'Look, my dear,' he cried, 'the sons of Nestor and Odysseus have graced us with their company.'

Still troubled by what had happened to her daughter, and aware how her own passionate behaviour all those years ago had disrupted the lives of these two young men, Helen greeted them almost shyly. Smiling at Telemachus, she said, 'Your build is much like your father's, but you have the look of my dear cousin Penelope about your face. Tell me, how is your mother?'

'She is well, lady,' Telemachus answered, 'but things go hard for us in Ithaca. My father has not yet returned from the war and there are those who insist that my mother must remarry.'

Peisistratus said, 'Telemachus tells me that Penelope's many suitors are making her life a misery.'

Menelaus looked back at Telemachus. 'Is this truly the case?'

'It is, lord. That's why I've come here hoping to learn news of Odysseus – either that he's certainly dead, which I pray the gods forbid, or that he's alive somewhere and we can look for him to return to us soon.'

Averting his eyes from the youth's frank gaze, Menelaus exchanged an uneasy glance with Helen. Telemachus did not miss that exchange and his young heart lurched at the immediate assumption that they knew his father to be dead.

But it was Peisistratus who said, 'Do you have word of Odysseus?'

'We do, we do,' Menelaus answered, drawing in his breath. He turned away, looking for his seat and sat down with his eyes closed, shaking his head. 'I blame myself for this. I should never have come to Ithaca all those years ago. I told him so the last time I saw him, outside Priam's palace at Troy. I should have left him in peace with Penelope, which was all he wanted. He was the best friend that a man could ask for, and they were happy together. My quarrel was none of theirs.'

'Is my father dead then?' Telemachus brought himself to ask.

Preoccupied with his own thoughts, Menelaus frowned up in surprise. 'No, far from it,' he said, 'or at least he was alive when I last heard of him. But the news was already old.'

'Then where is he?' the youth demanded. 'Why doesn't he come home?'

Anxious not to add to the hurt he was about to give to this sensitive young man, Menelaus chose his words carefully as he related what he had been told by the Phoenician Hylax about the choice

that his old comrade had made. The task was made more difficult for him by the fact that he had only a vague idea of the
events that had preceded that choice, but as far as he understood
the situation: Odysseus had been the cause of a major scandal in
an important cult centre of the Mother Goddess in a land to the
west. Having undergone initiations in that cult, he had seduced
one of its virgin priestesses, who then abandoned her sacred duties
at the Oracle of the Dead in Cuma and fled with him to her
island home of Ogygia. Reports both of the outrage they had
left behind them and of their subsequent life together had been
brought to Egypt by a Phoenician merchant whose trade took
him occasionally to Ogygia. According to his report, the priestess
was both young and beautiful. She was also deeply enamoured of
Odysseus, who had given up the roving life of a pirate and was
now living with his lover in great comfort and luxury. Menelaus
assured Telemachus that he had carefully questioned his source,
but as far as he had been able to ascertain, it was highly unlikely
that his father would ever return to Ithaca.

Telemachus received this news in silence, biting his lip; but in
the very efforts he was making to remain impassive, Menelaus
saw the disappointment and anguish he had caused. 'You must
try not to think too badly of your father,' he said. 'Odysseus is a
good man. And war does terrible things to us all. If you can find
room in your heart to do so, you should be glad he's managed
to find some peace after the long years of suffering at Troy.'

'Ithaca is not at peace,' Telemachus answered. 'My mother is
not at peace.'

'I understand that,' Menelaus said quietly.

Helen reached out her hand to cover his. 'This is not the news
that Telemachus hoped to hear,' she said. 'He must be astounded
by it — as I confess I was myself when I first heard it. The gods
know that I've been a fool for love in my time and have some
knowledge of these things; yet it amazes me that Odysseus would
behave this way. I can only think he too has been afflicted by the
madness of the goddess.'

'I think,' Telemachus said, 'if you will excuse me, that I need a little time alone.'

Menelaus watched as the youth politely lowered his head and backed away from him, before turning and hastening from the hall. Even though the wife that had once been lost to him was now at his side in this golden palace, tightly holding his hand as she too watched Telemachus walk away, the King of Sparta was overwhelmed once again by the unrelenting grief of the war. It seemed inexorable in the way it reached out, year after year, beyond those whom it had already killed and injured and widowed, to clutch the hearts of a new generation.

When Helen looked up at her husband, she saw the tears rolling down his face, and all the pain of their lives was present between them as she tightened the grip of her hand, silently affirming what both understood: that they must love one another now as best they could or all this pain would be forever meaningless.

'Come,' she whispered, 'Polydamna will mix the wine for us tonight.'

Furious with grief, Telemachus had already made up his mind to leave Sparta and get back to Ithaca as quickly as possible. He might have left immediately had Peisistratus not calmly persuaded him that it would be discourteous to his hosts and that they needed to rest before setting out on the journey home. But Telemachus lay on his bed in turmoil that night. Odysseus was nothing to him now. He would go home and care for his mother as best he could. And if Ithaca was to be saved from Antinous and the others, he would do it himself.

The following morning Menelaus pressed him to remain as his guest for a time, but the youth was adamant that he must leave. He was reluctant even to accept the gifts that his host sought to lavish on him. Horses and chariots were of no use to him on the steeps of Ithaca, he explained in embarrassment, while thanking Menelaus for his generosity.

'But you must at least take a gift for your mother,' Helen insisted as she saw her husband's face fall. She picked up a solid silver mixing-bowl, rimmed with gold, and pressed it into the youth's arms. 'This comes from Sidon,' she said. 'It is reputed to have been cast by Hephaestus himself. Take it, please. It will remind Penelope of our love for her.'

Sighing, Menelaus said, 'I would gladly surrender half my wealth if it would bring your father back to you. But surely, among all my possessions, there must be something you desire?'

Telemachus looked into his host's sad face and saw how strong was the man's need to offer some measure of compensation for the pain he had given. It would be cruel to refuse him. 'I wonder,' he said, 'did you bring papyrus with you when you came from Egypt?'

'Many scrolls of it,' Menelaus answered, a little surprised. 'Is that what you would like?'

'I have a friend on Ithaca,' Telemachus smiled. 'He will have a use for it.'

Telemachus was standing on the strand at Pylos saying farewell to Peisistratus when a stranger approached him out of the crowd that had gathered about the ship. His head was draped in a thick cloak and there was a hunted look in his intense black eyes. 'Are you the captain of this vessel?' he asked.

Telemachus frowned at the interruption. 'No, the ship belongs to my friend Peiraeus. I have merely commissioned her.'

'Then you may still be able to help me,' the man urged. 'I need to take passage out of Pylos as soon as possible. Where are you bound?'

'For Ithaca. But . . .'

The man grabbed his wrist. 'My life is at risk,' he said. 'If I don't get away from here today I'm a dead man. I beg you to take me with you.'

Telemachus turned to his friend, asking if he knew this man, but Peisistratus shook his head and demanded to know where the fellow had come from.

'From Hyperesia,' he answered, 'where I avenged my father's murder on the man who killed him. Now his kinsmen are hunting me down. I swear that my vengeance was lawful.' He held up his hands. 'I bring no pollution with me.'

'My friend has troubles enough of his own,' Peisistratus frowned, 'without involving himself in another man's feud. Why should he help you?'

When the stranger looked back at Telemachus, the intensity of his gaze was charged with a power that was deeper and more searching than mere entreaty. 'My name is Theoclymenus,' he said. 'I am of the lineage of the seer Melampus. Like him, I have the sight. Will you give me your hand?'

After a moment's hesitation, Telemachus allowed the stranger to take his palm. He looked down into it for a time before raising his eyes to study the young man's face. 'You are seeking something,' he said, ' . . . something very close to you. You believe it lost forever. I promise you it is not. There are hard ordeals to come, but that which was lost will be restored to you.' Then he gasped quickly three times, with his eyes closed. He uttered a little laugh. 'It will happen very soon . . . That which you have been seeking abroad, you will find waiting for you . . . in Ithaca.'

The Homecoming

Bright on the morning air, he heard the sound of laughter. Birdsong and laughter. The laughter of girls at play. Odysseus stirred where he lay in a litter of dead leaves under the boughs of a wild olive tree. His throat was dry. His limbs ached. He could feel the crust of sea-salt drying on his abraded skin. When he squinted up into the light he saw the sun already standing high in the sky.

Evidence all of it, against all expectations, that he was still alive.

Poseidon had raised the seas once more and this time the storm had wrecked him. The steering oar was wrenched from his grip. The small craft he had cobbled together on Ogygia was thrown over by the waves, and he was out among the clashing billows snatching at the air. When he surfaced again he saw the upturned bottom of his boat protruding from the waters like a dolphin's back. He swam for it, gasping, clambered onto the planks, and then he had no idea how long he had clung to the keel while the force of the tempest pushed him through the seas.

Eventually the skies had cleared. Bleached by salt and sun, he lay bobbing on his cockleshell in the swell. When he eventually lifted his head, Odysseus saw the grey rise of a coast within what would have been swimming distance for a less exhausted man.

Should he cling to his capsized boat, or let go and make a bid for the salvation of dry land? He lay with the sun glaring down at him, unable to decide. Then, barely conscious as the boat rose and fell, he saw the figure of a woman skipping like a sea-bird across the glittering crests. He could hear her voice beside him on the boat. 'Deliverance lies on land,' she whispered. 'Take off your clothes and commit yourself to the waves.' She held out her hands. He saw that she was offering him her long veil. 'Hold on to this,' she smiled. 'It will guide you ashore.'

But she could only be a phantasm of his exhausted mind; so he closed his eyes and clung on. He clung on until a wave stronger than most pushed his numbed fingers free of the keel and then the current grabbed him and the boat was gone beyond reach.

Treading water, he realized that his sodden clothes would make it harder to swim; so he tugged them off, and stared through the spray towards the distant shore. Only one way now to find out whether he had the strength to make it through the breakers between. With a prayer to Athena at his lips, Odysseus thrust himself forward on the next wave. He heard the boom of the surf. Closer inshore came the clash of water against rocks.

Had he survived all those days at sea only to have his body broken by land that might have saved him? Well, what difference now? He was all but dead already.

Odysseus surrendered to the current. Bashed against a rock, he clung there for a time, scarcely able to see for the salt spray. Then his fingers were sliding down green slime and he was buffeted by waves again. With his senses blurred and the breath sucked from his lungs he was washed to a place where he was gazing down into water so clear that he might have counted every pebble. A wave thrust him down into those green depths. His ears were singing like shells. Then stones were rolling round him, plucked and knocked together by the surf, back and forth, shushing one another as they were caught where the mouth of a river met the push of the sea. He could lie there if he liked, and quietly drown in a few inches of foam, or he could find the strength to stand.

Odysseus drank fresh water till his thirst was slaked; then he had pushed inland against the river's strong current till he found a culvert where he could stagger ashore. Not far from the bank he came across a copse of trees. Collapsing in the shelter of a wild olive bush, he covered his body with leaves.

And now the sound of laughter turned to squeals of dismay. He heard a voice cry out, a girl's voice, and when he looked in the direction from which the sound had come, he saw her running among the rocks of the river bank in a yellow dress, looking at where a ball was being carried swiftly away by the water sluicing between the stones. Then there were other girls gathering beside her, six or seven of them, all staring in dismay at the lost ball.

When the first girl started to venture into the current, a taller young woman wearing cornflower-blue called out, 'Oh let it go, Clymene. You'll never catch it now. We should be going soon anyway.'

He might have taken them for nymphs but for the cheerful practicality of that voice. These were only mortal girls at play in the sunlight on the river bank. When he raised his head to look more closely he could see the bright colours of the tunics and robes they had laid out to dry along the flatter rocks. Presumably they were serving-maids who had been sent out by their mistress that morning to do the laundry of some nearby house. But the sun was high, the clothes were dry by now, and some of the young women had already begun to fold them into piles. They would not be here much longer; if he wanted their help, he would have to stand up and show himself.

Wincing at the pain in his limbs, Odysseus got to his feet, brushed off the last leaves clinging to his skin, and realized he was stark naked. He looked around for something with which to cover himself and, when he found nothing, twisted off a leafy branch from the olive bush with his bare hands.

At the moment when he stepped out of the clearing, one of the young women looked up from the garment she was folding, saw his naked figure approach, and immediately screamed. The others looked first at her and then, following the direction of her eyes, turned to look at him.

Odysseus stopped in his tracks, astounded by the squeals of women who were running away now or holding on to one another for protection, frozen where they stood. Then he saw himself as they must have seen him – a wild man stepping out of the trees, his skin caked with salt, hairy, bedraggled, and naked but for the olive branch covering his manhood. All the more amazing, therefore, that one of the maidens stood her ground, refusing to be cowed.

'Forgive me,' Odysseus stammered, 'I don't mean to frighten you.'

Slender and proud, biting her lip, the girl said nothing but her eyes remained on his, unflinching. He saw at once that this was no servant. Her manner was far too composed. Accustomed to deference, she was not about to demean herself even before this alarming figure who took another two steps towards her, holding out one dirty hand in entreaty while the other held the branch over his loins. For a moment Odysseus wondered whether he should fall to the ground in the manner of a supplicant and clutch her by the knees. Had he been standing before a man he would have done so without shame, so desperate were his circumstances now. But even a girl as brave this one might feel threatened if he came too close; so he remained where he was, still a few yards away, and gave a rueful, beseeching smile.

'I'm sorry,' he said again, 'I'm not the savage I must seem. Just a shipwrecked mariner who has no idea where the gods have fetched him up.' As he saw her hesitate, a canny flash of inspiration came to him. 'Or even,' he added, 'whether you are a mortal like me or a goddess – such is your grace and stature . . .'

A half smile lit her face but still she said nothing.

Warily, one of the other girls stepped from behind a wagon that stood by the cisterns further upstream where two mules were grazing, and called out for her to come away. 'Nausicaa, please . . . . We've no idea who he might be.'

Though her eyes had swiftly glanced that way at the sound of her name, Nausicaa did not move. She looked back at him, swallowing, thinking quickly.

'I was at sea alone for many days,' he pressed, 'and now some god has cast me at your feet to beg for pity. All I ask is that you give me something to cover my shame and point me to the nearest town.' Sensing her warming towards him, he raised his eyes in appeal. 'I've got nothing to offer in return, I'm afraid – except my prayers that the gods grant you whatever your heart desires.'

Nodding her bright head, Nausicaa smiled. 'Your manner shows me that you're no villain, sir,' she said, 'and I can see you're no fool either. If Zeus has sent you here, it's with good reason. You shall have all our help.' Then she looked towards the wagon, calling out to her friends that there was no reason to be afraid. When they still seemed reluctant to come out of hiding, she laughed and told them to bring food and drink for this unfortunate stranger. A couple of the braver girls approached, one of them carrying a newly laundered cloak with which Odysseus hastily covered himself. Seeing that he was harmless, others began to collect food together for him – bread and olives, a fine goat's cheese, cold mutton, figs and grapes – and looked on with shocked fascination as he wolfed some of it down with the watered wine they had brought.

When she saw the famished man glance down in dismay at the dirty hands in which he held the food, Nausicaa said. 'I couldn't help noticing that your body is bruised, sir. If you wish it, my companions will bathe you in the river and soothe your limbs with olive oil.' But one of the younger girls was already giggling.

Flushing a little, Odysseus thanked Nausicaa for her kindness but said that he would prefer to bathe and oil himself if they would be so good as to stand apart a little. Taking the flask of oil they offered and a finely embroidered tunic that they brought for him to wear, he walked down to the bank with as much dignity as he could muster and looked for a place among the rocks where he could cleanse himself unseen. The river water had grown warm in the afternoon sun. Odysseus found it refreshing, but as he washed the brine from his body, rubbed the oil into his limbs, and used his fingers to brush out the tangles of his hair, he was conscious of the women chattering together in the sunlit glade.

They looked up in surprise when he stepped out from between the boulders in the viridian green tunic embroidered with golden threads. The unkempt wild man had vanished, and a well-dressed fellow with wet, slightly grizzled hair stood in his place, embarrassed by their frank attention.

'Thank you,' he said. 'I'm feeling much better now.'

Nausicaa stepped towards him, smiling; then she glanced back at the others. 'What did I tell you?' she said. 'He's a handsome figure of a man. I dare say any one of you would be pleased to marry him.'

Though he was startled by her candour, Odysseus was able to hold her gaze without diffidence now, and saw that she could not be more than fourteen years old. Most of the others were older, but clearly the authority was hers, and she wore it with a bright insouciance that both impressed and amused him. And now that his nakedness was covered, his confidence had returned. It seemed that the gods had been less cruel than he thought.

'I was wondering,' he smiled, 'might there be something else to eat?'

Politely restraining her curiosity about the stranger, Nausicaa sat by the rug on which more food had been arranged for him. As he ate, she chattered about how a strange half-waking dream had come to her just before she woke that day. ·

In the dream, she said, one of her friends had reproved her for leaving her clothes lying about the chamber and neglecting to wash them. She was told to ask her father for a wagon and then to take all the family's laundry down to the river and wash it clean. 'Except,' she announced with an elated smile, 'it wasn't really my friend at all, for at the end of the dream I saw her fly away to the cloudless heights of Mount Olympus and I knew that I'd been visited by Divine Athena herself. So I immediately went down and told my father what I'd dreamed. He gave me a wagon at once and I collected all the dirty clothes I could find, and we brought them here to the cisterns. And we've had a lovely day of it, singing as we beat the clothes against the rocks, and then swimming and playing with our ball. But now I see what my dream was truly about,' again she favoured Odysseus with her eager smile, 'because if Athena hadn't visited me and told me what to do, I certainly wouldn't have come down to the river today, and then I would never have found you, and that would have been terrible! So you see the gods have been kind to both of us!'

'They've certainly been kind to me,' Odysseus agreed. 'I'm glad that you feel so too. But you must tell me more about yourself. I still don't know who you are, and I don't even know where I am, for that matter.'

'You've landed on Scheria,' she said, 'which is the most beautiful island in the world, and my father, King Alcinous, is lord over all the Phaeacians. His city isn't far from here and you'll meet all our nobles there. It has two fine harbours and a splendid temple to Blue-haired Poseidon. We're a great sailing people, you see.'

And a most reclusive one, Odysseus thought, for the Phaeacians were famous for keeping themselves to themselves on their northern island, having neither the need nor the desire to trade with the kingdoms of the south and east. Every now and then, on his own voyages of exploration, he had caught sight of one of their dark ships running swiftly before the wind, but only rarely, and he had never come close to overhauling one. It was a worrying thought that these seafarers were devoted to Poseidon, who had shown no love for him; but if this girl's candour and friendliness were any guide to the temperament of the Phaeacians, he had nothing much to fear from them.

Yet the longer he listened to her chatter, the more unusual Nausicaa came to seem to him. If she had the self-possession of a king's daughter, she displayed none of the spoiled hauteur that often went with it, and neither coy self-regard nor any gloss of sophistication spoiled her wildflower freshness. She was unblemished by life, as yet innocent of sexual passion and its wounds, and still on the threshold of everything. It lifted his heart just to look at her.

'Once you've eaten your fill,' she was saying, 'I'll take you into the city and introduce you to everyone. I'm sure my parents will be delighted to meet you, and . . .' She looked up, frowning, at where one of the older girls was clearing her throat to attract attention. With a hint of impatience she said, 'What is it, Philona?'

When Philona indicated that she wished to speak privately, the two young women stood briefly whispering together, closer to where the others were already loading the folded clothes into the wagon. Nausicaa came back to Odysseus with a slightly discomfited air. 'I'd forgotten that we have to go past the shipyard on our way to the palace,' she said. 'Now that you're looking so distinguished, if the sailors see me keeping company with you they're sure to start gossiping. Some of them can be rather coarse, you see, and they're always teasing me about who I'm going to marry and when. It's all quite ridiculous, but there's the question of my good name . . .' She glanced up to see if he understood. When she saw him nod, she smiled and said, 'So we've decided it's best if you follow on behind the wagon as we go into town, and then wait for a while by Athena's spring in my father's park. You'll find your way into town easily enough from there. Just ask anyone where the palace is, and then go right through into the great hall. The King will almost certainly be in there.' Her eyes darted aside as a further thought occurred to her. 'But I think you should approach my mother, Queen Arete, where she'll be working at her loom. Clasp her by the knees and beg for her aid and once you've won her sympathy, they'll both do all they can to help you.' Nausicaa glanced up at him with an eager smile. 'What do you think?'

'I think,' Odysseus said, 'that all sounds very wise.'

★   ★   ★

Two nights later Odysseus sat in the great hall of King Alcinous, listening to the blind bard Demodocus singing the story of how the crippled god Hephaistus had revenged himself on Aphrodite when he learned that his wife was cuckolding him with her lover Ares. Waiting till they were lost deep in each other's embraces, Hephaistus had thrown a finely forged mesh of metal netting over the God of War and the Goddess of Love, trapping them together in her bed; then he called the other gods to ridicule their naked embarrassment.

Demodocus was renowned throughout all Phaeacia for the beauty of his voice and, looking about the hall, Odysseus smiled to see the entire assembly sitting spellbound beneath the bronze panels and blue enamelling of the palace walls.

From the first, Alcinous and Queen Arete had made him warmly welcome in their kingdom, and though their sons had tried to treat him with disdain on the field of sport earlier that day, he had soon silenced them by the strength with which he hurled a discus far beyond the mark their throws had reached. Nausicaa had stood watching him throughout, urging him on and warmly applauding his success. She was smiling across at him now, her fingers playing with the braided tresses of her hair that glistened in the light from the fire.

These Phaeacians were good people. Queen Arete had immediately responded to his appeal for aid when he threw himself down as a supplicant before her. Recognizing the green and gold tunic he wore as her own handiwork, she asked him how he had come by it; and when she and her generous-hearted husband learned how bravely Nausicaa had helped him, they seemed well-pleased with the friendship that had flourished between this stranger and their daughter. Even her discountenanced brothers had come round quickly enough from their defeat on the sports field and had lavished him with gifts before putting on a display of dancing that left him filled with admiration. Yet the truth was that these people knew almost nothing about him still. Though this was already the second night he had passed in their company, they were too discreet to ply him with questions, and he had volunteered no information other than that he had been ship-wrecked by a storm while sailing eastwards from Ogygia. If they thought it strange that a man should sail the seas alone, not one of them remarked on it; nor – great seamen that they were – had they asked about the kind of ship he sailed. Having for so long preferred to keep themselves to themselves, the Phaeacians were not about to intrude on anyone else's privacy without invitation.

Yet sooner or later something must be said, for Odysseus was aware that Nausicaa was falling in love with him, and he was growing concerned that he might injure those tender feelings that the girl was too innocent to conceal. So he was not entirely at ease as he listened to Demodocus sing of the passion of Ares and Aphrodite. The toils of desire entangling the god and goddess resembled too closely the golden chains in which he and Calypso had been bound together on Ogygia for the past six years. And Odysseus sighed as he thought of her now.

Even though Macareus had been appalled by Calypso's act of transgression, he had known suffering enough of his own to have sympathy for a desperate young woman who reminded him in many ways of his sister Canace. At her request he had agreed that he would do what he could to pacify Circe's rage against her on his return to Aiaia, and that he would try to explain why Odysseus had decided to answer her plea for aid. If he sensed a deeper, unspoken and perhaps as yet unrecognized collusion between the Ithacan and the beautiful renegade who had thrown herself on his mercy, Macareus said nothing of it; but it was with a heavy heart that he watched *The Fair Return* put to sea that day. He was puzzled too by Odysseus' gruff demand to know whether the Lady Circe had ever taken him to her bed. How could such a thought ever have crossed the Ithacan's mind?

As for Odysseus himself, he had no clear idea why he was doing what he was doing except that he knew he could not leave another young woman to die. He had watched Iphigenaia and

Polyxena die, and he had been given a premonition of Canace lying in her blood. None of those girls had he saved from the dreadful fate awaiting them. But this girl he could save. Out of a newly compassionate feel for life that was the true harvest of his initiations in Aiaia and Cuma, he was determined to do it.

Yet he was aware that Calypso's defection from her sacred service was an act of betrayal in which he was now complicit. He was betraying the goddess into whose mysteries he had been initiated; he was betraying Circe who had been his guide into those mysteries; and though he suspected that neither breach of faith would pass without some price being paid for it, he had not yet acknowledged another deeper betrayal that was he was about to perpetrate.

Always superstitious, his crew were unhappy about taking Calypso on board, for how could anything but trouble come from upsetting the gods of a shrine? They became still more disgruntled when they heard Odysseus order Baius to turn the cutwater westwards. They might have only a vague idea of their present location but they knew that Ithaca lay to the east, and that Elpenor still lay unburied at Aiaia to the north. So what was the captain up to now? He had been acting strangely since he came back out of the Underworld, but he would say nothing of what had happened there, and they felt offended by his indifference to their concerns. Yet when a deputation came aft to address their complaints to him, Odysseus merely told them that they would be home soon enough. Meanwhile they should hold their peace.

His ill-temper reflected his own uncertainty, for though he tried to give as little attention as he could to Calypso where she stood by the prow with her hair blowing in the wind off the sea, or rested in the hold beneath the afterdeck, he found that his eyes kept straying towards her. Also he was stirred by the desire to talk to her more intimately, but not until they made camp on the eastern coast of Sicily was he able to seek her out and demand a fuller account of her reasons for abandoning her sacred duties at the Oracle of the Dead.

She seemed wary and reticent at first, as though the certainty she had shown before boarding the ship had evaporated while they were at sea. When he saw how her eyes kept shifting nervously away along the strand to where the Libyan boy Hermes squatted on his haunches making sad music with his pipes, he decided to make a gentler approach.

'Tell me more about the Oracle,' he said. 'Is it very ancient?'

'Very.'

'And the gods of the underworld . . . they are truly present there?'

'Yes . . . when they are honestly invoked.'

'Is that not always the case?'

'Sometimes the power is . . . It is not always present.'

His voice was tighter as he said, 'What happens then?'

She hesitated before answering. 'The priests will have learned things about the seeker from his friends who wait above . . . while he is in the Painted Room. It is possible to know how to answer him in a way that . . .'

'In a way that leaves him believing it is the god who speaks?'

'Yes.'

'And in my case?'

She turned her face earnestly towards him. 'There was no deception.'

'How am I to know that?'

'Because you were there . . . you saw for yourself how the shade entered me.'

He resisted the intensity of her appeal. 'It was dark and I was confused. I don't know what kind of drug had been put in my water, but I'm sure there was something. I was in no state to see whether a deception was being practised.'

'I swear to you that the Goddess was present between us.'

'But you've already broken your oath to the goddess you serve. Why should I trust your word?'

'Surely you must know by now?' she said.

Odysseus frowned. 'What? What must I know?'

'Did you not see how I was?'

He thought for a moment, frowning. 'Only that you seemed frightened by the power that possessed you. But you were wearing the Gorgon mask . . . how can I know what you were truly feeling behind it?'

He felt the hot reproach in her eyes as she glanced his way again before once more averting her gaze.

'Tell me,' he said, 'was that the first time such a thing had happened to you?'

'The Goddess has taken possession of me many times.'

'Then I don't understand why you would forsake her,' – again he caught the hot flash of her reproach – 'except that it must have been a strong force to make you break your sacred bonds.'

'Yes,' she answered almost dully, 'it was a strong force.'

'But what force could be strong enough to make a priestess risk the fury of her goddess?'

She turned to face him then, her eyes a proud, unrelenting blue.

'You,' she said. 'My love for you.'

And immediately turned away again.

His outward manner in those first moments suggested shocked bewilderment, but it concealed a deeper shock of recognition. He had desired this woman since he first set eyes on her. Hers was the first face he had seen on returning from that long journey into dissolution in Circe's chamber. After that darkness in which his entire person had melted down like metal in a forge, her face had appeared to him as bright and lovely as the face of day itself. It had brought the promise of new life. And somewhere, without knowing what he was doing, he had been looking for that face everywhere ever since. Twice he had seen her – in the moments after he had broken the figurine of the goddess, and then again in the hot glade where, out of his fury and frustration with Circe, he had lifted Mopsa's skirts. And how inevitable it now seemed that it should have been Calypso – the Hidden One – who was concealed behind the hideous Gorgon mask in the House of

Persephone; that it should have been she through whom his mother's shade had chosen to speak; and that she, in her turn, should now, symbolically at least, be smashing the figure of the Goddess by forsaking her duties at the shrine in order to follow him.

Yet how doubly strange that Calypso had been nursing her own desire for him throughout all those weeks without him suspecting it. The force that had them in its grip was Fate. Or so it had seemed at the time, when she first began to draw him under the spell cast by the power and urgency of her confession.

She told him that she had loved him from the day she first saw him walk alone into Circe's palace resolved to rescue his friends. She told him that she had often spied on him from concealment, both when he came into the palace and as he went about his daily business in Aiaia. He had become, she said, the lodestone of her life, so that when his stubborn masculine will at last collapsed, and she was called by Circe to assist with the healing rites that were performed over him, she felt as though she was watching with tender care over the remaking of the man who must one day belong to her alone. She told him that it had been no accident that she had been present when he broke the ancient figurine of the Great Mother, and that she had even been following him on the day when he infuriated her by succumbing to Mopsa's wanton sensuality. But Calypso had known that a time must come when he would descend to the House of Persephone in the Oracle of the Dead and she would be waiting for him there.

Never in all his life, not even when he and Penelope had first begun to love each other, had Odysseus felt himself so exclusively the object of a woman's desire. Listening to Calypso's passionate contralto voice was like being wrapped about by silken bands that left him feeling both held and confined; yet also enlarged. For if she was young – at least twenty years younger than himself – she possessed a degree of wisdom that was quite startling in its pene-tration; and she valued aspects of his character to which the world had been blind for many years. Where Circe had often left him feeling foolish and unripe, he began to bask in the way that Calypso fortified his self-esteem by recognizing the power of his intelligence. She claimed that it was more than mere resourcefulness, for its strength lay in his ability to perceive new relations between things in ways which revealed hitherto unsuspected possibilities. And his true courage lay, she declared, not just in military prowess, which many men could boast, but in his willingness to render himself vulnerable to experiences that transformed a man in the very depths of his being. Above all, Calypso believed that he possessed a capacity for love as deep as her own. Together, she insisted, they might celebrate a passion such as few mortals were privileged to know. All that was needed was for his wisdom and his courage to trust their love and follow it.

Of all of this, Odysseus was, at first, less confident than she. Her intensity alarmed him because he knew that if he answered its call, the whole course and compass of his life must alter. Yet he also knew that the ordeals of the war had already changed him beyond recognition. He was no longer the man who had left Ithaca many years ago. Were he to return there, Penelope would scarcely know him; and what he had undergone on Aiaia had given him, he believed, a more exhilarating sense of feminine power than anything he had ever known in the simplicities of his married life.

'I watched the old Odysseus die,' Calypso avowed, 'and I have seen you reborn. If I am here with you now it is only because I too have undergone such transformation. I believe that the powers of both god and goddess have come to meet in us. They have done so for a purpose, and the deepest betrayal would lie in our failure to honour what their meeting asks of us.'

Listening to the voice of the blind bard of the Phaeacians echoing through the hall in Scheria, Odysseus sighed to remember how swiftly, and impulsively, his life with Calypso had begun. And there was no denying that they had given themselves to each other with a passion that seemed at times as divine as that which had once tied Ares and Aphrodite in its golden fetters. In the rapture of their lovemaking, Odysseus had come to understand for the first time the true strength of the power which had possessed Paris and Helen many years earlier, and thereby dragged the whole world into a disastrous war. And even now, for all the storms of mutual hurt which had blown between them, Odysseus could not entirely regret the passionate years he had spent on Ogygia with Calypso, though his sighs deepened at the memory of her face as he left the island.

Those sighs did not pass unnoticed. Queen Arete, who was sitting beside him, remarked that her guest seemed sad and wondered whether there was some solace he might be offered. So sympathetic was her smile that for a moment Odysseus was on the point of confessing all his troubles, but he had no wish to cloud the general air of conviviality in the hall, so he merely said that he had been thinking of the comrades he had lost at sea and how much they would have enjoyed the comforts of this handsome palace in which he was fortunate to find himself after his own narrow scrape with death.

'We count ourselves fortunate to have you among us,' King Alcinous said, and then leaned closer to Odysseus, smiling confidentially. 'By the admiring glances my daughter Nausicaa keeps giving you, I judge she counts herself lucky too. She's of marriage-able age, you know, though she seems to disdain most of our young men. However, I'm beginning to wonder whether she thinks a husband might have been cast up at her feet by some friendly god?'

Briefly Odysseus averted his eyes in embarrassment, only to see Nausicaa gazing at him from where she sat among the maidens further down the hall. She flushed at once as their eyes met, and glanced away. 'I could never consider myself worthy of so fair a prize,' he prevaricated.

But Alcinous had not failed to observe his moment of discomfiture. 'Or perhaps you're thinking of your homeland,' he said, 'and longing to be away? If that's what your heart desires, friend, one of my ships will certainly take you there. But tonight you shall have the best of our entertainment. I swear you'll find no finer bard than our Demodocus between here and Egypt.' Raising his voice, the king called across to the hearth where the blind bard was drinking from a silver goblet.

'When you're refreshed,' he said, 'give us your song of the fall of Troy.'

Before Odysseus could think of a polite way to suggest some other theme, Demodocus put down his goblet and retuned his lyre. A hush fell over the hall. The minstrel lifted his voice and Odysseus found himself listening to a heart-stopping account of how he had conceived the stratagem of the Wooden Horse, and how he and his companions had entered Troy, and of the devastation that had fallen on the city during the course of that terrible night.

Unaware that the man of whom he sang was seated among his audience, Demodocus gave voice to a paean of praise for the courage and intelligence of Odysseus; but so painful were the memories it evoked, and so great the gulf between the horror that Odysseus recalled and the stirring beauty of the poet's verses, that long before the song was over, tears were streaming in silence down the Ithacan's face.

Everyone else was so caught up in the song that only Nausicaa observed his distress. Rising from her place, she crossed the hall to comfort him, and when Alcinous saw what was happening, he put his hand on the stranger's arm. 'The song moved us all,' he said, 'but it seems to have affected you so profoundly I can only think you were among those who fought at Troy . . . or perhaps that someone dear to you was killed in the war for that noble city?' And when he saw that Odysseus had regained a measure of control over his breathing, he added, 'Come, friend, I think it's time you told us something of who you are.'

Seeing the small eddies of grief still shaking through his body, Nausicaa said, 'Won't you at least tell me your name?'

He lifted the grief in his eyes to meet the concern in hers, and heard the girl draw in her breath as he answered, 'My name is Odysseus. Odysseus of Ithaca.'

Many years earlier, in the draughty hall at Iolcus, when he was still a young man, Odysseus had persuaded the hero Peleus to unburden himself of his sorrows. Now during the course of that night in Scheria, Nausicaa performed the same tender service for him. Almost as though speaking of another man – an old friend that he had known and cared for well – he told them of how his heart had been shaken by the fall of Troy and of the way his life had been haunted by images of that atrocity. He told them of the death of Hecuba in Thrace, and of how he had lost his cousin Sinon and many comrades in the skirmish at Ismarus. He told them of the great tempest that had scattered his fleet and how, having failed in that storm to double Cape Malea, he had fetched up on the shore of Libya. He told them of his encounter with Guneus and of the fruitless journey he had made to the shrine of Neith beside the great salt lake where Athena was born. He told them of what had happened among the wind-callers of Aeolia and of the loss of the *Swordfish* under the assault from the Laestrygonians. He told them how he had come to Circe's palace on Aiaia and how his life had been transfigured by the healing rites that he underwent in her care. Less freely he spoke of his initiation at the Oracle of the Dead at Cuma and how the shade of his mother had spoken to him there. And then, more haltingly, he tried to explain how it was that, instead of returning home to Ithaca as he had intended, he had fallen under Calypso's spell and remained with her on the island of Ogygia.

Once again he was weeping as he told how his crew had grown restless there and he had allowed them to take his ship roving through the western seas; but they had met with no good fortune and, in the end, they had landed half-starved on the island of Thrinacia where they had killed and eaten some of the sacred Cattle of the Sun. Not until a long time after his ship had failed to return did Odysseus learn how the god had taken his vengeance on them. Damaged in a storm, *The Fair Return* had lost steerage-way and been sucked down by a whirlpool in the narrow straits between Italy and Sicily. All his old comrades were drowned in the wreck except for the Libyan boy Hermes. Found clinging to a spar by a Phoenician merchantman, and stricken with grief at the loss of his friend Eurylochus, Hermes had eventually managed to make his way back to Ogygia.

But by that time things were going badly wrong between Odysseus and Calypso. Oppressed by her exclusive demands, increasingly guilty that he could no longer honour the passion that had brought them together, he was further estranged from her now by his grief for the death of all the friends and comrades he had loved. Eurylochus, Baius, Grinus, his herald Eurybates and the rest . . . all gone. Odysseus blamed Calypso for keeping him at her side when he should have been at sea in *The Fair Return,* watching over his crew, seeing them safely home. His complaints grew ever more unjust. He had thanklessly betrayed Circe's trust for her. Had it not been for her sacrilegious passion, he would have been at home with the wife who loved him many years ago. He would have met and come to know his son. He would have been happy as he could never hope to be happy, rotting away in amorous sloth on this uneventful island.

Yet even as he ranted, Odysseus saw the unfairness of the hurt he gave; so he turned his rage against himself, which only made Calypso weep more grievously, and the day ended with them making love in tears once more.

Yet the harm was done. He had quarrelled with her before, but never with such rancour, and out of the heat of his grief and rage he had said things which had a terrible ring of truth about them. His words had trespassed beyond hitherto unspoken bound-aries, and they could never be taken back. Both understood it, and neither knew how to cope well with the silence that resounded in their wake.

Odysseus spent more and more time alone, and with each

passing day he found he was filled with longing to return to Penelope. His dreams ached with images of her patiently working at her loom or nursing the infant Telemachus in her arms. In his waking hours he recalled the respectful care she had always shown to his parents, and how quickly everyone on Ithaca had come to love her. Penelope was all modesty and grace and good humour, quick witted and with a sprightly tongue; and if their youthful lovemaking had never been quickened by the same sensual flame that burned between Calypso and himself, the fault was his; and it had been, in any case, as beautiful as it was tender.

The more he thought of these things, the more inconceivable it seemed that he could have forsaken such a wife for the madness of war, or that he had not hastened back to her as soon as he felt himself fit to do so. There were so many things he was sure he had come to understand about himself, and his relation to the feminine powers of life, during his stay in Aiaia; yet no sooner had he come away than life had expanded around him again, and left him floundering. Yet how was it that after all the transformations he had undergone, he had so quickly allowed himself to become trapped by the sexual allure of a woman half his age?

But that was not the whole story. Odysseus understood that if Calypso had dared to renege on her most sacred vows, it was entirely out of her love for him. It was through that love that she had glimpsed a vision of a richer life than that of an unrequited virgin serving the gods of the underworld in the halls of the dead. Acting bravely on that love, she had put her life at risk to be at his side, and her desire for him remained undimmed. And there was more, much more; for in taking off the hideous Gorgon mask she had worn in the House of Persephone, and revealing the love that lay behind it, she had confirmed the truth of everything he had begun to learn on Aiaia.

He remembered how Calypso had first made that truth utterly plain to him when he tried to tell her what he had come to see in the solitude of the Painted Room at the Oracle of the Dead. 'Of course,' she had answered smiling, 'that is exactly how it is.

446

If you refuse to know the radiance of the goddess in her darkest
aspect, and to include that darkness in your rites, then she will
return again and again in the image of your own dark violence.
And the theatre in which she will perform her operations on
your heart and mind is war; and if you ask why that should be,
she will answer it is because she cannot finally be left out of
count, and you will have left her with no other way to speak.'

Her words had struck him with the force of revelation. In those
moments all the ordeals of his life had seemed to fall into place
with visionary clarity. Out of that shared vision Odysseus had at
last renounced the life and values of a warrior. Forsaking Ares for
Eros, he had chosen love instead, and devoted himself to a quiet
life of peace on Ogygia with Calypso. And for a time that life
had seemed complete; so when he tried to speak to her now
about his increasingly wretched condition, it felt as though every
word he uttered was a betrayal of that vision. Certainly she experienced it so. It was a betrayal of their vision and a betrayal of
their love, and she swore she would die sooner than let him go.

Meanwhile, the boy Hermes looked on with his sad Libyan
eyes, comforting Calypso as best he could when she was left
distraught by his unhappy master. One afternoon, towards dusk,
when Odysseus had been missing for several hours, Hermes went
looking for him. He found him diving in a fathom of clear water
where the carcass of an old fishing boat lay submerged on the
sea-bed among a spit of rocks at the foot of a cliff.

Odysseus broke the glassy surface, gasping for air as he shook
his head and saw Hermes staring at him.

'Can you keep a secret?' he shouted. 'Come here and look at
this.' When the Libyan boy did as he was bidden, Odysseus said,
'I think the bottom's holed and some of the planks are rotten;
but if I can dig the sand out of her bilge, I could haul her out
and get her fixed up pretty quickly. What do you think?'

Hermes shrugged. 'You want to go fishing?' he asked.

Smiling, Odysseus shook his head and said, 'I want to go home.'

★ ★ ★

Nausicaa's eyes were already filled with tears as she heard of the final bitter quarrel between Odysseus and Calypso. It had been, he said, impossible that she would not discover that he was working to build a boat, and he left her in no doubt of his intentions. Her rage was fired by grief. She would have taken an axe and smashed the planks to matchwood if Hermes had not prevented her.

It was he who told her that a love that was not freely given was no love at all; that he had watched them both suffering now for many weeks; and that something must change were the affection they felt for each other not to burn itself out in hatred. It was Hermes who persuaded her, as she recovered from a frenzy of tears, to seek the guidance of the gods. He told her how the oracle had worked at Lake Tritonis. He brought her two pebbles, one black, one white.

Carefully, Calypso formulated a question in her mind. With a prayer to the gods, she swirled the pebbles in a golden bowl till one of them jumped out. The black pebble lay on the ground before her.

On the morning that Odysseus was to put to sea in the little cockleshell craft that he had rebuilt with the tools she brought him, Calypso stood beside him on the shore. She had made sure that plenty of food and water was stored in the locker at the stern. Everything was prepared but still she could not let him go.

Holding him tightly by the wrist, she said, 'There is still a thing between us. A thing that I have never dared to say to you.'

'Say it now.'

She looked away along the strand. Her breath was coming very fast. 'When you stood before me in the House of Persephone,' her voice was barely a whisper on the wind, 'and your mother's shade was speaking through me . . .'

'Yes?' he encouraged her.

'You heard me say that the world you knew was gone forever.'

'Yes.'

Now she confronted his eyes directly for the first time. 'It was not the Goddess who spoke those words,' she said. 'Nor was it your mother . . .'

Odysseus stood, scarcely breathing, feeling the breeze against his face.

Weeping silently, she glanced out into the shimmering blue light across the sea. 'I forced myself to say them because it was what I wanted to believe . . . I wanted you to believe it too.'

In the silence between them he heard the surf breaking against the shore.

'That is why I knew that I must leave the Oracle,' she confessed at last. 'The Goddess left me in that moment . . . I knew she would not return. I had only you, and I wanted only you.'

Odysseus released his breath in a sigh of pain. A moment later he said, 'I think she has made us both suffer for putting our desires before her truth.'

'No,' Calypso shook her head, 'it is we who make our suffering. I blame only myself.'

'Then we must forgive each other,' Odysseus said, 'for I know how I have hurt and wronged you too.'

They stood together in silence for a long time. With Hermes at her side, Calypso watched through blurred eyes as he pushed out the little boat and hoisted his sail. It flapped at first; then billowed in the breeze blowing off the land. The boat sallied among the breakers. In the moment before Odysseus pushed his prow eastwards round the steep fall of the cliff, he turned to bid a last farewell to the woman whose love he was betraying even as he sought to stay true to a deeper loyalty of the heart, but she had gone.

Only Hermes stood waving on the shore.

As he told his story in the great hall of King Antinous at Scheria, Odysseus could no longer remember how many nights he had passed at sea; only that he was exhausted, famished and parched with thirst by the time a big wave spilled his boat and he fetched up half-drowned on the Phaeacian coast.

'And I think I would have died there,' he said, looking back gratefully into Nausicaa's eyes, 'had you not come so bravely to my aid.'

Firmly she controlled the waver in her voice. 'How could I have done otherwise?' she said, and raised her eyes in a brave smile. 'In return, I ask only that you will not forget me when you come home to your wife.'

Wondering once more at the undemanding candour of the affection there, Odysseus studied her young face. 'Since coming to Scheria,' he answered, 'I have vowed to forget nothing of what has happened to me during all these years away from Ithaca. But of all the people I've met, and all the marvels I've seen, I know that my greatest pleasure will always lie in memories of you.'

An hour before dusk, two days later, the ship on which Telemachus had sailed back from Pylos beached in a quiet cove on Ithaca. During the course of the voyage he had consulted his friend Peiraeus and the soothsayer Theoclymenus about the best course of action to take on his return.

'Antinous and the others are bound to be suspicious of what you've been doing,' Peiraeus warned. 'They didn't like it when you asserted yourself at the council. I think you're going to have to be very careful.'

Theoclymenus asked who he was referring to; when he understood more of the situation on Ithaca, he nodded and said, 'Now I see it.' He looked across at Telemachus. 'I didn't care to say so before, but when we met, I sensed a shadow across your life. Peiraeus is right. These men are dangerous to you.'

'That's why I've decided not to go straight back to the palace,' Telemachus said.

'That makes sense,' Peiraeus said, 'but what will you do instead?'

'I've been trying to imagine what Odysseus would do. It's obvious I can't take on that gang alone, so I'm going to need all the help I can get. I've just remembered how quickly Antinous backed down at the Spring Festival when the shepherds came to my aid. My grandfather told me that Eupeithes did the same thing years ago, after that business with the Taphian pirates. I think if I can rally enough support among the common people, we might force them to back down again.'

Peiraeus nodded thoughtfully. 'But remember there's a lot more at stake now. It's the kingship they're after. They won't give that up easily.'

'Which is why I intend to rally the shepherds in my father's name.' Telemachus glanced away over the receding horizon. 'I know that he's not coming back, but *they* don't know it, and people like Eumaeus and Philoetius won't settle for anyone else as king if I can make them think there's half a chance he'll return.'

So it was agreed that Telemachus would leave the ship where his landing would not be seen, and make his way to the hut of Eumaeus the swineherd, who was best placed to help him gather support among the common people. Peiraeus would take the ship on into port and begin to spread the word that there was now good reason to believe that Odysseus was still alive. His story would say that Odysseus had been detained on Ogygia by the enchantment of a witch; and the hope was that the prospect of Telemachus returning with his father would discourage the more faint-hearted suitors and unsettle them all.

Darkness was falling by the time Telemachus crossed the wooded hillside beyond Crow Rock to where Eumaeus kept his large herd of pigs penned behind a fence of split oak and a neat series of stone walls hedged with wild pear-trees. He approached down-wind of the swineherd's hut, trying not to disturb the boars where they were snouting through the turned ground of their sties; even so, the dogs must have heard him and began to bark. Somewhere a sow was upset by the racket and her piglets began to squeal. A moment later the door of the hut creaked open and Eumaeus was standing there with an oil-lamp in his hand.

'Who's there?' he called.

Telemachus stepped out of the gloom, hissing, 'It's me, Eumaeus. I've come back. I need to talk to you.'

'Just a minute,' Eumaeus grunted and turned back into his hut. Puzzled by the delay, Telemachus waited in the familiar, rich smell drifting from the sties until the door swung open again and Eumaeus said, 'All right, you can come in now.'

When he stepped inside the hut Telemachus was surprised to see another figure sitting by the table with a trencher of pork and some slices of bread before him. He wore what appeared to be a torn and dirty blanket hunched up around his shoulders. Casting a quick glance at the youth, he pushed his fist to his brow in a gesture of salutation and then returned his attention to his meal.

'I didn't think there'd be anyone with you,' Telemachus said.

'It's only a beggar who knocked on my door in the name of Zeus,' Eumaeus said. 'I've given him food and shelter for the night. But what about you, young master? I thought you were out on the high seas looking for your father.'

'I was, and I've had word of him, but . . .' Telemachus glanced uncertainly towards the stranger. 'I need to talk to you alone, Eumaeus.'

'Oh never you mind him,' the swineherd answered. 'He's fallen on hard times, that's all, after being shipwrecked in the war. He's a good enough fellow in his way. Says he knew your father well when they was at Troy together.'

'This is Odysseus's boy, is it?' the beggar asked from where he wiped his greasy lips with the back of his hand. 'Good man your father was! Always kept an eye out for me.'

'What's on your mind, boy?' Eumaeus said. 'You've got an agitated look about your eyes.'

'Can we trust this man?' Telemachus demanded. 'My life may hang on it.'

'He's all right,' Eumaeus nodded reassuringly. 'I've told him about the troubles we've got here on Ithaca. You can speak free.'

'If you're about your father's business, boy,' the stranger said, 'you can trust me as sure as if Odysseus was here himself.'

Telemachus frowned at the man uneasily; but the swineherd's instincts were usually sound, and he was eager to tell him of his plans; so he took the cup of wine he was offered and began to explain that he needed help in recruiting the support of the island's shepherds to throw the suitors out of the palace. 'I know that my father's alive,' he said. 'I heard it from King Menelaus in Sparta. Once the shepherds know it, surely they'll stand up for him against that rabble?'

'You've been in Sparta, boy?' It was the stranger who spoke.

'I have.' Again Telemachus frowned at the man uncertainly.

'And what word did Menelaus have of your father?'

Telemachus glanced back at Eumaeus, who nodded once more in reassurance. 'That he's been on Ogygia for many years. Under a spell of enchantment.'

'A spell of enchantment, eh? Well, I reckon it would take something of the sort to keep Odysseus away from his wife and son.' The stranger sniffed and pushed his plate away. 'And on the strength of this report you mean to rouse the island against those louts who are making your mother's life a misery? Is that it?'

'That's exactly what I mean to do . . . if I can.'

'You have doubts?'

Telemachus flushed. 'I came here to talk to my friend Eumaeus, not to you, however well you may or may not have known my father.'

'Oh we were very close, he and I. And I can see you've got something of his spirit. But I wonder if you've inherited his brains? It seems to me this plan of yours might start a bloody war across this island. Is that what you want?'

'I want that rabble out of my house. I want my mother to be able to breathe freely again. I want to believe that I'll sit on the throne of Ithaca one day. And I can't see how else to do these things. If I have to fight for them, then I'll fight.'

'And not worry too much about who else gets killed, eh?'

'My father didn't seem to worry too much about that when he took off for Troy. Why should I start worrying now?'

The stranger heaved an audible sigh and sat, nodding, at the table.

'This fellow's been a warrior in his time,' Eumaeus put in. 'You might do well to listen to him, Telemachus.'

Becoming more heated, Telemachus said, 'It's the Feast of Apollo the day after tomorrow. They'll be demanding a decision from my mother.'

'I know, I know,' Eumaeus said, 'but we need to think about it carefully.'

'It's too late for thought. We have to do something.'

'People who don't think,' said the stranger, 'tend to do the wrong thing.'

Telemachus ignored him. Turning to Eumaeus, he said, 'How are things at the palace?' he asked. 'Is my mother all right?'

Eumaeus scratched his head, 'She's as well as can be expected with a gang of drunkards eating her out of house and home. Apart from worrying herself sick about you, that is. You'd have been wiser to tell her what you were doing, boy.'

'Then she would have tried to prevent me,' the youth retorted. 'Like Mentes said, there's a time when a man has to stop listening to his mother.'

'Then Mentes was wrong,' the stranger said. 'You should always listen to her – though whether you do as she says is another matter.'

'You may have *known* my father,' Telemachus snapped at him, 'but that doesn't give you the right to speak to me as though you were.'

The beggar scraped back the bench on which he sat and got to his feet. As he did so, the dirty blanket dropped from round his shoulders revealing a richly embroidered robe beneath. Staring directly at Telemachus with narrowed eyes, he said, 'I am your father, boy. Odysseus has returned to Ithaca.' But his eyes were smiling as he added, 'It would be good if you showed him a little respect.'

The two of them talked far into that night while old Eumaeus slept, but at first their exchanges were uneasy. Telemachus took a

long time to recover from the shock that had been sprung on
him, while at times Odysseus was so emotional that he could
hardly speak at all. There was so much to say, and all of it so hard
to say, and he could feel the heat of his son's unspoken anger
tautening the air between them. So his joy in his son mingled
with pangs of sorrow and self-accusation for all the lost years
when he might have been watching this fine boy grow into the
figure who sat nervously across from him, wanting to love this
father he had never known, yet uncertain how it could be done.

Eventually the boy demanded an answer to the question with
which he had been living almost all his life: 'Why didn't you
come home a long time ago?'

It took a long time for Odysseus to answer, and when he was
done he was still uncertain whether or not his son understood
that to live one's life is not so simple as a youth who has barely
embarked on it might think.

He ended his account of himself by telling how a Phaeacian
ship had dropped him in the quiet Bay of Phorcys early that
morning. 'They're good people,' he said, 'but they like to keep
themselves apart from the world, so I couldn't persuade them to
stay. They gave me precious gifts of silver cauldrons and tripods
which I concealed in the Cave of the Nymphs.' He glanced up
at his son. 'If anything happens to me, you should look for them
there. Then I met a shepherd boy outside the Temple of Athena
who told me what was happening here; so I sought out my old
friend Eumaeus, knowing I could count on him to shelter me
till I worked out a plan of action. No one but you two knows
that I'm back yet – not even your mother. But I'm glad that the
gods have given you and me this chance to get to know one
another before we do what we have to do.'

And only then, with their attention concentrated on the urgent
task awaiting them did they begin to connect with greater confidence. Odysseus questioned Telemachus carefully about conditions
in the palace, wanting to know more about each of the suitors
who had taken up residence there, and where their main strength

lay. Because Eumaeus had already told him that Antinous was the principal troublemaker, he was unsurprised by his son's hostility towards him.

'Perhaps I should have taken him to the war with me after all,' he said. 'I might have made something of him.'

'He's worthless,' Telemachus replied. 'No one can do anything with that sort of vicious bully.'

Remembering that, in any case, almost everyone who had gone to Troy with him was dead, and that he was lucky to be alive himself, Odysseus drew in his breath and said, 'What about Amphinomus?'

'He's a snake. In some ways he's the most dangerous of them all.'

Worried by the pang of hatred that had crossed his son's face, Odysseus forced himself to ask why Telemachus should think so. Heatedly the boy glanced away, unwilling at this moment to look directly into his father's troubled eyes.

'Because most of the others are mere brutes, 'he said, 'but Amphinomus . . . Amphinomus has wormed his way into my mother's affections.' When he looked up again, Telemachus saw the pain his words had caused. Wondering whether he had already said too much, he glanced away, scowling. 'It's a rats' nest. We have to clear it out. That's why we have to rouse the shepherds.'

Odysseus studied his son for a long time in silence. Much of him felt proud that the youth was showing so resolute a spirit – he was growing into the kind of young warrior he would have been glad to have fighting at his side at Troy. Already he loved the boy, though he could see he was going to have to work hard before Telemachus would feel free to express his own love in return. He could see too that the boy's passions were volatile, and too visible across his honest features; and there was so much anger in the flash of his stare and the dour set of his jaw. Telemachus had courage, yes, but of the impetuous kind that could cause harm where it meant to do only good.

Quietly he said, 'We don't need the shepherds. We can do this together.'

'Just the two of us? Alone? That isn't possible.'

'We won't be alone,' Odysseus answered. 'I've already talked it over with Eumaeus. He'll be there and Philoetius will come. There may be others.'

'Even so – there are so many of them . . . from all over the islands.'

'I know,' Odysseus said. 'Which is why we have to use our heads. Is my bow in the armoury still?'

'Yes. And it's in good condition. I've been taking care of it.'

Odysseus smiled at his son. 'Have you managed to draw it yet?'

'I haven't tried. I've just kept it oiled and made sure that the string is sound.'

'Good. Now listen to me carefully. This is what we're going to do.'

At the time I knew nothing of this encounter. I didn't even know that Peiraeus had put into port that evening and was already spreading the word among the townsfolk that there had been news of Odysseus. I was kept far too busy at the palace, entertaining the sots who had been left behind when Antinous and a few of the more hard-bitten suitors put to sea two days earlier with the intention of lying in wait for Telemachus and making sure that he did not get back alive.

Having learned about the planned ambush from some loose gossip in my hearing, I was close to despair. Never in my life have I found it harder to sing. The mood of the suitors had deteriorated since Telemachus had defied them at the assembly and then disappeared. With their patience already running out, they were more truculent now; and though it was true that the worst of them had gone with Antinous, the rest were even rowdier than before, drinking too much and making free with the serving-women, one or two of whom had grown shameless in their behaviour. I knew that if I shared my knowledge of the ambush with Penelope and Lord Mentor it was too late for them to do anything about it, and both would worry themselves to distraction. Still worse, if Penelope openly accused the suitors of treachery, as I feared that she might, anything could happen to her. So, rightly or wrongly, I decided to consign Telemachus to the care of the gods and keep the bad news to myself.

When it became clear to me that Amphinomus was also ignorant of what Antinous planned to do, I wondered whether I should confide in him; but Telemachus' suspicions had begun to colour my own views, and I wasn't sure whether I could trust Amphinomus not to have me silenced. After all, he too might profit from the death of Telemachus. So again I kept silent. Such, I regret to confess, was the confused state of my feelings at that time.

During this time, Penelope was, of course, in great distress. Her one thought throughout the years of her husband's absence was that she must protect the interests of her son, and it was for that reason, as much as out of her loyalty to the memory of Odysseus, that she had refused to commit herself to any other man. But now Telemachus was gone and she had no idea what had become of him; and though she did all she could to maintain an outward air of calm control, inwardly she was frantic with anxiety.

To add to her worries, the date of Apollo's summer feast was almost upon her and she knew she would be unable to keep the suitors at bay beyond that point. She knew too that, though their collective behaviour was a public disgrace, the suitors had a point: Ithaca could not be left to drift this way for ever. Somewhere, I suspect, she must have been making up her mind to marry Amphinomus, when Eumaeus came to her the next day and asked if he might have a private word. He tried to allay her anxiety by saying that Telemachus was at his hut and quite safe, but her insistent questioning forced him to reveal the plot against her son's life. Obeying strict instructions, however, he said nothing of her husband's return.

By now, word had got about the town that Peiraeus' ship was

in port. His course had brought him by a roundabout route in order to drop off Telemachus, so his ship had passed unseen by Antinous. But someone must have reported its arrival to the ambush-party the next morning because Antinous beached his ship on the strand before noon and immediately led his angry followers up to the palace.

The other suitors were in the courtyard throwing javelins and playing quoits. When they learned that Telemachus had slipped the net, they grew uneasy. Not all of them can have had much enthusiasm for the plan in the first place. Now that it had gone wrong they were fearful of the consequences. They were arguing amongst themselves when Medon the herald appeared in the courtyard, saying that their presence was required in the great hall by the Lady Penelope.

As I had feared, Penelope had been outraged by the news of this threat to her son's life and was determined to make the conspirators face her fury; but the men she confronted that after-noon were a less confident bunch than they had been only a day earlier. Their plans had gone awry, they didn't know where Telemachus was, or what kind of support he might be mustering, and by now some of them had heard the rumour that Odysseus was alive and might be about to return. So most of them stood shifting uncertainly before the proud woman who descended from her apartment when they were all assembled. Accompanied by Eurycleia and the closest of her women, Penelope was dressed in one of her finest gowns and kept her face veiled. She carried in her bearing all the authority of a queen.

'I have born patience with you all for as long as I can, gentlemen,' she began, 'and I have done so because you agreed to remain patient with me while I allowed a just amount of time to elapse before accepting that my husband would not return. But as I have waited I have been watching you. I have seen you consume the wealth of this noble house with the appetite of ravening beasts, I have watched you devour its food, drink its wine, and debauch the more stupid women who serve me with your licentious ways. And all of this I have endured because I believed there was some justice in your case that, if Odysseus failed to come home, the islands must be given a strong new king. But now I have learned that there are those among you who have been conspiring against the life of my son, and this I will not endure. Am I to choose a husband from among those who would murder my child? Tell me, is that the heartless kind of woman you think I am? And is such base behaviour what the people of these islands must come to expect of their king? I am waiting to hear what you have to say.'

When not one of them spoke, she said, 'What about you, Antinous? Your voice is usually loud in this hall. How do you answer this charge?'

'Madam,' Antinous replied, 'I have no idea where your son might be or what has befallen him. The last time I saw Telemachus he was insulting the council by leaving before its deliberations were complete. If harm has come to him since then it has nothing to do with me.' Defiantly he stared at the men around him, particularly Amphinomus who frowned back at him with intense suspicion.

Eurymachus spoke up then. Because he was among those whom Antinous had left behind at the palace to keep an eye on things, he may have felt less pressure of guilt, and he was anxious to dispel the tension.

'I can't imagine who would have made such an accusation, or why they would have made it,' he said, 'but I assure you, my lady, there's not a man among us who would dream of laying hands on your son. Everyone here knows and accepts that Telemachus is his father's rightful heir. Our only expectation, now that Odysseus has failed to return, is that you will choose a husband strong enough to act as king until your son comes of age. We mean only well by the boy – but if the gods should have seen fit to shorten his life-thread,' he added, looking around at his cronies, 'no one here can be held answerable for that.'

An uncertain murmur of assent rose around the hall.

Amphinomus stepped forward, 'I can speak only for myself,' he said, glowering at the others, 'but I swear I would die sooner than let anyone harm a hair of your son's head.'

Flushed and uncertain, fearful of the future, and grieving for her absent husband, Penelope stared for a time at these men she neither trusted nor cared for. She was about to speak when Antinous reasserted himself.

'As for the rest,' he said, 'tomorrow is the feast day of Apollo. You can put an end to your cares, Lady, simply by making up your mind.'

Penelope held him for a time in her incinerating stare; then before anyone else could utter a word, she turned on her heel and ascended quickly back to the refuge of her apartment where she was free to release her feelings in her tears.

A foul-mouthed beggar called Irus had been hanging about the courtyard for several weeks now, keeping the suitors amused by his scurrilous humour. He woke up from his customary doze just as that confrontation was ending and saw another ragged beggar entering the yard. The ancient hunting-dog Argus, who had barely stirred from his place in the shade since Telemachus had left, lifted his grizzled head at the newcomer's approach and wagged his tail. As the beggar crouched down, the dog tried to get to his feet but lacked the strength. The tail flapped once more; then the dog's head fell back in the dust. The newcomer stroked its wiry, flea-ridden fur for a time, whispering under his breath; then he rose and looked up towards the door to the hall where some of the suitors were coming out into the hot courtyard muttering together.

The incident would have meant nothing to Irus except that he had never known the animal do anything but growl at everyone but Telemachus. He took it as a bad omen that a strange beggar encroaching on his patch should have been given a friendly reception. Pushing himself to his feet, he gathered his rags about him and said, 'Piss off, greybeard, there's nothing for you here.'

The newcomer turned to look at him with narrowed eyes. 'I've never heard of a man down on his luck being turned away from the house of Odysseus,' he said. 'It seems to me there's plenty of room here for both of us.'

'It seems you've also not heard that Odysseus is with the fishes,' Irus retorted. 'There'll be a new master here this time tomorrow and he'll have nobody begging for his scraps but me. So on your way, before I throw you out.'

Antinous had heard the exchange. 'Here's something new,' he shouted, eager for the distraction, '—an honour duel between beggars. Come on, let's see you fight it out. My money's on Irus. And there's a roast goat's paunch for the winner.'

The newcomer frowned at the ground. 'I'm not looking for trouble,'

'But you've found it,' said Irus, tucking his ragged smock up into his belt to reveal his scrawny legs. 'Put your fists up and let me knock you down.'

The men had begun to crowd around, egging them on and making wagers, when another voice rose above the din. 'Until my father gets back, I'm the host here!' Telemachus shouted. 'One more mouth to feed will make no difference.'

Shocked by his unexpected appearance, all the men fell silent for a moment. Antinous was the first to recover. 'So you've come home to watch your mother's wedding, have you?' he glowered. 'Well, you're not spoiling our fun today. Come on, Irus, let's see you give this bag of bones a blow about the chops.'

Irus lifted his fists to his face, sniffed, flicked his nose with his thumb, and let fly with his right. The newcomer leaned so that the blow glanced past his chin, then drove his left fist into Irus's stomach and caught him with his right as his head came down. Everyone heard the beggar's jawbone crack. A second later Irus fell to his knees, spitting teeth and blood.

The crowd of suitors stared, astounded, for a moment; then they began to laugh and applaud. As they did so, Telemachus slipped away into the hall. Evidently undismayed that his fancied contender was beaten, Antinous shouted, 'We'll have a new king of Ithaca tomorrow, so it's just as well we have a new king of beggars today!' Turning to the winner he muttered, 'I owe you a goat's paunch, fellow,' and crossed to where the wine was being poured.

Amphinomus approached the beggar, taking care not to brush too closely against his clothes, and handed him a goblet of wine. 'Your luck seems to be improving, friend,' he said. 'Here's to better fortune still.'

The beggar poured a libation, took a drink and said, 'And you seem to be more of a gentleman than these others, sir. Amphinomus, isn't it? Prince of Dulichion?' When the other smiled, he added. 'I wonder that you consort with them.'

'If any of them were friends of mine, they've long since ceased to be so.'

'Then why are you here?'

'Because of the Lady Penelope. Why else? A man would be a fool to lose the chance of making her his wife.'

The beggar gave a canny smile. 'I hear tell that you've half done that already.'

Frowning, Amphinomus stared at the beggar in disgust. 'Whoever told you that is a base liar,' he said, and strode away.

Telemachus, meanwhile, had made his way up to his mother's apartment where he found her in tears; but her weeping stopped as soon as she saw him at the door. Uncertain whether to hit her son or hug him, Penelope met him with an outburst of furious relief. Where had he been? How dare he go off without consulting her? She'd been out of her mind with worry. Didn't he know that his life was at risk? Did he care about nothing but following his own rash will?

Telemachus let her rage wash over him for a time; then his stern voice astonished her to silence. 'That's enough now. I did what I had to do because there's no other man around here to do it. I dared to do what I think my father would have done in my place. And I'm back, alive and well, aren't I? Now do you want to hear what I have to say or not?'

When she had calmed down a little, he told her about his fruitless visit to King Nestor in Pylos, and then about what he had learned from Menelaus in Sparta.

'He gave me cause to believe my father is alive,' he said, and for the first time in many months he saw the light of hope break in her eyes.

'Where is he?' she demanded, clutching him by both arms. 'What's happened to him? When is he coming back?'

Freeing his arms from her grip, Telemachus said, 'The news was already old when Menelaus received it, and that was nearly a year ago. He heard that Odysseus is on an island called Ogygia – that he is under an enchantment there. A woman – some say she is a goddess – had him in thrall.'

For a long time he felt his mother searching his face. Then she uttered a little gasp of breath as though jarred by a stab of pain, and seemed to sag before him. Penelope averted her face, looking towards the window where the afternoon sky hung its fierce blue glare. The sound of coarse laughter rose from the hall below. She looked at the loom on which the finely woven shroud on which she had worked for years hung glistening in the light, almost complete. And she had lavished such care on it, stitching and unpicking, and stitching again, the gold and silver threads, the green of the hills, the sea's translucent blue, the intricate motifs of ships and beasts and birds through which she had told the island's story. Well, this portion of her work would serve its purpose one day soon. Old father Laertes could not have long to live; and would she rather, she wondered, have preferred to learn that Odysseus was also dead than that he lay in thrall to some other woman on some other island? Was there no faith left in the world? Had the war consumed all hope that life might still run true again?

Penelope looked back into the anxious face of her son.

'Tomorrow is Apollo's feast,' she said. 'What am I to do?'

'What do you want to do?'

'Right now,' she sighed, 'I think that I would like to die. But I cannot do that; so I will try to sleep instead. Perhaps some dream will come to help me.'

She turned away. Telemachus knew that she wanted him to go, and half of him wanted to run weeping from the room in any case; but he was under instruction from his father.

His lip trembled as he said, 'Do you remember the story you told me about my father's bow – how he once loosed an arrow through the handles of the axes he had set in line?'

Penelope shook her head impatiently. Why couldn't the boy leave her alone?

'What of it?'

'Make it a trial,' he said. 'Tell them you will only marry a man who can prove himself worthy to replace Odysseus. Have the axes set in line again. See which of them can even string the bow, let alone pass the arrow through the axes.'

She turned to look at him again. 'They will never accept it.'

'When I was in Pylos,' he said, 'I made a new friend. He has the sight. He told me that there are still ordeals to come, but that all will be well in the end.'

'They will never accept it,' she repeated, not daring to believe.

'Shame them,' he said. 'They won't dare to refuse.' He held her pensive gaze for a moment and then turned away. At the door he stopped as though struck by a fresh thought. 'There is a new beggar come to the court,' he said. 'He seems a decent man. You might also shame them into treating him a little better.'

My singing was interrupted by a disgraceful episode in the hall that night when Eurymachus threw a stool at the beggar for rebuking the loose behaviour of Melantho, one of the serving-maids he was bedding. The stool missed its target but hit one of the wine-stewards who fell to the floor, dropping the full jug he held. Immediately Telemachus jumped to his feet in disgust, berating the drunkards who had turned his home into the worst sort of tavern. I was fearful that things might turn very nasty then, but Amphinomus spoke up, reminding the suitors that this was the eve of Apollo's feast. He persuaded them that they should all pour their solemn libations to the gods and then take to their beds in preparation for the next day. Medon the herald and I left the hall together at the same time and sat, sharing our worries about the future in the quiet night outside.

As soon as we had gone, Telemachus and the beggar set to work collecting up the javelins from their racks against the walls of the hall and began to take them through into the armoury. When old Eurycleia demanded to know what they were doing, Telemachus said that the behaviour of the suitors had become so unruly that he wanted to reduce the risk of violent quarrelling the next day. 'This fellow is giving me a hand in return for his meal,' he said. 'Get you off to bed, good mother. I shall be there myself as soon as this is done.'

So the beggar was in the hall, sitting by the embers of the fire, when Melantho passed through, on her way from the kitchen to spend the night with Eurymachus. She couldn't resist the opportunity to insult him again and was getting a mouthful in return when Penelope came out of her apartment, having heard the entire exchange. Chastising the maid for her shameless manner, she dismissed her from the hall, and asked the other servants to make up the fire and bring rugs so that the beggar might pass a more comfortable night. She was about to turn away when the beggar said, 'My old friend Odysseus would be proud of his good lady if he could see how she is comporting herself in these trying times.' And Penelope stopped in her tracks.

'You know Odysseus?' she asked.

'I know him very well,' the beggar said, 'and I have good reason to think it won't be long before he's seen in Ithaca again.'

Though her heart must have quickened at the words, she said, 'Beggars have come here before hoping to profit from such claims.'

'Believe me,' the beggar answered, 'I wouldn't lie about a man who is as dear to me as my own life.'

I happened to come back into the hall at that moment. When Penelope saw me enter she asked me to play something soothing on my lyre while she questioned this newcomer more closely about the news he had brought. So I watched the exchanges between them from across the hall, picking up a few words here and there as he told her the story of how he had first met Odysseus many years earlier and the things they had done together. He ended with an account of how he had recently learned at the court of the King of Thesprotia that her husband had survived a shipwreck in which all his men were lost. Odysseus, he claimed, had been washed up on the island of the Phaeacians, from where he intended to make his way home as soon as he had recovered some of his lost wealth.

After he had finished, Penelope sat in silence for a time, staring into the fire.

'Only the gods know whether your tale is true,' she said at last, 'but it has cheered my heart a little. You shall have your reward.' Turning to her women, she told them that this man was now to be honoured as a guest of her house. She ordered them to make up a proper bed for the beggar, and asked Eurycleia if she would be so kind as to wash his limbs before he slept between clean sheets. Then thanking him for his kindness, she retired to her apartment.

Many times in the following years I would ask Penelope whether or not she had recognized her husband in the hall that night behind the disguise of his beggar's rags. Each time she merely smiled at me, lips slightly pursed, and looked away.

Therefore I think she did; but she hadn't seen Odysseus for many years, his face had aged, and his disguise was good, so I may be wrong. One thing is certain however: that his identity was discovered not long after Penelope had left.

Eurycleia brought oil and a basin of water to wash his limbs and was saying what a kindly woman her mistress was and how harsh the fates had been to deprive her of her husband for so long, when she pushed back the ragged skirt of the beggar's tunic to sponge his legs and gasped to see the white ridge of a scar running along the outside of his thigh. She looked up into his face and was about to cry out when Odysseus lifted a hand to silence her. Startled by the menace in his eyes, she sat back, knocking over the basin of water at her side.

'Say nothing,' he hissed. 'All our lives may depend on it.'

'Foolish of me,' Eurycleia gasped, starting to mop up the water with the sponge. 'I'll just get you some fresh water . . . then everything will be right as rain.'

When the suitors assembled at the palace the next day, Eumaeus and Philoetius the stockman were in the courtyard, penning the animals that would be sacrificed later in the grove of Apollo. Already the morning heat hung close and heavy on the air. Antinous glowered at the beggar where he sat on the steps in the shade of the portico as if waiting to accost him. 'What are you hanging about for still?' he demanded. 'Haven't you caused enough trouble?'

'You still owe me a goat's paunch,' Odysseus replied.

'Talk to me like that,' Antinous came back at him, sweating in the sun, 'and I'll stuff it down your throat. Now get out of my way.' He strode through the doorway into the rich smell of roasted heifer already drifting from the palace kitchen, and then stopped in surprise when he saw the line of axes that had been set up along the length of the hall.

Eurymachus and Ctessipus stood beside him, equally puzzled by the sight.

'What is all this?' Antinous growled, and stepped back outside to demand an explanation from Eumaeus.

'Don't ask me what it's all about,' the swineherd shrugged. 'They were here when we arrived.'

'The young master ordered them to be set up,' Odysseus said. 'I understand there's to be some kind of sport today.'

Antinous scowled at him. 'There'll be sport all right if Telemachus tries to play fast and loose with us again. Where is he?' He went back into the hall, shouting for Telemachus while the others sat down at the tables waiting to be served.

The maids were already dishing out the food and wine in the din of the crowded hall when Telemachus came through to join them.

'Good morning, gentlemen,' he smiled with a surprisingly casual air, 'I trust you all slept well and that you've made your solemn offerings to the god this morning, as I have just been doing.' Without giving Antinous time to do more than scowl in response he looked across at me. 'Phemius,' he called, 'play something for us. Play something in honour of the Archer God, whose summer feast we celebrate today.'

His voice recalled me from a memory of the day, years earlier, when Penelope had told Telemachus about his father's stupendous feat with the bow. Thinking quickly, I tuned my lyre and began to sing the hymn which opens by telling how all the gods tremble when Apollo enters the house of Zeus; but even as I began to sing, it was clear that my efforts would get scant attention, for Antinous was already demanding to know why the axes were standing there.

'You'll find out soon enough,' Telemachus replied. 'All you need to know for now is that my mother has found a way of determining which man here is truly worthy to be her husband.'

'So it will be decided today?' Amphinomus said.

Telemachus gave him a disdainful frown. 'Didn't you think that she would be as good as her word?'

'I never doubted it,' Amphinomus answered stiffly.

Telemachus scowled across the tables where all the suitors were gathered now. 'Eat your fill, gentlemen,' he said. 'The Lady Penelope will join us shortly.' But his insolent manner, and the uncertainty of the occasion, and the close heat of that summer morning had left them unsettled. Though they ate and drank as usual with no thought for the cost, the mutter of their conversation was subdued and intermittent until, in a coarse attempt to lift their spirits, Ctessipus got to his feet, shouted, 'Gentlemen, we're forgetting our duty to feed the poor,' and hurled the heifer's heel-bone across the hall at where the beggar sat by the hearth.

Having guessed that something of the sort was coming, Odysseus merely leaned aside so that the bone fell harmlessly among the ashes.

Instantly Telemachus leapt to his feet. 'It's as well for you that your aim was as bad as your judgement,' he shouted. 'If you'd harmed that man I'd have made you answer to my spear.'

I had already stopped singing. Now the entire hall fell silent. Ctesippus was already elbowing his neighbours aside to get up from his bench when the voice of Penelope came down from the balcony above the hall. 'Be silent, Telemachus,' she commanded. 'This is the sacred Feast Day of Apollo. There will be no violence in this house.'

Grave and stately, accompanied by Eurycleia and her attendants, she came down into the hall. As always when she joined the suitors in the hall, her face was veiled, but now they saw that she was carrying a bow-case in her hands.

When she reached the hearth in the centre of the hall, not far from where the beggar sat, she said, 'You were promised that you would have my decision today and I will try your patience no longer.' She slipped the bow from its leather and held its sleek length up for all to see. 'This bow once belonged to Lord Odysseus. No one else has ever strung it. A long time ago, when he was a young man still, he used this bow to shoot an arrow through twelve axes that stood in line,' with a sweep of her arm she gestured across the hall, 'like these I have had placed for you here. My decision is that I will give myself to whoever proves himself as worthy as my husband. Here is the bow.' Turning, she pointed to the quiver held by Eurycleia. 'Here are the arrows. And there are the axes. The rest, gentlemen, is up to you.'

Again there was silence. The suitors looked from Penelope to the line of axes that stretched for a distance of some twelve strides with their bronze rings fixed at an awkward height. One of them released a nervous, scoffing laugh. Leodes, the drunken priest of Apollo, shrugged and said, 'That rules me out. I couldn't hit a barn door right now.'

'How do we know this feat was ever done?' Antinous demanded and looked around at his discomfited cronies. 'Did anyone here see it?'

'I saw it,' Eurycleia said with a triumphant smirk on her face.

'And who would doubt a lady's word?' the beggar put in.

Antinous scowled at him. 'You stay out of this.' Wiping the grease off his hands, he looked across at Penelope. 'Let me take a look at that bow.'

'Wait!' Still smarting from the way his mother had rebuked him before the suitors, Telemachus crossed the floor and took the bow from her hands. 'This will be a test of manhood,' he said, 'and I'm sure that none of you wants to be humiliated in my mother's sight. Go to your apartment, mother, and take these women with you. I'll be judge of what happens here. You will be called when the thing is done.'

Astounded by the firmness of his tone, Penelope was about to protest when Eurycleia took her by the arm, saying, 'Come, my lady, let's leave these men to their sport.' Penelope looked back at her son and saw the resolution in his eyes.

Drawing in her breath, she turned and went back up the stairs.

As soon as she was gone, Telemachus said, 'I've looked after this bow for years and I don't believe there's one of you fit to draw it. So come on, Antinous . . . if you want to be the first to make a fool of himself.'

'I wouldn't want any one to claim that he hadn't been given a fair chance.' Antinous looked around at the gathering. 'What about you, Leodes? Let's see if you can at least string it for us.'

Pushed on by the men around him, Leodes got up and took the bow. Seeing that the string was already fastened to the bottom notch, he stood the bow on the ground, applied his weight to it, and tried to pull the loop at the far end of the string towards the top notch. He strained there for a time, puffing his cheeks till the veins were red, but the bow hardly bent under his strength.

'What's the matter, Leodes?' Ctessipus guffawed, 'string too short?'

'You come and try, if you like,' Leodes gasped. 'A man could break his heart trying to string this bow.'

'Here, give it to me,' a Samian called Pellas said impatiently, but he too failed to make much impression on the strength of the yew. Having watched two others try and fail, Eurymachus said, 'This bow's been standing about for years. It must need greasing. Let's get some tallow heated up. Then I'll show you how it's done.'

More drink was served while the tallow was heated. Lavishing his admiration on the bow, Eurymachus gave it a thorough waxing and, when he was satisfied, he too tried to string the bow and failed. 'It's this horn that's spliced into the wood,' he said. 'It's got no give in it. It'll take three of us to get the bloody thing strung!'

'Take your time, gentlemen,' Telemachus said, 'my mother is a patient woman.' He looked across at me where I sat next to Medon the herald. 'Play something calming for them, Phemius. It may improve their mood.'

'Odysseus was always a crafty sod,' Antinous glowered. 'Let's think about this. There has to be a knack to it.'

The suitors gathered round him, examining the bow, arguing heatedly about the best way to string it. They were no more aware than I was that Eumaeus and Philoetius had entered the hall, having locked the doors from outside and brought swords, spears and shields from the armoury.

Quietly Telemachus walked round the wall, past the great hanging, to stand beside them. At the same moment the beggar got up from the hearth, saying, 'I had some experience with bows like that one when I was a younger man. Perhaps I could give you gentlemen some advice.'

'You can keep your advice to yourself, clown,' Antinous snarled.

But Amphinomus got up from where he had been listening to the arguments in silence. 'We don't seem to be making much progress on our own,' he said dryly. 'Let the beggar at least have a look at the bow.'

'And what if he strings it?' Eurymachus retorted. 'What kind of fools will that make of us?'

'At least you might get the chance to loose an arrow,' Telemachus put in.

'He'll never string it,' Ctessipus jeered. 'Let him have a go. It should be good for a laugh.'

Antinous glared across at Telemachus. 'If it turns out that there's some trickery to this, I promise *you* won't live long enough to laugh over it.' He turned back to the beggar. 'Here, let's see you rupture your guts.' Handing over the bow, he crossed the floor to the table where the wine jar stood.

Aware now that something strange was happening, I lowered my lyre and watched the beggar test the strength of the string and caress the length of bow in silence. With his lips slightly pursed, he nodded at it, smiling. 'It's a long time since I held such a bow,' he said, 'but I seem to remember it's done like this.'

Quickly he turned his back on the crowd of suitors so that it was difficult to see quite what he did; but when he turned around again, the bow was strung. Holding its tautened curves out before him, he plucked the string. The air warbled to the note it sang.

Gasps and oaths must have been uttered around me, but I heard none of them. Like everyone else I watched, stupefied, as the beggar picked up the quiver and walked to the head of the line of axes, near to where Telemachus stood with Eumaeus and Philoetius at his side. Slipping an arrow from the quiver, he nocked it to the bow and aimed its point at the axes. Then he uttered a laugh, lowered the bow and said, 'No, I'm afraid that's beyond me these days. But I can still do this.' He raised the bow again, swung it to his right and released the arrow. A moment later it pierced the throat of Antinous where he stood, mouth agape, with the wine jar in his hand. The jar fell first, shattering against the flags.

★   ★   ★

Afterwards, Odysseus swore to Penelope that what happened next was never his intention. Yes, he had meant to kill Antinous. The man was irredeemable; out of that entire unruly rabble, he was the one that most deserved to die, and his death should have been enough. From the moment he fell and Odysseus shouted, 'Did you never think to see me back, you dogs?' all the rest understood well enough that their rightful lord had returned to Ithaca. It should have ended there.

But Odysseus had forgotten that his son was also a casualty of the war. Like Neoptolemus and Orestes before him, he was a warrior's son. He too believed he had a thing to prove. He too had a hoard of hatred loaded in his heart.

Even as Odysseus fitted the arrow to his bow, Telemachus gripped the spear that Eumaeus passed to him. Watching the body of Antinous crumple to the floor, he raised his arm to shoulder height. With the fierce sound of his father's voice shouting at his side, Telemachus released the spear.

The point plunged into the stomach of Amphinomus with such force that it pushed him backwards. He fell against a table, scattering dishes with his arms. He lay supported there for a few moments with the shaft of the spear sticking upwards from his stomach like a mast. When he tried to lift his head, blood spilled from his mouth. He spluttered on it, blinking in bewilderment. Then he too fell to the floor, pulled over by the weight of the spear.

I heard someone cry out, 'They mean to kill us all.'

From Odysseus's mouth broke an anguished cry of the single word: 'No.'

It might have been a simple denial of that accusation or a futile attempt to prevent his son from doing what he had already done. But nobody was listening. The hall was too full of fear. I saw Leodes scrambling for cover. Someone tipped over a table and three or four men crouched behind it. But with a courage that can only have been born of desperation, Eurymachus drew the short sword he always wore at his side and hurled himself towards Odysseus.

With no other means of defending himself, Odysseus raised
the bow again and loosed another arrow. At short range it went
straight to his assailant's heart. Eurymachus sagged at the knees
and fell forwards, smashing his forehead against the stones of the
hearth. A moment later a spear thrown by Eumaeus brought
down the man standing next to him who was about to throw
a knife.

Everything was confusion then. Some of the men tried the
door and found it locked against them. Others looked for spears
in the racks and found them empty. Panicking, they started to
shout. More tables were thrown over. I could hear someone whimpering. Only then did it occur to me that my own life might be
in danger. Cowering down behind the silver-studded throne that
stood by the rear wall of the hall, I covered my head with my
hands.

With all the leaders dead, Pellas shouted to some of the
others to make a rush for the armoury and bring back spears.
Odysseus raised his voice, ordering them to do no such thing.
If they came out peacefully, he promised, their lives would be
spared.

The men crouched uncertainly across from the entrance to the
passage. 'Don't believe him,' Pellas called. 'It's another of his tricks.
You can't trust him.' Still the men hesitated, 'There's four of us
dead already,' Pellas called. 'They won't stop there.' Two of the
men ran for the armoury then. A third followed,

'See what they're like,' Telemachus snarled. He stared, panting,
at his father. 'It's a rats' nest, I tell you. They have to die.' He
hurled another spear, which was deflected by the edge of the table
behind which Pellas crouched.

'Enough,' Odysseus shouted. 'It's enough, enough.'

But while they were staring at each other, Pellas picked up the
spear.

Seeing what he was doing, Philoetius shouted a warning just
in time for Odysseus to push his son away. The spear flashed
between them. It tore the sleeve of Telemachus' tunic and scored

his left arm before falling to the floor. The boy stared down, trembling, at the cut; then he looked back into his father's eyes.

Odysseus was gazing back at his son, appalled that he had come
so close to death. He closed his eyes and gritted his teeth, but a
fierce shout leapt out of his broken heart. As once before, that
night at the fall of Troy, frenzy combusted inside him like a burning
barn.

Turning, he saw the men hurrying out of the passage with
their arms full of swords and spears. His first arrow wounded one
of them in the shoulder so that the weapons fell clattering on
the stones. The next punctured the lung of a man who got up
from behind a table to reach for a spear. The third bounced off
the shield with which the last man coming from the armoury
had thought to equip himself. All the suitors were under cover
then, whispering as they distributed the weapons. I could hear
four of them planning to lift a bench for cover and charge at
Odysseus with his spears. But the veteran of Troy acted first.
Throwing down his bow, he grabbed a sword and shield from the
pile that his allies had placed beside the door and leapt across a
fallen table where he swung the blade down into the flesh of
cowering men. Others rose to their feet with weapons or tried
to scramble away; but Eumaeus and Philoetius were there with
spears to stab them as they rose. Telemachus leapt to join them,
brandishing a sword.

From where I crouched with my head in my hands, I could
hear men shouting and screaming as they died. Somewhere, Leodes
was begging for mercy, crying out that he was a priest and that
he had tried to talk the others out of their evil ways; but his
pathetic pleas were cut short as Odysseus sliced his sword into
the priest's neck. Utterly frantic now, some of the suitors were
slipping in blood as they vainly tried to get away from him; others
put up a fight with what weapons they could grab, only to fall
under the herdsmen's swords and spears.

Uncertain what to do, terrified beyond all thought, I heard the
hoarse sound of panting close to where I hid, and that of someone

else coughing on his blood as he clutched at a hanging and dragged it down from the wall. Then the throne was pulled to one side. Its feet scraped across the stones. When I looked up I saw Odysseus standing over me. His beggar's rags were drenched with blood. He was muttering profanities. His eyes were a madman's eyes. The sword hung above his shoulder, poised to swoop.

I must have shouted something then; or Telemachus must have seen me, I don't know which, but the boy grabbed hold of his father's arm; he was crying out that I was his friend; that I should be spared; that now it had to stop. I saw blood on his arm. I saw the tears streaming down his face.

Eurycleia is the first of the women to come down. Drawn by the prolonged silence, she descends step by step, looking across the confusion of the hall at the fallen tapestries, at the blood trickling with spilt wine among the stones. Quickly her eyes scan the bodies that lie sprawled between the tables and benches. She sees Eumaeus and Philoetius standing together by the opened postern door. Then she catches sight of Odysseus seated on the silver throne. His elbow rests on one of its studded arms; his head is down, his face covered by a blood-stained hand. Telemachus stands trembling beside him.

The cry released by the old nurse begins as a gasp of relief, but when she raises her fists beside her face, her voice lifts in a savage ululation. It is the only sound in the stillness of the hall, like an old eagle shrieking over its kill.

Then she is stamping out her dance of triumph as she yells.

'Enough!' Odysseus shouts again. 'Enough.'

Seeing Eurycleia stare in amazement, he shakes his head, incredulous at the dead who lie around him. 'Gloat in silence, old woman . . . I know these men,' he whispers hoarsely. 'These are my people . . . Gloat in silence, if you must.'

Again the hall falls still around him.

From where I sit with my back against the wall, clutching my lyre to my chest, I see Telemachus glance uncertainly at his father; then he too sits down on the stone floor with his shoulders shaking, holding his head between his hands.

And this is what Penelope sees when she comes down from her apartment, scarcely breathing, her face pale as a shade, uttering not a sound.

At first Odysseus does not know that she is there. Only when she catches her breath does he look up. She has stopped by the body of Amphinomus where he lies with one arm thrown out, sprawled across a fallen bench, his costly garments pooled in blood, the spear lolling over him.

Penelope looks at him for a long time before raising her eyes to gaze at her husband. Odysseus sees the dismay and bewilderment in her face. He too catches his breath. As if in fulfilment of a dreadful dream, the hand he reaches out to her is wet with blood. His shoulders begin to shake. But he tries to speak.

'This is not . . .' he begins, and falters. 'This is not as I wanted it to be.'

Penelope watches her lord slump back on the silver throne in his bloody rags. She glances across to where her son is sobbing quietly and sees that his cheek is streaked with blood where he has wiped a boyish hand across it.

Her instinct now is to gather them both to her sides, but both man and youth are too concussed with shame even to look at her. So she stands between them, at a loss what to say or do, knowing that shock and anger, sorrow and fear, are all present in the numbed tumult of her feelings, but accepting for now that only an immense patience will suffice if all these wounds of war are ever to be healed.

Again Odysseus tries to speak; again he fails.

He looks up, expecting to meet reproach and judgement – the stone face of the goddess – in her eyes; he finds instead only the compassion of her careworn human face.

'I know,' she whispers, reaching out to him. 'Be still now. Soon there will be time for words.'

And as once, long before him, Menelaus wept, Odysseus is weeping now, weeping for his wife's pain and his son's lost youth, weeping for his love of them; weeping for the faith he has broken and the errors he has made; weeping for all the comrades who have died, for the dead of Troy and for these dead who are assembled round him; weeping from the deeps of his mortal heart for all that is gone from him forever, and for all the present grief of things.

The Winnowing Fan

My work is almost done. When I first began to tell the story of the war at Troy I was already an old man. My sight is weaker now and my fingers tremble each time I unroll one of the scrolls that Telemachus brought home from Sparta. They were a gift I prized; one of such value that they remained stored away untouched for more than forty years. And now, by the time I bring these stories to completion, the last inches of papyrus will be covered in script.

One remaining story tells how, on his departure from Troy, the hero Demophon was given a locked casket by his Thracian concubine with the firm instruction that he must never open it unless he decided that he was not going to come back to her. No one knows what the woman had hidden inside the casket, but when Demophon unlocked it and looked at the contents, he was instantly driven mad.

A strange story, of dubious provenance and probably untrue, except in so far as it resumes the whole insanity of the war.

The fate that finally caught up with Neoptolemus was no kinder. Having won back most of the lands lost by Peleus, and deserted Andromache for Hermione, he soon discovered that his new bride's womb was barren. When he went to Delphi to demand of the oracle why he should be made to suffer this affliction, he encountered Orestes who was also at the altar beseeching help from the god. A struggle broke out between the bitter rivals. At the end of it, the son of Achilles lay ingloriously dead, and Orestes seized Hermione for himself.

So eventually, when Apollo saw fit to dispel the Furies of madness that had roosted in his mind, Agamemnon's son became King of Sparta after all. From there, as the years went by, he gradually extended his rule across the strife-riven kingdoms of Argos.

Meanwhile, Peleus and Thetis, at whose ill-fated wedding the first seeds of the war were sown, were desolated by their grandson's untimely death and, for the first time in forty years, they agreed to meet. At the funeral games held for the shade of Neoptolemus, they were at last reconciled to each other in their grief.

Many years later, when he was a man at peace, content with his quiet life beside the hearth, listening to the tranquil chatter of the women at their looms, or to the sound of the sea breaking against the cliffs at dusk, Odysseus talked to me about the time when he and Penelope had also found their way back into the comfort of each other's arms.

'I thought that I had understood something about the dark face of the goddess during my time with Circe and Calypso,' he confessed, 'but I was still a mere novice in such matters. Not till I got back home to Penelope did I begin to grasp what power the goddess has at her command when she decides to put a man through the ordeals of the heart.'

When I answered that this surprised me, given the degrees of initia-tion he had undergone in Aiaia and Cuma,' he said, 'But an initiation is only that. It's just a start, a new beginning, a preliminary to the longer course of things. And there are few things harder to reach than an honest reconciliation between a man's pride and a woman's truth.'

There had been times, he admitted, when he grew restless with the difficult struggle between Penelope and himself. In many ways it would have been easier for him to commission a ship and take to the seas again, looking for what other marvels the world might hold for his distraction. But each time he lost patience with the struggle and made to leave, he was stopped in his tracks, as if the love between them had a will of its own.

And then, quite suddenly, after a last passionate conflict that exhausted all the bitter residue of pain and frustration, they looked across the space between them, and saw that they had passed beyond remorse and forgiveness to the place where there was only the love left, and they were free to come together as the husband and wife they had always truly been.

Everything altered in those moments. It was as if the whole island had been holding its breath, caught between hope and dread, desiring this reconciliation yet fearing that it might never happen. But when Odysseus and Penelope came out of their chamber together and joined the people who were dancing in the soft air of the night outside, everyone who was gathered there instantly sensed how their world had been renewed. The music lifted in response to the knowledge. The dance gathered pace. I watched the lord and lady smiling at each other with the conspiratorial air of a man and woman who have just made love and shortly intend to make love again; and I remembered how I had seen them dancing once, many years ago, at the naming-feast of their son, in that last happy hour before the wind of the coming war gusted across the ocean to blow them apart.

Yet watching them together now, everyone saw that, having won once more the love of a woman in whom the bounty of Hera and the passion of Aphrodite were matched to the wisdom of Athena, Odysseus was not about to leave her again.

So he took pleasure instead in helping Telemachus to equip a ship and choose the men who would sail with him — northwards to Scheria at first, where he met Nausicaa and brought word to the Phaeacians of his father; and then out to the far west, driven by his own desire to see what he might find.

Meanwhile there were the islands to be ruled.

Old Laertes lived long enough to rejoice at his son's return. He even played a part in preventing the feuds that might have followed the day of Apollo's Feast. The most menacing threat came from Eupeithes, who tried to rally the kinsmen of the other dead suitors in a bid both to avenge his son Antinous and to seize the throne of Ithaca. For a time the islands might have collapsed into civil war. But too much blood had already been shed, and every honest man could see that Odysseus had never intended the massacre that took place in his hall. They also saw that there was no better king to be found among them.

So after an uneasy stand-off between Eupeithes and the others, a settlement was reached. With the help of Menelaus, generous compensation was paid and Odysseus set about the long task of ensuring the peace and prosperity of the islands at a time when, all around them, the world was in turmoil still.

After the death of Neoptolemus, resistance to the Dorian invaders quickly crumbled. Iolcus fell before their renewed advance; then all of Thessaly was lost. Soon their iron weapons were cutting a swathe down into Locris. Already losing control over Attica and the western kingdoms, Orestes lacked the authority to count on even half the number of men his father had once raised, even though the threat was to the homeland now. So, long before Mycenae was sacked by the Dorian horde, it was clear that if Troy had been utterly destroyed by the war, the High Kingdom of Argos could not long survive its consequences.

Everywhere order was breaking down. Men grew lawless, the roads became unsafe; piracy and cattle-lifting were rife again. By that time Odysseus was more than sixty years old, but he was still vigorous, and when raiders began to disrupt the hard-won peace of Ithaca he resolved to put a stop to their depredations.

A watch was kept along the coast and he instituted a system of alarms, using bullhorns and signal fires. The band of militiamen he organized were too late to save a hamlet in the north from ransack and murder, but when, only days later, a strange ship was sighted closer to home, he was ready to resist them.

Afterwards men argued about how things had gone so wrong on that high summer afternoon. Some blamed the heat, for there was no shade on the torrid beach and men's tempers were running short. But the militiamen were tightly disciplined. As ordered, they kept under cover while the strangers came ashore. Then they advanced with Odysseus at their head, shouting and banging their spears against their shields.

The intention had been merely to scare them off, but perhaps the landing party panicked at the unexpected sight of so many spearmen coming at them. Perhaps Odysseus incited them by his angry shouts, or maybe he said something that the foreigners misunderstood. Whatever the case, everyone stood by in stunned astonishment as a young man with tousled red hair reached for a primitive stingray spear and hurled it at Odysseus.

Because of the heat, Odysseus had gone down to the beach without his armour and his shield was slung low at his side. The barb of the spear entered his chest and penetrated straight to the heart. By the time his shocked men had run across those few yards of sand, he was dead.

Already the strangers were retreating through the shallow water to where they had anchored their ship. The armed guard were so stupefied by the death of their lord that they were slow to pursue them. For that reason, the red-haired fellow was able to climb aboard his vessel and shout back at the shore.

'My name is Telegonus,' he called. 'I came in peace. I came in search of my father Odysseus. But I see he has not taught the men of Ithaca how to welcome strangers as we do in Aiaia. Tell him I came. Tell him my mother Circe sent me.'

Then he turned and barked an order at the men scrambling for the oars, and the boat pulled out into the quiet bay.

Telemachus was away from Ithaca at that time on his long voyage into the west, so I stood beside Penelope as the offerings were made for Odysseus' shade.

'It is as Teiresias foretold,' she sighed, gazing at her husband's body where it lay at rest under the brazen sky in the rich garments she had woven for him. 'Death came to him from the sea after all . . . and it seems to have come easily.' Then she added something which left me puzzled. 'But we can be thankful,' she whispered, 'that he had long since planted his oar.'

Later, after I had sung my paean at the great feast with which we consigned Odysseus to the Land of Shades, I asked her to explain what she had meant.

'It was another thing that Teiresias prophesied,' she answered. 'Something that became the very root of our life together.'

I saw her deliberate a moment before confiding in me further; but then she must have recalled that I too had a great love for Odysseus and that the truest memorial to his deeds might one day be found in the stories I told of him; so Penelope admitted me to what was the most decisive moment of their later life.

'When he was at the Oracle of the Dead,' she said, 'Odysseus was told that he must one day go on a long journey to a place where men would not know an oar for what it was when they saw it. He assumed that Teiresias meant an actual journey . . . and perhaps the soothsayer thought so too. Certainly there were times in the days when things were hard between us when he threatened to leave and go roving in fulfilment of that prophecy rather than endure any longer the demands and limitations that our life together made on him. But he never actually left — though at times I feared he might do so, And then one night, when he had begun to understand that all the hard things happening between us were only the labour of a wiser love trying to get born, he was visited by a dream.'

In that dream, Penelope told me, Odysseus had gone on a long journey, far into the heart of Libya. Travelling alone, taking nothing with him but the great steering oar of The Fair Return, *he had walked for mile after mile through an arid terrain, crossing mountains and deserts and wilderness in the course of a single night.*

At last he came to a place where a man wearing a wide-brimmed hat with a light cloak thrown across his shoulders, waited at a crossroads.

'Why do you carry a winnowing fan with you?' the Libyan asked.

'Why do you call this a winnowing fan,' Odysseus answered, 'when you can plainly see it is an oar?'

But when he held out the oar to demonstrate the mistake, he saw how it might indeed have been taken for the kind of wooden paddle that the harvesters use to make the draught that separates the wheat from the chaff when the time comes to winnow the garnered crop.

The man smiled at him then. 'Don't you know who I am, Odysseus?'

Astonished that this Libyan should know his name, Odysseus peered more closely into a face that was neither strange to him nor yet quite familiar.

'It's been a long time since we last met, but surely you haven't forgotten me?' The smile broadened into a familiar grin. 'I stole a flower for you once.'

Looking more closely into a dark face that had been much younger the last time he saw it, Odysseus said, 'Hermes?'

'Who else? Don't you know that you'd be lost without me? And it seems you need my help again. Harvest time has come and there are things to be done. Here's what you have to do. Take this winnowing fan that used to be an oar and plant it deep in the ground; then offer up a ram, a bull and a breeding-boar to Poseidon. A tree will grow from your oar. A tree even stronger than the one from which you built your marriage bed.'

And with that Hermes gave a little chuckle, shook the white-ribboned wand that he now held in his hand, and disappeared.

Having listened in wonder to Penelope's account, I said, 'So it was truly the god in his dream!'

'And perhaps also at Zarzis, and again on Aiaia, and while he was building his boat on Ogygia.'

'But was it clear to Odysseus what his dream must mean?'

Penelope smiled. 'Haven't I said that it formed the root of our life together? Where he had once used only the oar to steer his life, always questing outwards, not searching for what lay hidden within, now he had begun to make use of the winnowing fan. He sorted the wheat from the chaff in the granary of his heart; and then, as Hermes had bidden him, he freely made an offering of the wild energy that had driven him for so long. In so doing he became a deep-rooted tree. After that, there was no more talk of roving.'

Penelope stood up, gathering the folds of her dress. 'Now if you will forgive me, Phemius, I wish to be alone.'

And with her customary grace, she stepped through the hall's noisy heat to pray for the voyaging soul of Odysseus in the silence of the night outside.

Glossary of Characters

Deities

Aphrodite Goddess of many aspects, mostly associated with Love and Beauty

Apollo God with many aspects, including Prophecy, Healing, Pestilence and the Arts

Ares God of War, twin brother of Eris

Artemis Virgin Goddess of the Wild

Athena Goddess with many aspects, including Wisdom, Power and Protection

Boreas God of the North Wind

Dionysus God of wine

Eris Goddess of Strife and Discord, twin sister to Ares

Eros God of Love, son of Aphrodite

Hephaestus God of fire and craftsmanship

Hera Goddess Queen of Olympus, wife of Zeus, presides over marriage

Hermes God with many aspects, including eloquence, imagination, invention. A slippery fellow

Neith Libyan Goddess of Lake Tritonis

Persephone Goddess of the Underworld, wife of Hades and daughter of Demeter

Poseidon	God with many aspects, ruler of the Sea, Earthquakes and Horses
Zeus	King of Olympus, ruler of the gods

Mortals

Acamas	Argive warrior, son of Theseus
Acastus	King of Iolcus
Achilles	son of Peleus and Thetis, leader of the Myrmidons, father of Neoptolemus
Aeacus	King of Aegina, father of Peleus and Telamon
Aegisthus	son of Thyestes, cousin to Agamemnon and Menelaus
Aeneas	Prince of the Dardanians
Aeolus	King of Aeolia, father of Canace and Macareus
Aesacus	priest of Apollo at Thymbra
Aethra	mother of Theseus, once Queen of Troizen, now bondswoman to Helen
Agamemnon	son of Atreus, King of Mycenae, High King of Argos
Agialeia	Lady of Tiryns, wife of Diomedes
Aias	Locrian captain
Ajax	Argive hero, son of Telamon, cousin of Achilles
Alcinous	King of Scheria, father of Nausicaa
Amphinomus	prince of Dulichion, son of Nisus, friend and suitor to Penelope
Andromache	wife of Hector
Antenor	counsellor to Priam
Anticleia	mother of Odysseus, wife of King Laertes
Antilochus	son of Nestor
Antinous	son of Eupeithes, suitor to Penelope
Aerope	Queen of Mycenae, wife of Atreus and mother of Agamemnon and Menelaus
Arete	wife of King Alcinous and mother of Nausicaa
Astyanax	son of Hector and Andromache

Atreus	King of Mycenae, brother of Thyestes and father of Agamemnon and Menelaus
Axylus	a Zacynthian sailor
Baius	helmsman on *The Fair Return*
Briseis	Dardanian maiden captured by Achilles
Calchas	Trojan priest of Apollo who defects to the Argives
Calypso	priestess of Aiaia, sibyl at Cuma, and lover of Odysseus
Canace	daughter of King Aeolus and sister of Macareus
Capys	son of King Priam
Cassandra	daughter of King Priam
Cheiron	King of the Centaurs
Chryseis	daughter of Apollo's priest in Thebe, captive of Agamemnon
Cinyras	King of Cyprus
Circe	High Priestess of Aiaia
Clitus	sailor on *The Fair Return*
Clymene	Andromache's serving woman
Clytaemnestra	Queen of Mycenae, daughter of Tyndareus & Leda, wife of Agamemnon.
Ctesippus	son of Polytherses, suitor to Penelope
Deidameia	daughter of King Lycomedes, mother of Neoptolemus by Achilles
Deiphobus	son of King Priam
Demodocus	bard of Scheria
Demonax	captain of *The Swordfish*
Demophon	brother of Acamas. Son of Theseus
Diomedes	Lord of Tiryns, Argive hero
Diotima	wise woman on Ithaca
Dolon	fisherman of Ithaca
Doricleus	counsellor at Mycenae

Electra	daughter of Agamemnon & Clytaemnestra
Elpenor	Ithacan warrior and sailor on *The Fair Return*
Eteoneus	chief minister of Sparta
Eumaeus	farmer and herdsman of Ithaca
Eupeithes	a nobleman of Ithaca and father of Antinous
Eurybates	Herald of Ithaca
Eurycleia	servant of Anticleia, formerly nurse to Odysseus
Eurylochus	lieutenant to Odysseus
Eurymachus	suitor to Penelope
Eurynomus	son of Aegyptius, suitor to Penelope
Glaucus	captain of the *Nereid*
Grinus	Ithacan warrior and sailor on *The Fair Return*
Guneus	Thessalian warrior and captain
Halitherses	soothsayer of Ithaca
Hanno	nomad of the Garamantes
Hattusilis	Emperor of the Hittites
Hector	eldest son of King Priam
Hecuba	Queen of Troy, wife of Priam and mother of Hector
Helen	daughter of Tyndareus/Zeus and Leda. Queen of Sparta, wife of Menelaus.
Heracles	hero
Hermes	Libyan boy
Hermione	daughter of Menelaus and Helen
Hylax	Phoenician trader
Icarius	Spartan nobleman, brother of Tyndareus, father of Penelope
Idas	Counsellor in Mycenae
Idomeneus	King of Crete
Iliona	Queen of Thracian Chersonese, wife of Polymnestor and daughter of Priam
Ilus	Grandfather of King Priam

Iphigenaia	daughter of Agamemnon & Clytaemnestra
Irus	Ithacan beggar
Jason	hero, leader of the Argonauts
Laertes	King of Ithaca, father of Odysseus
Laodice	daughter of King Priam
Laomedon	King of Troy, father of Priam
Leodes	priest of Apollo in Ithaca, suitor to Penelope
Macareus	son of King Aeolus and brother of Canace
Marpessa	serving woman to Clytaemnestra
Mastor	Ithacan warrior and sailor on *The Fair Return*
Meda	Queen of Crete and wife of Idomeneus
Medon	Ithacan herald
Meges	leader of the Dulichians
Melantho	serving woman to Penelope
Memnon	Trojan ally, leader of the Ethiopians
Menelaus	King of Sparta, husband of Helen, brother to Agamemnon
Menestheus	Argive captain, King of Athens
Mentes	Taphian ambassador
Mentor	nobleman of Ithaca
Molossus	son of Neoptolemus by Andromache
Mopsa	woman of Aiaia
Nauplius	King of Euboea, father of Palamedes
Nausicaa	daughter of King Alcinous
Neoptolemus	son of Achilles, also known as Pyrrhos
Nereids	fifty daughters of the sea-god Nereus
Nestor	King of Pylos
Nisus	King of Dulichion and father of Amphimonus
Odysseus	Lord of Ithaca
Orestes	son of Agamemnon and Clytaemnestra

Palamedes	Prince of Euboea, son of King Nauplius
Paris	son of King Priam, lover of Helen
Patroclus	son of Menoetius, beloved friend of Achilles
Peiraeus	friend of Phemius and Telemachus
Peisenor	herald of Ithaca
Peisistratus	son of Nestor
Pelagon	bard of Mycenae
Peleus	son of King Aeacus, father of Achilles
Pellas	Samian suitor to Penelope
Pelopia	daughter of Thyestes and second wife of Atreus, mother of Aegisthus
Pelops	father of Atreus and Thyestes, grandfather of Agamemnon
Penelope	daughter of Icarius, cousin to Helen and Clytaemnestra and wife of Odysseus
Perimedes	sailor on *The Fair Return*
Phemius	bard of Ithaca
Philoctetes	Aeolian archer
Philoetius	herdsman of Ithaca
Philona	friend of Nausicaa
Phoenix	Myrmidon warrior
Polites	Ithacan Lieutenant and sailor on *The Fair Return*
Polydamna	wise woman to Helen
Polydorus	youngest son of King Priam
Polymnestor	King of Thracian Chersonese
Polytherses	Lord of Same and father of Ctesippus
Polyxena	daughter of King Priam
Priam	son of Laomedon, King of Troy, also known as Podarces
Pylades	son of King Strophius and friend of Orestes
Sinon	cousin to Odysseus
Sthenelus	King of Mycenae
Strophius	King of Phocis and father of Pylades

Talthybius	Argive herald
Teiresias	Prophet at the Oracle of the Dead at Cuma
Telamon	father of Ajax and brother to Peleus
Telegonus	son of Odysseus and Circe
Telemachus	son of Odysseus and Penelope
Terpis	father of Phemius the Ithacan bard
Theano	high priestess of Athena in Troy, wife of Antenor
Theoclymenus	seer from Hyperesia
Thersites	Argive soldier and kinsman of Diomedes
Theseus	hero, King of Athens, conqueror of Crete
Thesprotus	King of Sicyon
Thetis	daughter of Cheiron, wife of Peleus and mother of Achilles
Thrasymedes	son of Nestor
Thyestes	brother of Atreus, uncle to Agamemnon and Menelaus, father of Aegisthus
Tyndareus	King of Sparta, father of Clytaemnestra and Helen, husband of Leda

Acknowledgements

Because the truth of myth is subtler than the truth of fact, myths never take a fixed and final form. Even among the early poets and tragedians of Greece, there were many variations, both of detail and substance, in the way those powerful tales were told. So any reworking of such mythic material must either choose among the available alternatives or tell it differently again. For that reason, and because I wanted to tell this story in a new way for our own time, readers already familiar with Homer's *Odyssey*, with the *Oresteia* of Aeschylus, and with the Trojan plays of Euripides, may have found that aspects of this novel ran counter to their expectations. Nevertheless my debt to those poets is immense, as also to Book VI of Vergil's *Aeneid*, to Ovid's account of Macareus in his *Metamorphoses*, and to Herodotus' description of the various tribes of Libya in Book IV of his *Histories*. If this novel encourages readers to return to those incomparable sources, or to visit them for the first time, then perhaps the unscholarly liberties I have taken with them will be justified.

There are debts to contemporaries which should also be acknowledged. Once again Robert Graves proved a provocative guide through this mythic terrain, particularly in his comments on the story of Odysseus in *The Greek Myths*. I should have been quite unable to follow Odysseus on his journey through the underworld without R. F. Paget's bold, pioneering work to uncover the Cumaean Oracle of the Dead, as recorded in his book *In the Footsteps of Orpheus* (The Scientific Book Club 1967), and without the further research into that important site reported by my friend Robert Temple in his *Netherworld* (Century 2002). For inspiration about the nature of the rituals on Aiaia, I drew on Normandi Ellis's translations from the Egyptian Book of the Dead in *Awakening Osiris (Phanes Press 1988),* and I found Peter Kingsley's illuminating study of Parmenides, *In the Dark Places of Wisdom* (Element Books 1999), to be an invaluable study of incubation rituals (as well as of so much else) in the Velian culture of Hellenic Italy. I strongly recommend all these books to those who wish to know more about the oracular and initiatory rites that lie behind this work of fiction.

Then there are other friends to thank: Sarah Tregellas, who sent me photographs of Ithaca, an island I hope to visit one day; Keith Sagar who generously shared his thoughts on the *Odyssey;* Jules Cashford who nurtured my faith in this enterprise, and John Moat whose wise good humour focussed my imagination. The encouragement of my editors Jane Johnson and Emma Coode was there for me throughout, as was, indispensably, the patient help of my wife Phoebe Clare.

L.C.
The Bell House
2004